MW01127279

RHAPSODY

The First Volume of the Muse Chronicles

David P. Jacobs

RHAPSODY
The First Volume of the
Muse Chronicles
Copyright © David P. Jacobs
Published 1 September 2012
ISBN 978-1479249138

The right of David P. Jacobs to be identified as author of this
Work has been asserted by him in accordance with sections 77
and 78 of the Copyright, Designs and Patents Act 1988.

All rights reserved. No part of this publication may be
reproduced, stored in retrieval system, copied in any form or by
any means, electronic, mechanical, photocopying, recording or
otherwise transmitted without written permission from the
publisher.

This is a work of fiction. Names, characters, businesses, places,
events and incidents are either the products of the author's
imagination or used in a fictitious manner. Any resemblance to
actual persons, living or dead, or actual events is purely
coincidental.

Cover design by Anelia Savova
https://www.crowdspring.com/user/Ann_RS/

In loving memory of Miss Norene Wood
who was, and always will be, one
of the greatest muses that ever lived.

"If a man does not keep pace with his companions, perhaps it is because he hears a different drummer. Let him step to the music which he hears, however measured or far away."

Henry David Thoreau

"Sing in me, Muse, and through me tell the story . . ."

Homer

CHAPTER 1: REQUIEM

To fully comprehend the events of the day Annette Slocum died, one would have to examine how she lived the first thirty years that preceded it. Annette lived a life of isolation with her husband Lyle. She might as well have lived alone as he hardly acknowledged her presence. This was something that she often preferred, as Annette's already limited social skills were barely utilized. Very plain looking, Annette was a pale-skinned woman. Brown hair fell limp around her shoulders. Bags crept steadily around her blue eyes with each passing year. Annette was thin and of average height. Her features weren't anything spectacular. Had she worn makeup or attempted to change her blandish wardrobe or felt any true satisfaction in her life, Annette might have been quite striking. But that wasn't the case. In short, Annette never stood out in a crowd and, more often than not, blended into the wallpaper or couch cushions at the parties Lyle forced her to attend.

Lyle, on the other hand, was easily recognizable with the handle-bar moustache, a comb-over and charismatic personality that drew customers to him with the same effect as a bug-zapper attracting pests. Lyle, a new and used car salesman, excelled at selling automobiles. He worked constantly: day-in and day-out, mornings, nights, weekends, and even holidays, through rain, sleet, snow and dust storms.

The lot in which Lyle worked was decorated in anxious triangles of plastic which frequently attempted to escape from their poles. Annette often thought of herself as one of those colored flags; forever attached, she hoped that a strong enough wind would someday rip her from their eventless marriage. Annette never spoke this feeling out loud to Lyle, primarily because she wanted to be a faithful housewife to her husband in spite of his neglectfulness and, secondly, because she rarely even spoke at all.

Annette was a quiet, respectful and dedicated servant. Every morning she awoke at five-fifteen, as if an inner alarm clock had jostled her from a dreamless sleep. She then ambled into the shower and silently lathered herself in soap bubbles and generic shampoo that gave off a hint of stale peppermint. After her shower, Annette abandoned her towel for a house dress that was as plain as she. In that dress and her peach house-slippers, she fetched the morning paper at the end of the driveway. Annette then cooked Lyle's breakfast over the kitchen stove. Every morning it was the same two vigorously scrambled eggs, five crisp strips of bacon, a stack of waffles coated in thick maple syrup, a small bowl of sliced cantaloupe and a mug of coffee.

Over the years she had timed this morning ritual so perfectly that the greasy fumes of the sizzling bacon would begin to coax Lyle from his sleep. By the time she would have set the plate and coffee mug, Lyle would have climbed out of bed, completed peeing, checked to make sure his handlebar moustache hadn't accumulated any lint from the bedcovers, and pruned the sculpted facial hair to perfection. Lyle would amble into the kitchen wearing only his dirty white briefs with a bit of a belly spotted with hair arced above the elastic.

Once Lyle met the plate, breakfast would begin. Lyle consumed every crumb, sliver of fruit and drop of coffee while Annette resignedly enjoyed a meager helping of grapefruit and granola, washing it down with water from the faucet.

After ten years of marriage, some couples might despise the way the other chewed food or chugged liquids. Conditions were slightly different in the Slocum household. Annette didn't really care how Lyle ate his eggs or bit the bacon or the way the

2

metal fork would scrape against his teeth as he tugged the fruit from its prongs. What Annette cared about was the lack of reaction to the food he shoveled. There were no groans of satisfaction to imply that he enjoyed what he'd eaten.

Within seconds the meal would be inside the belly of her husband and little particles would clutch to the moustache that made him Lyle. He read the morning paper as he ate which also dug emotional canals under Annette's skin. It was as if she didn't exist. She was there only to cook his meals, clean his underwear and, occasionally, be there to pleasure him sexually – but even then he wouldn't acknowledge her. Every so often, she simply laid there and fantasized about something better.

Before Lyle left for work in his usual ironed dress shirt, pressed pants, and blue and green striped "lucky" tie, he would give his wife a quick, wet, furry kiss on the cheek. When the sound of his maroon-hued 2004 Honda Civic purred down the driveway and street, Annette blossomed. She would excitedly open the windows to allow a light breeze while she did her housework. Depending on her mood (and the weather) Annette ignored the dryer all together and hung the laundry outside in the backyard, delighting in the sound of the shirt fabric as the wind rippled through it.

When the housework was complete, Annette would walk briskly to the nearest library. Lyle kept a spare, weathered, champagne-colored 1979 VW Beetle in the driveway on the chance that the one he'd regularly drive off with wouldn't start. Annette hardly used it, as she preferred the trek on foot.

At the library Annette celebrated her love for reading. She often devoured books and pressed her nose to the ink and paper. Perhaps it was the tang of grease from phantom fingers that had recently thumbed through it or the lingering, aged odor of mildew and dust; but, regardless of the exact smell, the collected aromas nearly brought her to tears every time. With the use of her library card she would cycle through three books, taking the old ones back and returning home with the new ones. In these few quiet hours in the late afternoon, she would read and daydream. Lyle would then return home to devour another meal in silence. He would then watch whatever game was on (furthering the silence between them). After they went to bed, if the book was good enough and Lyle was fast asleep, Annette would lift his sleepily wandering arm that wrapped around her waist. At the kitchen table late at night was where Annette enjoyed reading the most. She never required much sleep. Reading for her was all the rest she needed. In truth, Annette felt more comfort in the spine of a library book than she felt in Lyle's arms.

She found herself immersed in the tumultuous adventures of Paul and Helen in Elizabeth Kostova's *The Historian*. Author Carlos Ruiz Zafón kept her equally enthralled with main character Daniel's attempts to unravel the dark mysteries of an elusive fictional author named Julian Carax in *The Shadow of the Wind*. Her literary affairs were spent in the company of Dickens, Dumas, Hawthorne and Wilde. Her adventures spanned from the historical romances of Jane Austen to the dark and macabre of H.P. Lovecraft. There was no story that Annette wouldn't read.

She would often wonder to herself where Lyle dredged up his charismatic qualities. It was what had drawn them together in the first place. But as the years passed he seemed to reserve it only for the potential buyers and never for her. Lyle never beat her or abused her. He didn't speak to her in any condescending tones; he just didn't seem to acknowledge her in any way.

The night before she died, while a moth flitted about the light fixture of the kitchen ceiling, Annette wondered if it were possible to divorce Lyle and marry a library. The thought of Lyle's stunned face brought about a mischievous grin which grew more impish. Annette imagined the library structure sporting a tuxedo. This notion sounded a bit far-fetched however. What seemed more likely was Lyle to sweep her into his arms and up the stairs in the same romantic fashion as Rhett Butler carried Scarlett O'Hara. But even then that fantasy seemed just as improbable. She let out a dejected sigh and continued reading Margaret Mitchell's *Gone with the Wind*.

As the hours passed, a wave of despair washed over her. Even after she had served his comforts, Lyle probably wouldn't even acknowledge her if she had, indeed, walked out the door with a suitcase. He would, in all probability, continue to shovel those damn eggs every morning, scraping the fork with his teeth while wearing his dirty white briefs and scanning the paper.

Annette supposed that being "happy" was relative; as long as she had her library books and Lyle didn't throw them out, she'd stay. Annette often wondered to herself if anyone would read her own adventures if they were scribed on paper. The thirty years leading up to her death, Annette would have thought not, but the events on the day she died proved otherwise.

*

The day that Annette Slocum died started off like any other morning. Her eyes fluttered open at five-fifteen. She rose out of bed, showered, and lathered her mousy brown hair with the peppermint shampoo. She then abandoned her towel for a colored floral house dress on the verge of turning grey with age. She then opened the front door and, with her peach house-slippers hugging her feet, obediently retrieved the paper from a tumbleweed-type bush that haunted the mailbox at the side of the road.

Across the street, in a cream-colored pants suit with matching heels, was a woman perceivably ten years older than Annette. The woman's long hair waved radiantly in the morning breeze. As the rising sun on the horizon struck this stranger, Annette thought the Woman in the Cream-Colored Pants Suit resembled a passenger standing on the deck of a great ocean liner while waving to the shore as the boat drifted away. In actuality, both were standing on opposite sides of the street. Regardless of the proximity between them, the strange woman had indeed waved, an odd sort of behavior coming from a woman Annette had never met.

Annette, the ever-so-anti-social being that she was, didn't wave back; instead, she turned and hurriedly retreated back into the house where she fixed Lyle's breakfast and stewed in confusion. The woman had waved as if she had known Annette, but Annette certainly did not "know" her! As she scrambled Lyle's eggs, Annette wondered which party her husband had dragged her to that a woman *like that* would have attended.

The more she scrambled the eggs, the more Annette weeded her way through a labyrinth of perplexity. Annette wasn't able to place the woman and she ran through a list of possible explanations as she crisped Lyle's bacon. The woman couldn't have been a friend from her childhood. Annette had not had any friends. Even the bridesmaids at their wedding had been relatives of Lyle's, and *that* woman was too beautiful to be in any way related to her husband. This was followed by a startling thought that perhaps Lyle was having an affair. Annette thought she'd ask about it over breakfast.

When the opportunity arose, however, she noticed that a few crumbs sprinkled Lyle's handlebar moustache (as they had every morning). If Lyle had been having an affair with someone who accepted the morsels of food regularly caught in his facial hair, then whatever her identity, she was without a doubt worthy of having him. Then again, if the woman across the street *had* been Lyle's mistress, why would she be waving happily at Annette? If Annette was a mistress and she was about to announce her affair, she would walk up slowly and worrisome with the need to confess plastered across her face.

Annette didn't muster enough courage to ask Lyle. Therefore Lyle left for work and Annette scrubbed the dishes. As it was one of those beautiful days, she put the laundry out to dry and then sat in a battered lawn chair watching the breeze tease Lyle's shirts. The pleasure of observing this task was short-lived as Annette spotted the woman. This time the woman was in Annette's own back yard, watching the fabric from the other side.

They locked eyes for a moment, the strange woman and Annette. The woman then smiled and carefully said "Hello" as if addressing a hesitant child or a skittish cat. She said nothing more, but simply stood there and continued smiling a little too pleasantly for Annette's tastes. The woman acted like a friend but Annette wasn't buying the act.

"Whatever it is," Annette suddenly found her voice. It was timid and quiet like the afternoon air. "Lyle doesn't accept soliciting." Lyle accepted soliciting. In fact he welcomed any man who had something to sell and often swapped business cards. Yes, Lyle even sold cars to strangers on his doorstep to poor unwilling prey.

"I'm not soliciting, Mrs. Slocum." The more words the woman spoke, the more Annette caught a subtle British accent. "I've come to talk."

Talk? If there was one word in the English vocabulary that Annette despised the most it was the word "talk." Annette couldn't even remember the last time she'd uttered a full sentence, save for what she'd said to the stranger before her. *"The woman certainly isn't here to confess to an affair,"* Annette thought. *"Nor was she selling spare parts to a vacuum cleaner. What then, is she here for?"*

Annette wasn't about to find out. The woman had obviously known Annette, as she had spoken her last name, but Annette wasn't too keen on keeping a conversation with a complete stranger. Annette turned and surrendered the laundry to the strange woman.

"Mrs. Slocum, please! Give me five minutes!" The woman called after her but, by that time, Annette was already inside the house dead-bolting the door and closing the curtains. "Aren't you the least bit curious as to why I'm darkening your doorstep?"

The woman's muffled voice could still be heard despite Annette's best efforts to cloak it. Annette picked up the phone to dial the police but as the dial tone hummed in her ear she quickly realized there was nothing outside; there was no voice or footsteps, only a curious silence that prompted her to put the phone back on the receiver. Annette peeked through the curtains to find the perimeters of her private kingdom were vacant. Perhaps the woman had been a ghost. The thought prompted the hairs on Annette's neck to stand on end. How else could she explain the woman's sudden absence? Annette then chortled; she had never believed in ghosts and didn't even now. There had to be a perfectly logical explanation for the woman's arrival and departure.

Once Annette convinced herself that the coast was clear, she bundled up the books she had most recently borrowed and, surveying of the front porch a final time, escaped the house with the car keys. The spare VW Beetle protested as she revved the engine. Annette made sure the doors were locked and the windows rolled up. She felt a bit better about things once she was safely inside, alone, as she preferred.

The drive to the library was far more scenic on foot but, considering that the unknown woman who knew her by name was stalking her, Annette certainly didn't want to take any chances. The drive only took five minutes. Once the Beetle was parked in the lot that surrounded the library, she fled for the front stairs.

"Thank you," said the male librarian behind the desk as she slipped the old books in the return bin. Annette whisked past him with her eyes to the floor, in search of something else to devour.

She liked libraries because they, too, were quiet. Occasionally there was a ruffling page, or clicking of computer keys, or the sighing sound of copy machines, but nothing obtrusive by any means. The world outside the books was chaotic; but, within the books, all was controlled and predictable.

Annette wasn't sure if it was the book she had in her hand or the fact that, beyond the shelf, the woman was watching her; either way, she sighed and put the book back where she'd found it. Annette moved to a different shelf but, no matter where she moved or how she tried to hide, the woman was there, on the other side, with her eyes peering over inquisitively.

There was no way Annette could feel comfortable pulling three novels from the shelf with *that woman* skulking around predatorily. With the prospect of going home empty-handed, Annette snaked disappointedly through the aisles. What had started as a typical hunt for the perfect book suddenly converted into a game of hide-and-seek with Annette at the whim of this persistent Woman in the Cream-Colored Pants Suit.

Annette soon found herself crouched in the magazine section. The woman's matching heels were clearly visible behind the periodical shelves. The front door, which yawned open, was before her, several feet away. Annette wondered if she could she make it past the circulation desk, out the door, down the steps, and to the car fast enough. Once inside the Beetle she'd be alone again: something she yearned for.

The woman's cream-colored shoes were *still* visible beyond the periodicals. Bracing herself, Annette took a deep breath and bolted for the door. She dared not look back to see if the woman was gaining on her, but she felt that her tenacious admirer was once again in pursuit. There were two heavy sets of running footsteps on the pavement outside: hers and those of the woman. Annette spotted the Beetle, ripped the keys free from her clinched left hand, flew down the stairs and shut herself in the car, locking the doors. Annette was able to see her, barely out of breath, standing defeated two parking spaces away. Annette regained her composure and started the ignition; the sound of its whining motor was as soothing as the sound of shirts swishing in the washer. She closed her eyes.

"This would go a lot easier if you would talk to me," the woman whispered in her ear. Annette's eyes shot open to find the woman sitting next to her in the passenger seat looking slightly frazzled. "I'm here for a specific purpose that will no doubt change the entire course of your life. Now if you please, hear me out for five minutes. And then I'll be on my way."

"Get out of my car," Annette managed to squeak, but the woman didn't budge.

"Mrs. Slocum, it's vitally important that you pay very close attention to what I have to tell you." The woman said this as she opened her jacket pocket, sticking her hand into the folds. Annette felt the granola from breakfast try to pry itself from her stomach. The woman was no doubt going to pull out a gun and shoot Annette, but if that was the case then two questions erupted. Who would want to kill Annette and why?

Annette certainly didn't wait to find out. She opened the car door, unbuckled her belt and fled to the parking lot.

"Mrs. Slocum!" The woman, she could hear, was behind her again. Annette ran to the road to escape her captor. The woman raced after her and they both wound through the traffic. Drivers' horns blazed in aggravation. As Annette dodged the cars, she wished she was home. Even though it wasn't much of a life, it was *her* kind of life. She took the quiet and boring matrimony with Lyle, not for granted like before, but as something she wanted, something she knew, something she feared she'd probably never see again.

Indeed, it certainly wouldn't be something she would see again. A blue Cadillac convertible, with its top up, barreled down the road. Annette wasn't fast enough. With a sickening crunch Annette's body toppled over the hood, cracked the windshield, and flopped back to the ground. The woman in the pants suit stood aghast. The envelope which she had taken from her pocket fell to the street as all traffic paused. From inside the envelope rolled out a bright orange peg that rotated, then ceased motion, next to Annette's left ear.

The day that Annette Slocum died began like any other that had preceded it. Some people would call her death the end of a tragically boring, unfulfilled life. For those who had sent the Woman in the Cream-Colored Pants Suit, it was the exact opposite. For them, Annette's life finally began. By the time anyone even looked around to see who or what Annette had been running from, the woman, the envelope, and the bright orange peg had vanished entirely.

CHAPTER 2: AN INSTRUCTIONAL VIDEO NARRATED BY NATHANIEL J. CAULIFLOWER

Annette woke to the sound of a water cooler belching its bubbles. It was the oddest sound for her to hear since she'd been hit by a car moments before. Or had she? Waking in this small room was like waking from an elaborate dream she'd been having for thirty years. It felt as if Lyle, the house, the rippling shirt fabric in the afternoon breeze and the smell of the ink on the pages of a library book had all been pieces of a fragmented illusion brought on by an overabundance of pizza before laying down for an afternoon nap.

"That's impossible," Annette told herself, certain that two seconds ago she had been splattered all over the road in front of the library like a dismembered mannequin encircled by her own blood. As life had been taken from her, she had detected a swarm of people crowding around the unforeseen misfortune. Now she was alone and completely intact, sitting in a chair next to a water cooler. To Annette, the water cooler was a foreign object with as much charm as a toad croaking unhappily while perched on a lily-pad.

The waiting room in which Annette found herself had nine chairs in a row, eight of which were empty, and all the same color and shape as the one underneath her. The room was small and windowless and no bigger than a walk-in closet. It had barely enough room for the nine chairs, let alone the water cooler with its irritating belches. A single clock ticked the seconds away silently on the wall before her. There wasn't even a table with magazines as one would expect from most waiting rooms. There were, however, two doors: one to her right and one to her left, both closed, keeping whatever was behind them at a concealed distance.

"Who was that Woman in the Cream-Colored Pants Suit, and where is she now?" Annette wondered to herself, shifting to a more comfortable position. Annette was a woman who had an around-the-clock routine and the woman who had ultimately brought her to an end had spoiled it. The fact that her life, which had once had a specific pace, rhythm, and reason, was suddenly thrown into upheaval unnerved Annette even more.

If only she could see that woman one more time, she would . . . Annette wasn't quite sure what she'd do. Silently stare at her in fury? Would she reach beyond her insecurities and spout a monologue about how her life had been ended unfairly? Or would she do something drastic like whack her assailant over the head with the water cooler jug? Annette didn't have to wonder very long as, within seconds of these thoughts, the door to her left opened. There, in the doorway, stood her enemy.

"You . . ." Annette seethed. She was hardly one for histrionics so, as a substitute for jumping from her chair and strangling the woman, Annette sat and simmered.

"I'm afraid so, Mrs. Slocum. Can you follow me, please?"

Annette spied the other closed door to her right. If she could make a quick escape, she wondered where it would lead. Unfortunately for Annette, it seemed that the woman would follow her even now, after death, wherever she fled. Annette figured she was already deceased so what harm could it do to follow her? She stood, brushed the wrinkles from her faded floral house-dress, and faced her fate. The woman released yet another smile, perfect teeth beyond her Barbie doll veneer, and held the door open. The woman wore pearl earrings, the surfaces of which glistened in the waiting room light.

On the other side, Annette found a rather long plain hallway with doorless offices. Annette could see from a quick glance that each office had their own interior designs specifically installed for their occupants. The woman walked fast and Annette struggled to keep up, therefore did not have time to investigate the offices further. Annette did see that each office had a private post box. Each one varied in color, size, and shape; some post boxes even had different languages written on them. Annette followed the woman to the very end of the hall where there was a tenth door.

A rather skinny man in an argyle sweater and tight-fitted jeans stepped out of the doorless vestibule. He was in his late twenties. His hair was a maintained crew cut with highlights. His eyes were hazel-green. He held in his hand a plate of chicken Marsala fettuccini topped with steaming mushrooms. To Annette, the pasta dish smelled divine. As she didn't know this man and didn't feel comfortable speaking to a complete stranger, Annette kept this thought to herself.

"I was hoping you'd get a chance to try the new dish, Mr. Richardson," the woman said to him. She then made introductions. "Mr. Richardson, this is Mrs. Slocum. She'll be staying with us for a short while."

When Mr. Richardson smiled Annette spotted dimples. "New to the afterlife, huh?" he asked Annette, offering a handshake. Annette looked at Mr. Richardson's hand. She nervously shifted her eyes to the woman.

The woman then said, "You'll have to excuse Mrs. Slocum. She's a bit frazzled from having recently collided with a Cadillac." But Annette wasn't frazzled. The woman was simply trying to be polite in lieu of Annette's lack of response.

"I see," answered Mr. Richardson who seemed intrigued on Annette's last moments.

"You two will have plenty of time to talk later, I'm sure," the woman told Mr. Richardson and Annette. "In the meantime, keep up the good work, Mr. Richardson." With that, Mr. Richardson respectfully ducked into his own doorless office.

The contrast of the simple hallway where Annette stood to the aesthetic cedar balcony of Mr. Richardson's office was breathtaking. A star-filled night sky could be seen beyond his balcony. There was also a comforting spring breeze that brushed its way through the door to Annette's cheek. It was as if the hallway was an actual gateway to Mr. Richardson's private *world* rather than to his office.

Annette whispered, "This isn't Heaven, is it?" To this, the woman laughed, leading Annette into the tenth office at the end of the hall. Annette took that as a "no."

"I'm afraid Heaven will have to wait for you, Mrs. Slocum. Besides, I'd much rather be here than there any day."

The tenth office was a conference room. It held a long rectangular table surrounded by nine swivel chairs and another water cooler. Serving dishes had been placed on the conference room table. The dishes were virtually empty save for a spot of vegetable oil in one, a lone mushroom in another, and a bowl that housed one single piece of discarded lettuce. There were used China plates, glass goblets, and also silverware that were waiting to be bussed.

"Please excuse the mess, Mrs. Slocum," the woman told her. "Our chef, Mr. Cauliflower, should've taken care of these dishes before your arrival."

Annette wasn't worried about the dishes. Instead, her attention was on one of the walls where a brilliant mural had been hung. The mural looked as if it had been painted sometime during the Renaissance. It featured nine beautifully naked women dancing in a garden, each wearing laurel leaves around their heads. Annette studied it with fascination as the woman took her seat at the head of the table. The woman placed the blood-spotted orange colored peg before her then took a cup from the dispenser and filled it with fresh water. Bubbles brought Annette's attention from the mural. Like the other woman, she sat down.

"You're no doubt wondering what this place is, Mrs. Slocum," the woman assumed. "It's a very special office for a very special function. You, Mrs. Slocum, have been hired by Management as a muse."

"A muse?"

"Exactly." The woman dunked the orange peg into the water rinsing off the blood. Once the peg was cleaned she squeezed the cup in the palm of her hand and, as if by magic, the cup disappeared into thin air or imploded in on itself, Annette wasn't sure. "My name is Fiona, and I've been instructed, due to the unexpected circumstances, to train you."

"Train me?" Annette still wasn't sure she grasped the concept of being a muse. Fiona produced a remote control from her jacket pocket and pressed a button. As the florescent lights in the conference room dimmed, the mural was covered by a movie screen that lowered and clicked into place. As the movie started, Annette was reminded of a black and white news reel. Big words made of block letters popped on the screen. The movie was then narrated by a male's booming voice.

"'*Musing and You*' brought to you by Management. Narrated by Nathaniel J. Cauliflower." Annette turned to Fiona and noticed she was shaking the orange peg dry, inspecting it, and wiping it clean with a cream-colored handkerchief. Annette turned back to the movie and the narration continued. "Since the beginning of time, muses have been inspiring the world around them - painters, writers, sculptors, dreamers and lovers: you name it, they have done it. According to Greek mythology, there were nine. Born of Zeus and Mnemosyne, they each had their own private field of expertise: Terpsichore was the muse of dance; Urania, muse of Astronomy; Thalia, muse of Comedy; Melpomene, muse of tragedy; Clio, muse of history; and the four muse poets: Polyhymnia for sacred poetry; Euterpe for music and lyric poetry; Calliope of epic poetry; and Erato of love poetry. Each had worked tirelessly, for centuries, criss-crossing backwards and forwards throughout time until, one day, they hired replacements and retired. These replacements had been randomly chosen, given offices after their deaths, and trained by the very first muses in the universe's history. As time progressed, these 'First Generation Muses' had filled their quotas and hired the next generation of replacements, and the Second Generation progressed to the Third. The Third passed it on to the Fourth, and then they passed it on to the Fifth, and so on . . . which means if you are watching this training video, you are now one of the elite. You, dear muse, are one of the Ninth Generation."

"So basically, I'm replacing you?" Annette asked Fiona who, in turn, said nothing. She simply kept her eyes on the training video. Annette followed suit. Nathaniel J. Cauliflower continued.

"Now we know what a muse is, so let's talk about what a muse does and, more specifically, how they do it."

It was at this moment that a poorly drawn animation filled the screen. Annette suddenly remembered why she preferred books over television. She had been raised in a house that encouraged imaginative thinking. Her father had only kept a television for special occasions such as weather reports and presidential speeches. Even then, the picture on their television had been mostly static. In her youth, Annette's father had encouraged his children to go out and experience life or read a book and discuss it over dinner.

The instructional video went on. "First introduced in the year 1967 by Hasbro, the Lite-Brite board had been created to allow artists to create pictures by the use of translucent colored pegs when inserted into a grid covered by opaque black paper. A light bulb inside the device, once activated, had caused the peg colors to illuminate. A muse in training," Nathaniel J. Cauliflower preached, "is given an empty Lite-Brite board but for a slightly different purpose. You see, dear muse, envelopes are delivered to a muse's post box and inside each envelope is a colored peg. Whether it's blue, green, yellow, purple, pink, red, white, orange, or cream with bright red polka-dots, the peg is then taken from the envelope and placed into the Lite-Brite board. That's when things for the muse become quite complex. The office folds and unfolds like an elaborate pop-up book. The colored peg transports you into the corresponding life of a specific person, place and time. Once there, it's up to the muse to decide how to proceed. Your job, as the muse, is to inspire the person in that specific page of his or her very own story. Once the inspiration job is done in the allotted time, the book is closed and the muse is returned to the office to await the next peg. This process repeats itself until the entire Lite-Brite board is full. Then, and only then, will the muse retire with a replacement starting a brand new board."

"To fill an entire Lite-Brite board, that'll take forever," Annette thought to herself. In her post mortem denial, she was eager to return to the safety of her library books.

"There are several things to think about before venturing forth, dear muse: the first is the water cooler. Water is a conduit, a necessity for traveling from place to place. Drinking the water lubricates the transition of traveling through these passages. Without it, the journey would be excruciating." Annette wasn't too thrilled that the water cooler was imperative. She had to get used to the obnoxious gargling bubbles each time she took a drink when all she wanted to do was be rid of them.

"Second," the narrator marshaled, "time for the muse is circular, which means that you can travel both forwards and backwards through time. Remember that past, present and future exist both harmoniously and simultaneously. Therefore, don't be surprised if you're inspiring a person suffering from vertigo to bungee jump with his friends one moment and, then, inspiring the painting of the Sistine Chapel the next.

"Third and most importantly: Do not, under any circumstances, leave an envelope unattended. The window of time, or the page of the person's pop-up book, is only open for a limited interval and can only be opened by you: butterfly wings and earthquakes, dear muse! First finish one job before moving onto the next." Annette had read enough science fiction to know that changing one thing in a past timeline might result in a greater change in the future. She hoped a colored peg wouldn't send her to the Jurassic period, where she might accidentally step on a twig. Then, when she would come back, the human race would have evolved into something like a jelly-fish. "You now play a vital part in humanity, dear muse. No one you inspire is too great or too small. No task is ever out of your control. You, by yourself, hold the reins to inspiration. You can and will inspire anyone."

The instructional video ended, the screen receded into the ceiling, the lights brightened and Fiona stood. "Well, there you have it, Mrs. Slocum."

Annette stayed in her chair, once again peering quizzically at the mural. The painting acted like an endorphin as it pulled disjointed memories from her. The memories were of nothing in particular: a mixture of names, faces, and plots of library books. It seemed that now she was dead, Annette's beliefs and reminiscences, once dormant in life, currently buzzed around her head like a swarm of gnats.

"Shall we check out your office, Mrs. Slocum?"

Annette was looking forward to seeing her new office as much as a non-flosser looks forward to a tooth-cleaning from a dentist, but she dutifully followed Fiona anyway.

"Take it from me, Mrs. Slocum, someone who has been here since the First Generation." Fiona spoke reassuringly to Annette as they walked. "Orientation can be a bit overwhelming. Everything will make sense in time."

Fiona's cream-colored heels clipped the tiled floor beneath them and the conversation took a different direction. "Now," Fiona said. "The office is a green one, Mrs. Slocum. The light bulbs used in the hallway ceiling help reduce and conserve energy. Even the envelopes that Management sends us are biodegradable, though Mr. Cauliflower prefers we simply recycle them. It was his idea to modernize. He called it an 'earth-friendly operation.'"

"Cauliflower the chef?" asked Annette.

"Mr. Cauliflower: our chef, our instructional video narrator, our colored peg aficionado – he wears many hats, as you'll see. You'll meet him in due time, Mrs. Slocum. I'm sure of it. He was a Second Generation muse. He's the one who prepares the colored pegs and delivers the envelopes to the post boxes." Fiona went on with her orientation. "You'll notice that we don't rely on clocks in this office. You saw one in the waiting room but we don't rely on it. Muses measure increments of time by the amount of colored pegs that accumulate in one's own board. And speaking of the waiting room," Fiona then stopped and turned to Annette to make sure she was paying attention. "I must ask you not to open the waiting room door until you retire. Mr. Cauliflower uses that door to deliver his envelopes and his gourmet dishes, which Management has allowed him to do for centuries. But a Muse must never trespass back into the waiting room before their board is full. Butterfly wings and earthquakes, yes?"

Annette nodded sheepishly.

Fiona stopped in front of an office and gestured inside. "Behold."

Annette gasped as she stepped through the door of her office. She was expecting four drab walls or perhaps a windowless cubicle-type space to start off with. Instead, Annette had been given a room that was much more elaborate. Annette stood in a three-story library with arched stained glass windows. Rays of sunlight shone down upon stained wooden floors. The polished bookcases stretched so high Annette figured she would need a ladder to reach the top shelves. Her eyes, which traced the height of the shelves, finally settled on a great crystal chandelier which decorated the ceiling. Unfortunately for Annette, each shelf was void of books.

There was a single desk in the lobby of this library accompanied by a swivel chair with a padded leather seat behind it. There were two extra swivel chairs for company. On the desk was an empty inbox and beside the inbox was the Hasbro Lite-Brite board.

"Envelopes are delivered to your post box," Fiona told her "and once they arrive, you're asked to use the *inbox* to store them. Mr. Cauliflower asks that when you're done, please place the used envelopes back into the post box so that he can re-use them." But Annette wasn't listening. She was too distracted by the ornate details of her own personal empty library. In the place of recognizable stories from the Bible, Annette's stained glass windows had impressively constructed murals of the original nine muses.

"There *is* one thing the instructional video didn't show." Fiona propped herself against the desk, arms folded, a serious look on her face. Fiona made sure Annette was paying attention before continuing. "Most envelopes are white but occasionally one will arrive in your post box that's violet."

"Violet?"

"No one is too great or too small, it's true. But the violet ones are the toughest of cases. They're the ones that'll literally push you to your limits if not beyond. If you see one of them, open it immediately, take time to assess the situation, and execute. If you fail, consequences could be disastrous."

Annette nodded.

"I'm serious, Mrs. Slocum. There was once a muse here who had one peg left: one peg before she could retire. When the last envelope came, she felt she was more than ready for it. She cracked open the envelope and found the peg. Can you guess what happened, Mrs. Slocum?"

"No. . ."

"Evangeline, a Second Generation muse, was taken to a neighborhood of duplexes where at least fifty mailboxes were lined along the street. All she had to do was find the right mailbox to place a harmless letter into. You would think that it would have been easy as most letters have an address for the proper recipient. However, in that particular instance, the letter in Evangeline's hand was to be intentionally misdirected. The address on the letter was not supposed to be the address of the mailbox. So Evangeline had fifty mailboxes to choose from. Only one of them had been destined to receive it. Are you following me Mrs. Slocum?"

Annette simply stood looking askance.

"Try as she might, Evangeline failed in that moment. The letter in her hand had not been delivered to the proper address. The client who had been destined to receive that letter went on uninspired which then caused a chain reaction. We, as muses, provide the catalyst for change. When a client goes uninspired, all the individuals that *they* were to inspire as a result also go uninspired . . . so on and so forth. That was seven generations ago and we're still trying to pick up the pieces!"

Annette looked slightly horrified.

"Now I've frightened you. Forgive me. . ." said Fiona, suddenly regaining her managerial attitude. "I've only stressed the importance of this story to emphasize the true impact that you, as a muse, will have on the world. Have no fear, Mrs. Slocum. Any situation, however bleak, can be fixed over time. That's why we have Mr. Cauliflower." Fiona was suddenly lost in thought. "I suppose it was his relationship with Evangeline that brought about that disaster. But that's another memory; another story for another day."

Fiona's grim demeanor brightened as they both heard the click of Annette's post box. Annette turned to the hallway expecting to see her postmaster, but Nathaniel J. Cauliflower had already disappeared. Annette's post box was blue, snorkel-shaped and from the United States. Inside her post box she found a single envelope. Annette was relieved that the envelope was white, especially for her first try. It was light in the palm of her hand as it only carried a small weightless thing inside.

"So . . ." Annette sighed as they both looked down at the seemingly harmless envelope. "I guess this is it."

"You open the envelope," Fiona encouraged.

"I open the envelope." Inside was a green peg that fell into her free palm while she held the envelope with the other.

"You take a drink of water." Fiona handed her a cup of water from the office's water cooler. Annette took a drink, chasing her hesitance with a dramatic gulp. "Then you fit the peg into the Lite-Brite."

"Then I fit the peg into the Lite-Brite." Annette once again thought of butterfly wings and earthquakes. She had never in a million years thought she'd be standing here as a muse, in this office, with a gurgling water cooler and, of all things, a Lite-Brite board. She fit the green peg into the Lite-Brite and, for a moment, nothing happened. They stood there uncomfortably. "So. . ." Annette sighed. "Have you ever had a violet envelope?" Annette's and Fiona's eyes met but, before Fiona could respond, Annette's office and empty library folded and unfolded like an elaborate pop-up book. Thus, Annette's after-life occupation had begun.

CHAPTER 3: ANNETTE SLOCUM'S INITIAL INSPIRATION

There was something hauntingly familiar about the place where the green peg sent Annette. Annette's office had unfolded into a page of someone else's life: the backstage of a concert hall. The lights were dimmed so low that the surroundings were bathed in deep velvet. A sliver of golden light peeking from under the closed crimson curtains suggested the presence of an eager audience awaiting the performance. Annette couldn't decode the details of various conversations she overheard.

What had she been sent to do? Annette couldn't place the theater or, for that matter, time period. And yet there was still a familiarity that troubled her. Annette peeked through the side of the curtain and hoped to catch a tie or dress or hairstyle that suggested a time or place. At first, Annette spied the box seats and wondered if, perhaps, the green-colored peg had sent her to the pop-up chapter of Abraham Lincoln's assassination. But the iconic hat was not present and the clothing of the spectators was far more current.

"Looking for something, Mrs. Slocum?" Annette spun to find Fiona peeking through the curtains behind her. "Don't be alarmed. I always accompany new muses on their first inspiration. Why are you observing the audience?"

If Annette had possessed a reasonable aptitude for conversation, she would have explained the strange familiarity of the theater; but alas, her words were few and remained as scarce as they always were. Annette peeked through the curtains again. As she did, a new wave of memories crashed on the rocky shores of her mind. Daydreaming in the late afternoons while Lyle had worked at the lot, Annette had remembered all sorts of things: snippets of events, faces of half-forgotten individuals she'd encountered in her childhood, and words of encouragement from her father's lips.

It just so happened that, at this particular moment while she stood backstage, a memory scuttled from the depths of her subconscious like a crab emerging from the water onto a beach. In this recollection, the year had been 1987.

Annette had been eight when her father took her and the rest of the family to a concert. The task of finding several seats in the front hadn't been easy and it certainly wasn't cheap either. Considering that this concert was to be Annette's initial encounter with a live violinist, he had spared no expense in making sure the family had the best view. Eight-year-old Annette's baby blue dress had swished as her two older brothers, Franklin and Michael, had led the family's caravan through those who had been seated and flipping through their programs. Annette had been next to last in the family's line, protected safely by the parents that had conceived her: beloved Mom and Dad.

Now this moment was replaying. Adult Annette watched this past scene repeated itself and was quelled by an unsuspected urge to shout out to her family from behind the curtain. She decided against it. How Annette longed for the good old days when expectations were easier and before the harsh reality of adulthood tainted the blissful moments of youth.

A new set of emotions passed over her. The first was exhilaration as she entertained the possibility that, perhaps, she had been sent to inspire herself. Annette wasn't sure how the colored pegs worked. Had she been sent to a chapter in her own private pop-up book? Had the green-colored peg actually been hers all along? Annette turned to ask Fiona these questions. However, Fiona was too focused on the present details. Annette feared that if she asked these questions it might, in some twisted way, hinder the inspiration. The second was mystification speckled with dread; if this wasn't her own pop-up book, whose could it be? Annette's eight-year-old self wasn't the only one in the audience. Hundreds upon hundreds of people were out there. So then who was the intended recipient? The third emotion that crippled her was more a physical reaction – a stomach tied in knots and forehead glistening with sweat. For a few seconds Annette's lungs refused oxygen. The backstage began to shift precariously as if she were standing on a sheet of ice dislodged from a glacier drifting out to sea.

The envelope that arrived in her post box had been a white one, hadn't it? Surely there wasn't some mistake; surely Management hadn't meant to send a violet one instead? Was it normal to have a mentor on the first job? How was she supposed to find the person she had been sent to inspire if there were hundreds of potential contestants?

"Mrs. Slocum, you've gone pale," Fiona consoled, pulling Annette from her worries. "There's no need to panic. Let's assess the situation. You have a concert hall full of people."

"A violet envelope nightmare," Annette croaked.

"No, Mrs. Slocum. Not a nightmare. The green peg sent you back here behind the curtain. Not out there in the audience. So what does that tell you?"

"That the inspiration job takes place backstage?" Annette attempted a deep breath, "Or on stage in front of an entire audience." She'd wished she'd brought a paper sack to avoid hyperventilating. The sickening feeling returned. Fiona patted Annette reassuringly on the back, guiding the muse's eyes from the audience to the near-darkness backstage. They scoured the shadows in hopes that Annette's intended would manifest itself. Hopefully, Annette thought, with a big sign that read "Inspire me."

The stage behind the curtain had been cleared of everything except a music stand, a stool, and a dramatically painted backdrop of a garden in full bloom at sunset. It was clear from the professional look in Fiona's eyes that the surroundings were like any random location a Lite-Brite unfolded: A place of clues and puzzle pieces that, when fused together, revealed the muse's task.

Alas, to Annette, the puzzle pieces were already collected like a painting in the great museum of her past; unfortunately, the light bulb displaying the mental work of art had fizzled out years ago. Outside the curtain in 1987, eight-year-old Annette had been taking in the sights, sounds and general awe of her first concert experience. Behind the curtain Ninth Generation muse Annette tried desperately to recall these memories and sift through them.

Annette hated keeping the arrival of her eight-year-old self a secret from Fiona; she just didn't want to expose the irregularity. If there even was one, Annette certainly didn't want to risk it and wind up facing some great wrath. She feared that seeing her eight-year-old self had somehow changed something. Annette was here to inspire someone. Not to gawk at a past version of her family.

"Mrs. Slocum, your eyes have glazed over again."

Annette said guiltily: "Sorry."

"The green peg sent you backstage. So what does that tell us about your inspiration's vicinity?"

"That the person I'm meant to inspire is close by?"

"Very good, Mrs. Slocum. Now, why don't we take a look around?" In contrast to the crowd on the other side of the curtain, the number of the backstage crew was considerably fewer. There were several stage hands, a stage manager and, she assumed from light under the door, whoever was in the dressing room. None of the crew members seemed to notice the two women as they skulked in the gloom.

From beyond the dressing room door, Annette could hear a bow gliding along the strings of a violin. The music called to her from beyond the door. Annette closed her eyes. The sound somehow coaxed the memories out of Annette's mind where she had kept these stale images captive when she met and married Lyle. Suddenly, they escaped and danced before her in thought.

"I want you to listen to the music, Annette." Her eight-year-old self had craned her ear to her father's lips to better hear his whisper. The lights had been dimmed in the auditorium. "Allow the violin to paint a portrait in your head, then tell me about what you imagined when we go out for ice cream." Eight-year-old Annette's father had scruff on his face and it had grazed gently against her ear. It had made her smile. It also made the older Annette beam as she remembered it.

25

Annette's eight-year-old self had watched as the violinist walked across the stage with instrument in hand. He had been in his fifties and clad in a pressed tux with his graying hair slicked back with gel or sweat, young Annette hadn't been sure. It hadn't really mattered as she had promptly closed her eyes and, like everyone else around her, became still. The violinist had touched the bow to the string. From it had come a sound young Annette had never before encountered. It had pulled her thoughts from her like a crafty bandit.

"Mrs. Slocum?" The voice came from somewhere far away. Annette was barely even sure she heard it. The sound of Fiona's voice was nothing more than a tiny particle of dust in the universe she was envisioning: something akin to fiddlers dancing around a fire, or recalling the sharp crisp ripple of Lyle's shirts caught by a breeze, or the subtle turning of a page in a library book. These images and more swirled playfully about her. "Mrs. Slocum!"

Annette's eyes shot open. The mental fiddlers exited into the shadows, the wind died down in the backyard, and the imagined library book was closed and shelved. She found Fiona next to her. "Mrs. Slocum, will you be inspiring your person or not?"

The past was repeating. The violinist, whom Annette had caught warming up in the dressing room, was now before the audience giving the performance. As Annette's eight-year-old self had collected mental images, the adult Annette was unsure how to proceed. Annette was determined to remember anything that would help her. She needed more time. While the violinist stroked the strings, the backstage, where the green peg had sent her, was beginning to refold. No one from among the audience, or stagehands, not even the violinist, could detect it. But Annette and Fiona were more than aware of the change.

"We don't have long, Mrs. Slocum!" Fiona whispered. "Inspire! Now!" Annette didn't know how to inspire. She didn't know how to do much of anything outside of retrieving the paper from the mailbox, cooking Lyle's breakfast, doing the daily housework and picking out library books. As the song ended and applause followed, the ground below Annette's feet began to rumble. The lights began to flicker. "Mrs. Slocum, execute!"

Annette wracked her mind for any abnormalities of the performance. She tried to picture herself eight years old and once again watching the violinist. She even went so far as to pray to God (something she hadn't done since she married Lyle.) And then it struck her. As the backstage collapsed, Annette flung herself on stage in front of the audience and grabbed the instrument and bow. In a thunderclap, the stage disappeared and Annette landed on the floor with the violin and bow gripped between her fingers.

Only it wasn't Annette's office where she lay. It was a different floor with a shag green carpet. The place and time to which Annette had been flung evaded her detection but one thing was for certain: it was night. Moonlight poured in from the curtains of a small window above her. A window air conditioner unit rattled relentlessly.

With the purloined violin, she stood carefully surveying the partially moonlit room. She was in a seedy hole-in-the-wall hotel. It was a space designed for a single bed, a chair that threatened to cave in, a prehistoric television with tinfoil-draped antennae and a bathroom that no amount of scrubbing could sterilize. Even though at night colors fade and, to the human eye, everything is a variation of grays and black shadows, to Annette the spectrum did have a color: green. It was puke green for the walls, forest green for the carpet below her - except where the moon hit it and then it was closer to jade.

The man lying in the bed was fast asleep and in combat with nightmares. It looked like he had been dipped into a vat of deep turquoise paint. Whoever he was, Annette had a very strong pull on her muse-in-training heartstrings that this was the person she had actually been assigned to inspire. She wondered that if this was the man she was destined to inspire then what was the point of sending her to the concert hall to lift the violin?

"Put it in the chair, Mrs. Slocum." Fiona appeared behind her in the moonlight as a ghostly apparition. Annette held the violin to the moonlight. Its surface shined majestically. "Put it in the chair and we'll return to the office."

Annette held it to her ear and listened. "Do you hear that?"

"Hear what?" The violin was humming even though the strings remained untouched. Starting quietly with a gentle hum, the music then grew in intensity. The man in the bed stirred in his sleep. "Mrs. Slocum, he's about to wake."

Annette wondered where the music was coming from as clearly the violin itself remained quiet. The music grew to a maddening intensity and reverberated off the walls. It was shaking the tin foil above the television. Fiona reached for the violin and, as she did, the man in the bed shot up from the pillows and opened his eyes. For the first time in what Annette felt had been years, a complete stranger looked her straight in the eyes.

He was in his mid forties with matted hair, an untrimmed beard, and bags under his eyes. Whatever events that had led him here to this room were obviously taxing. It was even more surreal as Fiona urged Annette to hand him the violin, which she did. As the violin and it's companion bow touched the man's fingers, the music that troubled the room stopped. Fiona urged Annette to say something inspiring but Annette was still the same anti-social woman as she'd been in life. Before she said anything, or attempted to say anything, the room shook and a thunderclap ripped her from the inspiration.

Annette and Fiona stood in her office again with the water cooler belching its bubbles. "Job well done," Fiona complimented her pupil, patting Annette's back. Annette simply looked to Fiona in bewilderment. "It's probably a good thing you didn't say anything. Don't worry. 'Hello, my name is Mrs. Slocum and I'm a muse. Please take this violin and play to your heart's content.' Then the men in white coats would have arrived."

Fiona stared at Annette's face which hadn't changed since they left the hotel room.

"Well say something, Mrs. Slocum."

"What's he supposed to do with a violin?"

"Play it or use it as a flower-pot. What does it matter? What matters is that you've completed the initial inspiration. You should be proud. You're one peg closer to retirement. And look," Fiona said as she pointed. Another envelope was already waiting in Annette's post box. "Now don't get hung up in the details, Mrs. Slocum. It's not our place to question why: we're only to actively take part in a single moment within the page of a person's life. Be satisfied that you did well on your first case."

"Where are you going?" Annette blurted out.

"You have your envelopes; I have my own." Fiona turned her attention to the ceiling of Annette's private library, winked, and exited the office.

The more Annette sat in her swivel chair and considered why the man in the hotel room was destined for the violin, the more another concern began to occupy her mind. Annette recalled the concert in the past and how the violin had never actually left. A muse had not jumped out onto the stage. *Nothing out of the ordinary had happened then.* Annette had a sneaking suspicion that there were many more mysteries to encounter. As she opened her second white envelope, she was resigned that nothing would ever be "ordinary" for her again.

CHAPTER 4: JIMINY CRICKET REINCARNATED

Life, unlike great blockbuster movies, does not come with a soundtrack. If life had come with one, Annette would expect the place to which the second colored peg had sent her to be accompanied by a haunting lullaby played on an oboe. The cream-colored peg with red polka dots transported her to a warm rainy afternoon without thunder, lightning, or anything more spectacular than water drumming the windows.

Annette stood in a tiny diner where waitresses wore frilly aprons and white tennis shoes. Four people were present in the early morning hours. Five if you were to include Annette. There were two waitresses who both looked equally unsatisfied with life. There was a fry cook who only appeared every so often to set a plate on the pickup counter. And then there was a pathetic-looking man who sorrowfully munched his eggs. Annette didn't recognize any of them; in fact, nothing about this place seemed remotely familiar to her so she sat at a lonely table in a far corner and assessed the situation. To Annette they all looked in dire need of inspiration but only one of them would receive her "special treatment."

Annette hadn't eaten lunch on the afternoon in which she had died; hunger was setting in causing her stomach to rumble. If she hadn't recalled her body smashing against the windshield of the blue Cadillac before the library, Annette would have dismissed her hunger as a faint memory from being alive. But she knew she had died. Hadn't she? Was her hunger real? Why was she hungry if her stomach was, in reality, either splattered across the ground or opened for autopsy somewhere in a morgue?

"I didn't hear you come in, Honey," commented one of the waitresses who now hovered over her. A bell dangled inside the diner's front door but Annette had not entered the diner from it. "Coffee?"

"Water, please," Annette whispered.

"I'll give you a minute to look over the menu," said the waitress whose name tag read "Madge." She handed Annette a menu and opened it to the dessert page. "I'd recommend the peach cobbler. It's a bit early for it, I know, but it's worth a try." Menu selections danced before Annette as Madge delved into the dishes displayed in the pristine plastic-reinforced pages. "If you've got the stomach for it the bacon, egg and cheese platter, is always a customer favorite. Or you can go with a basic old hamburger. If you do that, make sure that you order it medium; if you say 'well done' it comes back a lump of coal; if you want it rare, it moos while you eat it. I'll give you a minute to decide."

Madge then left the table and walked past the sad-looking man and his eggs. "Everything okay, Hun?" He didn't acknowledge her in the least but she didn't stay long enough even if he had tried. If Annette ordered anything, how would she pay for it? She decided not to tempt herself any longer by studying a menu which she couldn't order from. Instead, Annette watched the Man with the Eggs and let her mind wander.

The man had moved on to a helping of brittle hash-browns, she observed. He was clean-shaven with bloodshot eyes, pale cheeks, and a flat-top haircut. His fingernails were long and dirt-caked. Annette wondered who this man was and what had brought him here. Where was he going? Was he stuck within a private purgatory of his personal pop-up book as she had once been before she had discovered life between the pages?

"Excuse me," Annette whispered inquisitively to Madge, as the waitress set the water on the table.

"Decided yet, Hun?"

"Not quite, but what can you tell me about him?" Now they were both staring at the man.

"Oh." Madge the waitress cocked her hip. "I'm not really sure, to tell you the truth. He started comin' in five days ago. Every morning since he sits there and eats his eggs in silence. He tips well and leaves. He's never spoken to anyone as far as I know. Strange, huh?"

It appeared to Annette that the man shared similar feelings about communication but was that enough to mark him as the one she was meant to inspire? The violinist had meant nothing to her but when she saw the man lying in the hotel bed her heart-strings had hummed. Perhaps the one she was meant to inspire in the diner would strum her heart-strings too. If that were the case, then the Man with the Eggs would simply be a man with eggs and nothing more.

By the time Annette pulled herself from her thoughts, Madge had abandoned the table. The muse continued to survey the two waitresses and the fry cook. Madge looked to be in her mid-forties, possibly fifties, and seemed like she'd worked in this diner her entire life. *"Did Madge have a hidden ambition,"* Annette wondered? If she did, Annette was certain she wasn't the one to provide it for her heart-strings didn't hum.

The fry cook appeared intermittently. He seemed to Annette to be in his mid-thirties with a healthy amount of facial hair that hadn't seen a razor in a few weeks. The color of his beard was dark as the hair on his tattooed forearms. He, too, looked like he'd been part of the diner for his entire life. Whoever it was that checked the order slips and cooked the food wasn't Annette's client.

A plate of fresh-baked bran muffins was on the counter. Ghostly steam emanated from the plate. The aroma of the buttered bread made Annette salivate at the prospect of snatching one unnoticed. Had she been reduced to stealing bran muffins to get by?

The waitress who hadn't yet approached Annette's table stood refilling the donut tray. Annette understood that her job entailed inspiring someone but this was torture! There they were: glazed sugary lumps of paradise displayed under the lights of the diner. She'd never been much for donuts but, as she was practically starving, Annette didn't really care what she ate as long as it was inside her belly. Unfortunately, now was not the

32

time to indulge herself. So she tried her best to inspire despite her ravenous appetite.

As the waitress stacked the glazed donuts, Annette caught something in her eyes; the pupils of which were magnified four times their actual size by obnoxiously thick lenses in black frames. The waitress hungered not for the baked goods before her but for something else. Something undefined yet as crisp as the pages of a new book. Before Annette knew it her heart-strings were teased like a bow on the strings of a violin and, as if by some invisible force, Annette was soon standing in front of the counter.

The waitress, whose name tag read "Doris," looked to find Annette and forced a smile. She held a donut aloft with a pair of tongs. Her glasses were hideous, no doubt about it. No words were spoken between the two, even as Annette was lifting her hands. Like before, the landscape began to rattle jostling Annette's attention, which meant that, in a few seconds, the inspiration would soon conclude. While Annette was distracted, the donut slipped between her fingers to the floor. Its glazed exterior plopped on the ground between them while the man was standing to pay. For a moment, the rattling stopped. The three of them stood in awkward silence staring at the wasted donut. The man kept his eyes to the floor as though his pupils were pulled by gravity.

Doris bent down to pick up the donut but the man beat her to it. Their hands met followed by their eyes. And then the most unexpected thing happened: the man, after five days without responding to anyone in the diner, said three words.

"Here you go."

The man handed Doris the donut and left the diner without even batting an eye in Annette's direction as if she were invisible.

Doris didn't acknowledge the donut or the fact that Annette finally seized the moment to snag a few bran muffins. Instead, Doris simply stood there like a deer caught in headlights as the rain drummed on the glass door the man had exited from. Annette slumped back in her booth. She secreted the bran muffins inside a few napkins and privately nibbled a few crumbs as the rattling started again. The silverware setting in front of Annette shook, as did the water in the glass, and before she could do anything else the pages of the pop-up book folded and unfolded.

Annette knew better than to assume she would land back in the office she had departed from. So it came as no surprise that she found herself reduced to the size of a cricket and standing on Doris' left shoulder. Doris was in a Honda Civic much like the one in which Lyle drove off in the mornings. Annette was sure it was in considerably worse shape from the mildew smell that exuded from the cushions. Rain poured down relentlessly and more heavily than before. Through the windshield Annette spied a funeral and could make out the Man with the Eggs standing beside and staring down at a closed casket in the rain. In the driver's seat of her Honda Civic, Doris also watched this sad spectacle.

Throughout the funeral, the rain pounded the hood of Doris' car. Annette's mind began to whirl. Here she was in a stranger's car much like Fiona had occupied hers unbidden at the library. If Annette were to speak, would Doris listen or bolt for the street to be promptly pulverized by another blue Cadillac? Annette was earnestly praying that the past wouldn't repeat itself and that she wouldn't inadvertently cause a death instead of an inspiration.

Completely unaware that Annette was standing on her left shoulder, Doris grabbed a tissue from the glove compartment. Annette, not used to being the size of a cricket, squealed and held tight to Doris' shirt fabric. When Doris righted herself, the muse took a breath and spoke.

"Why don't you go and say hello to him?" Annette's voice was so quiet it was barely audible over the rain; obviously it was loud enough as Doris spun. Swatting at Annette and thinking her a bug, Doris caught sight of the tiny Annette long enough to know that she was dealing with a tiny human instead. The bran muffins that Annette had stolen earlier, which had also shrunk to microscopic crumbs before the swatting, toppled in between the seat cushions. Bewildered, Doris the waitress held Annette aloft in the palm of her hand and asked:

"Where did you come from?"

"I'm not really here. I'm a figment of your imagination."

"You're some figment," came Doris' response. Doris then studied Annette's features. From Annette's angle, Doris' eyes were humongous. "You were in the diner earlier weren't you? You're the one who didn't catch the donut. Who are you and why are you so small?"

"Think of me as your own personal Jiminy Cricket. Why don't you go to him and say 'hello?'" Annette asked again. Doris studied the Man with the Eggs through the front window. The rain was reflected by her thick lenses. A look of surrender spread across her face like margarine on bread. "Oh, come on," Annette interjected. "I saw that look you two shared in the diner."

"I can't go to him and say 'hello.'"

"Why not?"

"Because that's not how things work out with me. That's why."

"What's so difficult about it?"

"You wouldn't understand." Doris looked at the man standing in the rain and sighed. "Even if I did say 'hello,' I'd stutter my words and he'd think me an idiot."

"Better for him to think you're an idiot than not think of you. At least if he thinks of as an idiot he'd be thinking about you." Annette wasn't quite sure where this encouragement was coming from; it was as if she were possessed by a peppy cheerleader. To counter her excess in dialogue when she retired to her office after the inspiration, Annette planned to sit in silence - absolute silence.

"Look," came the words from Annette's throat, "at least do something above stalking him in your car. Get him a card or flowers or a trip to Cancun. You obviously want to, Doris . . . all I know is that I wouldn't be here playing your conscience if you weren't meant to speak to him. So put yourself out there because someday you're going to be like whoever is inside that casket. You don't want to spend the rest of eternity wishing you'd done something do you?"

As if thirty years of pent-up words had suddenly burst open the floodgate, Annette found herself pouring out a variation on the advice her father had spoken to her before he had walked her down the aisle to marry Lyle.

Annette remembered the moments that preceded her changing her last name to Slocum. She stood in the back of the church draped in a spectacular wedding dress that had worked miracles on her rather drab facial features. Her father took her by the arm and started to walk but Annette wouldn't move. The bridesmaids, flower girl, five-year-old ring bearer, congregation, and Lyle were awaiting her arrival.

"You look beautiful, Annette." Her father smiled, fitting the veil over Annette's face. Annette spied that the flower on his jacket was a little crooked but said nothing. "Are you sure this is what you want to do?"

Annette nodded but inside she wasn't sure if this was what she wanted to do or not. It seemed like a good idea at the time. Pachelbel's "Canon" ended and the music for Annette's walk down the aisle erupted soon after. Her future was only a few steps away. Between the doors were hundreds of faces turned in her direction. Annette let out a gasp of fear.

"Annette," her father whispered. "Don't think about the people. Think about my arm in yours." He once again held out his arm and Annette took it. Annette swallowed hard and fought back the apprehension. "Just do me a favor, won't you?" her father said.

Annette turned her eyes from the people's faces to her father. "Don't let your marriage to Lyle define you. He's a good man, yes, and he'll make you very happy, no doubt about it. He'll be able to support your family. Annette, if you ever listened to your old man about anything," he took a breath and smiled. "Don't forget to find things in your future that inspire *you*."

"You're not a figment of my imagination, are you?" Doris the waitress asked. Annette wasn't sure how to respond. "Who are you, really?" Annette shrugged her shoulders. The flesh of Doris' hand was as pliant as a pillow.

"It doesn't matter who I am, Doris. Stop wasting time! That man isn't going to be in your life forever!"

"You know what?" Doris puffed with a newfound precarious confidence. "You're right." Doris brought Annette's tiny body to the dashboard, switched off the ignition, fumbled for the umbrella under the passenger seat and unfolded it outside of her car door. Underneath the umbrella seconds later Doris turned to Annette with a burning passion in her eyes. "If I sound like an idiot, I sound like an idiot. I am human, after all…"

"That's the spirit." Annette forced a smile as the car's pop-up page folded and unfolded. Sitting in her swivel chair empty-handed, Annette wondered what her life would have sounded like. Would there have been any sound? Certainly not brass, woodwind, percussion, or string . . . then what? Could it be, Annette wondered, that her life had been one with no sound? If that were the case . . . what sort of life had that been?

CHAPTER 5: RELIEF FROM THE RANCID REVIVAL OF ROTHCHILD

Twenty-nine inspirations had passed for Annette following her return from Doris' pop-up book. She took the used envelopes from her inbox and placed them in the post box outside her office door to be picked up by Nathaniel J. Cauliflower. "*How was it possible that individuals were so uninspired,*" Annette wondered? There had been a time of art and music: a time in which composers had composed, when painters and sculptors created something from nothing that would eventually be housed inside museum walls, and when history had been filled with great inventions and groundbreaking innovations which had passed from one era to the next. Now, as she visited the modern world, Annette found her clients worried less about their own originality and focused, instead, on more day-to-day matters that were chained to the mundane: the commonplace world of stocks, paychecks, healthcare and the life of the unemployed.

As she sat and contemplated such things, Annette was limp in her swivel chair staring at the sunlight in its luxurious luminescence. The daylight outside the stained glass windows of her personal library was caught in an eternal afternoon. Though this sight should have brought forth a sense of happiness, Annette's thoughts were anything but joyful. A memory as hot as a heated oven kissed her senses leaving behind an unshakable stinging sensation. In this memory Annette could see the face of her childhood adversary peering down from the branches of a tree. His name was Jonas Rothchild.

*

Eight year-old Annette enjoyed resting under the shade of trees. The trees on the playground were particularly pleasant but there was noise around her: basketballs crashing against chained hoops, tennis shoes scuffing the gravel, and screams and laughter from fellow students running about the yard. Annette often preferred some place quiet as an alternative. The tree that Annette preferred over the others was in the park just off from the man-made lake behind the pavilion. It was quiet in the late afternoons. The wind rustled the leaves and distant birds twittered from one branch to the next.

It so happened that, on a particularly warm afternoon, as young Annette was nestled nicely against the trunk of the tree, an apple dropped from the branches hitting the top of her head. Eight-year-old Annette looked up from L'Engle's *A Wrinkle in Time*, rubbed the top of her head, and hoped to ease the mild pain. She then cast her eyes through the branches. A face peered down out of the leaves at hers: a grinning orangutan named Jonas Rothchild. Sunlight behind him caused his face to obscure in shadow.

"Whatcha readin'?" asked Jonas. Young Annette's eyes turned to the thrown apple which had rolled to the left of her knee. She had picked it up and turned it this way and that in her hand. Another apple was jettisoned to the ground. "Hey, I'm talkin' to you!"

Not happy in the least that the stranger had intentionally tried twice to knock her unconscious, young Annette stood, closed the book, and swept quickly out of range.

"Hey!" yelled Jonas, who climbed down from the tree. Annette looked over her shoulder to find his slender figure was draped in a black tee-shirt and dirt-covered jeans. His hair was dust-coated. She stopped running for an instant and stood waiting for the boy to apologize.

"My name's Jonas," said the boy, staying exactly where he remained beneath the tree. "What's your name?" Young Annette turned her back to him and continued to walk. "What's your *name*?" he called out again from behind her but ever-so-antisocial Annette didn't reply.

39

"You can't run from me!" Jonas yelled after her as she disappeared from the path. "Eventually you'll have to say *something*!"

*

Annette looked away from the sunlight that draped through the stained glass windows hoping that, by doing so, she could stuff the memories of Jonas into the murky abyss from which they had crawled. Even after attempting to do so, Annette could not shake Jonas' revival in the back of her mind. She worried that the office might cause Jonas to manifest as part of her scenery. Annette spun, half expecting to see Jonas standing in her office doorway.

There was someone standing in her doorway but it was not Jonas. The man named Mr. Richardson stood with two plates on one arm along with silverware and cloth napkins. He was about to knock politely on the doorframe to announce himself when Annette had turned. Mr. Richardson apologized if he had startled her. His dimples were once again visible as he smiled and said: "Hungry?"

Annette looked at the plates on Mr. Richardson's arm. The chef Nathaniel J. Cauliflower had prepared personal Cornish game hens adorned with garlic and rosemary for each muse. Mr. Richardson had taken it upon himself to bring Annette hers.

"Not too bad for your first meal here," he offered. Steam rose from the glazed hens carrying the garlic perfume with it. Considering that she had not eaten anything since before she had been struck by the blue Cadillac, Annette stepped aside to allow Mr. Richardson access. "Nice digs!" Mr. Richardson observed as he stepped through the threshold and observed her office.

"You must be a reader," Mr. Richardson said as he sat the plates down on Annette's desk. "A library with empty shelves is pretty sad, you know? I suppose that's the nature of the beast. Management gives us offices of locations in which we're familiar but then somehow manages to remove the one thing that really makes our space complete. For you it's a library

40

without the books. If you ever get a chance to visit Fiona's office, you'll find that she sits in an art gallery with empty frames. Mr. Hill, whose office is straight across the hall from yours, has a greenhouse without the seeds and roots. And then there's the office of Mr. Andrews who's been attempting to recreate his beloved Ship of Dreams. And then there's Harriet who hasn't done anything with her office. She just sits in a drab little cubicle with empty egg-shell walls. I'm hoping she'll do something with it someday but that's her decision. Have you met Harriet yet?"

Annette, who had already taken to her Cornish hen with gusto, finally looked up and shook her head.

"You remind me of her in a way," Mr. Richardson said. "She too was quiet when she first arrived. But death has a way of helping anyone through that I suppose. Just as death has ways of making us remember."

He extended a hand while the other sifted through the contents of his plate with a polished silver fork. "I'm Lucas, by the way. Lucas Richardson." Lucas' dimples deepened on the sides of his cheeks as he picked apart his own hen. Annette blushed and turned her eyes back to the plate. "Not much for conversation, huh? Well that's alright. If you're not careful, Annette, you'll have me talking your ear off. Fiona can sometimes come off a bit dry during orientation. That's why I like to take it upon myself to be the more personal welcome wagon for new muses." Lucas attended to his own plate. He took a bite of the hen and savored its flavor. He groaned in satisfaction and took another bite. He went on: "I'm what Management would call a Seventh Generation Muse and it seems like my employment here has been going on forever. Mr. Hawkins, Ms. Simonton, and Mr. Hill are all Eighth's: even Harriet. Harriet's an Eighth. Mrs. Donnelly's a Ninth Generation, like you. Mr. Andrews is a Sixth; he's been here forever. No one's been here longer than Fiona. I've been trying to map out the genealogy of the muses. I haven't gotten very far though."

Lucas looked proud of himself when he said: "I *have* managed to crack the color code of the pegs. Management doesn't mention it in the instructional video but each color stems back to a specific original muse. My personal peg color was green. The muse that green corresponds to is Euterpe, the Muse of Music and Poetry. Which I suppose is appropriate considering my affinity to the guitar. That's one thing Management allowed me to have in my balcony, a guitar. But I don't play much anymore. It brings back too many unwanted memories."

Annette nodded.

"What's your story, Annette? Any special dreams, unfulfilled urges? Any unwanted memories?"

Annette thought to herself for a moment. Did she have any special dreams or unfulfilled urges? Sure, she had liked to open the windows in the middle of a nice afternoon. She had adored hanging Lyle's shirts on the line, and had loved the breeze fluttering the fabric. Surely there was something she had always wanted to do but for the moment nothing came to mind. On the other hand, when she thought of all the things she'd rather *not* remember, an entire laundry list unfolded before her.

She could feel the memories of Jonas Rothchild breathing in the shadowy recesses like a mechanical beast lying in wait in a horror house on Halloween. Instead of bringing Jonas up, Annette let slip another concern. "Have you ever had a violet envelope?"

"Ah, so you do talk!" Lucas cheered. Annette blushed. "Have I ever, Annette! Three."

"*Three* of them?"

"Three, indeed," Lucas offered what was left of his Cornish hen to Annette but she declined. "And boy, they were like walking across broken glass with your bare feet, you know? The first one was a movie theatre. I mean, try and inspire someone in a movie theatre! That show was packed."

"What happened?"

"Well, cutting right to the chase, I had to find a guy who wanted to put his arm around this girl he was sitting next to and liked a lot. I mean, how could I have known that's what I was supposed to do, you know? These colored pegs don't really come with an instruction booklet. It's all about instincts. *Anyway.*"

42

How Lucas said the word "anyway" fluttered something inside Annette. She had a strong suspicion that the muse beside her was gay but that was the least of what made him Lucas. Annette could tell there was something deeper: a hidden room within him that had rarely opened since he had been given the muse position. "The guy stood up to refill the popcorn and there was like this pull on my heart-strings."

"Like he was the one you were meant to inspire and no one else?"

"When I discovered him, it sort of hit me. Like he was a short story I've read a hundred times. Some people call that 'pull' inherent when a muse is hired," Lucas shrugged. "But only Management knows how it all works, you know?"

"And the second violet envelope?"

"The second was to a race track, Annette." Lucas' face turned grim. "A disaster if there ever was one. I mean, try to inspire someone who's riding a race car past checkered flags to reach a finish line."

Annette tried to imagine herself in that kind of situation. She'd never been one for excitement. Bright lights, loud noises, and a crowd of spectators made her nervous.

"How does working as a muse suit you?" asked Lucas.

"Inspiring individuals," Annette rolled her eyes. "Well, it's complicated."

"Ha! To put it lightly!"

"Well . . ." Annette began. She had never been one for story-telling but she regaled him with the events of past inspiration jobs to the best of her ability. "I didn't realize the office could really 'fold and unfold like an elaborate pop-up book.' I don't know what I was expecting. But there it was – one minute I was one place. The next moment I was in another." Annette caught herself. She was actually having a conversation. It frightened her.

"Go on . . ." Lucas coaxed.

"I guess I was expecting something different. The world's grasp on inspiration isn't what I thought it would be. For example:" Annette sat forward. Looking into Lucas' eyes made her feel uncomfortable. She looked at the remains of the hens instead. "A donut drops to a café floor resulting in Doris

43

the Waitress to gather gumption to tell someone 'hello.' Not to mention the violin! I stole that violin from a concert and handed it to some random stranger in a hotel room. For what? How could dropping a donut and handing someone a violin change the course of their personal histories?"

Lucas thought of something and opened his mouth to reply.

Annette had more to say: "And for that matter how would my life have changed if I hadn't run from Fiona outside the library? What could she have possibly said or done to change *anything*?" Annette fell silent, contemplating such mysteries further.

"If there's one thing I've learned, Annette," Lucas' serious face was as expressive as his smile, "is that trying to figure out what it all means is futile. Time is circular as the instructional video taught us. To try and decipher *why* we do the things we do . . . well, I don't think we're supposed to *know* why. That's up to Management, you know? Still that doesn't stop us from being curious." Lucas winked playfully and finished off his hen. "You mentioned a library. What else was there besides the library?"

Annette shrugged. "Nothing really."

"So there's nothing to say about your life outside the office, huh?"

"Life was fairly uneventful," Annette told him. "Except for . . ."

"Yes?"

If Lucas had stood beside her during childhood he would have found countless times in which her school bully, Jonas, had tormented her. Annette prayed the memories of Jonas wouldn't resurface from the depths of her brain the way children dare not tread through darkened, fog-filled cemeteries.

There came a sound from the hallway. While they had sat there talking, Nathaniel J. Cauliflower had delivered more inspirations to Annette's post box. By the time she reached the hallway, Mr. Cauliflower had already disappeared.

"We'll save more conversation for a later date," Lucas promised. "Had your fill?" he asked. Annette nodded and Lucas gathered their plates. "Well Annette, don't be a stranger. I'm two offices down from you and across the hall from Mr. Andrews. If you're ever in need of a change of scenery that is."

Before he left, Annette asked him: "Those violet envelopes . . . how far do they push you?"

Lucas thought for a moment with his eyes searching for the right words. "Let me put it this way: the third violet envelope sent me back to September 9th, 2001 - a day that I remember living before I was brought here. I thought that I was given a second chance to save as many people as I could, even if I was to inspire only one. But I couldn't just convince one - I wanted to convince them all. I'm only one man; I couldn't get everyone off of those planes or out of the World Trade Center even though I wanted to, you know? But that's the crux of it. Management only affected a handful of people but trying to understand how these people were chosen would be an even greater headache."

He seemed to be encountering his own dark thoughts. Annette could see that his eyes were starting to glisten with a hint of emotion which he quickly waved away.

"So . . ." Lucas smiled once again. His dimples deepened. "Welcome, Annette, to our humble corner of the universe." He turned to go then stopped. "I almost forgot." Lucas handed Annette a stapled handwritten packet complete with a map of the musing offices and their occupants along with a list of the peg colors and the muses they represented. There were several pages on his personal procedures on dealing with violet envelopes. "It's a packet I give to everyone when they first arrive; a little more casual of an orientation. Godspeed, Annette." And with that he was out the door.

Annette sat Lucas' packet on her desk. She planned to flip through it on her next break.

There was a white envelope waiting in her post box. She cracked open the lip of the envelope and out plopped a red peg. She wondered what muse the red-colored peg corresponded with. For that matter, Annette wondered about her own colored peg. If she remembered correctly, hers had been orange. Who was her original corresponding muse? Did the color have any special weight on the kind of inspiration given to the client? If so, how would her life have changed had she not been run over by the Cadillac? With a drink of water from her water cooler, she fit the peg into the Lite-Brite. The office then folded and unfolded.

She found herself up an apple tree. Below her was a man who Annette figured was the famous Isaac Newton. She plucked an apple from a branch and aimed it directly over his head. As the apple collided on Newton's head below, the leaves around Annette were combed by a breeze. While she thought about it the tree suddenly reminded her of one she had once climbed in her childhood to escape her other siblings. She found the branches, leaves, and patches of sunlight in Newton's tree soothing. However, the longer Annette enjoyed the tree the more the brick wall that safeguarded the memories of being bullied in school by Jonas soon began to deteriorate issuing forth the first recollection of her adversary . . . followed by the second encounter.

*

After the incident with the tree in the park and the bludgeoning apples, Jonas appeared in young Annette's classroom the very next day with a miserable announcement to boot. His family had moved from another state and he had not only been scheduled to learn in the same classroom but had been assigned in the desk directly behind Annette for the rest of the year. As he passed her desk, Jonas' eyes were locked on hers while the left side of his mouth curled upwards in a sneer.

*

Coming out of her memory, Annette found herself in her swivel chair once again and staring at the sunlight as it washed over the empty shelves of her library. Her heart was racing and the palms of her hands were sweating. She had to remember that Jonas wasn't in her life anymore. Neither was her husband Lyle, for that matter. She had a job that allowed her the opportunity of inspiring the world and, for once, Annette had something even greater than a plate of Cornish hens garnished with garlic and

46

rosemary, or a tree under which she could read, or a school bully haunting her memories.

After thirty years, Annette had found in Lucas Richardson someone she could potentially call a friend.

CHAPTER 6: STAFF MEETINGS AND SUNSETS

The first time Annette Slocum had ridden an airplane she and Lyle were on their honeymoon to Las Vegas. It was a smaller aircraft with little wiggle room. On one side of Annette was Lyle and, on the other, was a vacant seat. Annette looked forward to the instant that the door at the front of the plane would close so she could move over and stare out over the wing. The plane had already finished boarding so this prospect had potential.

Lyle had already been napping; the overture of his snore-symphony had begun even though the plane had not yet left the tarmac. If she moved over one seat for a better view, there would be no protest from him. From where she sat, Annette looked out the window but the view was limited. She watched as the afternoon sun ducked behind a cloud. She watched attendants fuel the plane and she guessed that the rumbling underneath was from airline workers storing the cargo into the plane like stuffing into a Thanksgiving turkey.

"Excuse me," a male's voice spoke. Annette's heart plummeted as she looked up to see a dangerously skinny, rugged man with a developing beard. He was wearing a tweed jacket, buttoned-up shirt, and black silk neck-tie. The glasses the man wore on the bridge of his nose led Annette to believe he was some kind of college professor even if he only appeared to be in his early twenties. He was carrying a book with him, something by John Steinbeck, but his hand covered the title – it might have been *Grapes of Wrath* or *East of Eden*, judging from the size of it. She wasn't sure as Annette begrudgingly stood and sacrificed the potential window seat to let him by. Inside she was furious but said nothing.

She spent the rest of the flight between a snoring Lyle and the man with the book, while a wave of prickly embarrassment washed over her every time she cast her eyes out the window. The flight was turbulent and, more often than not, the discomfort Annette felt was doubled by nausea. While Lyle was holding on to the dreams in his head, and the man was reading John Steinbeck, Annette anxiously clutched the vomit bag and hoped to God she didn't actually have to use it.

*

Annette had never been a fan of airplanes so one might imagine her mood when a green peg sent her to one. Perhaps it was the proximity of the seating, or the scuff marks on the small windows, or the stuffiness of the atmosphere but, regardless of the exact aversion, Annette felt uneasy. The green-colored peg was indifferent to Annette's feelings. Here she was sitting next to a man who, like Annette, found comfort in the sky outside. He was in his seventies with graying hair and a face blemished with wrinkles. He wore a muted green dress shirt. His sleeves were rolled and his brown suit tie was loosened from his collar.

The sun was setting over the horizon with a remarkable orange glow that could only be formulated in dreams. Orange was dotted with deep purple as clouds hovered regally. Bright watercolors were reflected below by an expanse of ocean. It was only when a flight attendant walked by with a cart and asked if Annette wanted anything that the conversation between muse and inspiree began.

The client said to Annette: "Oh. Hello."

Annette could've said hello back and introduced herself formally but she didn't. Once again silence overtook her.

"I would like a coffee, please," the man requested of the flight attendant.

Annette then found her voice and asked for water.

"Where did you come from?" the man beside her asked as the flight attendant poured his coffee.

49

"I was cramped between two obese women and needed an aisle seat." Annette lied.

He added cream to his coffee and looked at her quizzically. He then asked her: "Have we met before? You look familiar."

"I don't think so," she told him.

"Ah . . . well, it's always nice to have company."

Annette felt the pull on her heart-strings which meant that she had met the right person. But what didn't follow was the feeling that she would know how to inspire him. The color of this man's peg was green so she knew that the original muse was Euterpe, the Muse of Music and Lyric Poetry. But there were no musical items to hand to this man as she had previously done with the violin. What existed was an emptiness that Annette couldn't place. She hadn't a clue how to help her client; what could Annette do to inspire someone on an airplane besides simply sit and talk?

"So . . ." Annette sighed, taking a sip of her water. "Are you a frequent flyer?"

"Yes, I suppose I am." The man said nothing more but quietly sipped his coffee and returned his attention out to the horizon. Annette understood if he wanted to be quiet but this was not one of those moments for her to be shy.

"So what do you do?" Annette forced the conversation.

"I quietly sit and watch sunsets from airplane windows," he answered.

"Does that have good pay?" Annette hoped that last comment would put a smile on the man's face as it certainly added a tiny grin to hers.

"When I'm uninterrupted, yes," he murmured only loud enough for Annette to hear.

The sunset was beautiful. Annette couldn't argue with that. But there had to be more to this man than coffee and watching the sky. Annette feared she had little time left and she didn't know what else to say. She had exhausted her efforts so she sat there and watched the sunset with him in respectful silence. Once the sun set and the sky was nothing more than a quilt woven of stars, he finally spoke again.

"That was rude of me, I apologize. I always take time to watch the sunset, no matter where I am. That way if I died I could say, 'well, at least I got to see the last sunset.'"

"I like sitting in the backyard listening to Lyle's shirts dry on the clothes line," Annette suddenly realized how ridiculous that sounded. However, she said nothing to correct herself.

"Lyle?"

"My husband. Well, *ex*-husband I guess. Are you still married after a death?" Annette consulted the ring on her finger.

"'Till death do us part.' The answer is in your wedding vows." He instinctively turned back to the window.

"Then I suppose he wouldn't be my husband anymore?"

The airplane then began to rattle. It didn't seem to faze the man beside her at all but Annette took the turbulence as a sign it was time to inspire him as the pop-up book page in his life was about to unfold.

"You know what's even better than watching every sunset?" she asked him as she stared into the plastic water cup before her. "Watching every sunrise. When I was married to Lyle, I would wake up every morning at five fifteen and, while I cooked his breakfast, I'd occasionally look out the window at the sun on the horizon. Sort of like an opening scene to an opera."

"Instead of a dismal end," he added dryly.

"I didn't mean it like that," Annette said, suddenly feeling a wave of guilt. Her client held his cup of coffee and stared into it. She asked him, "What's your story?"

"My story?" The man asked. "It's not important. I'd hate to bore you with the details."

"Bore *me* with the details?" Annette sighed, taking a sip of her airplane water. "*My* life is the boring one."

"I work for a living. Like my father and my father's father before him: a genetic flaw in my family history. We're all workaholics." The man took another a sip of his coffee. "Not a sunset goes by that my mind isn't elsewhere. Conversations with employees, incidents that need problem-solving, numbers which need crunching . . ."

The airplane began to rattle again. Any minute now the current inspiration job would end and Annette still needed to inspire him.

"When I lay awake in bed at night the life that I've missed because of work flashes before my eyes. For years I'd come home after my children were tucked in to bed. Then I'd leave before they'd even awakened for school. My wife practically raised them single-handedly, you see. But," the man beside her shifted his feet to a more comfortable position, "my children have all grown and have children of their own. Watching sunsets reminds me of fireflies in the summertime. When I was a little boy, I'd catch one and hold it in my hand." After sipping his coffee he added, "Here the old man goes again slipping into memories no one wants to hear."

"I'm fond of your memories," Annette told him, hoping that he'd be inspired before the airplane refolded. Another sip of coffee brought an intermission to his story.

"There are so many mornings I wish I'd stayed around, had breakfast with my children, packed their lunches in paper sacks, or taken them to school," he intoned before falling silent. Then his eyes widened, "You're absolutely right, my dear. This whole time I've been wasting my life watching sunsets when I should've been watching sunrises instead." He held the coffee up to toast. "Here's to sunrises."

Annette raised her own plastic water cup up to join him. "To sunrises." They both took a sip of their drinks. Annette sat her cup on the tray table. *Where were the anxious rumbles now,"* Annette wondered? Had it been just turbulence she had mistaken for the turning of the pop-up page?

"Tell me, my dear, what *did* happen to Lyle? How did he finally meet his end?" The rumbles suddenly returned, seemingly determined to extract the muse from the location. Annette figured she was already on her way back to the office, so what did it matter if she spoke the truth?

"Nothing's happened to Lyle. At least that I'm aware of." The airplane, the star-filled sky, and the man with the coffee were then replaced by her personal library, the water cooler and Lite-Brite board. As Annette sat once again in the swivel chair, she thought again about Lyle. If her marriage to her husband had ended the moment when her body collided with the blue Cadillac in front of the library, Annette should feel like an empty shell; dried shed skin from a snake as she simply sat staring at the wall. Instead she felt alive and slightly empowered by the adrenaline of her musing position.

A knock on her office door interrupted the thought of the former Mrs. Slocum.

"Staff meeting." The person in her doorway was a strict-looking female muse in a gray blouse and navy-blue skirt. This muse's hair had been placed in a tight-fitted bun intensely secured by a fistful of perfectly arranged bobby-pins. Annette didn't say anything in response. The muse, impatiently, spoke again. "Are you coming, Annette, or aren't you?"

Annette reluctantly pulled herself from her swivel chair and followed the muse down the drab hallway, past the other post boxes and offices, and into the conference room. All nine modern day muses, including Annette, were there. She recognized Lucas instantly as, from his seat, he waved. When Annette realized she was the only one standing she gave a small wave in response and sat in the only empty chair at the conference table.

Fiona stood regally from her swivel chair and called the meeting to order.

"Mrs. Slocum is new to our sanctuary and introductions are required. This is Mr. Richardson, whom you've already met, then Mrs. Donnelly, Ms. Simonton, Mr. Hill, Mr. Andrews, Mr. Hawkins, and Harriet." As the names were mentioned each modern day muse raised a hand and waved, or simply acknowledged Annette with a slight nod of the head (except Harriet, the strict-looking muse, who stared at Annette with daggers for eyes). She at first wondered what Harriet's problem was and, secondly, why Harriet's was the only first name mentioned. Annette would never remember these names and hoped Fiona wouldn't quiz her on them.

"Let's begin the meeting, Muses." The screen that had once been used for the instructional video was now used to project a presentation. Harriet took down the minutes. "There's been a noticeable difference in our production since the last staff meeting Muses," Fiona told the lot. "In our previous meeting we discussed the breathtaking incline of our inspirations. Since we met last, however, the number of our inspirations has actually declined in a staggering rate. Can anyone tell me why that is?"

"Perhaps the more modern the world becomes our clients grow less accustomed or susceptible to inspiration in general," said Mr. Andrews.

"Well put, Mr. Andrews," said Fiona. "The amount of envelopes that the office has received since the last staff meeting has decreased by nearly double. While Mr. Cauliflower is working with Management to arrange for more inspirations we must take extra care with the inspirations we *do* have. I've recently spoken with Mr. Cauliflower about the efficiency of your inspirations. While you're fulfilling the needs of our individuals, Mr. Cauliflower believes that with a little more attention and focus, we can truly make an even more lasting impression in the lives of our clients." Fiona turned her eyes on Lucas. "Mr. Richardson?"

"Fiona?"

"Would you mind telling your peers about your most recent inspiration? What was the situation? What would you have done differently to create an even more resonant outcome?"

"In the most recent inspiration . . ." Lucas thought for a moment of his recent encounter and then continued. "It was in a seafood restaurant where a little girl wanted to see one of the lobsters outside of its tank face to face. No one was really paying attention to the girl so I took it upon myself to extract a lobster and show it to her."

"And how would you have handled that in a more effective way?"

Lucas shrugged. "Unclipped the bands from around the lobster's claws and shown her what it can really do?"

The other muses gave a slight chuckle including Annette. Fiona and Harriet were not amused.

"What do you want me to say, Fiona?" Lucas asked her. "It's not like we're given all the time in the world. We go, we inspire, and we come home."

"Precisely my point," said Fiona. "You go, you inspire, and then you come home." She turned her eyes to the rest of the

54

muses. "Let's see a show of hands, Muses. How many of you think of your own personal lives when you're on an inspiration job?" Everyone looked around the room. No one raised their hands. "Don't be shy. No one's in trouble."

Mr. Andrews was the first to raise his hand. Lucas was next. Annette sheepishly raised hers halfway. Much to Annette's surprise, Fiona even raised her hand. Harriet's hand didn't rise in the slightest.

"Muses, I understand more than anyone what death does to one's memory. Desires that were once dormant and nightmares that were netted down are suddenly exposed. Management has given you offices to ponder such thoughts in a place familiar to you. But you must understand that there's work to be done. How do you expect to inspire the client properly if you're lost in your own thoughts? When you're out on an inspiration, you must leave thoughts of your previous lives in the office. You must be clear-headed in conquering the challenges that lay before you when you travel."

"So you're saying that we're not allowed to think when we're out inspiring?" asked Lucas.

"I'm saying that the offices are designed to be your personal refuge while you're here. When not on inspiration jobs, think about your past lives all you want. But when you go out to inspire you must focus on *those* precious moments instead. Your office and your thoughts will be waiting for you when you return."

Lucas continued to speak in defense of the others: "It's not like we have control over the memories, Fiona. If I see a praying mantis on an inspiration my mind automatically reels to the last time one landed on my shoulder. The memories are also extremely descriptive, as you well know. They're hard to ignore."

"Believe me, Mr. Richardson," Fiona tried not to look saddened by her own thoughts. "I know all too well what memories have the ability to do." She swept away the evident emotion from her face. "Mr. Cauliflower asks that we at least *try* to focus a little more. And I think with a bit of concentration and hard work we can make that happen."

Lucas crossed his arms and sneered. "And will the great Nathaniel J. Cauliflower be reining in his own thoughts like the rest of us?"

"We'll *all* make a more honest attempt. Including Mr. Cauliflower," Fiona spoke with a more hardened edge to her voice. "Muses, I don't think Mr. Cauliflower's demands are unreasonable. He and I ask that you inspire the world. But how do you intend to motivate the world if you're distracted? You're here to *instigate*, muses; this isn't a weekend retreat."

"Then what are our wages, Fiona?" It was like a badminton match between Lucas and Fiona which would have made the conversation more entertaining had they rackets and birdie. "You expect us to inspire yet we get nothing in return?"

"Nothing in return?" Fiona frowned. "Isn't the satisfaction of doing a job well enough compensation? What about the lessons you receive? And what of retirement parties, Muses. Have you forgotten about those? The growth of your soul is your wage. You've no financial obligations, creditors, telemarketers stalking your phone lines, no bigotry or spite . . ." these last few words caused Fiona's tone of voice to falter. "You are *protected* here, Muses. Never forget that. May I remind you that each of you has your own private office -"

"Doorless office . . ." Lucas interrupted in a forced cough. "You give us an office but take out vital pieces that truly make it a home."

"What you're saying, Mr. Richardson, is that it isn't enough. You're not satisfied. You want more from Management?" Fiona looked at the ceiling. "Well that's human nature, I suppose . . . always wanting more than what you already have."

"Annette agrees with me, don't you, Annette?" Lucas boldly volunteered.

Now Fiona turned her eyes to Annette who, in turn, looked to the table like a scolded adolescent and reddened. She wasn't quite sure why she felt the need to look guilty or why she was blushing. She hadn't intentionally stolen anything but she had become the current target nonetheless. Harriet, with daggers for eyes, was bad enough but to see the same look from Annette's employer was agony for her.

56

"It's not right to deprive a reader such as Annette of her books, or of Mr. Hill his plants, or *me* of . . ." Lucas' steam quickly deflated as he caught himself before saying any more. "Oh, never mind."

"Alright, Mr. Richardson," Fiona turned back to the table and broke her connection with Annette. "I'll confer with Mr. Cauliflower who will take the request to Management. Perhaps we can come to some kind of compromise." Fiona dismissed the meeting. The other muses stood from their chairs and began to exit. Fiona gestured for Lucas and Annette to stay put in their chairs. Harriet also continued to sit in her chair. Fiona then said to both Annette and Lucas: "I appreciate that you two are forming a friendship. But please, for the sake of my title and reputation, keep the rebellions to a minimum?" As she sternly instructed them, the other muses filed out with backward glances.

Lucas nodded. Annette nodded. Everyone else meandered back to their offices. Annette waited several minutes before heading to her own office. She wanted to avoid awkward conversation with the others. The hallway was quiet, as she preferred, when she left the conference room with Fiona following closely behind. As Annette passed by Fiona's office she could tell from her peripheral vision that her employer was mentally burning a hole into the back of her head.

Annette felt a memory creeping up her esophagus with the consistency of vomit. "Think of sunrises . . ." she whispered to herself. "Think of sunrises," she repeated. But the memory brought about a feeling of dread despite her words.

*

"Annette?" The voice from the front of the classroom could barely be heard as her attention was drawn from a stone-walled jail cell in *The Count of Monte Cristo*. "Annette, are you with us?"

Ten-year-old Annette looked up from her book. Her eyes cast a line out to the sea of young faces who had taken on the same expression as the teacher and stared at her waiting for a response. Her mouth went dry. Her heart began to beat irregularly fast. Her face went numb. She had been so enraptured in Edmond Dantès' adventures that she'd failed to take part in the discussion of long division on the blackboard. Ten-year-old Annette was horrified at this time and, as each second passed, she felt the sting of an emotional whip cracking against her shoulder blades.

"Would you come to the board, please?" asked the teacher who was a portly woman with flushed cheeks, wispy hair and wore a flowered dress that aided not in hiding the shape of her sagging breasts. The teacher's chubby fingers held a piece of chalk while white particles spotted her forearm.

Ten-year-old Annette stood from her desk and slipped the book onto the seat. Rain pummeled the windows of the classroom as Annette began to walk to the board. Her steps were heavy and the thudding in her ears had the intensity of a bass drum struck with fabric coated mallets. At the start of the new school year, Jonas had been moved three chairs ahead of hers. She was too distracted to notice Jonas' foot strategically in her path. A flash of lightning and a roll of thunder helped to accent her stumble.

The trip in her step caused a few chuckles from the rest of her peers when Annette toppled forward but managed to regain her composure. She turned her eyes back to Jonas who had stealthily tucked his foot back under the desk where it belonged. It was clear from the look on his face what an adversary he truly was.

All eyes were on Annette accompanied by a few snickers from fellow peers about the fumble in her step. She took the piece of chalk and placed the tip of it to the problem she was instructed to solve.

As Annette stared at the board, she felt a trickle of sweat on the side of her face. Her under-arms were moist with perspiration. She excelled in math; long division wasn't the issue. Somewhere behind her, Jonas was watching her. Somewhere behind her he was well aware of his actions and was proud of them. Thirty pairs of eyes were upon her. Mouths were turned up into mischievous smirks. She wondered why the teacher hadn't said anything. Hadn't she noticed Jonas' foot in the aisle? It certainly hadn't been the first time Jonas had done something to plot her awkwardness. Annette wondered how much longer she would have to endure his torture. Much to her dismay, in all this worry Annette's world before the class became fuzzy. The blackboard seemed a million miles away. Annette fainted before her classmates.

CHAPTER 7: THE MUSE'S CORNER

After the staff meeting Annette had inspired many different individuals, including a barista, an acupuncturist, a doctor preparing himself for surgery, an orthodontist, a burly individual selling alcohol and spirits, a night club owner, a pianist and a professional dog walker. She had inspired each to the best of her abilities but she still had not come any closer to understanding why Management had her do the things she did.

Annette inspired two others as well. The first was the mathematician Archimedes while he was lying in a grimy basin. As the mathematician discussed his theories, Annette held her nose and silently pleaded with Management to deliver her from the wretchedness. When the mass that was Archimedes submerged deeper, Annette made a comment about the volume of the bath water. His eyes glazed like the swirling of suds. Archimedes then jumped up from the bath sending the bath water in all directions.

Annette, who had been accustomed to fleeing an immediate area at a moment's notice, jumped out of the water's path. He stood naked in the tub holding out his hands. "Eureka!" Archimedes shouted. "Eureka!" he said again, this time louder. Annette watched as the mathematician left the bathroom without a towel. From the window, Annette watched Archimedes streak down the street screaming the word "Eureka!" over and over.

The latter peg, thankfully, sent Annette to a familiar face: the Man with the Eggs. It appeared that the story of Doris had been only half of the equation. The man who nibbled his breakfast in the diner for five consecutive days currently sat in a chair before her in a house that had fallen into disarray. Annette thought it was normal for a person to neglect scrubbing the scum from the shower stall or to run the dishwasher an extra cycle to break away hunks of grease from a pan. Someone grief-stricken certainly wouldn't have washed windows or beaten the rugs. But, eventually, even the most emotionally weak soul would have moved on. As if it hadn't been obvious enough how much misery this man had lived in while she and Doris were stalking him at the funeral, Annette's closer inspection proved that he was far worse off than heartbroken and that his condition showed no signs of letting up.

Annette was invisible to him. Even her voice didn't have any effect whatsoever on the situation. Annette, in fact, was the perceivably ghost of whoever had been in the casket the Man with the Eggs had been mourning. The man had simply sat in a catatonic state wallowing in his own self-pity and watching re-runs of *Leave it to Beaver*, *My Three Sons*, and *Wheel of Fortune*. The doorbell occasionally rung yet the man didn't stir from his position and didn't even bother to look up in acknowledgement. The house began to roar after some time passed. Annette knew that she had better do something fast or else the man would go uninspired.

"Would it have been so terrible if the Man with the Eggs had gone uninspired," Annette thought to herself. *"What was one side of the equation without the other?"* She wasn't able to speak and was invisible to him so how could she possibly have an effect under those circumstances? Annette approached the man hoping that perhaps her hand touching his face, or possibly brushing the stubble atop his head a bit, would've secured his attention. Her fingers went straight through him and she fumed words only audible to her. There came a rustling sound in the attic then as if someone had been listening and trying to give her a reply. It was the sound of fluttering envelopes but nothing more; Annette was sure of it.

The doorbell rang again, then again, followed by silence. Annette found herself at the front door and, out of reflex, reached for the doorknob. Remembering what had happened when she had touched the man's face, she reached for the metal knob anyway. Much to her surprise, her fingers fit around the metal.

There was a heavy breeze that aided Annette's attempt to crack the door ajar and it had rippled through her hair. There, on the front doorstep, was a simple funnel cake dusted with sugar. She expected a package or a stern note from a bill collector - but a funnel cake? The randomness of the choice in dessert was almost humorous. Annette picked up the funnel cake and brought it inside. Closing the door, her eyes gazed upon the powdered sugar. Sweeping a few grains with her index finger she licked the skin clean. The rattling pop-up book atmosphere startled her causing her to drop the cake. It landed face-down on the floor of the foyer.

The doorless personal library, water cooler, and Lite-Brite instantly reappeared.

"All right Annette. So here's my list." Lucas found Annette standing as she had stood in the foyer. Handing her several used white envelopes with his handwriting scrawled over the paper he said, "I know I've only got a few pegs to go but Management only knows how far they're spaced. And I'd hate to waste the time I have left between the remaining colored pegs by recounting the sum total I've already inspired, you know?"

"Uh . . . list?" Annette could hardly make any sense of his handwriting but made an attempt to decode it anyway. "Why are you giving this to me?" Annette looked up to Lucas but he had already fled her office. Annette sat with Lucas' list in her hand, more confused than ever.

"Hello, Annette," barked another muse upon entering her office. Harriet reminded Annette of an A-type student at a prestigious boarding school. Her hair was rolled in a tight bun, her clothes were pressed and crisp, her eyes were filled with knowledge (or disdain, Annette wasn't sure) as they passed over Annette's Lite-Brite board. "Figured as much. You know, Annette, by the time that I'd been here as long as you've been now, I had *twice* the number of pegs in my Lite-Brite board."

Annette instantly hated her. There may not have been a great number of pegs in Annette's Lite-Brite, but it was hers. Not Harriet's. She was proud of the work she'd done. Annette wanted to say this to Harriet to defend herself yet she said nothing.

"Fiona mentioned that I'm going to take her position after she retires," Harriet puffed proudly, "something that I've personally strived for since the moment I found myself in that waiting room. Harriet, by the way." They shook hands. "Here's my list. You'll find Betty Friedan's *Feminine Mystique* and a few others. But please keep my order confidential." And with Harriet's list in Annette's hand, Harriet turned and marched out the office leaving Annette as confused as she had been when Lucas had handed her his own list.

"Dalai Lama?" Annette read aloud wondering if the great Buddhist teacher on the list had truly had any profound effect on Harriet's attitude.

Over the next few minutes Annette came face-to-face with the other five muses she'd seen at the conference room table, each of whom presented their own private lists to her. Annette was absolutely confused. The lists were titles of books but the last place she had visited that had books had been the library where she had eventually met her demise.

Annette found the opportunity to ask Fiona shortly thereafter after she heard the click of her post box. The envelope she discovered inside was not white nor was it violet. Instead, it was a soft baby blue that reminded her of an afternoon sky. Fiona knocked quietly on the door, announcing her entrance.

"I don't understand," Annette began. "I've never received a blue envelope before."

"That's because Management has decided to send you, yes *you*, Mrs. Slocum, on a special project. Do you have your lists?" Fiona explained.

"Yes." Annette had already sorted the lists into a neat stack and alphabetized by the muse's last name.

"You still have someone you need to inspire, of course. However, Management has decided to give you a bit more time for the inspiration *and* the errand."

"Errand?"

"I can't give your fellow Muses the missing pieces to their offices but I can at least supply them with something else. And that 'something' is books. What the Muses need is their own solace, a comfort, and hopefully the passages in the books of their choosing they will find a suitable substitution." Fiona handed Annette a cup of water from the cooler which Annette brought to her lips. She drank the liquid in preparation to depart. "You, best of all, should know about the power of the written word, Mrs. Slocum. That's why *you* are being sent on this mission." Fiona, who was visibly hesitant to leave Annette's office, stopped the blue-colored peg before it touched the Lite-Brite board. "Wait, Mrs. Slocum." Fiona then produced her own list from her cream-colored jacket. "I'd prefer if this stays between us?"

Annette then said "Without money, how am I to . . .?" But Fiona had already left the room. In tiny almost illegible handwriting the list on the slip of paper had the collected works Emily Dickinson, Robert Frost, and Kurt Vonnegut, and the novels of Isaac Asimov, Robert Heinlein and Danielle Steele. Annette tucked the various lists into the blue envelope. She fit the blue peg into the Lite-Brite board and watched as the office promptly folded and unfolded to its destination.

As the pop-up book around her finally settled Annette found herself in a quaint underground bookstore nestled quietly in the basement of a much larger building. The humidity in the place was nearly unbearable but the ambience (with its tiled floors, boxed fans, and mismatched rugs) was enticing. Books of various subjects and age were stored on shelves. There were volumes of history, a few biographies (with the faces of strangers), and children's books with printed dogs, dragons, and other creatures. But it was the fiction section that piqued her interest the most. Annette ran her fingers along the spines, casually flipped through newly printed dust jackets, and pretended she was a normal person who hadn't been struck by a Cadillac and employed as a muse.

"I'm in Heaven," Annette whispered to the present shelf while placing the book back in its spot. "It has to be Heaven."

"Not quite, but close to it." The response came not from the pages of the book but from a woman nearly twice the muse's age. "I'm Gwendolyn Mansfield." Annette looked at Gwendolyn Mansfield's outstretched hand and suddenly realized she was supposed to be shaking it. "Let me know if you need anything. I'll be right over there." Gwendolyn retracted her hand from the unrealized handshake and pointed to a small desk. Atop which sat an old brass cash register and mounds of personal paperwork.

"Actually, I have lists," Annette said, suddenly remembering her manners. She brought her own hand out for a handshake. It was an odd sort of moment and made the muse blush. "Lots of lists, actually," she added. Gwendolyn Mansfield smiled genuinely, shook Annette's hand despite the awkwardness, and took the lists. She brought to her eyes a pair of spectacles that had been dangling from a chain.

"I don't see anything here that I can't handle. Why don't you have a look around while I collect the books?" Annette nodded and continued flipping through the dust jackets of the literature section. Thankfully, the books were there to soothe her. Silent and splendid, the printed words on the inside pages were picturesque paragraphs. The dust jackets on the hard-covers were flimsy yet new. If Management had somehow forgotten her and left her to spend the rest of eternity within these walls, Annette would've been content. She chose a title she'd never read before and hugged it to her chest like a child coveting a security blanket or stuffed animal.

From the periphery of Annette's eye she could see a man in a black suit and tie with gray hair glancing from a book to her direction. Several seconds passed and Annette couldn't shake the feeling that she was being closely watched by the Man in the Black Suit and Tie.

Gwendolyn Mansfield passed in front of the Man in the Black Suit and Tie with her back to him to address another bookseller who had recently returned to reorganize the history section. "Making any sense of it, Adam?" she asked.

"It's an eyesore if I ever saw one. It'll all have to be redone."

"Well, I couldn't have thought of a better man to fix the history section than my own son." She said to him with a maternal pat on his shoulder.

Upon seeing Adam, Annette's thoughts of the man quickly darted away. Annette's heart-strings tugged immediately at the sight of Adam who was restocking several of the history books several feet away as his mother passed by him. Adam was dangerously thin and hadn't shaved in probably a good two weeks. To her, his beard resembled the plush face of the teddy bear Annette often carried throughout her toddler years. Adam was as plain-looking as Annette. His eyes were a mud brown and framed by wire rimmed glasses. The color of his eyes matched the hue of the shaggy hair on top of his head. Annette knew she'd met her inspiree.

As if to confirm her assumption, there was a roll of thunder. Annette approached Adam. "Into history, are you?" she observed while running her fingers along several spines.

Adam Mansfield looked from his work and gave a half smile. His hair looked like a bed of brown feathers atop his head. How Annette wanted to brush it from his eyes and feel the fine ribbons against her fingertips. *"So handsome,"* she wondered to herself. The thought bathed her face in red.

"Fiction?" Adam asked, gesturing to her hands.

"Sorry?"

"You're holding a work of fiction."

"Oh..." Annette hurriedly set the book upon the shelf but it didn't want to stay. The spine tumbled to the floor fluttering the pages. Adam was quick to recover the book and, in that moment, the muse's and bookseller's hands touched. It was a trivial moment in the grand scheme of the history books he re-shelved but they shared it anyway. "Have you always wanted to be a bookseller?" she asked.

"It runs in the family. My mom and dad were booksellers before me. So were my grandparents. Somewhere in the family tree I hear we had a family member or two in a library in Egypt . . . but who really knows?"

"Who really knows?" Annette shrugged her shoulders. The roll of thunder returned signaling that the end was quickly approaching. "But the question remains unanswered," she reminded Adam.

"Have I always wanted to be a bookseller?" Adam asked aloud. "I guess. 'Cause what else would I do?"

"See the world?" The muse once again shrugged her shoulders. "Find out if everything you read in the history books is true?" There was a glint in the eyes of her bookseller and a smile that stretched across his lips.

"We've seen one another before," Adam offered.

"No, I don't think we have."

"On an airplane . . . to Las Vegas?" Annette shook her head and suddenly recalled the airplane ride and the man who had taken her window seat. Another awkward moment passed between them as she considered that she may not have been as plain as she had originally thought back when they had met. Someone had actually remembered her from years prior! Adam asked "Thirteen years? Does that sound right?" Annette wasn't sure. Time was circular in the office so piecing together a proper time-line caused a slight headache to form. She had married Lyle in 1999 and died in 2009. That made the current year 2012, if she calculated it right.

Gwendolyn Mansfield had already gathered the books from the various compiled lists. The spell that Adam had Annette under was suddenly brought to a screeching halt. It had come time to pay for her books but she wasn't given any money to do so. As the Man in the Black Suit and Tie checked out before her, Annette's heart raced with the possibility of thievery. Surely Fiona hadn't intended Annette to steal these books! Thunder once again rumbled beneath her feet. Annette pretended to check her housedress for a wallet knowing full well she was empty handed when it came to appropriate funds.

"I must've left my wallet back at the office," Annette told them once the Man in the Black Suit and Tie had left the store. Other than that she was unsure exactly what to say! Fiona had expected her to bring these books back to the department. The only question was . . . how? Annette traced her fingers along the spines of the collected books thinking of her next move. Eventually she nervously apologized and ducked from the register to the stairs leading up to the ground level.

"Wait!" Adam Mansfield called after her. "What's your name?" Adam asked, pushing open the front door of the bookshop with his backside. The open door ushered in sunlight.

"Annette."

"I'm Adam."

"Annette," absent-mindedly repeated, Annette felt stupid. The humiliation of her stupidity caused her to blush even more. He was handsome, even behind the beard that covered his face. As she stood there in the doorway Annette imagined her hand in his, their fingers interlocking, and his lips on hers. She tingled all over.

"I'd like to see you again."

"You would?"

"Is there a phone number I can call? I'd like to take you to dinner."

He walked her through the door and out to the sidewalk above. Annette felt odd yet euphoric. She dared not look to find him staring for she too might stare back. Although she did absolutely nothing but share a spare minute, engaging in small talk, Annette had inspired him. Now he was asking for her phone number.

"I . . . don't have a phone . . . anymore."

"Well how can I reach you?" Annette didn't have the heart to tell him that they'd probably never see one another again. Instead, she said nothing and stood awkwardly on the sidewalk as if waiting for a train that was scheduled to arrive.

"Which car is yours?" Adam asked finally, turning his brown eyes to the parked cars around them. "I can at least walk you."

"I . . . I didn't drive here," she stuttered. How could she tell him the truth without spoiling this fine moment? The rumbling started again in the distance and a roar of thunder pounded a cloudless sky. Annette turned her eyes to the sign painted above the independent bookstore. *The Muse's Corner.* She almost gave a laugh. Adam turned his eyes from her to the store sign. The back of his head faced her as his pop-up book refolded.

Fiona was waiting in the personal library office for Annette to return. Annette, when she finally got her bearings, sighed and accepted defeat.

"I'm a terrible employee," she told her employer.

"Why do you say that, Mrs. Slocum?"

"But it's not like you gave me much of a choice. You sent me to the bookstore without money? How was I supposed to bring the books back without . . ." Annette then fell silent. What brought Annette to this silence was what she found on the shelves that had once been empty. Every single book that she had touched in the *Muse's Corner*, including the ones that had been on the counter upon purchasing and the history books that she had gently grazed the spines with her fingers, were now present on her library shelves.

"From now on, Mrs. Slocum, any book that you touch *there* will appear on the shelves as an exact replica *here*."

Annette stood speechless, unsure of what to say. Finally she uttered a single word that best described how she felt inside. She said in wonderment: "Fascinating."

*

Eighty-two white envelope inspirations had passed in the course of Annette's employment. The details of her life had altered dramatically over the short length of time. So much that her subconscious stirred and her soul seemed to progress through a metamorphosis. As the books were placed in her own collection Annette was designated as the department's librarian. She was astounded that being the center of attention didn't affect her negatively as it once had. Annette was no longer an outcast; she was a hero. She was a beloved figure in the muse office and the equivalent of Santa with his crimson bag on Christmas Eve.

When all was quieted in the office, Annette made sure to recycle her empty envelopes into her post box for Nathaniel J. Cauliflower to pick up. Annette felt strangely confident to explore the area surrounding her own private abode. She paced the hallway of the musing office and peered into the offices she had been told about in an earlier conversation with Lucas.

Exploring the hallway further Annette found a bathroom at the opposite end of the hallway from the conference room. It had a toilet, a shower stall with a curtain spotted with a various assortment of pastel crustaceans, and a medicine cabinet which held spare unopened toothbrushes, pain medications, cotton swabs, dental floss, women's and men's deodorant sticks, a shampoo bottle that, when opened, gave off a scent of ripe tangerines, various bars of scented soap, fluffy towels, and nail clippers. Beside the toilet was a stack of outdated travel magazines and a robust roll of toilet paper. On the back of the door was a hook where a black hoodie was draped.

What intrigued Annette most about the bathroom were the toothbrushes to the left of the sink: nine of them rested in various holders; all of different colors (each corresponding to the various hues of the Lite-Brite pegs) nestled perfectly, with different names imprinted on their handles. Fiona's was white, Mr. Richardson's was green, and Annette's was orange. It was interesting how seeing that toothbrush made Annette feel like she belonged here even more. She recalled having flipped through Lucas' notes. The white pegs went with Thalia, the Muse of Comedy. Annette's color, orange, stemmed from Polyhymnia, the Muse of Sacred Poetry. The red pegs, upon inspiring Isaac Newton, Annette discovered stemmed back to Urania, the Muse of Astronomy. However, knowing this information only brought more unanswered questions.

Annette stood in front of the waiting room door. She had been asked by Fiona not to open it again. She wondered what would happen if she did? Would she return to her life of peace and quiet blissfully unaware of the proverbial pulleys and gears? How she longed to return to the stillness. How Annette longed to return to a world of library books and shirts fluttering in the afternoon breeze. But Annette didn't open the waiting room door. Something stirred within her now. Something she couldn't explain. It was as if the very fabric of Annette's DNA felt somehow changed but only slightly.

The haunting music that Annette had first heard in the green-slated hotel room during her first inspiration had returned. Like before, bow on string hummed angelically somewhere above and below her. As the mysterious violinist soared through another masterpiece, the strings were plucked barbarically in mimicry of chicks scratching for feed. Even though the music remained long enough to leave a chilling impact on Annette it was as mysterious as a cloud on the horizon. Eventually, it faded to silence.

Annette found herself at Fiona's office door outside of the conference room. Fiona sat behind her desk with a faded sheet of paper which had seemingly survived for several centuries. Her employer was lost in thought as she consulted the aged paper. Annette wasn't sure what was on the paper exactly but it was enough to capture all of Fiona's attention. Annette decided to come back later. She turned to the hallway only to be stopped by Fiona.

"Did you need something Mrs. Slocum?"

Annette stepped into Fiona's office. She pulled out a spare swivel chair and sat. Fiona took in Annette's presence and leaned forward in her own swivel chair. She took a deep breath and said with confidence: "I'm ready."

"Ready for what, Mrs. Slocum?"

"To hear what you had to say at the library right before my death."

Fiona studied Annette for a moment. "Oh," Fiona said finally. Annette waited for Fiona's explanation. She had inspired eighty-two individuals and now she wanted to know how Fiona would have inspired her. Fiona had been determined to tell her something on that afternoon. Unfortunately for Annette, Fiona now had nothing to say.

"Harriet mentioned you were retiring soon," Annette coached. "When I first arrived here, you mentioned that you'd rather be here than anywhere else."

Fiona continued to study Annette. "You are mistaken, Mrs. Slocum."

"But you yourself said . . ."

"I said that I'd rather be here than *Heaven*, Mrs. Slocum."

"Where would you go, then?" Annette wanted to know.

For several seconds Fiona sat lost in thought. Annette had known what it had been like to get lost in thought. She sat and let Fiona's private memories take over. Fiona shook these memories away and hesitantly presented the old paper from within a desk drawer. She sat it on the desk top before her and Annette. From Annette's perspective it looked to be a letter written in quill and ink. Upon further inspection she found that the words were in French. Annette did not know French and therefore couldn't readily decipher its message.

71

"It's true that my retirement is eminent," Fiona began. "You feel satisfied with yourself after eighty-two inspirations – and you have every right to feel that way, believe me." Fiona's strong managerial appearance soon sagged into exhausted. "But I grow so tired, Mrs. Slocum. Millions of inspirations have gone by. I've filled and emptied so many boards but Management keeps sending me more without a retirement in sight. Each peg has been repentance for the life that I led before. They've been my own Hail Mary's and Acts of Contrition. One of these days I hope to have my own retirement party. To walk through the waiting room door and live again."

"Why would you want to go back there?" asked Annette. "You said we were all protected here in this office."

"To find *him* again," Fiona lifted the letter. "To be in his arms again would be the real Heaven. Even if it is only just one lifetime more."

Annette had always fantasized about the kind of love which Fiona had spoken of. It seemed that ten years married to Lyle had somehow brought a cynicism to Annette's heart. "What did you do in your previous life that was so awful?" she asked Fiona.

"We all have skeletons in our closets," Fiona looked at Annette. "When we die, we think we're free of them. Alas, they're still there. When humans think of Judgment in the afterlife some imagine there's a deity with scales; where all of our hatred, spite, achievements and generosity are weighed. The real Judgment is within."

A silence passed between them. Fiona's pearl earrings twinkled in the lights of the office.

"On the day that you died, these were the words that I had wanted to say to you. Life is the adventure. You'd been missing out on all of it. Depriving yourself of such happiness. I suppose Management did right by sending the Cadillac your way. Who knows what will come of it?"

Annette wasn't sure what to say. She couldn't see herself as important or in charge of a team as much as Fiona had been.

"Perhaps Management made a mistake," Annette sighed.

"Management doesn't make mistakes," Fiona countered, "only new opportunities." The letter was then tucked safely

72

back into Fiona's desk drawer. "Have no fear, Mrs. Slocum. You're only eighty-two envelopes into this position. Tomorrow may hold even *more* paths for you to take."

Annette stopped by Lucas' office before returning to her own. She watched from the doorway of his private star-lit balcony. Lucas sat at his desk staring at his guitar which sat propped against a wooden rail. He wasn't aware that anyone was watching him. Lucas reached for the guitar half out of impulse but then retreated from it. His eyes turned to the doorway. Annette, startled, ducked back into the hallway.

"Annette?" Lucas called to her. "Don't hide. Please?"

Annette then shamefacedly poked her head out from around the corner.

"I gave you an open invite, silly. Don't feel ashamed for catching me in a memory. Come in. Have a seat."

Annette did as she was told. It was a beautifully everlasting spring evening in Lucas' world. A surf board was propped opposite the guitar. She wasn't quite sure what Lucas was going to do with a surf board in an office like this. Annette imagined he had a plan to overturn the water coolers in the hallway and the thought brought a smile to her face.

Noticing the direction of her gaze Lucas said, "It's always been one of my dreams, you know? When I was alive I wanted to go surfing like you see in all those beach movies. Sort of a strange dream, I suppose. Maybe in a past life I was more athletic, hence the desire, but when you grow up in the heartland of America where there are fields of corn for miles around it kind of makes that difficult. Yep, I grew up in the Midwest but didn't stay there. I wanted to venture out and get a little perspective on life. California, maybe, but never made it. I did make it to several other states though; eventually landed in Oregon. Have you ever been to Oregon?"

Annette shook her head.

"Beautiful state! Perhaps a colored peg will take one of us there; I can show you. See that's where I died before I found myself in the waiting room."

Thankfully, the Lite-Brite board on Lucas' desk distractedly sparkled. Filled with colored pegs, it looked like a painting by Georges Seurat.

73

"Really something, you know?" Lucas sighed blissfully and followed her gaze again. He leaned back in his swivel chair. "Only five more pegs and then I'm out of here."

Annette, out of fear of losing the one person with whom she had ever truly connected, sat beside him. They stared at the untouched guitar without speaking until they were both swimming in their own confidential recollections. They remembered days that they had once lived along with the riddles and perplexities that had served to torment them.

*

A thunderstorm clouded the skies outside of *The Muse's Corner* as the Man in the Black Suit and Tie stood waiting patiently for it to open. He held a black umbrella which aided very little in keeping him dry. Gwendolyn Mansfield had already let herself in locking the door behind her. The man checked his silver cockpit watch. The hands that lingered on the Roman numerals told him that the bookstore would open in precisely ten seconds. There came a flash of lightning. He looked to the sky just in time to watch as the electrical tendril disappeared from view. By the time he had looked back at the bookstore, Gwendolyn had unlocked the door.

"Good morning," he told Gwendolyn.

"Good morning," Gwendolyn said to him in return. "Come in from the storm before it washes you away."

"Oh, the storm isn't so bad," said the man who stepped inside and closed his umbrella shaking the drops outside the door. "I happen to enjoy thunderstorms very much. In fact you could say that I collect them in a way."

"Collect them?" said Gwendolyn as she started down the stairs to the bottom floor. "How so?"

"The way some people collect nice days in their minds I suppose," the man said as he followed her. "Thunderstorms have always brought me a sense of peace."

"Perhaps you should be a meteorologist," Gwendolyn said with a smile.

"As a matter of fact, that's exactly what I am," he told her. "You probably covet your books the same way I do my storms, wouldn't you say?"

"Is it that obvious?" she gave a laugh. The sound of tumbling books caused Gwendolyn to jump. "Excuse me." Gwendolyn raced around the corner to come to the aid of her son.

"Everything's fine," Adam said. "I suppose it was only a matter of time before the wood on this ancient bookcase gave in."

The man then looked on to the pile of history books that had fallen.

"I guess I'll have to start back at square one again with a different bookcase," Adam told his mother. Shaking her head Gwendolyn began helping her son in cleaning the mess.

"I'd love to stay and help," said the man "but I only came to inquire about one of your customers before heading off to cover a shift."

Gwendolyn looked at Adam who nodded. She then stood and gave her full attention to the man. "Which customer would that be?" she asked.

"The woman who came in yesterday. The one in the house dress?" he asked. "I was wondering if you could tell me her name."

"I'm not sure . . ." Gwendolyn said.

Adam then said "Annette. Her name was Annette."

"Annette?" asked the man. "Are you sure?"

"Do you know her?" asked Gwendolyn.

The man's face turned dark. His eyes were as cold and treacherous as the storm that raged outside. He was lost in thought and, from the looks of things, the thoughts were not satisfying.

Gwendolyn once again asked "Do you know her?"

The man's face brightened. He smiled like a gentleman. "No. I must have her mistaken for someone else. Someone I *used* to know. Someone who's been dead for three years. She has one of those faces, I guess." And with that his eyes returned to the darkened, angry state they had been a moment before.

Adam stood from the work now protectively standing beside his mother.

"I'll leave you to your work," said the man. "I wish you good luck in reconstructing your history section." He then, with the umbrella he had brought with him, left the concerned Mansfields and *The Muse's Corner*. He climbed into his vehicle and locked the doors. Before turning on the ignition he pulled a filing box from the front passenger seat and lifted the lid. Inside he found several library books each with Annette's childhood name written on the cards. He then took out a copy of Wilde's *The Picture of Dorian Gray* and studied it in the storm's flashes of lightning.

He opened the front page of *Dorian Gray* to find an aged obituary from three years prior. Annette Slocum's face stared back at him from the clipping. It had most certainly been her in *The Muse's Corner*. The man was convinced beyond any doubt.

He shook his head and said to the obituary "One of those faces."

A flash of lightning tore through the sky. A rumbling protest of thunder shook the clouds. The man watched the storm with a look in his eye that matched the ferocity above. He didn't drive away from *The Muse's Corner* until the storm had passed.

CHAPTER 8: COUNTER-CLOCKWISE

After the events concerning the Man in the Black Suit and Tie in *The Muse's Corner,* and shortly after Annette had left Lucas Richardson's office, Annette had worked through each of her inspirations with deftness and deportment. She had inspired a man pulling golf balls from a lake near the green, a woman operating a carousel that repeated the same melody in a mall food court, a hair stylist, a potato chip inspector, a receptionist, a carpenter, a busy mother trying to maintain peace among her three children in a playground, a television talk-show host, a museum curator, at least fifteen individuals stuck in cubicles without fresh air or sunlight, several passengers wedged in afternoon traffic in their respective vehicles, countless retail clerks, and other individuals who seemed trapped in the routine particulars of everyday existence. Annette had begun to lose track of the occupations of the many clients she inspired. Envelope after envelope Annette had inspired over one hundred and fifty individuals. Thankfully, none of the envelopes that had been filtered through her post box were violet.

Her Lite-Brite board was already well over a quarter of the way full which meant two things: first that she had barely enough time to read any of the books that she had brought back from *The Muse's Corner* and, second, that she was well on her way to retiring and never having to worry about her own memories of Jonas Rothchild, staff meetings, and the prospect of a violet envelope.

When Annette returned from her most recent client, she collapsed into her swivel chair and took a few sips of water to calm her nerves. Though she seemed to have gotten the hang of the inspiration jobs, her antisocial abilities were sometimes brought to the test. She had to force herself to interact with strangers or else the method of musing wouldn't have been administered successfully. Finally her post box was empty and she found time to relax. She took these few moments to sequester herself in comfortable silence.

As she sat there drinking her water, Annette's eyes trailed past the rays of sunlight shining down from her library's stained-glass windows. They rested upon a foreign element on the second floor that she had not before seen: a polished cherry oak cabinet with glass windows. Annette swept up the stairs to investigate the piece of furniture further. Nine antique golden frames had been placed on the shelves behind the glass. Five of the frames had black and white photographs inside while the other four remained empty.

Annette recognized Fiona's smile and the shoulders of her cream-colored pants suit. Inscribed on the frame were the words "Fiona, First Generation." Beside Fiona's frame was a face that she didn't recognize: he was a bald man in his thirties with a clean-shaved face, round spectacles, a crisp white dress shirt and suspenders. Even though the man before her looked considerably younger, he reminded Annette of the male subject in Grant Wood's painting *American Gothic.* The inscription on the frame read "Nathaniel J. Cauliflower, Second Generation." In another frame was a young man, possibly in his late teens, with sculpted features as if he'd been a living Greek statue. "Icarus, Third Generation" is what the frame beneath his portrait had read. There was another portrait of a Russian dancer "Anna Pavlova," the frame had displayed, "Fourth Generation." The last individual was an African American male poet named "Paul Lawrence Dunbar," who was of the "Fifth Generation."

Annette's eyes once again settled on Nathaniel J. Cauliflower's photograph. "So there you are," Annette said to the picture.

In all the time she'd spent in the office, she had not yet seen him in the hallway. She had only tasted his culinary creations and heard the click of her post box as he had delivered her envelopes. Finally she was able to put a face with a name albeit through a single photograph.

Inscribed on a gold plaque were the words "The Nine Greatest Muses in History." Below this plaque was a unique combination lock. This lock could only be opened by maneuvering ten small marble discs with assorted letters. Apparently one had to decipher a ten-lettered word to gain access into the drawer. Annette frowned at the prospect of this riddle but mulled over it anyway.

"What do you know about Nathaniel J. Cauliflower?" Annette later asked as Lucas brought along two plates of Cauliflower's delectable ratatouille between inspirations. She shoveled a fork full of the meal. "My compliments to the chef," she took another bite, "but honestly, Lucas, why have I never seen him?"

"He's a private man. Something you of all people would appreciate," Lucas accented his words by poking the fork into the air. "I've asked Fiona several times about him but she gives such vague answers as to his past. She's been in his office several times and told me about it. Apparently *his* little asylum is a rotunda where he keeps his seven most favorite obsessions organized inside glass cabinets."

"Seven obsessions?"

"Fiona mentioned that he has the most impressive collection of fountain pens, assorted beakers, science equipment from the 1800's and ornately hand-tipped globes made out of brass. She said that Nathaniel also has an entire wall devoted to all the portraits of every muse that ever set foot inside this department. Portraits that he himself painted! There's also a breathtaking assortment of kerosene lamps lighting the office. Fiona tried to take an accurate count once and failed. There were too many! She also mentioned his vast collection of the encyclopedia of destinies; thousands upon thousands of volumes telling him the pasts, presents, futures, colored pegs and life themes of our clients."

Something fluttered deep within Annette upon hearing all of this. Especially about the encyclopedias.

"What I wouldn't give to get my hands on my volume," Lucas told her. "Just to see what it all meant, you know?"

"I hear you," Annette agreed. Perhaps if she too had been standing before the encyclopedias she would divine the reason why her first client had to have the stolen violin. She would then have found out why the donut had to drop for Doris in the diner.

There was one inspiration she recalled to Lucas about when she had been sent to the time of the cave men to complete the task of helping to create the wheel; it hadn't been easy. She also told him about inspiring the painter Picasso; Annette had felt dwarfed by his genius. She even told him about Emily Dickinson and her hidden poetry.

"Did you know that Emily Dickinson was a recluse?" Annette asked Lucas as she took another bite of ratatouille. "She wrote poetry, beautiful poetry at that, but she kept it locked up in a drawer of her desk, bound in bundles."

"Did you meet her personally?" he inquired, visibly interested as he leaned forward.

"No. I thought maybe I was there to inspire a poem which would have been interesting, but . . ." she replied.

"What did Management send you there to do?" he interrupted, impatiently.

"To inspire her sister to find the poems in the drawer," Annette shifted in the swivel chair. "It was a tricky situation, though. Do you ever find yourself on an inspiration job in which you're invisible and unable to say anything?"

"Sometimes," he confirmed.

"Makes me feel weird," Annette confessed, "as if I were a ghost residing in someone's walls. Reminds me of how I felt at my wedding with Lyle, actually. I was the center of attention but it was as if I stepped out of myself that afternoon and watched the event from the punchbowl."

"Weddings make me melancholy," Lucas said. "Always have. I played a lot of weddings in my day back when I was alive. My old trusty guitar and I were inseparable. Teaching music had its benefits but about the only time I was happy was when I played my guitar."

"I've never heard you play," Annette told him.

"No, you haven't." Lucas' eyes glazed over. "No one has. I haven't played since I've been here. Too many memories, you know?" He fell silent now. Annette stopped chewing mid-bite. Lucas was caught up in a memory. From the looks of his face it was not a pleasant one. She recalled finding him in the office reaching for and, then, retreating from the guitar. Lucas had the same look in his eye then that he did now. Annette had been careful not to ask him what his thoughts had been. Now, she was intrigued.

"Lucas?"

"I'm here, Annette." Lucas smiled, breaking the silence. "Do you ever wish you could go back? See the reason for things?"

"Sometimes."

"Not just talking memories here but actually *going* back and witnessing every detail exactly as it was?" Annette nodded. "What if I told you there was a way to do so without flipping through Nathaniel J. Cauliflower's encyclopedias?"

Lucas brought out an object from the pocket of his jeans which he kept balled up in a tight fist. Annette wasn't sure what the object was but, regardless, it seemed that Lucas was debating whether or not to share it with her. Instead he chose to gather the empty china plates thereby storing his secret object for another meeting.

"I've got to get back to work and so do you." As he stood from the swivel chair, there came the sound of Annette's post box closing. Nathaniel J. Cauliflower had once again delivered her envelopes and already disappeared before Annette could catch a glimpse of him.

As Lucas turned to the hallway with plates in hand, background music began to play. More specifically, the haunting music that had first plagued Annette in the green hotel room could be heard. The indistinct violinist had returned. It wasn't the first time she'd heard the music in the muse offices. The origins of the violin music eluded her more often these days; so often that, whenever it seeped through her office walls, she eventually asked Lucas if he had heard it too. All other times Lucas would have said no but today Lucas stood in the hallway with his eyes cast quizzically to the ceiling.

"You *hear* it, don't you?" Annette asked him with a new-found validation.

"Management has outlawed CD players and DVD players. So unless it's a rebellious muse . . ." Lucas thought aloud.

"It's not a rebellious muse, Lucas. That violin music is coming from somewhere else."

Fiona also heard it as did the other six muses Annette had encountered. All nine muses stood in the hallway listening to the plucked strings as a captive audience to the fiddler. When the music ended, Lucas finally spoke.

"Paganini."

"Paganini?" The name Lucas had spoken sounded more like an Italian sandwich than a person's name to Annette. "Who's Paganini?" she asked aloud but no one would answer her.

Instead, Fiona turned to the eight other muses and posed her own question. "Who here inspired Paganini?" It seemed that all other eight muses knew of Paganini even though no one seemed to have inspired him. When Fiona realized this was the case she checked each office and the conference room in a radical fierceness for speakers or rotating discs in mechanical devices. She came up empty-handed.

"Can someone please explain where Paganini's music is coming from?" Fiona calmly addressed the stunned muses who were still gathered in the hall. As on many occasions in the past, the music fell silent causing the inquisitive crowd eventually to disperse into their separate offices. The hallway was once again as quiet as it had always been.

Annette stood in the hallway. She couldn't help but think that the music was her fault. It was during her first inspiration job that she had heard the stringed instrument and, considering this was the first time anyone but her had actually heard the music, Annette deduced that it hadn't happened *before* her arrival. Then again how could it have been her fault? Annette didn't even know who Paganini was so how could she be directly responsible for the music?

"Hey, Annette," Lucas took her hand and passed along a violet envelope crumpled up into a ball. "My time here in the musing office is falling short so in case we don't have the opportunity to talk again, here's a little present you might like. I

82

uh . . . didn't want to give it to you quite yet because I hoped there'd be more of these kinds of meals in our future. But just in case, you know?" And with that Lucas headed back to his office leaving Annette alone.

Traipsing past several offices to her own, she unfolded the crunched-up violet envelope hoping that Lucas hadn't passed along an inspiration job that would cause her grief. She was pleased to find something else entirely. Inside the envelope was a white sheet of paper that looked like it had been ripped from his personal instruction booklet. On the page Lucas had scribbled a message with a blue Sharpie marker.

> **Annette,**
> **Discovered a nifty trick my first day here. Thought you might enjoy it. Or at least it might help explain the ever popular question "why?" Rotate the colored pegs counter-clockwise for a client's past; rotate them clockwise for the future. Remember, Annette, like the instructional video said: "You can and will inspire anyone," no matter how fixed or seemingly impossible.**
> **Your friend,**
> **Lucas**

"Your friend," Annette read aloud letting the words roll sweetly off her tongue. The bond between them was official now and she felt that, with these words, she'd been accepted into a tightly-sealed secret society. A swarm of thoughts buzzed busily about her brain again. Annette wondered how her life would replay if the bright orange peg on Fiona's Lite-Brite board was twisted counter-clockwise. What sort of past would it show? Annette's memories seeped from the vault she kept them in. As she sat in her own swivel chair moments later, she remembered back to when she was ten years old sitting under a giant oak tree.

*

It had been recess in 1989. While other kids were playing ball, running around on the track, or pretending they were astronauts by launching themselves off see-saws, ten-year-old Annette was reading a book. The title of the book in her hand was Tolkein's *The Hobbit* which parted Annette from the rest of the world around her.

"Look at her," spat Jonas Rothchild contemptuously who had been standing with ten other boys on a nearby hill tossing a football. "The little bookworm is reading again." Young Annette had been the topic of everyone else's conversation because she was considered "weird." She talked about how she loved authors who had been dead for years. And there was the obvious fact that she was so socially detached from the rest of the school's happenings that didn't help matters either.

Her two older brothers Franklin and Michael, who as growing boys would have rather thrown themselves into the path of an oncoming well-thrown football than have become social outcasts, stood with the other boys who harassed young Annette. Her brothers had never spoken a word against Annette but simply stood there with Jonas because they wanted to be part of something greater than the world of "fabricated nonsense" that was literature.

While young Annette sat there engrossed in a novel that was as heavy as she, the boys stalked her like a pack of mountain lions in anticipation of their prey. Soon she was surrounded and the only thing that brought her from the book were the two words: "Hello, Annette."

It was Jonas who had spoken. His bull-dog head was haloed by the sunlight behind him. Ten-year-old Annette said nothing as she looked up to acknowledge his words and then returned to her book. Jonas took the book from her, closed it, and threw it over her head past the remaining yard. It eventually landed in the street. Ten-year-old Annette ran after the book, but the traffic was horrible. (Even at this young age, Annette found herself dodging cars.) Alas, the book was irretrievable and, in seconds, was disassembled by a tire. As Jonas laughed, Annette's brothers stood there wordlessly to see what she'd do next.

It was young Annette against the world; however, she wasn't about to go down without a fight. Her social skills were inadequate but, after seeing the book torn to shreds like a fish gutted for supper, she threw a series of punches. Within seconds, four of the ten boys hit the ground and the rest of them fled the scene . . . except for Jonas who, sporting a red mark on his cheek from Annette's fist, watched as she attempted to rescue *The Hobbit*.

"You took out four boys?" her father said, obviously impressed. They were seated at the dinner table that night. "Single-handedly?"

"It's not lady-like to hit a boy," Annette's mother admonished. "I would hope we've raised you better than that." Ten-year-old Annette wanted to tell her parents that Franklin and Michael, currently sitting across the table from her, were also present and witnessed her humiliation as bystanders. But, because she barely said anything at all, she continued eating in silence throughout the meal.

"Don't get me wrong. I'm proud that you stood up for yourself, Annette," her father said as he put a hand on hers. This stopped Annette from silently scooping mashed potatoes. "The next time they pick on you, though, speak as a main character in a book would speak: with strength and confidence. Annette, reasoning is better than fist-fights and, in ten years, everything will have changed. As you grow older, think to yourself how you want to be remembered."

"It was a library book," ten-year-old Annette mumbled to her mashed potatoes.

"Well, there's no saving it now," said her father. "We'll go out and buy a replacement tomorrow."

As young Annette crawled into bed that evening, she found the same copy of *The Hobbit* that had been thrown into the street on her pillow. The card on the inside back cover bore her name, written in cursive. Making it all the more intriguing, someone had meticulously stitched it back together in apparent concern.

*

85

As the events of her childhood have proven, Annette had trained herself not to fight with fists. Hardly one for histrionics, Annette hadn't whacked Fiona over the head with the water cooler in the waiting room before she had become a muse. As she had grown older, Annette had firmly believed that she was more than a fist-flailing monster. Unfortunately, the plan backfired and Annette had not developed into the hero she had expected herself to become. Instead, Annette had been converted into a doormat that remained in an eventless marriage for ten years.

As a muse, Annette sat in her office and stared at the pegs in the Lite-Brite board wondering how her life had been remembered by others. Chances were, considering her limited social skills, there hadn't been much that anyone had reminisced about at her funeral. If Annette hadn't run out into the road but had sat and listened to what Fiona had to say the on first day they had met, would her life have changed? If so, then how?

Annette certainly couldn't barge into Fiona's office and rotate the bright orange peg clockwise. Nor could she peer into her own volume in search of her destiny. Instead she decided to do the next best thing. She would revisit some of her own pegs in the hope that they would reveal to her some common truth about how a life is changed through celestial intervention.

Annette hesitantly reached out her index finger and thumb, squeezed the tip of a familiar green peg, and rotated it counter-clockwise. Annette was then thrust counter-clockwise in time to the very first chapter in the life of the turquoise man in the green hotel room's pop-up book.

CHAPTER 9: JONATHAN'S STORY

The first chapter in someone's life is typically measured by the moment a baby exits its mother's womb but, for the green peg, the "beginning" was in Jonathan's tenth year. He was sitting at his kitchen table one spring afternoon working a math problem that was giving him much grief. No doubt the twenty that would follow would be even more afflicting. Sunlight, chirping birds, and playful childhood laughter from the neighboring yard distracted him from his mathematics and musings. But he knew additional bad grades and even more wasted afternoons spent trying to catch up on his schoolwork would follow if he gave in.

Annette sat with him at the kitchen table and was completely invisible. She was more as a spectator than an actual piece of the puzzle. Seen or unseen, both Annette and her charge heard the music emanate from the attic. It was an odd sort of sound for Jonathan to hear. It reminded him of a dinghy gliding along the surface of a lake carved by deep waves with its bow snapping a few waves acting as speed-bumps. The music was like a body of water: smooth and luxurious one moment and erratically barbaric the next. Its broken melody caused him to turn his eyes from the numbers.

Jonathan was the type of boy who loved to climb trees or venture up jungle-gyms in pursuit of a better view of the playground. So it was hardly a great feat for him to ascend the rickety ladder into the dark and moldy shadows of the upper floor. Annette followed him closely, careful to be extra silent so as not to disturb what had already been set into motion.

The music peaked Jonathan's interest as it intensified while he crouched next to some abandoned luggage. However, the boy found that the music wasn't coming from the attic as he'd originally thought. Instead it came from above and below it. Jonathan wondered if an old record player had been triggered by a rogue squirrel. It was then that his eyes caught a brass object resting on a stack of brittle and faded newspapers like a beaten and rusted trophy. Jonathan had never seen anything like it yet somehow he knew that this object, with its keys, mouthpiece, and horn, was something akin to the reverberating composition that disturbed his world.

Jonathan deduced that the music was coming from somewhere else when he saw that the instrument was untouched and realized it was silent. He rummaged a path through the forgotten boxes and moth-eaten winter coats that dangled on wire hangers. Within minutes, he was cradling the brass instrument in his lap. He considered the trumpet. The music that had coaxed him up here came to a dramatic conclusion and, in response, Jonathan licked his lips and pressed them to the mouthpiece.

The horrific noise was nothing as spectacular as the music he had heard; in fact, it reminded him of the sounds that would radiate from his Grandpa's bowels after ingesting fruit salad at Thanksgiving dinner.

"John?" His mother called from the rectangle of sunlight in the hallway below. "John, what are you up to?"

"I thought I heard music," he tried to explain. Judging by his mother's response "what music?" Jonathan knew he was the only one who had heard it. "There was music coming from up here so I followed it." But the attic was quiet and stale as a sepulcher; the ghostly music had ended and was replaced by only the sound of the afternoon breeze stretching against the side of the house.

"Come down here and finish your homework. Then you can help me with dinner," she called. Jonathan reluctantly set the instrument and the obstacles back in their original positions. Taking one last look at the trumpet, Jonathan abandoned the darkness for daylight. As he descended the ladder and retreated back to his math problems, he wondered if and when the mysterious music would return.

The following Friday came as swift as the wind. Jonathan rode his bike to and from school and the following Friday was no exception. Every afternoon, he would ride past Main Street. Jonathan never took the time to examine any of the shops. The world would glide behind him with the silkiness of an ice-skater. That is, until that particular day when the music Jonathan had heard two weeks earlier prompted his wheels to come to a dead stop. As fate would have it, he stopped his bike in front of a music store where acoustic and electric guitars and a single shiny sapphire drum set were displayed in the front window.

After stepping through the front door, Jonathan surveyed his surroundings. The haunting music blended in with his discoveries. The smell in the store was a sundry scent of sweat, saliva, brass polish, and printed paper. Somewhere in the store, someone was testing a guitar strumming the strings and singing a wordless tune. Another customer flipped through music books as she hummed several measures. A third individual plunked random notes on a keyboard. Instruments dangled from the ceiling: some brass, some wood, some with strings, and some with mouthpieces the size of Jonathan's entire head. If the hanging instruments were the stalactites hanging from this cave, the stalagmites were piles and displays of music books with pages, the white paper sheets littered with black ink measures, notes, and scales. The store was a true museum of sound.

The music that had originally led him to such an establishment continued to coax him forward through such riches. One instrument in particular seemed to be waiting for him: a single violin with wood that reflected a heavenly ray of sunlight shining from a nearby window.

He glided his fingers across the strings. Happily, the mysterious music he'd heard in the attic had found its twin. As if he suddenly understood the unknown music that called to him, Jonathan knew that someday that particular violin would be his. Jonathan toyed with the notion that if he *owned* this violin he might comprehend where the original music had been coming from and why. Closing his eyes, Jonathan imagined himself standing under an awning with the base of the violin beneath the left side of his chin, the neck cradled by his fingers, and the bow held out to play the strings.

"Music lessons?" When Jonathan's aspiration was addressed over chicken and dumplings later that night, the news came as quite a shock to his parents. Annette's mouth watered as Jonathan's mother served a steaming bowl drenched in yellow broth.

"Yes, music lessons," he repeated. Trying to convince his parents to invest in music lessons was as arduous as promising he would do better in school. Jonathan tried to explain that music lessons were different: it wasn't about unsolved mathematical problems and misplaced homework. The music lessons were something he actually wanted and would do anything to have.

"Well," Jonathan's father stuffed a bit of dumpling into the right side of his mouth while the left side formed a verbal compromise, "I suppose, if you were to continue studying hard and raise those grades . . ."

"I will!" Jonathan promised. The excitement and volume behind Jonathan's voice took both parents by surprise. "I'll study really hard, and I'll ask Mrs. Simmons for extra credit." There was a look of recognition behind his parents' eyes that to Annette seemed to say, "I suppose if he really wants the music lessons, we'll see a drastic improvement." Jonathan could see this meaning as well. He smiled with his cheeks showing optimism with youthful dimples.

Indeed, the drastic improvement took place. Annette watched with fascination as days and months roared by like a BBC documentary set on fast forward. Jonathan would drive his bike to and from school. Each time he would pause to stare in the window of the music shop where the violin that he desperately desired stood unattended. When he wasn't at school or atop the jungle gym at recess watching the playground antics, he sat at the kitchen table with spare sheets of paper and open school books. The mysterious violin music, that only Jonathan seemed to hear, played throughout this strenuous endeavor like a playful puppy nipping at his heels.

Eventually the speed of the days came to a screeching halt as Jonathan rode home on his bicycle proudly waving an "A" on his report card. His mother and father were pleased and announced that, if Jonathan washed up the dishes, there'd be a surprise waiting for him in the foyer. Soap suds splashing, scrub brush scrubbing, the music stayed with Jonathan until each dish was cleaned, dried, and put into the cabinet. Jonathan knew this was the moment that the violin was his. After finishing his hard work, Jonathan tossed the towel into the hamper and ran into the foyer to find his reward: the battered trumpet Jonathan had discovered in the attic many months before.

Mom and dad stood towering over the young boy and the trumpet. They were unaware that the silence had been caused not by sheer joy but from crushing disappointment.

Now the trumpet sat on Jonathan's bed. The boy paced back and forth and spouted a dramatic tirade about the injustices of life. "I worked my butt off and all I got was you! You! A stupid, beat up old thing that sounds like a half-starved goose on his death-bed!" The trumpet took each insult and said nothing as all trumpets in this particular situation are prone to do. "Why couldn't you have been a violin, huh? Why couldn't you have strings and wood and sound like an angel?" Jonathan now had the trumpet clutched between his fingers. He hoisted it in the air for more impact with the floor when his father came into the bedroom and seized it.

"This was my instrument in high school, young man. Let's not be wondering how many pieces it can dismantle itself into. As much money as we're spending for music lessons-"

"I wanted a violin!"

"This was mine in high school, John," his father repeated. "It may be a little old but it still has some 'oomph' to it." Jonathan's father pressed the mouth piece to his lips. Twiddling the keys with his fingers, he played a song from memory. To Jonathan's father it sounded decent; from Jonathan's perspective it was awful. "See? It was the best thing that ever happened to me, Jonathan. It's because of this trumpet that I met your mother."

"But I wanted a violin!" Jonathan insisted.

"Then you should have said 'Dad, Mom, I want a violin,' instead of simply asking for music lessons," his father countered. "You didn't specify *which* instrument. Your mother found you in the attic with my old trumpet . . ." The trumpet was placed in Jonathan's hands again. "There you have it: passed down from my generation to yours."

"I want a *violin*." Jonathan's temper was typical for a young boy but Annette identified a similarity between this boy's anger and hers on the day Fiona stood in the waiting room with her. Jonathan and his father stood like two bulls in the same ring. It was his father that moved to resolve the simmering situation between them.

"Buck up, John. Treat the trumpet as trumpets should be treated or you'll be in a heap of trouble." His father then abandoned Jonathan and the trumpet. In spite of the door between them, Annette had a feeling his father could hear Jonathan's final protest: "Then spend the money on the violin instead. Forget the lessons! I'll teach myself!" He shouted even louder now. His voice was choked with tears. *"I'll teach myself!"*

Annette watched as the hours flew by: Jonathan's first music lesson with the trumpet when all the other trumpet players were happy with their instruments; Jonathan's first concert where his eyes should have been on the music when he watched another violinist from afar as he strummed the strings of a violin. Finally, riding home from school with the trumpet case attached to his bicycle when Jonathan stopped and stared into the window of the music shop where, through the glass, he could barely see the instrument he truly coveted.

"And how did that make you feel?" Suddenly a woman's voice was behind Annette and, as she turned, Jonathan's room filled with cigarette smoke. Annette found herself in a small tavern with a familiar face. How Fiona managed to squeeze herself into the life of Jonathan was beyond her. Was this before Fiona had become a muse or after? Fiona sat next to the now adult-Jonathan with an air of patient assurance. While Fiona took a sip of daiquiri, Jonathan sat beside her on his own stool with his face cradled in his hands. His green and black striped tie dangled like a tear drop.

"This is insane. It was only a trumpet, for God's sake," the man who was Jonathan, grown-up, said.

"Maybe it's not about the trumpet," Fiona pointed out.

"It's not like my parents neglected me. I had a good education and they put me in Boy Scouts where I learned how to be a man, I guess." Jonathan shook his head, showing a sliver of a smile. "You know, it's funny."

"What's funny?"

"Those math problems. Can you believe that I kept working diligently on them? I thought that if maybe my parents would see how well I was doing in school, they'd change their minds, chip in, and buy a violin for me. In high school I excelled in Calculus and even went on to pursue a degree in accounting which I later chose as my profession."

Jonathan lifted his head. He was a clean shaven handsome man. Of course the last time Annette had actually seen him had been in the hotel room when he had a beard covering his face. But it had been his eyes: his eyes were still the same.

"Then I met Elaine. We got married, had two kids, and after a while the need to impress my parents faded away. I never forgot about the violin but I sort of grew up, I guess." Jonathan went on. "I'm stuck in a dead-end marriage with a woman who doesn't love me anymore and children who I've intentionally spoiled so they wouldn't end up like me. And here I am talking to a strange woman in a bar."

Fiona, playing the mysterious woman, asked: "Do you think things would have been different had you received the violin?"

Jonathan shrugged his shoulders.

"I've got to go," Jonathan stood, straightening the creases in his dress shirt. "Elaine's probably got lunch prepared."

"Before you go, might I suggest something? Get yourself a violin. Right now, on the way home. While you're at it, pay for music lessons. It's never too late to start."

"You don't think I've thought about it, going back to the music store?"

"Maybe you have; maybe you haven't - or perhaps you're still waiting for permission." There was a look in Jonathan's eyes: a look of hope. "See where it takes you," she said.

Jonathan headed for the outside world with a spark of joy behind his eyes as he called back to Fiona. "How random, running into you."

Time roared forward and Annette found herself staring into the music store on Main Street. The same violin was still sitting there in the window. As the adult Jonathan finally became the proud owner of the long-awaited prize, Annette felt satisfied with how it was all shaping up so perfectly. The only thing that bothered her was Jonathan hadn't *bought* himself the violin. No, she'd *handed* him the violin when she was transported to his squalid hotel room, when he was ten years older and considerably less elated. She wasn't sent back to her office, either . . . no, the story continued.

Jonathan sat the violin on Annette's invisible lap next to him in the blue Cadillac. As he drove down the street to his home, Annette had a nauseating numbness in the pit of her stomach. Jonathan was driving too fast, snatching momentary glances of the violin he'd just purchased. Nothing could stop him now. Annette could see the youthful enthusiasm burning in his eyes like coal in the winter as he strummed the strings of the instrument while his other hand guided the steering wheel.

Jonathan wasn't expecting the cars swerving in front of a library up ahead. Before he knew it, with a sickening crunch, a woman's body, Annette Slocum's body, rolled up the hood and slammed into his windshield.

Annette had been sitting in the automobile with the man that had run over her.

Instantly Jonathan stopped the blue Cadillac and watched from the review mirror as onlookers raced to the corpse which lay on the ground like a dismembered mannequin in a pool of her own blood. He took one last look at the thankfully still-intact instrument and then abandoned the violin to see, for himself, the devastating damage he'd unintentionally inflicted.

Annette then sat with him in a prison cell. This was where Jonathan would spend ten more years pining over the violin. The music would return more frequently: sometimes when he took his communal showers and at other times atonally narrating his meager lunch of burnt macaroni and bread that was stiffer than cardboard. More often than not, the music would sing him to sleep as the moon and stars would shine down through the ceiling bars of his cell.

Ten years passed fluidly and the length of those days raced like a quick afternoon storm in spring. In those ten years, his wife and children had visited and sat behind a plate glass window while they talked over phones. As the years progressed and the children and his wife grew older, the frequency of their visits dwindled leaving Jonathan and Annette to wonder on some days whether they were ever coming back at all. On his wife's last visit Elaine sat on the other side of the glass with the phone poised to her ear.

"Did you bring it like I asked?" had inquired Jonathan. Elaine nodded. "Show it to me."

She brought the violin into view: what was left of it. The last time he had seen the violin was the day of the accident. While Annette had not been spared the violin certainly had. Unfortunately for Jonathan, in the many years he'd been in the prison the violin had been broken into many pieces. Upon seeing the remnants of his hope, Jonathan's eyes had swelled in discomfort.

"This will be the last time I visit you, Jonathan," said his wife. "Your true love will be waiting here for you when you're released." Elaine sat the violin on the counter, placed the phone receiver back on the hook, and left.

In the last year of his sentence, Jonathan and the violin music had been alone. He spent his days counting down to the moment the walls and bars that surrounded them would break away. Jonathan had transformed from the thirty-year-old Annette had discovered in the bar with Fiona to the bearded man with matted-hair that she had seen on her initial inspiration. The music was relentless in its pursuit to charm Jonathan through the days.

He was released on a bright and sunny Tuesday. The violin was returned to him in the same mangled condition as it had been when his wife had brought it to him. Carrying what

95

was left of his only possession, he shielded himself from the sunlight with his hand, hailed a cab, and went home.

Home, like his wife and children, had changed over the years. Annette could see in the backyard a swing-set that once had a polished red exterior was now sporting spots of rust. The pool was choked with leaves. A neglected trampoline was unused throughout years of winters and summers. It had frozen over, thawed and frozen again. Annette recognized the blue Cadillac sitting in the driveway. Beside it were three more cars each progressively more expensive than the one before.

Jonathan and the invisible Annette stood and took in this depressing sight even as his wife, who had noticeably wrinkled since last they spoke, exited the front door with a watering can in attempt to revive the weed-infested flower-beds. Annette wondered for a moment if Jonathan was, too, invisible. His wife didn't even look up to acknowledge his presence. Jonathan took a deep breath and, with the violin's strings hanging like the tentacles of an octopus, took a few steps forward. As he did, another man came out of the house and wrapped his arms around Elaine's waist.

They giggled like children as he tried to pry the watering can from her hand while she tried to douse him with the water inside it. Annette could tell from the look in Jonathan's eyes that he knew he had been replaced. The life that he had known (or more specifically the life that he had fantasized about for a brief moment in the bar ten years ago before) had been stripped from him.

"I've never made her laugh like that," Jonathan whispered. Annette wondered if he was talking to *her* but she figured he hadn't as he held tighter to the violin and dejectedly turned back to the street. This was probably better, anyway. Who needed a house when it was already filled with someone else's memories? Who needed a family when they didn't even consider him part of it anymore? Who needed a violin when the music that Jonathan had once felt inside of himself had finally gone silent?

The cab was gone so he'd have to trek on foot. He and Annette walked down the road through the afternoon and well into the night. With what little money he'd had in his pockets on the day he had hit Annette, Jonathan purchased himself a week's stay in the hotel room of a horribly dilapidated building. As the man slept each night the music lulled him through his nightmares. Annette sat on the bed and stared at him while he dreamed. She wished there was something she could do or something she could say to bring him out of this funk but there was nothing to say or do that would change the way he was feeling.

And then another Annette arrived: the shy and timid Annette Slocum who had promptly taken the violin from the violinist in the concert hall. Now there were two Annettes in the room: the one from her past, taking in the various greens of the seedy hotel room, while the present Annette took stock of her past self. She stayed still on the edge of the bed hoping that her presence there wouldn't disrupt the hand of fate.

"Put it in the chair, Annette," Fiona had whispered into her past self's ear.

"Do you hear that?" the past version of Annette had asked. The music returned once again. This time so strong that it shook the tin-foil on the television antenna.

Jonathan stirred from his sleep as the music had risen to a crescendo. He looked directly into the past Annette's eyes. Fiona had ordered Annette from the past to say something, anything, but she hadn't. The invisible Annette knew what she had wanted to say: "It will all turn out all right. Take the violin and be happy. Strum the strings and remember your childhood!" But the past Annette Slocum had said nothing as she placed the violin and bow in Jonathan's hands. A thunderclap signaled the end. The pop-up book page suddenly closed the book of Jonathan's life story and, suddenly, Annette found herself back in her office staring at the quarter-full Lite-Brite board.

There was an envelope waiting in her post box and inside that envelope yet another peg. Standing in Annette's office doorway was Harriet. Her arms were folded with pride.

"That envelope has been sitting there for a good ten minutes."

Annette said nothing. She opened the lip of the white envelope that waited for her.

"The instructional video said that envelopes can only be opened for a limited time and it's been sitting here unattended for ten minutes. Where were you?"

Annette wanted to defend herself and tell Harriet that it was Lucas' idea to turn the peg counter-clockwise but she wasn't ready yet to socialize with someone with whom she wasn't comfortable enough, let alone a muse who seemed to have it out for her. Annette wanted to lie and tell Harriet she hadn't consulted the colored pegs and, perhaps, an inspiration job had taken a bit longer than expected. She knew that Harriet, Ms. Future Management, would never buy it. Annette was too emotionally exhausted to fight with Harriet or to later backtrack on a lie. So Annette simply sat defeated in her swivel chair with her face flushed.

"I'm on to you, Annette. That look on your face. I've seen it before. It's a look that screams the truth: you've been rotating pegs. Not a wise choice! Not at all! Before you consult another colored peg, consider the muse who sat in this office long before you. One peg left and it sent Evangeline to a neighborhood of mailboxes. Need I remind you of the flop that ensued?"

Harriet went on to recite the recent drama including the toll of uninspired individuals that had followed. Annette knew all too well of the circumstances. Midway through the lecture, she finally stopped listening to Harriet. Annette sheepishly nodded her head in agreement that she'd leave the pegs alone. Apparently content that her job of being Fiona's lapdog had been accomplished, Harriet uncrossed her arms and left Annette to her thoughts.

"You rotated one, didn't you?" Lucas was standing in her doorway now, his face marked with sympathy. Annette said nothing - how could she? What could she have said that would make it all right? Lucas took a seat in one of the empty swivel chairs, intent on keeping Annette company.

CHAPTER 10: "OH THE SHARK HAS MANY TEETH DEAR . . ."

Nathaniel J. Cauliflower had recently set up a new meal in the conference room of the musing office. Nine plates had been set of blackened mako shark served with seared cucumber and grilled watermelon. Along with the dishes, Cauliflower had poured nine sparkling china goblets of pinot noir. The centerpiece of the table had been a watermelon gutted and sculpted into the general shape of a shark scouring the deep.

Annette sat in the conference room. She didn't want to take a bite as the display was so lovely. Eventually she took a fork and bit into the grilled watermelon.

*

The last time Annette had eaten watermelon, she had been twelve years old and eating a sliver of the fruit that her mother had prepared on that morning. Sunlight poured through the leaves of the great tree. She was sitting underneath the tree when, somewhere in a nearby field, boys were playing. Annette wouldn't have any of it.

The juice of the watermelon would have soaked the pages of *Dracula*. To avoid tarnishing the book, Annette kept a separate towel to wipe her fingers. The process of eating a bite of the watermelon while finishing a page was almost comical: Annette would take a bite, savor it in her mouth several seconds, abandon the watermelon, clean her fingers with the spare towel, wipe them dry on the sides of her dress, turn the page, and take another bite of the fruit.

Twelve-year-old Annette was barely noticeable while she ate her lunch; she faded into the background like a shadow. Unfortunately for Annette, there were a pair of eyes that kept a close watch on her movements. They belonged to Jonas Rothchild. It seemed to her he would make it his personal life's mission to find her weaknesses and destroy whatever happiness she had left inside. This day was no exception.

"Why do you do that?" He asked.

Annette dared not look up from Bram Stoker's masterpiece. She thought the vampire in the novel would have been far more attractive than the real-life monster above her.

"Why do you clean your fingers before turning the page?" He wasn't given a response to his question so he then asked another: "I've been meaning to ask, Annette, how you managed to stitch Tolkien back together. I kept turning it over and over in my head. That it may have been a duplicate seemed like a logical conclusion but the dust jacket was torn in the upper left corner and the card in the back of the book had your signature. It was also stamped with the same due date. It was the exact same book. The only question is . . . how?" But Annette didn't know how and, even if she did know, she certainly wouldn't have confided the secrets to Jonas. "Why don't you *say* anything, Annette?"

Annette sat the watermelon down and lifted her eyes from the page. For a moment underneath the tree, it seemed that twelve-year-old Annette *would* say something. Jonas was, for once, speechless as Annette cast her eyes to his. Instead of saying anything however, Annette took the spare towel, wiped her fingers dry on the side of her dress, and turned to the next page. When her fingers reached for another bite of watermelon, Jonas snatched the fruit away quicker.

"Ask for it." Jonas smirked. But Annette had no intention of asking for it. If she had asked for the watermelon, it would have proven that Jonas had power over her. Twelve-year-old Annette wasn't quite sure how to proceed at this point. Her eyes darted from Jonas' and the watermelon between them. "What are you waiting for, Annette?"

For several awkward seconds, Jonas kept a close watch on Annette, who carefully set a bookmark into the current chapter, and closed the book. As she stood from the grass, Jonas snatched *Dracula* from her lap and replaced her bookmark with the sliver of half-eaten watermelon. Jonas tossed the book to the ground, turned, and left her alone with the juicy mess.

*

"Annette?" Lucas waved a hand before Annette's face.

Her glazed-over eyes came back to full attention. Lucas had joined her at the conference room table. It was the bite of grilled watermelon that had herded her thoughts.

"Sorry, I was lost in yet another memory."

"Where were you?"

"It doesn't matter," Annette shrugged her shoulders and took her first bite of shark. She groaned happily. "Someday I hope to actually meet this Cauliflower guy to get his recipes."

"I know, right? Fiona said that when she visited his office, she found an entire gourmet kitchen which spanned for half a mile. Imagine the amount of counter space and storage! She said he had at least a hundred rolling pins and five times as many pots and pans. She didn't see any cookbooks though. He must have them all memorized."

"Every recipe?" Annette scoffed. "Memorized?"

But Lucas once again fell silent. Lucas had met him before; Annette was sure of it the way his eyes glazed over in memory. "*Anyway*," Lucas recovered from his silence and took a bite of his own piece of shark. "I only have one peg left."

"One peg?"

"Only *one* and you know what *that* means. I'll be out of here: long gone. Vamoose. Finito. No more." A bite of grilled watermelon went to his mouth. Annette suddenly realized that this was probably the last time they would sit and share a meal together. So Annette sighed and sipped her pinot noir.

"Lucas?" she asked him. Lucas acknowledged her with a grunt as he took another bite of his shark. "What memories come back to you?"

Lucas swallowed the shark and slowly turned to Annette. "All sorts of memories, really," he told her thoughtfully.

"I didn't mean to pry." Annette blushed. Lucas took Annette's hand and pulled her out of the swivel chair. "Where are we going?"

They gathered their plates and goblets and scurried to Lucas' office where Annette and Lucas continued the conversation.

"The first day I got here, Annette, the *very* first day, Fiona showed me the instructional video in the conference room and then led me to my office where I found the Lite-Brite board. You'll see, Annette. At the end of every employment, Fiona empties the Lite-Brite board, sweeps the office of any personal belongings, and prepares for the next muse."

Annette tried to imagine the previous muses that had once, also, sat at her desk. Had they been plucked from their own lives in the same brutal manner as she? Whom had they inspired? What had become of those muses after their retirement?

"But mine *wasn't* empty, Annette," Lucas continued as he led her to his own personal starlit balcony. "There, in the face of my Lite-Brite board, was a colored peg: one harmless little green peg. At first I didn't think anything of it and figured it was left over from the previous muse, right?" Annette nodded. Lucas shook his head. "But no, this peg was different."

Lucas opened a drawer of his desk to reveal a magazine clipping of a surfboard as it scraped against a giant curved wave, a black moleskin journal with ballpoint pen, a photograph of a young man whom she guessed was his lover before Lucas had died, and a single green colored peg, which he lifted from the cabinet so Annette could get a better look.

"This is your peg?" Annette inquired.

"Spectacular, isn't it?" In truth, the green-colored peg was the same as any other peg she'd seen before, but to humor him, Annette nodded. "What it was doing in my Lite-Brite, I'll never know, but the point is this: after Fiona helped with my first inspiration, I rotated it counter-clockwise."

"What did it show you?"

Instead of plugging the peg into his own Lite-Brite, Lucas rushed out from his office down the end of the hall to Annette's. She followed close behind him with her helping of shark in hand hoping there were no violet envelopes in the post box. She was pleased to find it was still empty. Lucas inserted the peg into a random spot lower than the others on Annette's Lite-Brite grid. Lucas tightened his grip on her hand, and with the fingers of his spare hand he rotated the peg counter-clockwise.

The office folded and unfolded as it had many times before until, at last, Lucas' first chapter was set on display like a Faberge Egg at a prestigious auction house. In quick succession, Lucas' story flipped with the same frequency that Jonathan's had.

Even before he was born, Lucas Richardson was serenaded by a guitar. As Mrs. Richardson sipped iced tea in the summer, the windows opened to let in a mildly cool evening breeze, Mr. Richardson sat with her. His green guitar pick strummed the strings as his fingers created chords. No words were sung, but the simple bliss of music brought the baby inside Mrs. Richardson's belly to peace.

"He's calmed down a bit," sighed Mrs. Richardson happily.

Mr. Richardson smiled, setting the guitar on the cushions next to him. He carefully leaned over and brushed his cheeks against his wife's belly. For several minutes, the parents lay in silence. A strong current of wind shook a curtain into the air.

"Keep playing," said Mrs. Richardson. And Mr. Richardson did just that. In fact, Mr. Richardson played for his son for years afterwards. Lucas couldn't fall asleep at all unless his father strummed the guitar. Night after night, the pick strummed the strings to deliver Lucas into the land of dreams. But as Lucas grew older, so did his father.

"Someday, Lucas," said Mr. Richardson one morning over breakfast, "you'll need to meet someone else who'll play the guitar for you." Young Lucas was too naïve to understand that his father was getting older and he was unaware that his father's body was slowly retaliating against itself.

"Cancer," the current muse explained to Annette as they ate their meals during the impressive dinner theatre. As time roared forward, Annette and Lucas both watched as Mr.

Richardson's body was tormented by tumors. "The peg doesn't show it, Annette, but he was a music teacher . . . my music teacher . . . he changed the lives of so many people." A single tear ran along Lucas' cheek. "If only I could have changed *his*."

"But you did, Lucas." Annette swallowed, sweeping away her own set of tears. She dared not think of the losses in her own life. Annette's father had also passed away and those memories threatened to resurface. But this was Lucas' time and he needed her.

The moments that followed were silent. His father died and no one played the guitar for him. It was too emotionally painful for Lucas to pick up the instrument and learn to play it alone. In his sixth grade year Lucas' substitute English teacher, who happened to be Fiona in a cream-colored pants suit, handed the students an assignment. They were instructed to go out and explore the world around them and document all the things they saw, which led young Lucas on an expedition through the surroundings in which he felt immersed: dried-up creek beds, old bridges, woods in his backyard and nearby caves. Sometimes Lucas stood atop a hill overlooking his neighborhood, eyes closed, and feeling the wind rush against his cheeks. At night, after his mother thought he was asleep, young Lucas lifted the glass of his window to discover the lawn where he would spread out a blanket. He slept under the stars and heard the hooting of owls, the scratching sound of raccoons in the neighbor's trash, and the meowing of stray cats in the moonlight. Lucas wrote it all down in a tiny moleskin journal.

One night, as he lay staring up into the craters of the moon, young Lucas heard a sound from far away. Someone was playing a guitar. The music pulled Lucas from the blanket and, under the moonlight, he scribbled the images that came to mind.

Fiona, in her role as substitute teacher, read aloud the passage from his work and, for the first moment in his school years, Lucas swept his eyes across the classroom. He spotted a boy several rows in front of him who had shaggy brown hair that reminded Lucas of a sparrow's wing as it beveled in a curve above the boy's ears. This boy turned to find Lucas staring at him and Lucas immediately blushed bowing his head in embarrassment.

After the lesson ended and they were to go on to their next class, Lucas waited around a little longer than normal to avoid having to speak to the boy several desks ahead. However, the boy had waited for Lucas outside the classroom door; their meeting was inevitable.

"What you wrote," said the boy. "It's inspiring."

"Is it?"

"I'm Gabriel."

"Lucas." Their friendship sparked at that moment and soon they were inseparable. As days roared on and their friendship grew all the more defined, Lucas spent the night at Gabriel's house. He only lived several blocks away and, as fate would have it, Lucas discovered that Gabriel had a balcony. And on that balcony, before he went to bed, Gabriel would play a guitar; the sound of his music, of his passion, stretched out into the night.

"Gabriel played his guitar everywhere." Lucas told Annette. "He played at church for the youth group praise band and in the band at school. But his favorite time to play was late at night with the windows open. His fingers, as they strummed the chords, were experienced. As he played, Gabriel's eyes stared before him as if imagining notes on a page."

It was then that the current muse Lucas reached out to Gabriel but no contact was made.

Lucas went on: "When we were alone during the afternoons before his parents drove in from work, Gabriel would teach me how to play. I'd fumble on a chord but he'd wrap his fingers around mine and whisper the melody in my ear that he'd intended me to imitate. Though we never kissed, or were physical in any way, Gabriel and I shared something exclusively between us. He said his family was from California. He talked of the ocean, of the surfs, the seagulls and the warm winds. So often I fantasized he'd take me there, you know?"

As Lucas spoke, these details fluttered before the two muses. Time finally stood still on a single afternoon when Gabriel didn't attend class. In fact, he didn't attend for several days or even weeks. Teenaged Lucas visited Gabriel's home only to discover that the family had unexpectedly moved. Through the windows, Lucas could see that the rooms had been emptied; the walls were bare. For the longest time, teenaged Lucas sat in the doorstep and wondered what had happened to make Gabriel and his family depart so suddenly.

"Strange, you know?" Lucas continued his narration. "Gabriel was there one day and the next . . . an empty balcony. So I went exploring, you know? Got out of that town. Wanted to know what it felt like to surf, to experience all that I'd heard about. Never made it there. At least not while I was alive. I documented all sorts of things in the moleskin and even took up guitar. I eventually took a career in education: a music teacher, like my father. I eventually ended up in Portland, Oregon. I grew older with this notion that we'd find each other again. We'd meet. Pick up where we left off. I found him on the Internet but it was just e-mails. We were a country apart. Heck, a world apart. Me, a music teacher in Oregon; he worked in the World Trade Center. There were plans in the works for me to fly out there and see him. But one day, September 11th, 2001, I woke to find an e-mail."

The moments flipped in quick succession, one right after the other, until the living Lucas watched as the news coverage had replayed the attacks. After that moment, Lucas' guitar remained untouched and, as it had after the death of his father, his world had grown quiet again.

And then the muse arrived. Nathaniel J. Cauliflower stood in Lucas Richardson's classroom door.

Lucas, who was sorting music, looked up.

"Mr. Richardson?" asked Nathaniel J. Cauliflower.

"Can I help you?" asked the living Lucas.

"I sure hope so," said Nathaniel J. Cauliflower. But he didn't say anything more; he handed Lucas the violet envelope and left.

Opening the flap of the violet envelope, Lucas reached inside to find a single guitar pick. By the time Lucas ran out into the hall, Nathaniel J. Cauliflower had disappeared. And like that, Lucas' story reached its zenith.

As the modern-day muse, Lucas touched Annette's shoulder and guided her out of the story returning her safely to her personal library office with the gurgling water cooler.

"Wait... that's it?"

"No, there's more. There are too many memories, you know?" he replied.

"Nathaniel J. Cauliflower was your muse," Annette pondered out loud.

There was an uncomfortable silence that passed between them. It was evident that Lucas didn't want to show her the rest and, being a good friend, Annette didn't push the topic any further.

"Promise me something, Annette." Lucas said, finally, pocketing the green-hued peg.

"Promise you what?"

"That after I'm gone you'll find someone else."

"Someone else?"

"A friend. You've evolved so much since I first saw you in the hallway. You may not even know, you know?"

"Who would you suggest?" Annette's forehead furrowed at the thought.

"Harriet, perhaps?" Annette nearly choked on her own saliva. Lucas offered her a Styrofoam cup of water to help. "Now *Harriet's* story . . ." Lucas shook his head. "And I thought *I* had it bad . . ."

Annette's features frosted over. "She probably deserved what she got," she said, hastily.

"Oh come on," Lucas leaned back in his chair. "She's a great gal; you have to give her some credit." Annette scoffed in response. "Once you get to know her, Harriet's not the dictator she makes herself out to be."

"I'd prefer to keep my own version of Harriet, thanks." Annette stretched her arms around Lucas' figure. "I'm really going to miss you," she told him. Lucas smiled kissing Annette on the forehead.

"I've got one peg left, Annette." He tightened the distance between them. "Management only knows when it's gonna arrive in my post box, you know? We may have all the time in the world . . ."

*

Twelve-year-old Annette sat with her mother and father at the kitchen table; all three sets of eyes were set on the book that had been ruined by the slice of watermelon. "Well," said her father. "I'm beginning to think we should buy you books instead of borrowing them from the library."

She climbed into bed later that night after setting the watermelon-logged *Dracula* on her desk. She dreamed she was a seed drowning in the juices of a watermelon. Jonas' teeth took bites of the fruit, getting closer and closer to where she lay. Twelve-year-old Annette awakened with a start once again to find that her window had been opened. A cold breeze caused her shoulders to shiver. There, on her desk, sat the copy of *Dracula* in the same position that she had placed it before. Switching on her bedside lamp, Annette pushed the covers to the side with her bare feet, closed the window, and traced the closed novel with her fingers.

Just as before, with Tolkein's *The Hobbit*, Bram Stoker's magnum opus had been meticulously repaired. The pages were as fine as they had been earlier that morning. The printed words were unscathed by the pink juice. Clutching the book close to her chest, young Annette looked out the window and wondered if, perhaps, whoever had fixed her library book was out there in a puddle of moonlight out on the lawn. Annette barely spied a young man running off into the woods behind her house.

CHAPTER 11: HOW DORIS CAME TO HOLD THE TONGS AND DROPPED THE DONUT

Annette's post box was inundated. She found twenty-two white envelopes and opened them from the bottom of the stack to the top. The twenty-two white envelopes seemed a series with the same end goal: for lovers to begin a momentous journey toward encountering one another. In one instance, all Annette had to do was kick a tin can into the street and then watch the events unfold. In another, after forty-two years of individual solitude, two strangers met on a subway train when a tangerine was "accidentally" dropped from a plastic grocery bag. She also brought together a young man and a young woman by means of a discussion of subjects in a bookstore. She switched the scarves of two men and she brought them together to share a discussion on how it might have happened. She inspired a man and a woman who were taking the next-to-last jar of preserves and who hadn't seen one another in years but were meeting once again. They ultimately decided to share it.

Each colored peg from the twenty-two inspirations had been cream with red polka dots. Upon further inspection in Lucas' amateur guide, Annette discovered that the particular peg stemmed back to the muse Erato who had been in charge of love poetry.

When she finished with her inspirations and there were no envelopes waiting for her, she decided to attempt in cracking the code on the glass oak chest. She stared at the picture of Nathaniel J. Cauliflower and sighed. Why had he been so elusive? Sure he was a private man but he had to be seen eventually! Annette couldn't help but to wonder if perhaps Mr. Cauliflower was intentionally trying to avoid her.

She then considered his last name and bent down to the letters. She studied the letters for a brief moment before moving them with her index finger. Her heart began to beat faster as she caught a C in the first disc, an A in the second, and a U in the third. Eventually she filled in the other letters only to come up short:

CAULIFLOWE

There were eleven letters in his last name and the combination needed only ten. She turned the letters again and found another combination. Once again, her pulse quickened.

NATHANIEL

In this instance, Annette came up short with letters. His first name was too short, containing only nine letters. She frowned, absentmindedly turning the letters of the last disc until she came up with another combination.

NATHANIELJ

There were ten letters that seemed to fit but the lock remained fastened. Though she was back to square one, she felt as if she had made some progress at least.

Annette abandoned the code and went in search of the novels she had brought back with her from *The Muse's Corner*. However, the words didn't have the same dramatic effect on her as they once had. The paper didn't have the smell of fresh ink or of greasy fingers that had previously thumbed the pages. The book was simply a book and nothing more. What she wanted was something a book couldn't supply. What Annette desired was her own real-life love story. Although she had promised Harriet that she wouldn't rotate the colored pegs, the clear-colored red polka-dotted peg that encapsulated the history of Doris was too much of a temptation.

Annette licked her lips, cracked her knuckles, definitively stood up from her swivel chair, and crossed to the doorless doorway of her office. She checked to see if the coast was clear. Annette rotated the polka-dotted peg counter-clockwise with her index finger and thumb. Doris the waitress' life flipped casually to the beginning.

Time was rewound to Doris' Valentine's Day in first grade where she, like the other students, sat at her desk with a box donned in multi-colored macaroni shells. First-grade Doris wore thick black glasses, pig-tails tied in white ribbons, and frills on a festive bright-pink dress. Her mouth was pursed with concern as she peered into her Valentine's Day box. The box before her was completely and utterly empty. Annette was as invisible as she had been when Jonathan the violinist had bent over his math problems at the kitchen table. The lack of valentines in Doris' Valentine's Day box was as gut-wrenching for Annette as it was for young Doris.

First-grade Doris spun around in her chair to spy the other Valentine's Day boxes around the room. It was clear from her concerned expression that she had given everyone else one, even to the cute little red-headed boy who was flanked by far more attractive young females than she. Yet young Doris' box remained empty. Annette wanted to pick up some red construction paper and scissors, scrawl something inspiring, and put it into the box while the little Doris wasn't looking, but Annette's hand went through objects the way fish wiggle through water.

Doris' timeline fluttered before Annette; Valentine's Day after Valentine's Day, year after heart-sinking year. The boxes progressed from macaroni-speckled shoeboxes and paper hearts to carved wood from Doris' sixth grade shop class, but the number of accumulated Valentines inside the various containers, no matter how progressively elaborate, did not. The boxes, as the years went on, remained barren.

Doris had never been one of those stunningly beautiful women who provoked great paintings; her hair had always been flat, her black glasses repulsively thick and, because of her increasing unhappiness, her pale lips had formed a stomach-turning scowl of displeasure. That still didn't stop Doris from keeping her eye on various men throughout the years.

First it was Billy, the red-headed boy in the first grade who stared out the window, followed by Donald, the boy who

111

ate his own boogers, in the second grade. Next it was Elijah, the classroom snitch in the third grade, and then it was Donald again in the fourth grade after he realized that not eating his boogers was more attractive. Stanley, in the fifth grade, always bathed with the freshest soap. Shreedar, whose family had been from India, was her ideal mate in the sixth grade. Todd, the class clown in the seventh grade, then took the next spot on her ever-growing list. Andrew, whose ears were pierced and who had sported a spot of oncoming facial hair under his chin in the eighth came next. Following Andrew was Paul, who in the ninth grade sang tenor (and sometimes alto and soprano if he warmed up his voice enough.) There was even a time that Doris had a crush on the man who served Chicken Surprise in her high school cafeteria: an entire yearbook full of individuals who caused Doris' heart to quiver. Sadly, none of them seemed remotely interested in her.

It, then, came as no surprise to Annette when Doris actually found the one boy whom she had stalked several weeks before senior prom. His name was Wilbur and he, like Doris, had thick black glasses and the same dreadfully cheerless frown. The day she nervously asked him to prom, he was standing next to her waiting for his daily scoop of Chicken Surprise. When it came time for him to pay the cashier, he realized a hole had ripped in his pocket. Sometime between waking up that morning and that exact moment, all his change had dispersed.

"Here you go." High-school Doris shared with him the extra money she had brought in case she desired a second helping of Chicken Surprise from the man for which she secretly harbored feelings. Wilbur's grimace barely curled into a sneer but Doris knew the simple gesture made him happy.

"Thanks," Wilbur told her, as the newfound odd-ball friends sat together at lunch.

"Will you go to the prom with me?" Doris asked him when the lunch bell rang. Wilbur said "Okay," but there was something blithely unsettling in his response. As he put the corsage on Doris' wrist, he squealed like a girl when a roach skidded by. The boy she so desperately loved turned out to be gay; Doris went with him anyway, because she would be damned if fate would back-hand her yet again.

112

Even after she graduated from high school, Doris' unlucky streak continued. She did, however, have a best friend in Wilbur and, after a while, Doris slowly began to realize she would be much happier single than pining for men she would never be with. For a year after graduation she and Wilbur bet on which one of them would find someone first, for it seemed that they shared the same affliction.

Once Wilbur went off to college, he found someone as pathetic-looking as he. After he promised Doris it wouldn't affect their friendship, the bond between the two of them eventually turned sour. Doris was distraught yet again.

Doris decided to try to asphyxiate her desires by way of a college education. She earnestly delved into general studies for the first semester, soaking up anything and everything from anthropology to zoology. Accordingly, her four-year degree spanned eight years. The asphyxiation of her love for men became an immersion instead. Much to her dismay, by the time she walked across the stage in yet another black robe to receive yet another diploma, she had fallen in and out of love with twelve of her teachers, four teaching assistants, and a freshman straight from high school who was eight years her junior.

All of these men had no clue that Doris felt the way she did because Doris was too worried that she would be rejected. If a relationship had flourished, she feared it would promptly fall through. Thus, it was Doris' growing fear of rejection that kept her single and unhappy.

Once she graduated with her degree, she soon discovered her college education was practically useless. So Doris decided to wait tables at the diner down the road from her one-bedroom, one-bathroom flat until she decided what she wanted to do with the rest of her life.

Day after pitiful day, night after dark and lonely night, Doris dappled dish soap on dishes and swished sterile cloths across countertops and tables. She deposited hamburgers and hash-browns onto the tables of those who had requested them and refilled soft drinks and sweet teas. Doris stacked donuts and bran muffins with tongs and made sure that each made it safely into the display case.

Doris' hair remained matted, her glasses remained the same thickness, and her attitude became indifferent - that is, until one day, when she looked at herself in a mirror. Perhaps the problem with her unrequited romances had been caused by her appearance. She begged God for a make-over. She experimented with various beauty products and cropped her curly hair short, which helped a little. By using Lucille Ball's style as her guide, Doris transformed herself into a relatively attractive specimen. Even as she waited tables, Doris dreamed that a camera crew would someday invade the diner like Prince Charming or, perhaps climb a fire escape like Richard Gere in *Pretty Woman.*

Doris did a little research and found a television show looking for volunteers in need of a make-over. While eating microwave-zapped fettuccini, she wrote a sorrowful letter to the studio. Then one dreary rainy day, when it seemed that Doris' hope was dashed, Doris' prayers were answered by a phone call from the producers. By the next week she was seated backstage before a gigantic mirror that seemed to magnify all her flaws: the scar from the pimple she had picked in the fourth grade on her forehead; the bags under her eyes had taken the appearance of a misshapen clay statue; the inner criticism of general figure brought a feeling of great despondency.

"Well, let's see what we can do," said Fiona, who had taken on yet another façade as a make-up artist. She stood and made a mental list of all the characteristics she wished to change which, unfortunately for the protagonist, was an extensive inventory. "The problem isn't your features, child," Fiona said. "Make-up can only take us so far. You have to learn how to be happy. Give me a smile."

Doris strained a smile. Fiona looked disappointed and leaned in to speak privately in Doris' ear. "Imagine if a young man brought you flowers." So Doris imagined herself standing before a man offering flowers. Her face suddenly began to glow and her cheeks began to blush. "Now we can begin," Fiona said, brandishing the makeup brush.

It took over an hour but a general wash and conditioner made Doris' hair buoyant. Doris brought along contacts which she forcibly inserted onto the pupils of both of her eyes. Make-up was then professionally applied onto her face. Annette, who was observing inspecting the documentary, nearly fell asleep during this process, until time did its usual "fast forward" thing. Within seconds, Doris emerged onstage before a live studio audience as a changed woman. There was applause and cheers. Doris left confident in her brand new velvet blue suit accented by a freshly pressed handkerchief.

But it wasn't to last.

Time flew and Doris, still afraid of rejection despite her newfound beauty, once again sat in her living room devouring luke-warm fettuccini presented on a Styrofoam plate. The magic that Fiona the Make-Up Artist had performed was fading and, with each passing day, she would rewind and play her fifteen seconds of fame over and over again on the television. The happy version of Doris' former self mocked her before the studio audience. Doris continued her misery because it became clear to her that everything fades and that there weren't men waiting to offer her flowers. Doris didn't want to fight it anymore. She wanted a man who loved her for her obnoxious glasses and her blonde hair. She desired a man to hold the door open for her instead of running as she approached. She wanted a love that was requited.

Then the Man with the Eggs entered the picture.

Doris again stood before the donuts stacking them with tongs. It was a blustery day outside and the man brought a bit of breeze in with him as the bell above the door announced his arrival.

"Sit anywhere," said the waitress named Madge, who had brought water to Annette on her first visit. The current Annette took the seat opposite the man and watched as his grief-stricken eyes scanned the menu. Doris approached the table and they locked eyes. Doris then promptly dropped her notepad, excused herself, and disappeared into the kitchen. "What'll it be, hun?" asked Madge, who took Doris' place.

The man pointed to the eggs and, for the next hour, he sat and sipped coffee while swishing the eggs around on his plate with his fork chewing slowly. Finally, he paid with crinkled bills and left the diner. No words were spoken during the entirety of his visit. The same routine occurred for five consecutive mornings which rolled by like waves on a quiet secluded beach.

The fifth day was one that Annette remembered perfectly. Right on cue, a past version of herself materialized out of thin air and sat in a nearby booth. Annette watched from her new perspective as Doris lifted the donut followed by the rattling that drew her former self's attention. And so, as the donut dropped and the man stood to pay, he and Doris locked eyes yet again. "Here ya go," and he was soon out the door.

Annette again sat in the front seat of Doris' car while her former self had stood on the waitress' shoulder, no bigger than the size of a cricket. Beyond the windshield and the pounding relentless rain, the man stood over a casket. Former Annette's voice was so quiet and timid, the current Annette worried that Doris didn't hear it but she was pleased as Doris spoke with a newfound confidence over the pounding rain on her windshield. The pop-up book thunderclap followed as Annette was thrust back into the office.

She sat there in the swivel chair silently reviewing the events in Doris the Waitress' love life and felt an uncontrollable desire to parallel it to her own. She and Lyle had only gone on a few dates before he had proposed to her. Because of her antisocial behavior, Lyle had tried to extract words from Annette's mouth besides the common "yes" and "no" that he'd previously endured. Lyle had taken her to places like drive-thru windows, movie theatre concession stands, karaoke bars, and various parties of friends and fellow customers who had purchased new and used cars from him in the past. Lyle had hoped that she'd find her voice but, alas, Annette's words had not surfaced.

She wondered what sort of love story her marriage with Lyle had been; it hadn't been the least bit interesting, she told herself. If she were given another chance, would she do things differently or would her life play out the same as it had before? What if she was doomed to suffer in dead-end relationships and shackled down with eventless marriages? Now that she was dead, would she even get a second opportunity?

Adam the bookseller had asked for her number, hadn't he? As she sat looking at his familiar blue colored peg, which

116

was her key to the pages of the bookseller's pop-up, Annette wondered what sort of damage it would cause if she rotated it. Ultimately, she did nothing. Instead, she returned to the oak cabinet on the second floor of her private library.

Fiona had mentioned once that it was Nathaniel J. Cauliflower's relationship with a former muse that brought about the debacle with the misplaced correspondence. Annette anxiously bit her lip and turned each disc one by one. "E . . ." she said aloud to the cabinet as she turned the letter. "V. . ." she said as the second letter clicked in to place. On and on Annette went until, at last, the name was finished in the lock.

E V A N G E L I N E

Annette had before her a ten-lettered name to fit into the ten-lettered lock. She waited for something to happen. Were there gears inside that would twist and turn to allow access? There wasn't a handle to grasp or anything to open it any other way. Annette waited for at least five minutes. Nothing happened.

"It's not the right word," she sighed miserably. "If not Cauliflower, or Nathaniel J. or Evangeline, then what else could it be?"

CHAPTER 12: CAR, COMMENCEMENT, CHAMELEON

Annette had inspired a wide range of individuals, including a computer analyst, obstetrician, plumber, nanny, boat captain, window-dresser, and fire-eater. Surprisingly the more people she inspired, the more Annette felt comfortable while she had spoken, the less dread Annette felt when envelopes appeared in her post box. Sure, she had inspired in the same old faded flowery house dress that she had put on that fateful morning Jonathan's car had rounded the corner before the library, and she was still antisocial. She had a few more kinks to work out but Annette was adapting.

She and Lucas were inseparable; he would sit in a spare swivel chair in her office and accompany her on various inspirations while recollecting some of his own. They continued to share meals together in the conference room. Although Annette enjoyed his company, it was torture knowing that, at any moment, Lucas' last envelope would arrive.

"So tell me about Lyle," Lucas inquired over Nathaniel J. Cauliflower's pork roast. "How did the two of you officially meet?"

*

The circumstances in which she and Lyle had met were these. Annette was in high school, if "in" was the proper word for it. Boys were loud, obnoxious, and filled with too much testosterone. Girls talked about nothing but New Kids on the Block and crimping irons. Teachers (although they thought

Annette wasn't listening) gossiped about their students over cigarettes and coffee around the side of the building. Annette certainly didn't seem to have a voice of her own. The thought of conforming to any one group in particular was an insult to her and an affront to the possibility of the person she could potentially turn out to be. So she stayed quiet and, apparently, preferred it that way. Annette truly felt she didn't fit anywhere in the tapestry of her youth.

Annette's accumulated knowledge of all subjects resulted in stellar academic achievement. Annette's name was posted several times on the "principal's favorite" list but, because she was so quiet and, consequently, a splinter of flesh away from being absolutely invisible, no one knew who Annette was. Therefore no one took the time to congratulate her. Annette's silence made her appear stand-offish. Even if there was another social outcast who happened to wander into her territory, she would have deemed Annette as about as exciting as moss growing on the north side of a tree. Annette was even offered the chance to be the valedictorian but she quietly declined; the thought of having to give a speech terrified her.

"You don't seriously intend to live the rest of your life in silence, do you?" Jonas asked one day as Annette waited for her father to arrive in his car to pick her up after last period. She and Jonas had been enemies for years and were constantly at war. This day was no different than any other. "You've got all that knowledge in that thick skull of yours and what has it brought you? You may as well not even be alive."

Annette, who was reading Victor Hugo's *Les Miserables* as Jonas talked to her, looked up from the pages and simply stated, as matter-of-fact as possible, "I am alive."

"Are you? Truly?" Annette's eyes glazed over as she considered this. "Do you have *any* friends?" Annette pondered his question and shook her head. "And why do you think that is?" Jonas thumped the pages of *Les Miserables* with his forefinger. "Because your nose is always buried in a book; that's why. And because of that, you're anti-social, and because of *that*, you're a sack of flesh taking in air that *should* belong to someone who deserves it. Don't you think it's time for a change?"

Annette started to leave but she had to wonder: the conversation between the two of them could have been genuine; could it possibly be that Jonas might actually become a friend at some point? So Annette lingered a second longer than she probably should have to hear what Jonas had to say.

"What you need, Annette, is a drastic transformation in personality. I've been trying to separate you from the books for years but what I've finally realized is I can't do it myself. Ultimately, you're the one who has to break free. To really change, first, you've gotta ditch the book." Annette considered about closing the book and returning it to the library where she had found it. If the experiment didn't work, she would simply pick it back up again. There was simply no harm in at least trying, she said to herself. Jonas continued to speak. "And I know what you're thinking. You'll return the book and wash your hands of it, but no. That's something the old Annette would do. What you have to do. . ."

A warm breeze forced a strand of Annette's hair from her forehead and blew it around the other side of her face. Jonas took the book and flipped through each page with the same intention as a mob leader flipping through a stack of newly printed hundred dollar bills. ". . . Is burn it."

Annette almost felt faint. "Burn it?"

"You want to prove you're alive, don't you?"

Annette watched him flip through the pages of the novel. As her father's car pulled up the circle drive, Jonas handed the novel back to Annette. Seconds later, as her father's car pulled out onto the main road, Annette turned back to find Jonas, who was shrinking smaller and smaller on the road behind her, until his figure finally disappeared from sight.

Graduation came and went and the salutatorian who took Annette's spot gave an inspiring speech. Afterward, Annette scuttled across the stage. She shook hands with a few people, turned her head away from the camera at the end of the line, and slid back into her seat. How unpleasant that Annette's seat was next to Jonas'.

"So we've graduated," Jonas' face was pensive. "Congratulations. They say if high school doesn't kill you nothing will. I hate to tell you this, Annette, but it's not the case.

The world, the real world, is waiting for you out there." As another name was called to the podium, Jonas turned to Annette. "After today, Annette, we'll probably never meet again. So heed my warning. If you haven't burned the book yet, you'd better do it fast. The world doesn't take too kindly to the anti-social. How can you ask for anything if you don't sever the ties that keep you quiet?"

They parted ways for what Annette hoped would be the last time.

A conversation that decided her future occurred several nights later. "Have you thought about what you want to do?" asked her father. Annette poked the stir-fry with her fork, staring at the rice as if it held some clue to her future. "Your mother and I have picked out a graduation present though, initially, the decision was not unanimous. Mom wanted to use your savings to pay for whatever college you eventually choose. You have quite a healthy selection of prospects." Annette wasn't that interested in continuing school. College meant dorm rooms, and college meant study groups, college meant being even more social than one might have to be in high school. It was her parents who had spent the time and effort in applying for her. "However, your mother agreed that perhaps the money for your education would be better spent . . . on a car."

Annette looked up from the stir-fry.

"Tomorrow morning we'll find you one but you have to promise me something." Annette swallowed in anticipation. "Use the car to get out of this town and explore the world, learn in your own way, at your own pace."

Later that night, Annette carried a metal bucket out to the road. She could hear a conversation between her parents who had their bedroom window open. It was the voice of her father Annette heard first. "Just because she won't talk to you as she does to me doesn't mean she won't open up eventually." Annette stuffed a few leaves and broken pieces of tree bark into the bucket and had lit a match. "She's a remarkable girl, honey. I just wish you could see the potential that I see."

"She's an enigma to me," said Annette's mother. "And I fear that, even though she has potential, she'll never reach it due to her shyness." The words of her parents were drowned out by the sound of crackling wood. The light on the porch waned by the closeness and brightness of the small fire Annette had recently brought to a fine glow. She took one last look at the novel and made a wish the way some make wishes before tossing copper pennies into wells. She didn't wished she'd be more social. Instead, Annette wished that the mysterious individual who had rescued her previous library books would do the same with this one. She wished she could meet that individual after doing so and learn his trick . . . so that she could stitch herself back together properly in the same fashion.

The morning Annette's father took them to the new and used car lot was a cold and miserable one. Thunder above them bellowed like the stomach of a starved lion. Lightning was just as vicious. The rain caused the cement of the car lot to take on the look of transparent lizard scales. Colored flags thrashed about on the poles as her father pulled his car onto the lot. The brilliant hues were muted by the shadows of an ominous storm. It was one of those mornings when birds dared not chirp, when the roads remained vacant of the regular traffic, and a strong wind initiated a boxing match against the side of the car: rain versus metal. There were vehicles of every color, quality, shape, and size.

Lyle Slocum ran from the indoor office to their car with an umbrella. The soles of his shoes squelched in the rain beneath him with the same intensity as children jumping up and down in puddles. He was in his late twenties then with far more hair on the top of his head. The handlebar moustache had remained the same, since even that early in their lives together, and he wore the same type of crisp dress shirt and neck-tie as he would wear for the next ten years.

"Not a great day to be lookin' at cars, I'm afraid," Lyle said to Annette's father through the open driver's side window. "Lucky for you, today's free carwash day." Annette turned her attention to Lyle, scowling at his positive outlook on the morning. In return, Lyle winked at her. "What sort of car are you looking for?" he asked them.

"It's her graduation gift." Annette's father patted the top of Annette's hand.

"Well, how 'bout that." A subtle southern accent came from behind the handlebar moustache. "Hop on out, Little Lady, see if there's a car that catches your eye."

Lyle glided around the front of her father's car to Annette's passenger seat door, which she opened for herself. She found his hand poised in preparation to take hers and she took it gracefully. Under the safety of Lyle's umbrella, the pair walked through the aisles of cars the same way she did the aisles of a library. Annette's father had his own umbrella, and walked several feet behind them. But, at the moment, Annette and Lyle were alone.

Lyle inquired: "So you've just graduated?" Annette nodded. "Going to college?" Annette shook her head. "Eh, don't blame you. Always wanted to go to college but I followed in my dad's footsteps and fell into this profession. Maybe it's in the genes. Do you know about genetics?" Annette knew about genetics; she had excelled in every subject in school, but she didn't say this to the Man with the Handlebar Moustache. Instead, she simply nodded and cast her eyes out to the car lot around her. "Best to keep quiet when picking out the car, I understand. My parents were odd when it came to picking Christmas trees. They'd scan the rows of evergreens thinking that one would talk to them and, every time, I kid you not, they'd find one. The perfect one. Interesting, no?"

Annette nodded again. Her eyes finally set on a single vehicle.

"Ah, good looking car," said Lyle. It was a fine champagne-colored 1979 VW Beetle, a little aged, with a few thousand miles on it. Whether it was the paint or the way the lightning reflected off the surface, Annette knew that this was the car she was destined to have. "Like picking out the Christmas Trees . . ." Lyle whispered to himself.

Another customer's Mercedes pulled up to the office and, even from the distance and over the echo of thunder, its blaring horn could be heard. "If you'll excuse me," he said to Annette, opening the driver's side door. Then to Annette's father, "Have a seat inside the old girl. Be right back."

Once Lyle was gone, Annette climbed into the used Beetle. She pictured the places she would visit along with the sunsets and mountains she would see behind the wheel. Her father sat beside her imagining all of these places, too. If Annette had chosen a single second which she would replay in her mind for the rest of eternity, it would have been this: sitting in the driver's seat with one hand on the clutch and the other on the steering wheel while absorbing something similar to hope.

A figure passed behind the car. Half out of curiosity, she turned the rearview mirror to find Lyle standing with two other men: a father and son. The father's face was far from familiar but the son's face . . . Annette bit her lip and climbed out of the Beetle.

"What a coincidence," said Lyle to the father and son, "another customer's daughter just graduated." Annette and Jonas locked eyes for a moment. She was drenched with rain while Jonas was mostly dry under his father's umbrella. He waved at her with a smirk and she, trying to be polite, waved back. She secretly wondered if there was gas in the used Beetle so she could run over him. "So what do you think, Little Lady? Does the car talk to you?"

Annette nodded.

"What car . . . you mean *that*?" Jonas tried to suppress a guffaw out of respect for his father's reputation at the new and used car lot. "Well, I suppose it *does* suit you."

"How much for the Beetle?" asked Jonas' father.

"I believe the young lady here was interested." Lyle countered. "We have some new makes and models you might be interested in. You've never been interested in the used."

"How much is the Beetle, Lyle?"

Lyle turned his eyes to Annette, then back to Jonas' father, then to Jonas. Obviously on this dark and dreary day he was caught in the crossfire. He looked at Annette, smiled, and turned his eyes back to Jonas's father. "It's not for sale, Mr. Rothchild; if you'd like, there are a few more just as run-down but still capable enough for your needs."

Jonas' father frowned but followed Lyle anyway. When the morning turned to afternoon and the rain finally softened into a light mist, Annette signed the paperwork with her father's co-signature. The used Beetle became hers and, much to her amusement, Jonas left the car lot in something far less superior than he was anticipating: a terribly rusted 1957 Chevy two door sedan.

As Annette turned the ignition of her graduation gift, Lyle's knuckle rapped against her driver's side window. She then slowly cranked the window down by hand.

"Don't be a stranger now, Little Lady. My name's Lyle."

To which she responded "Annette . . ."

*

A blue envelope was discovered in the post box outside of Annette's office disrupting hers and Lucas' conversation.

"Well, it's not every day someone receives a blue envelope," Lucas seemed shocked as Annette opened the flap with her thumb. "What does it say?" Inside was a note from Fiona.

Mrs. Slocum,
There comes a time in every muse's employment for the muse to grasp a better understanding of the entirety of the profession. We've kept you in a comfortable zone in a language you can understand but it's a wide world out there. After Mr. Richardson's retirement party, Management has decided it's time to broaden your inspiration types. Meanwhile, please procure language books that will work best for your learning style.

A sip of water from the water cooler and a clockwise peg rotation later, Annette, with Fiona's permission, rotated the bookseller's blue peg clockwise. Instead of taking her to *The Muse's Corner*, where she was to purchase language books, the peg was far craftier. Instead, the muse was deposited into a booth at a familiar restaurant where she and Lyle had taken their first date. Adam sat alone enjoying a nice steak while reading a novel. Annette's face grew pale.

Looking up from the novel, Adam asked "Well, where did you come from?"

"It's complicated." Annette told him. "Eating alone?"

"Not anymore," Adam smiled, handing her a menu with plastic reinforced pages, closing the pages of his book, and turning his attention in whole to the muse before him. "How are you?"

"I'm-" Annette started. But before Annette could tell Adam that she was fine, a waitress approached the table to take her drink order - but not a typical waitress. Fiona stood with black pants, skid-free work shoes, and a black button-down dress shirt tucked in at the waist. "Confused," Annette finished, fitting herself into the booth.

"Can I take your drink order?"

"Water," Annette told Fiona, who had once again played the role of chameleon.

"Decided on anything to eat?"

"I'll need a minute."

"A minute it is: *no rush*," Fiona offered with a smile, departing the table to fetch Annette's water.

"Has she been your waitress the entire time?" Annette asked Adam.

"Dunno," he shrugged. "I don't really pay attention to those kinds of details."

"I didn't either," Annette held the menu in her hands but couldn't concentrate on any of the words, "until very recently, that is. She's a real chameleon, Fiona . . ."

"What's that?" Adam countered.

"Oh nothing. I'm thinking to myself . . ."

"Water for you," Fiona appeared with the glass, setting it down with the tip of the straw wrapped in paper. "Need any suggestions?"

Annette needed suggestions all right: as to how to proceed in this particular circus act. She flipped to the wine list, hoping for a libation to put her mind at ease.

"Why don't you surprise me?" Annette asked finally turning her eyes back to Fiona, who turned away from the table. Annette then feigned a smile to Adam who took a sip of his tea. *"This should be interesting,"* Annette thought to herself. And indeed it was. The small talk of the weather was tolerable as was the discussion of Adam's love for history and how he came to

126

work at the *Muse's Corner*. Annette found that she loved listening to him speak, even if it *was* about himself. By the time the steak arrived at the table, conversation had turned and it was now time to listen to Annette's thoughts.

"So," said Adam Mansfield, "fiction."

"Yep, fiction." Annette nodded, slicing a piece of steak with the knife.

"Any particular kind of fiction?" Annette looked up from the steak. "Romance?" Annette shook her head. "Science fiction?"

"Has its perks but most of it is far-fetched." Annette took a bite of her steak. "Which is probably why some enjoy it. I like the Classics most of all. Victor Hugo is my favorite." And then Annette went on to tell him of the library books in her childhood and of the burning of *Les Miserables* and how she had hoped she would meet the stranger. She was surprised, even elated, by how much she had spoken of herself to the bookseller. It wasn't until she stopped talking that she even realized that half an hour had passed where he had not said anything to interrupt.

After a second of silence, Adam said: "You're beautiful, you know that?" Annette choked on a sprig of parsley. "I'm serious, Annette. You're beautiful. And you were beautiful on the airplane."

"Clutching the vomit bag, oh yes," Annette scoffed, sucking the last particles of water from her cup through a straw. "Very beautiful."

"So what do you do, Annette, when you aren't disappearing and reappearing?"

"I'm a . . ." but how could she tell him she was a muse? There are some things you shouldn't bring up on a date and describing the afterlife was one of them. "I'm in community relations."

"Community relations," Adam repeated, with a look that said he wasn't buying it.

"Community relations," Annette repeated more convincingly while sitting back and rubbing her tummy. She was pleasantly full. At the end of the meal, Fiona the Waitress brought the check. Adam reached for it with one hand, while digging into his back pocket with the other. "Adam?" Annette asked him.

"I've got this, don't worry."

"That's not what I was going to say."

"Oh?" Adam asked with a raised eyebrow as he tucked his crisp paper currency into the leather pouch. Fiona arrived. "Keep the change," he told her. Adam then turned his eyes back to Annette. "What were you going to say, Annette?"

"I hate to ask this," Annette blushed. "But I need access to language books. Can you help me out?"

"You want to take our date to the bookstore?" Adam asked.

"Well . . ."

"I was going to take you out for frozen yogurt or sit by the river and talk for a while."

Annette wasn't sure what to say. His plan seemed simple enough but, considering that the plan involved *her*, Annette was speechless. Adam stood from the table and offered a hand to help her up.

She surprised herself by offering, "There's no reason why we can't do both."

Annette considered the time it would take to enjoy the frozen yogurt at the river, followed by a visit to the bookstore. Harriet would have her head for it that was for sure. Then again, Fiona had told her "no rush" at the beginning of the meal. Fiona passed by the table to help another guest. She took the time to tell Annette and Adam to "Have a nice evening!" Fiona then gave a wink that only Annette noticed.

As Adam walked Annette out the door, Annette turned one last time to see Fiona. Her employer had turned to another table where a man in a black suit had been sitting. It was as if the man was watching Annette and studying her every movement. The man nodded at Annette. Annette awkwardly acknowledged the man's nod and turned to Adam.

"Ready?" Adam asked Annette.

Annette smiled. "Lead the way." When she turned back to see the man, the unfamiliar person had already stood leaving his seat empty.

CHAPTER 13: IN PURSUIT OF THE PUBLIC SPEAKER

"Ladies and gentlemen, please welcome Mr. and Mrs. Lyle Slocum."

There was applause as the newlyweds entered the banquet hall, after taking pictures in the church. There they all were: Lyle's immediate and extended family members twice and three times removed. At a solitary table Annette's mother, father, and two older brothers with their dates were seated. The new Mr. and Mrs. Slocum cut a slice of their wedding cake. When they fed one another Lyle's handlebar moustache turned white with icing.

It was supposed to be the happiest day in Annette Slocum's life and, to anyone watching, her fear was masked with make-shift artificial joy. As she perched with Lyle and the wedding party, Annette sadly watched her own family discussing philosophy at their table. She wanted so desperately to tear off her veil, abandon the wedding dress, and toss the ring into the punch bowl; however, Annette had vowed herself to live a life to which she had not been accustomed and so she decided, right then and there, that her role would be a faithful, devoted housewife to her husband.

"I remember," her father began his toast with a wine-glass in one hand and microphone in the other "my own wedding day with Annette's mother. After we said our 'I do's', cut our wedding cake, and endured speeches by family and friends who preferred to roast us rather than toast our happiness, the bride and I took to the dance floor. The dollar dance followed and I danced with a woman whom I thought was a member of my wife's family. She was radiant: this woman who spoke volumes about her life while we shuffled our feet. And after her shoulder was tapped by my great-great grandmother who wanted a spin the woman disappeared. And I remember thinking to myself, 'When my wife and I have a baby girl, I want her to grow to be like the woman I've met. And she has: the radiant woman who will always remain my beloved child, sitting right beside one of the luckiest men alive." Annette's father hoisted the wine glass and finished the toast properly by draining the contents in one gulp.

The wedding gown that Annette wore had been a drastic improvement. Some people even called her "radiant" but, to Annette, the word "radiant" was only reserved for the color yellow. Annette simply received the compliments as flattery and, after several more speeches, she swept herself onto the dance floor where she and her father danced to several songs in silence. Once the evening was over, Annette and Lyle threw the bouquet and garter. Both the dinner mint bowl and the open bar were drained. Husband and wife retired to their hotel room to consummate their marriage. Lyle mistakenly thought Annette was crying because she was happy but Annette's tears were for the sorrowful change. She hoped that, before they made love, her copy of *Les Miserables* would be returned to her having been stitched back together. But there was no library book. Only a wedding ring. Regrettably, she already made the decision she would be faithful; she let Lyle believe whatever he wanted.

*

The haunting violin music returned once again, stirring Annette from her swivel chair. Memories of the steak dinner with her bookseller hovered in her mind. She wondered what the bookseller was doing now. Was he thinking about her as she was thinking about him? What sort of impression had she left? All she had were the language books that she had touched in *The Muse's Corner* after having eaten frozen yogurt at the river.

Without any clue on how Paganini's music had been permeating the ceiling and walls of the department, Annette paced back and forth down the hallway in hopes that the answer would reveal itself. She paced by the post boxes and peered into the various offices all the while nervously wringing the fabric of her house dress. Another thing that bothered her was the attendance of Fiona while she sat in the restaurant with Adam the bookseller. *"What sort of game was the Head Muse playing,"* Annette pondered. She was determined to ask Fiona about it when her employer had returned to the office.

Annette waited for Fiona to return. As she did, Annette's keen eye began studying the old photographs and portraits which had been hung on Fiona's office walls. There seemed to be nearly a dozen pictures of a young man she could only deduce was who Fiona had mentioned when she had previously shown Annette the letter. As Annette looked at these photographs, she recalled Lucas mentioning that the frames had once been empty. *"Did Management provide the subject after the last staff meeting,"* Annette wondered?

In the picture, the young man looked directly out into the office with otherworldly watchful eyes.

"Who are you?" Annette whispered. "When are you from?"

A sound several offices away pulled Annette from her various concerns; she heard Lucas sniffling attempting to fight back tears.

"Lucas?" Annette found him on his balcony sitting in his swivel chair with his eyes locked on an envelope he held in his lap. A violet envelope. "Lucas?" she said again, a little louder than the whisper it was before.

"Look at it," he said, not even looking up from the folded paper. "I never actually thought this day would come, you know? I mean, your first day you're given an empty Lite-Brite board and you think it'll take forever to fill it. And now here it is." Lucas scoffed, turning the blank envelope flap side up. "And of *course*, it's violet."

"Violet," Annette sighed swallowing a lump of apprehension while putting a hand on Lucas' shoulder for comfort. "Let's hope there are no mailboxes and misdirected letters where it sends you, right?" Even though Lucas was facing away from her, she could tell that the comment made him smile; maybe it was the way the skin around his temples tightened or the sudden intake of breath. So she bent down before him in an embrace. Her instincts told her to rub his back while he sobbed against Annette's shoulder. This is how the two of them sat for several minutes. Several of Lucas' tears dotted the violet envelope an even deeper hue.

"I'm sorry." That was all he could say while he fought back the remaining tears wiping his eyes with his shirt sleeve. "Fiona said the last envelope would be an emotional one, you know?"

"Did she?"

"How can you stand it, Annette?"

"Stand it?"

"They come in flocks, one after the other, fluttering as if they were once-stationary geese startled by a gunshot."

"Violet envelopes?"

"No, Annette. Memories. All my life I remember thinking . . . is that truly what I'm supposed to believe, that there's someone out there for me, or is the person I'm meant to be with actually *myself*? Is loneliness temporary? Could it be that the reason I've been so alone is because the purpose of a solitary existence is to perfect my soul? Or has it been punishment of some kind? All my life I've wondered why so many people have had relationships while I've remained perpetually single, you know? Others seek companionship and they get it, but not me." Lucas paused for a moment and Annette could see the anger and frustration of his situation flooding his face. "No, never me. I thought, maybe, if I got out into the world as a muse, I'd find the answers. When I traveled to all those places, I was invisible. And no, not just invisible like we sometimes are when Management sends us on inspiration jobs: much worse, actually. Sometimes it hurt so much, being alone, but I adapted to it, you know? Like preparation for the ultimate loneliness in the department. Nights would pass and I'd lay awake in bed wondering if I'd ever laugh again or ever truly be happy the way some couples are . . . or was I slowly fading like the death of a flickering flame on the wick of a candle?"

"But you had Gabriel."

"For a brief moment I did, Annette." His eyes began to glisten again. "Never anything you'd call official. We were too

132

young to know what it meant, you know? The attraction we shared . . . there were no words for it. When I decided to travel, he wanted me to stay . . . but staying in the Midwest was slowly killing me. I had to see the world and understand it better, you know? Gabriel and I would keep in touch by e-mail. It was in Oregon, Annette, when I was still alive. There was an e-mail from him in my inbox . . . a message saying there were terrorist attacks on the World Trade Center. He was in one of the buildings Annette, can't you see? Before he tried to get out . . . before Gabriel died . . . he . . ."

"One of your first violet envelopes had sent you to September 9th to save a few people . . ." Annette was now beginning to piece Lucas' history together – everything was quickly carved into a perfect circle.

"I tried to save Gabriel on that violet envelope," Lucas told her "but he wasn't my responsibility to save, Annette. Management just . . . let him go. And since I've been here, memories have been clawing at me with untrimmed nails. For the longest time I was so alone with no one to confide in, you know?"

"I'm sure Management had a specific reason to let Gabriel-"

"And then I met you."

"Lucas . . ."

"Oh sure, I was the muse to inspire Harriet. You think that would be enough to solidify a bond. But she's so guarded I don't feel comfortable talking to her about anything. But you, Annette, you *listen*. And not only that but you've rotated a few of your own pegs. You understand where I'm coming from. The Man with the Violin, the Woman with the Tongs, the Man with the Eggs . . . they mean something to Management. We all do. But what?" Lucas looked up from the violet envelope with bloodshot eyes. "What am I going to do, Annette?"

"Retire, supposedly." Saying the words caused Annette even more torment.

"Fiona said I'd have to make a decision pretty soon. Management gives you a full day between the last inspiration and the next stop. I've been to seven retirement parties; did you know that? Seven of them and each time I've thought – this is worth it, the rings of Saturn and the public speaker. But what's always tarnished the event had been the decision the retiring muse has to make. I guess I've got some thinking to do."

"Where could they send you?"

This was the first time that Annette had wondered that thought. Was where they sent you Heaven? Did the final destination have books and crisp shirts on clothes-lines that rippled in the wind? Annette could have speculated all different kinds of scenarios for the rest of eternity.

"Let's just say it's one of the hardest decisions I've ever made, you know?" Lucas looked down at his violet envelope, his fingers shaking. "I'd . . . sort of like to be alone for a bit." Lucas looked at Annette. "If that's okay."

"You know where to find me." Annette stood from her crouching position and turned to leave his office. Before entering the hallway she was stopped.

"Will you come with me," Lucas asked "on my last inspiration job, when I'm ready to open it?" Annette cared for Lucas more than she'd ever cared for her older brothers. There was a part of her that wanted to say "yes," that she would go anywhere with him, even if a violet envelope took them there. Annette wanted to tell Lucas that she wished wherever Management sent him, she could go too.

But Annette was terrified about venturing forth on a violet envelope that could potentially transform the human race into jellyfish or something with tentacles. So she did the one thing that made her the most comfortable: Annette said nothing at all and retreated to her office in silence.

*

It was with the same inactivity that Annette sat next to Lyle at the blackjack tables. All around them were whistling slot machines and people cheering as the jackpot jingled or a certain person's luck brought even more mountains of multi-colored chips to his or her hands. Cigarette smoke mixed with the stale stench of beer; above all, the not-so-subtle aroma of Lyle's musk wafted to her nose as he dripped with sweat after hours of gambling.

Eventually Annette gave up and retired to the hotel room where she switched off the lights. She pulled the covers over her head and remained still.

"Are you coming along or not?" Lyle playfully asked her one morning as he ruffled his thinning hair with the hotel towel. His chest hair was damp from the shower water, his eyes sparkled with greed, and his penis once again rose to its husbandly erection. After they made love Annette said she was tired and would be down later. She never did come down on that day or the day after that, and Annette preferred it that way. As Lyle spent most of their honeymoon gambling, the only thing Annette truly become acquainted with was the room service menu. She sometimes delighted in white tigers, magic tricks, or theatrical performances, but at night it was always the same; she lay in bed awake while Lyle's sleepily wandering arm found its way around her middle.

In the morning Lyle went to the crap tables and Annette watched documentaries on the television. She assumed that they would return home the following day and play house. At least that was the plan.

A phone call came at three in the morning. Annette was the one to hear it but, because she had never been the one to pick up the phone and answer it, she nudged Lyle, who answered. "Niello?" Annette was surprised when Lyle handed her the phone. She pressed the receiver to her ear. At first Annette thought that it was the individual who had rescued her library books; that they had found her at last. Annette didn't say anything. She simply breathed into the phone. Her heart beat was thudding in her chest.

"Annette, it's mom. I'm sorry to be calling so early, but honey, are you there?"

"I'm here," Annette told her mother.

"Honey, I'm afraid something's happened . . ." Annette heard a tissue being torn from a tissue box on the other end. "Honey, something's happened to daddy."

*

135

"A muse's retirement party in this office is always a pivotal event." Harriet said as she sat down in her own swivel chair while Annette pouted in the spare swivel chair by the water cooler. Fiona had given orders for Harriet to show Annette "the ropes" for retirement parties, much to Annette's chagrin. "It's a simple process. Out with the old; in with the new. But on a bigger scale. For the muse you've replaced, Fiona spared no expense on decorations and food. But the decorations weren't balloons and streamers and such; I'm talking candles, sparkling china, and stars."

"Stars?"

"Yes, Annette, stars. Sometimes, if there's space enough, Fiona brings out Saturn and its rings. Good supervisors try to trump their own previous parties. You'll get a chance to see the office like you've never seen it before."

She had seen Saturn before in a book of Hubble Space Telescope photographs but Annette had certainly never seen it "up close and personal."

"Now, as a Management policy, all inspirations are put on hold out of respect for the retiring muse."

"Which means no envelopes or colored pegs."

"Exactly. And, in that time to plan for the special retirement party, it's always been tradition that the muse who's worked here the shortest length of time has a very special job to do."

"Baking the cake?"

"No, Annette. Nathaniel J. Cauliflower takes care of the food. Keep up, will you?" With that retort, Annette hated Harriet even more. She was like the bossy older sister Annette would have hated to have. "It's your job to pick the public speaker."

"Sorry?"

"Follow me." Harriet stood from her swivel chair and ushered Annette to the end of the hall where there sat a beaten-up filing cabinet that had not been there before. "Open it." Annette did as she was instructed. Inside were thousands of envelopes packed as tight as sardines. "A modest collection of some of the greatest speakers who have ever lived in the entire history of the universe," Harriet said casually, thumbing through the envelopes.

"A modest collection?" Annette hated to see what an exhaustive collection would have looked like. Annette found that each envelope contained a polished colored peg. There was even an envelope with a black screw that looked like it had been accidentally tossed into a fireplace at some point in history. Harriet was quick to put the screw back into the envelope in which it had been discovered.

"I don't know how that one got inside there," Harriet confessed, keeping the envelope and black screw in a firm grip. "No one but Fiona ever touches this envelope."

"Why's that?"

"Why ask if it doesn't concern you?"

Annette rolled her eyes and picked a yellow peg to which Harriet shook her head disapprovingly. "What's wrong with that one?"

"Nothing, if you want to spend hours translating Socrates." It seemed that Harriet would be better at picking the public speaker so Annette tried to pawn off her position. "Trust me, I would do this job for you if I could, Annette. Nothing gives me greater displeasure than delegating responsibilities. But Fiona has me ordering a surfboard, the cherry blossoms, and a meteor shower. That's all I have energy to tackle this time around. Happy hunting."

"Wait," Annette said. Harriet stopped, apparently offended that Annette felt she had to have the last word. "We can bring people back here? Living people? To the office?"

"Management doesn't like it. They're lenient for the retirement parties but only to a point. Stick with the pegs in the filing cabinet only, Annette, *or else*."

"Or else what?" But Harriet was already down the hall and back in her own drab office. "Or else *what*?" Annette asked louder but Harriet obviously felt that all that needed to be said had already been said.

Annette was left standing alone in the hallway with the filing cabinet filled with unmarked envelopes and a putrid feeling gripping her intestines. Not really knowing which peg led to whom, Annette brought a handful at a time back to her office.

*

Annette and Lyle Slocum were sitting in the waiting room of the hospital, both staring off in their own respective silences. They were sorrowful-looking statues with props: a magazine in Lyle's lap and a cup of water in Annette's hand. These objects were as meaningless as the life that Annette had been hoping to fit into as Mrs. Slocum. Lyle looked at Annette and opened his mouth to speak, but Annette didn't meet his stare and certainly didn't seem to be in a talkative mood. He returned to his original position. The man on the other side of Annette had been reading his magazine and consulted his wrist, which he was disappointed to find was missing a watch.

"Damn it all," said the man. He turned to Annette. "Excuse me, Dear, do you have the time?" Annette had been too busy staring off into her own daydreams to notice this stranger talking to her, so the old man consulted Lyle instead. "Excuse me, Sir, what's the time?"

Lyle lifted his wrist, which was covered in his usual wilderness body hair, and checked the ticking hands. "Five thirty," he answered.

"Five thirty? My daughter's been in labor for four hours," the old man said. Lyle smiled and Annette knew that his smile meant he'd found someone to talk to and would most likely try to sell the old man a used car. Lo and behold, that is exactly what happened. Annette's father had been in the emergency room while Lyle made small talk with a complete stranger and attempted to make a sale on the best deals in his used car lot. Annette sat between them as Lyle listened intently to why the old man was there hoping that his attentiveness would bring about a signed contract.

"This is my third granddaughter in the past two years and, I'm telling you, I couldn't be more proud than I am right now. I only wish I was home more often to spend time with my family. However, someone has to make an income."

"I'll bet." Lyle bobbed his head up and down earnestly, though Annette was convinced that he really didn't care. Or maybe he did but, honestly, who knew when Lyle tried his hardest to make a sale. Whether it was in a hospital waiting room or in line at a grocery store waiting to check out, even if they were stranded on a desert island, Lyle would still have convinced potential customers that a used car was close to witnessing the face of God.

"And you, what are you two here for?"

"Annette's father is in the emergency room: a heart attack."

"Oh, Dear . . . I'm so sorry to hear that." The man spoke solemnly to Annette but Annette wasn't listening. She continued to stare off into the room again.

"Oh, we'll be alright," Lyle patted his wife's knee sympathetically. "Won't we, honey?" It was then that Annette's mother, who had been fighting the vending machines that wouldn't take her wrinkled dollar, arrived with a packet of cheese crackers.

"Annette, the doctor wants to see us." Annette stood up to leave and Lyle, the ever-so-persistent used car salesman, produced a card and handed it to the old man.

"Whenever you're near the lot, stop by for a visit."

"Oh," said the old man while looking at Lyle's card. "I do have a feeling that fate will most likely reunite us." As Annette walked away with Lyle's hand on the small of her back, the old man called out. "I'm sorry to hear about your father, Dear. I hope all is well."

*

Five billion, seven hundred fifty million, two hundred thousand, five hundred and eleven envelopes later, Annette had never before been so exhausted. What Harriet *hadn't* told her was that more than half of the public speakers would be grotesque and other-worldly. Annette felt like she'd lived through a demented science fiction novel. She'd seen enough tentacles, various shapes of eyes, exposed oversized brains, and mouthfuls of tongues to last her the rest of her eternity.

Thankfully, half of them were human and at least spoke commonly through orifices with which she was familiar. Only a minute fraction of the human entities, about half, could speak English. Even though the ones she actually had been able to understand had spoken with enthusiasm or overwhelming conviction, she had been disappointed overall.

"Well?" Harriet asked Annette as they stood before the filing cabinet stashing each envelope back inside. "Who's our public speaker?" She dared not tell Harriet that she hadn't chosen one. Annette stood there like a statue staring at her opponent. Harriet struck the top of the filing cabinet with a forceful fist. "Who have you chosen?"

Annette turned and headed back to her office. What was she going to do? Where was she going to go? What did Annette hope to accomplish? There wasn't even a door that Annette could close and lock to keep her marauder from stalking. Annette could hear Harriet behind her repeating the same question over and over. The more she heard the question, the more Annette knew she was in trouble. Annette saw a window before her and took it: as she took a sip of water, she touched a familiar peg and rotated it clockwise. Her office and the vehemently fuming Harriet disappeared in a thunderclap.

It was quiet where the peg sent her. The sun had not yet begun its ascent but Annette noticed that the nightly stars were already beginning to dwindle in number. She sat motionless on a porch swing. As the first light of approaching dawn brought the sky to a deep sapphire, Annette realized she wasn't alone. Next to the porch swing was a weathered rocking chair and in the rocking chair was the man whom Annette had inspired on the airplane. The two of them sat in reverence watching the sunrise. It was only when a shard of sunlight poured its rays onto the porch and turned the front lawn into a great emerald that the man even realized she was sitting there at all.

"Hello, Dear," said the old man, his creased smile accented by the wrinkles of his age. "I do believe you're right. Sunrises are far more glorious than sunsets." A morning breeze accompanied the chirping birds. To Annette, it seemed as if she were still alive. It seemed that Lyle was in the bathroom trimming the hairs on his handlebar moustache, the eggs were scrambled to perfection, and an afternoon of watching Lyle's shirts flutter in the backyard would be soon to follow.

"May I ask you a rather personal question, Dear?" he inquired.

Annette hated personal questions because they tended to lead to personal answers, which usually meant having to tell someone her miserable life story. As she was "in hiding" from Harriet and this man seemed genuine (if not paternal), Annette simply whispered "Yes."

"Are you, in fact, a ghost?"

"A ghost?" Now that she was dead, Annette really wasn't sure what she was. "A muse," the words had come from her lips before she even realized she had spoken them. It was the first time she had ever truly referred to herself as a muse to any of the people she had inspired. Thankfully, the man didn't call the local mental ward.

"After you literally disappeared from the plane, I asked the flight attendant where you'd gone. There was no record of you on the manifest. I supposed you were either a ghost . . . or an angel."

"Just a muse. Sorry to disappoint."

"Disappoint? My Dear, if only you had any idea how much your sunrise suggestion has inspired me!"

"How much *did* it change you?" Annette was eager to know.

The old man then looked at Annette. "Are you hungry?" This wasn't quite the answer Annette was looking for but the mere mention of food prompted her stomach to wrench in a growl. Apparently, attempting to uncover the public speaker had taken more out of her than she realized. He stood, offered his hand, and led Annette into his kitchen.

He offered Annette the use of his shower and to find a fresh dress in his late wife's closet while he cooked breakfast for his guest. Annette took her time lathering the shampoo in her hands; once the gelatin surface was reduced to bubbles, the aroma of fresh-picked strawberries kissed the tip of her nose. In a closet she found a yellow dress which she traded for her plain house dress. Staring at her reflection in a mirror, Annette witnessed a transformation. For the first time, she was truly content.

*

Although Annette had hardly gone to movies, she had certainly seen enough dramas to know that when a surgeon takes off his cap and holds it mournfully in front of him that a death has occurred. And so it was, on the early morning of what was supposed to be the happiest vacation of her life, Annette's father had died of heart complications during surgery.

Her father would give no more words of wisdom or further insights that would prompt her to grow. Annette sat in a chair beside her mother while Lyle casually slipped the surgeon his business card. If her father's life had been a book it would have been vandalized; the last few hundred pages would have been ripped out and only a tiny portion of evidence was left buried inside the spine. How she wished that the person who had stitched her library books back together would heal this moment in time.

Her father's funeral was lovely and sad. There was sunlight beating down on the casket as the pall bearers (which included Annette's two older brothers at the front) sat it gently on its stand. The eulogy coaxed Annette's desire to weep but the numbing uncertainty that enveloped her had won the mental battle. So she sat there emotionless gripping Lyle's hand on the lap of her plain black dress.

The preacher asked if anyone would like to say a few words about the deceased. Her mother stood and, while fighting her own tears, tears that butchered most of her words, told how they had first met in college in a literature class and how they had fallen in love and raised three beautiful children together.

Even Franklin and Michael had something to say: about how during the summer they would play catch with leather baseball mitts or fly kites in the park. They told about the way that their father would always build grand sand castles at a beach trumping the efforts of his own children. Annette, however, wasn't able to say anything. She sat there crippled by her emotions and fear of public speaking, as the afternoon sun began to set on the horizon.

Because she had been filled with such regret, Annette stirred from her sleep every morning before sunrise. Her dreams were filled with such horrible and lonely images. She cooked Lyle's breakfast day-in and day-out hoping that, somehow, by being a devoted housewife, God would forgive her for not wanting to speak at her father's funeral.

*

"Well, Dear, this Harriet sounds like a nightmare. As does Jonas."

"Tell me about it," Annette drank a glass of water from the tap while cutting another bite of pancake. "I mean, what's her problem? I've done nothing to her and she feels it's her personal responsibility to judge me on every little thing! 'Annette, there's an envelope and it's been sitting in your post box for less than a millisecond. Are you going to attend to it or not?'"

Annette even told the old man all about the envelopes, about the colored pegs, and the inevitability of the dreaded violet envelope.

"Well, the violet envelope doesn't sound that bad," he said.

Annette almost choked on her pancake. "Not that bad? Perhaps you didn't understand about Evangeline's misdirected letter fiasco. And Lucas, he's been through *several* of them!"

"And he came out intact."

"Yeah," Annette scoffed. She then sighed unhappily. "He asked me to go with him on the last inspiration."

"Well, that was nice of him. What was it like?" Annette stopped mid-chew. "You *did* go with him, didn't you, Dear?" It was obvious from Annette's face that she had not. "My Dear, we all encounter violet envelopes in our lifetimes and, yes, we may take a wrong step and ruin everything, but things will iron themselves out eventually. Your employer did say they were still trying to pick up the pieces of Evangeline's disaster. It may take a while, but things have a way of coming full circle in the end," he admonished.

Annette sat there in silence. His words were like salmon swimming up-stream to her beating heart. And suddenly it hit her. Annette set the fork down squinting her eyes quizzically. Leaning forward she asked, "How are you at giving speeches?"

A thunderclap deposited Annette back into her office where Harriet was still seething about her recent escape. Annette said nothing; instead, she removed the peg from her Lite-Brite board, placed it in Harriet's hand, and casually brushed shoulders on her way to the hallway. Annette's step as she headed to Lucas' office had grown from a subtle meander to an excited rush but, much to her dismay, Lucas was seen taking a final sip of his water and disappeared right before her eyes in a maniacal thunderclap. Annette instantly felt a pang of regret swell within her. Nothing could change the fact that he had gone to the violet envelope inspiration alone.

"He waited as long as he could, Mrs. Slocum." Fiona said from his office doorway. "I'm sorry." Annette sat in Lucas' swivel chair and studied the completely illuminated Lite-Brite board. Soon, Lucas would leave her and, once again, Annette would be without an actual physical account of what had happened with the violet envelope. Annette wasn't sure if it was fear or sorrow that she was feeling but what was for certain was that she suddenly realized how much she'd grown from the first day she arrived. She wanted to tell Lucas she loved him and how grateful she was that he had allowed her to blossom. Fiona turned to leave Lucas' office but Annette stopped her.

"Explain it to me," Annette demanded. "Why were you there at the restaurant?"

"I'm not sure I follow, Mrs. Slocum."

"You were our waitress when I last turned the bookseller's peg clockwise!"

"Was I?" Fiona looked up to the starry sky, winked, and left the office.

Annette sat back in Lucas' chair, hoping that the inspiration wouldn't take long. She would wrap him in her arms and apologize profusely and he would hold her, literally hold her, and say it will "all be okay." But after twenty minutes,

Lucas didn't return. With food in her belly and the reverberating resonance of the ghostly violin music that once again shook the ceiling, Annette closed her eyes and dreamed a long-forgotten memory.

*

One November afternoon, when she was still alive, snow began to fall and Annette sat in the Beetle with three new library books resting beside her in the passenger seat. A crossroads lay before her: Annette could have either taken the highway and explored or driven back to the house. She sat parked beside a curb for hours watching the snow blind the landscape beyond her window. Eventually, as the bulbs in the street lamps hummed to life, Annette returned home to her husband. As she kicked the snow off of her boots, Annette was lost in her own despair more than ever.

It was only when Annette discovered a parcel meticulously wrapped in wedding paper on her doorstep that her spirits lifted. As she and Lyle had already opened all of the wedding gifts, Annette wondered what it could be or, more importantly, from *whom* it could be. A tiny white envelope had been taped to the bottom. She opened the flap with her right thumb.

> **Annette,**
> **Sorry I couldn't get this to you any sooner. Hope this gives you peace in the present situation.**

Whomever had written the message had beautiful penmanship. It also looked as if the person had written a name but scribbled over it after giving it a second thought. She promptly opened the package and revealed an object that had nearly taken her breath away. In the palm of her hand she held the novel *Les Miserables* that had previously been burned at the end of her driveway and it had been miraculously repaired! Annette checked the note again a total of three times for some

145

clue as to who had restored the novel but she remained no closer to discovering her admirer.

She was certain she'd seen the handwriting before.

CHAPTER 14: LUCAS RICHARDSON'S RETIREMENT PARTY

"Annette?" Lucas' voice called but it was too far away for her to grasp on to. Annette was caught up in a dream: her father and mother were alive and dancing at their wedding reception. Annette stood in the dream where the ghosts of her parents were linked together: her father's arms around the waist of her mother in the wedding dress, and her mother's arms around the collar of his tuxedo. The yellow dress that Annette had picked from the old man's closet glittered like gold underneath the lights. If only Annette's feet had cooperated, she would have walked up to them, touched them, and whispered how much she missed them. But she remained immobile. When Lucas shook her a second time, the images broke away like a glass window ripped apart by a misguided baseball. "Good dream?"

"I don't remember." Once she awakened Annette truly didn't remember her dreams. Lucas grinned which coaxed a smile from her as well. She asked him "How was it, the violet envelope?"

"It was . . ." Lucas tried to search for the right words but only came up with "a nightmare as all violet envelopes tend to be."

Shifting in Lucas' swivel chair, Annette noticed that the office in which she'd fallen asleep no longer looked like a balcony. The wooden walls of the balcony had been extinguished and replaced by something far more miraculous: a fresh morning sky. She wondered, for a moment, whether perhaps she'd once again escaped into one of her colored pegs

147

but the old office still existed, or at least the shell of it remained. The floor on which Annette had walked back and forth on countless times before remained, and door frames still led into offices. The walls and ceiling were, at the very least, transparent.

In the daylight, Annette could see a great forest in which cherry blossoms fluttered in a breeze. The shifting pink petals, crisp as an image on a high-definition television, made a quiet soothing sound.

"Oh, Lucas . . ."

Lucas whispered in her ear: "Think this is cool? Cherry blossoms are only the beginning to the retirement parties. You'll see."

A breeze then coaxed a cloud of the cherry blossoms from the branches as if the surroundings were a shaken snow globe. Dancing from the branches to Annette's cheek, several petals kissed her and then elegantly mutated into spectacularly-hued butterflies.

As Lucas promised, there was more to this display than cherry blossoms and butterflies.

Upon further inspection of this phenomenon of a retirement party, Annette found beyond the hallways, where the offices should have been, an elongated terrace made of chiseled moss-riddled stone. As she looked over the edge of the veranda cherry blossoms, butterflies, and morning sky were reflected on the great placid sea. Below the water, Annette found gliding shapes as small as minnows growing in size to humpback whales.

"Come on, there's more." Lucas tugged the sleeve of Annette's yellow dress and led her back down the hallway to Fiona's office, where another transformation unfolded. While the terrace was evident in every other office, Fiona's office was a vast field with a fresh new carpet of grass, wild flowers, and great mountains stretched in the distance. Dancing in a field, illuminated by the morning light (four suns actually, now that Annette counted, brightening the sky with maddened intensity), were nine naked women with laurel leaves on their heads. They danced, carefree, to music only they seemed to hear.

"Are those . . . ?"

148

"The original nine muses, yes. They make an appearance at every retirement."

"What do you think, Mrs. Slocum?" Fiona stood with the two of them now, watching the first nine muses' movements. "They look happy, don't you think?" Fiona turned to Lucas. "Can you come with me, Mr. Richardson? Mrs. Slocum, will you be joining us?"

A surf board, brilliantly polished gold with blue trim, erupted from the ground in the hallway. Lucas shouted in glee as, outside the terrace, the water's surface curled in a monstrous wave. Surfing was one of Lucas' oldest desires and Fiona had managed to make it possible. *"Retirement parties truly are worth the troubles of inspiring the world,"* Annette thought to herself as Lucas found a wet-suit and put it on.

"Isn't it interesting," Fiona asked Annette as Lucas rode a wave in the distance, "how some individuals never find themselves playing out their greatest dreams when they're alive? Why do you think so many clients are blocked, Mrs. Slocum?" Annette shrugged her shoulders as a great tidal wave caused Lucas to shout in excitement. Fiona lifted the old man's green peg. "I like the public speaker you've chosen, Mrs. Slocum. I've pilfered through the filing cabinet myself yet I must have missed this one."

"Yes, well . . ."

"Buried deep in the bottom?"

"So what do you do with the peg?" Annette blurted, changing the conversation.

"Well, you'll put it into a Lite-Brite board, Mrs. Slocum, and retrieve him. When he crosses the 'bridge' to our offices, he'll plainly think he's having an elaborate dream. Then, after he says what he feels is important, you'll take him back home. When he wakes, he'll hardly remember anything at all. You'll never have to see him again. Unless . . ."

"Unless what?"

Plucked strings from Paganini's ghostly violin once again graced the celebration. Fiona pocketed the green peg without responding and disappeared down the hallway. The retirement party was indeed a collection of Lucas' greatest desires accompanied by the most spectacular sights chosen by

Fiona and supplied by Management: everything from the hanging gardens of Babylon in full bloom, to the very shelves that had once housed classic literature, and ancient scrolls from libraries that were erected and eroded centuries ago.

As morning crept into afternoon, eagles soared from the mountain tops that stretched across the horizon in all directions. Lucas glided with them as if he'd been flying with actual wings for years. As the four stars brought the sky to full glory of the afternoon, a single red balloon heralded a fair with the largest Ferris wheel Annette had ever seen, cotton candy, popcorn in cardboard red and white striped boxes, and even a man who told fortunes. As Lucas and Annette sat at the table looking down at the cards, Annette rolled her eyes at each prophecy. Since having his fortune told made Lucas happy, Annette tried to slap on an enthusiastic smile. Lucas laughed at the attempt but told Annette he'd rather she be herself than to accommodate him on his last day.

Two sets of muses, the old and the new, all celebrated the occasion and rode the great Ferris wheel a second, third, and fourth time. While she and Lucas were reaching the very top of the wheel, Annette's breath was nearly taken away as Saturn finally entered orbit. The planet's spherical shape was translucent at first like the barely visible crescent of the moon in the early summer evenings. Annette had never seen an object so large in the sky and couldn't help but stare in wonder at its face as the Ferris wheel carriage slowly descended for another round.

Saturn's façade grew even more splendid as the evening sketched its splendor. Mysteriously, a few more inches were added to the conference room table and nine more chairs gathered around it for the eighteen muses. They all sat together and watched a slideshow of Lucas' most memorable inspirations. Annette was disappointed when Harriet's inspiration, mentioned by her friend before, was not included in the presentation. Management supplied buttered popcorn and other sugary concessions but there wasn't much eating as the muses viewed the inspirations in awe. It was interesting to Annette how a single second in a person's life could dramatically alter the years that followed it. All of the insignificant moments were made to look all the more significant.

"Where's Nathaniel J. Cauliflower?" Annette leaned in to ask Lucas. "I thought he'd at least make an appearance."

"He set everything up while you were sleeping. Must have missed him." Lucas then excused himself and stood on the terrace with a man Annette recognized from his colored peg as Gabriel. Brilliant planetary bodies, star clusters, and nebulae filled the heavens as the two men then found lawn chairs and unfolded them for the performance.

A meteor shower, drawn across the evening horizon by an invisible carriage, acted as a heavenly disco ball swirling with Paganini's haunting violin music. Annette had never seen two gay men holding one another and, truthfully, it made her a bit jealous that Lucas was sitting beside his partner instead of beside her. But as this retirement party was all about *his* fantasies, she stayed quiet.

The hallway was dimly lit by ornate candelabras that burned timidly in the evening starlight. As Annette found her own private space on the terrace, she was happy to see that not only the planet Saturn had fully emerged, but Venus, Neptune, and Jupiter had also graced the skies. A cool evening breeze was pulled from the sea below her and, considering that the yellow dress she'd been given earlier had thin sleeves, Annette wrapped her arms around herself wishing she'd found a sweater vest in the closet instead.

"Here, put this on." A man's heavy winter trench coat was wrapped around her shoulders warming her instantly. Annette figured it was Lucas or perhaps even the man she'd deemed the public speaker. Instead, it was the bookseller Adam Mansfield. "Something wrong?" he asked.

"What are you doing here?"

"What do you mean?"

"You're here."

"Yes." Adam gave a sly smile.

"I didn't rotate your peg or pull you from whatever it is you were doing. But you're still here."

"Actually, if you really want to get technical about it, I'm asleep in my bed having a rather nice dream." Adam cast his eyes skyward and the reflection of Uranus was clearly evident in his pupils. ". . . About planets in the solar system." He then looked at Annette and smiled. "I'm really glad you're here to share this with me."

Annette's head was swimming. How was this happening? Worm holes in space? A rip in the fabric of time? Was destiny cracking open windows that normally remained padlocked? One thing was for certain, Annette didn't waste any time.

"You have to go."

"It's just a dream."

"No, it's *not* just a dream. Right now, you *think* it's a dream but, for me, this is reality. It's something much more than a . . . look, you have to go. If anyone found you here Harriet would most likely rip me limb from limb, reconstruct me, and rip me apart again."

"Just like Alaodae,"

"Who?"

"From Greek mythology. He was tied to a pillar in the Underworld by snakes and every day a screeching owl would come and torment him. Then there was this other guy who had his spleen ripped out continuously and it would grow back. Or was it the same guy?"

"Whatever. You can't be here. Please . . ."

"Annette." Adam held her closer now.

"Adam." Annette, impatient, tried to break away.

"I want to see you again."

"It's not right, Adam."

"What's not right?"

"Complicated. That's what it is, complicated. You and I are from two different worlds."

"Looks to me like we're from the same," Adam touched his nose against the tip of hers.

"We're in two different places . . ."

"No, we're not." Indeed, they weren't in two places as Adam brought his arms inside the coat warming her further. "Dinner the other night was great but I want to see more of you."

152

"I can't . . ." This was starting to feel like one of those kinds of romance books that Annette would've put back onto the shelf in search of something more tasteful to read. Adam was presumptuous to think that she would want to spend time with him. He seized her and placed his lips on hers, despite her mental objections. It was the finest kiss that Annette had ever experienced. They kissed for hours, or so it seemed, and as the meteor shower dramatically roared above and Saturn overlooked their tryst, Annette didn't care that her life had suddenly become a romance novel.

"Now, I'll exit stage left," Adam told her, holding up a hand to stop Annette as he removed himself from the trench coat. "Give it to me later. What say we have dinner again? My place? The next time you visit?"

"Okay," Annette found herself saying. Adam stepped into the shadows leaving Annette to her own thoughts and the cologne that clung to the coat's fabric. Her heart was racing as if a bit of her frozen soul had been placed on defrost in a microwave. But her elation was soon extinguished as Harriet appeared from the shadows.

"Well, aren't you full of surprises, Annette." She said nothing in response to Harriet's words, sheepishly buttoning the trench-coat around the yellow dress. "It's time to retrieve your public speaker. I'll show you to the Lite-Brite board."

Where the waiting room once had been stood a great archway and beyond was a grand staircase. Handing Annette a Styrofoam cup of water, Harriet removed a candle from the wall and held it aloft as they ascended into the darkness. Annette wasn't sure how many more steps the staircase had. After the hundredth and fiftieth stair she stopped counting. The stars that dappled the heavens twinkled like the countenance of a polished diamond. As they ascended further, the rings of Saturn separated themselves into specks of ice and dust revealing the muscles and tendons of the rings' motion.

The Lite-Brite board stood as a beacon, hoisted high into the cosmos. There were no colored pegs present on the board. Instead, Annette found the green peg in Harriet's palm.

"Like before, I take a sip of water?" Annette said aloud.

"Like before, you take a sip of water."

153

Annette took a sip of water and, also as before, a thunderclap brought Annette back to the same porch from which she had recently watched the sunrise. The old man sat there in his rocking chair holding a cup of coffee. In bewilderment, he took a sip. "I suppose . . . you've come to bring me to your offices?" He took hold of Annette's hand. Per instructions from his host, he retrieved one glass of water for Annette, and one for himself. After taking a few sips, they were fully prepared as the thunderclap announced their departure from the porch and entrance among the party.

From the platform Annette led her public speaker back down the grand staircase past Saturn's rings and, once again found the hallway, or what she deduced had previously been the hallway, before the transformations. With the air of a tour guide, Fiona stood poised in her cream-colored suit. "Well, Mrs. Slocum, I see you've managed to bring our public speaker in one piece."

"Fiona, this is . . ." Annette quickly realized that she had no earthly idea what the man's name was.

"Patrick. A true pleasure to finally meet the famous Fiona. Annette here has told me so much about you."

"Has she?" Fiona's eyes turned to Annette who in turn focused her eyes on Fiona's cream-colored shoes. "Well, we're very proud to have her with us in the department. She's truly one of my *best* muses." Annette looked up at Fiona, honored. "Would you follow me please, Patrick?" Fiona took Patrick's arm, for his attention had been drawn to the ever-incredible meteor shower. The conference room had been replaced by an auditorium decked in potted flowers, beautifully arranged. "I hope you didn't go to *too* much trouble, Patrick."

"Not at all, Fiona," Patrick assured her. "It's nothing award-winning but hopefully it'll be the speech you're looking for."

Dramatic lighting accented the stage. One of the original muses strummed a harp while Annette took a seat with the other seventeen. Patrick took to the stage and removed a pair of wire-rimmed spectacles before pulling out his speech notes.

"Well," Patrick consulted his notes. "I wish to thank Annette and Fiona and umm . . . Management, for this

154

opportunity." Patrick's eyes squinted as he looked into a spotlight as if in that light he was directly addressing the hierarchy. "Let's get down to it then, shall we?" Patrick took another look at his notes and turned his attention to his audience.

"I've never been one for giving speeches. In high school I had to give a speech in front of my entire class," Patrick lifted the palms of his hands several inches facing them out to the audience. "And felt those little pinpricks in my fingertips. My palms got sweaty and the classroom began to restrict upon itself." He brought his right hand to the frame of his glasses shifting the lenses while consulting his notes. "Now, here I am, nearly fifty years later, with the second speech of my lifetime, and my fingers, surprisingly, feel normal.

"Things have a way of evolving, I've learned over the years. For one, fifty years ago I rode a bicycle to school; now I travel by airplane. Fifty years ago I had considerably less arthritis and fewer liver-spots and wrinkles; now I'm falling apart. Fifty years ago it seemed that the future was limitless; now time is precious, like grasping at a fistful of sand and seeing it slip through my fingers. Fifty years ago everything was new; now it's all the same as it has been before.

"What haven't changed, Muses, are the teachers that one encounters throughout life. When Annette appeared . . ." Patrick seemed to hesitate now, taking a short breath, smiling at Annette ". . . in the seat next to me on the airplane, then later on my porch, I was immediately drawn to the memories between fifty years ago and today. When she asked me to write a speech for Lucas Richardson's retirement party, I made a few notes of the three types of great teachers that have influenced my life.

"There are three kinds of teachers: those who influence you in school, those who affect circumstances out of the school, and the teacher we find within ourselves. The ones you encounter within the bricks and mortars of education could be the literature teacher who reads novels aloud to captive students, the math teacher who makes extra time to tutor, a gym teacher who perhaps encourages an individual to climb higher on a rope, a history teacher who uses slides from personal expeditions or documentaries to further explain the miracles of the world, or a science teacher who creates analogies to aid in a better understanding of the elements.

"The teachers whom we discover outside of school come in the form of parents, grandparents, aunts, uncles, other family members, friends, coworkers and the media. As we grow older, the naïveté of childhood takes on a whole new aspect: one of family picnics where we learn the responsibility of cleaning our plates, reunions where the lessons of genealogy play a role, Sunday mornings when we learn the complexities of religions, museums where we understand the physical truths of history and where the world of adulthood responsibilities take precedence over following personal dreams. And it's in this adult world where the grim reality of today's society challenges us, where you, Muses, become the educators."

Patrick flipped to another page of his notes.

"But who teaches the teachers who inspire the world? How does one go from being uninspired to inspired, anyhow? A muse is given a Lite-Brite board and sent to a specific person, place and time. Muses take it on blind faith that inspirations have occurred, so clients have it within themselves to create change. The greatest teacher is the one you find within yourself. The first two teachers seemingly hold the most influence; they are the ones we remember and who affect us the most. The greatest teachers follow their own beliefs and form their own personal opinions regardless of what has been engrained. The greatest teachers remember the past, yes, but are able to disentangle themselves from those memories and make new memories. How many of you, Muses, can say that the memories of previous lives have no effect on your decisions: moments in history you'd redo, a bully who ripped out a few pages of a library book, a wounded soul keeping you from experiencing the moments that will truly define you?"

Patrick pocketed his notes and his eyes scanned the audience. "You've done great work, Muses. The world and those who know your occupation are most certainly grateful. But, think of the greater impact you would have on the world if you weren't affected by all that has come before. There are no mistakes, only new experiences: both good and bad. And when

156

those violet envelopes in life surface - believe me when I say there will *always* be violet envelopes . . ."

Annette shivered at the prospect of a violet envelope landing in her post box.

"Rejoice; don't cower. Stand tall and say, 'I may take a wrong step somewhere along the road, but at least I took that step. At least I had the guts and, most of all, *desire* to face the world outside of my comfort zone.' A muse or not, Lite-Brite or no, you can and will inspire anyone. Also, don't forget to always continue to strive to inspire yourself. The third type of teacher is a rare form, Muses, and to inspire someone to become that kind of teacher . . . you must *allow yourself* to become one first. Discard the memories that plague you, make new memories, seek new adventures." Patrick took a deep breath, lifted his palms once more, inspecting them with a smile. "Still here, Muses. No pinpricks in sight. Thank you for this opportunity."

Applause followed. "That was lovely," Fiona told Patrick, but Patrick was far from convinced until he heard it directly from Annette herself.

"Well, Dear?"

"It was wonderful, Patrick."

"Boring, wasn't it? Did it have any impact?"

"Patrick," Annette touched his face, tracing the crows feet beside his aged eyes with her finger. "I couldn't have picked a better person to give a speech at Lucas' retirement party."

"Really?"

"Well, you had a bit of competition with Socrates," she said with a laugh, then added "thank you for agreeing to this."

Annette made sure she carried enough water for Patrick as they once again ascended the grand staircase, past the heavens, and through Saturn's rings that continued orbiting the office's ceiling. They stood before the Lite-Brite board, green peg in Annette's hand, and watched as the meteor shower dwindled below the horizon.

"Ms. Annette . . . I just wanted to say thank you."

"It was Management that sent your peg."

"It was Management that brought us together, that's true, but as I recall, Management didn't ask you to repay me a visit."

"I'm sorry."

"Don't be sorry, Annette. You've shown me Saturn, you've shown me even greater sunrises, and a meteor shower! Out of all the colored pegs in the filing cabinet, you picked mine. And for all these things and more, I say, 'Thank you for being such an inspiration to me.'" Patrick hugged her at this point and drank his water from the office water cooler. "One more thing. You may not remember me, but I've never forgotten you. Ten years ago I asked if you had the time and your husband Lyle talked incessantly about his used car lot." A look of recognition spread across Annette's face then. Patrick released another genuine smile. "How I wished Lyle had stayed quiet so that you and I could've talked. You may not have said anything, but sometimes, Dear, silence speaks novels. So thank you for giving me another opportunity to spend time with you." They embraced tightly now. "Enough of this emotional stuff, Dear. You have a best friend who's retiring, a life worth living, and a great purpose to fulfill."

In a thunderclap Patrick was gone; all that was left of him was a little green peg that Annette carried with her down the grand staircase and fit back into her own Lite-Brite board in her office.

Annette followed the light of a single candle down the hallway where a small group stood before the now-exposed door to the waiting room. The candle was poised on a small one layer cake that had been wheeled in front of Lucas with a candle and wick. The candle flame flickered playfully on the wick's tip.

"All right Mr. Richardson, you know what to do," Fiona instructed as all the other muses (excluding Annette, as she had no idea what Fiona was referring to) held their breath. The tiny flame reflected onto Lucas' pupils as, for a moment, he silently collected his thoughts. Then he inhaled, pursed his lips, and blew out the candle with his breath.

"A very good choice." Fiona smiled that same radiant smile that Annette had first noticed long ago from nearby her and Lyle's mailbox. From under the door a bright light shone and Fiona twisted the knob. The waiting room, which Annette hadn't seen since her first day, still contained the same nine chairs, water cooler, and typical wall clock. The only difference was that the other door was now standing wide open, revealing the light of a million star clusters. Lucas started moving toward the light but Annette stopped him.

"Lucas!" He turned around and Annette ran to him. Her eyes were glistening with tears. They held one another and she whispered in his ear. "Don't go."

"There's a goodbye present in your desk drawer," Lucas whispered in her ear. "I wish I could stay . . . but it's time."

"I'm sorry I couldn't be there on your last violet envelope; I wanted to. I really did."

"You were there, Annette. Just as *I'll* be with *you* even after I walk through this door."

"You can't leave me alone here," Annette pleaded.

"We'll see one another again someday, I'm sure of it. In another life, perhaps." Lucas kissed the top of her forehead now and Annette took that as her cue to step away. "I love you, Annette Slocum." As the other seventeen muses watched, Lucas raised a hand and waved goodbye. He then stepped into the light and disappeared. The door closed quietly behind him.

*

There was an envelope waiting in Annette's post box. The white walls and ceiling had returned which meant that the elaborate decorations had, like Lucas, departed gracefully. She cracked open the envelope from her inbox and out popped yet another green peg. After a sip of water and a thunderclap, the office folded and unfolded like an elaborate pop-up book. The smell of formaldehyde, painfully evident, was accompanied by a mortician who stared down at a body on a slab. The music of Phillip Glass lilted from a CD player as he worked. This woman's limbs had obviously been snapped and repositioned back together. The corpse's face, though . . . *her* face . . . Annette immediately recognized it as her own.

"How did you get in here?" asked the mortician as Annette brought herself forward for closer inspection. Annette didn't say anything in reply. She just looked down at her corpse in sorrow. Annette stared at the shell of her former self. On the slab was a woman who had spent her life as a silent and devoted housewife to a husband who didn't even acknowledge her, a woman who spent the first thirty years trapped in the pages and spines of someone else's story. "There's really not much I can do with her," said the mortician, until he looked up and caught Annette's eyes. "Perhaps . . ." The mortician took to his work and within minutes transformed the face of Annette's corpse into the face that Annette currently wore. It had been days, possibly even years, since she had actually looked at her reflection but apparently her current image was filled with more life than she gave credit. On the slab now was the face Annette had always wanted.

"What do you think?"

Annette stared even harder at the cold shell of the person. She still said nothing. What could she say to the mortician who had been inspired? Annette simply brought her fingers to her lips in thought. Suddenly, the scalpels and make-up vibrated with rolling thunder. Annette was returned to her swivel chair and sat in bewilderment. Inside the drawer of her desk was a rolled-up violet envelope which, once flattened, revealed Lucas' gift: his colored peg.

Without Lucas there to keep her entertained, Annette once again found herself in front of the oak cabinet with the ten-lettered lock combination. She thought of Lucas as she fiddled with the letters. Eventually she discovered another word completely unrelated to Nathaniel J. Cauliflower or Evangeline.

DANDELION

But the word was only nine letters long, not ten. Annette sighed and gave the final disc several more casual spins to pass the time. She then descended the stairs, took a drink of water from the water cooler, and reached out yet again to the bookseller's peg. The old Annette Slocum would have rebelled against this but the new Annette suddenly felt a desire to trade in her old memories for new ones. She wasn't exactly sure how she was going to accomplish this grand of a change but Annette figured that another dinner with Adam the bookseller was the perfect first step toward that goal.

As Annette disappeared in a thunderclap, the final disc slowed its spin and stopped on a single letter, "S." If anyone had been in Annette's private library, they would have seen the complete word settle into place:

D A N D E L I O N S

If anyone had been in the office at that moment, they would have heard the subtle whirring of a triggering mechanism from inside the cabinet. They would have seen the cabinet door open wide revealing the secrets it contained

CHAPTER 15: THE GREAT NICCOLÒ PAGANINI

As another three retirement parties came and went, Mr. Hawkins, Mr. Hill and Mrs. Simonton were delivered through the door in the waiting room after blowing the candles out on their respective cakes. Just as before, the department switched from miraculous displays of cherry blossoms and meteor showers back into its white walls, earth-friendly light-bulbs, and gurgling water coolers. Each unique office of the retiring muses had been switched into different locations for their immediate replacements. The muse replacements were also Ninth Generation muses, same as Annette. They were no one special. They were simply "average Joes" picked to inspire the world.

Lucas' replacement, oddly enough, had not yet been chosen. Even after three retirement parties, Lucas' office still remained quiet and void. The balcony had been replaced by four plain egg-shell white walls. It was a box. Nothing more. As Annette looked in on the now vacant space, it seemed as if the very soul of the place had been surgically removed. In fact, everything in the office that had held any semblance of his existence had been removed. The Lite-Brite board had even been gutted of the colored pegs.

Though she had sworn to herself that she'd strive for future experiences, Annette still found herself bound to a swivel chair wrapped in the warm trench-coat Adam the Bookseller had given her at Lucas' retirement party. She rotating Lucas' colored peg the way some would listen to scratchy records of yesteryear. Though Lucas was no longer in the office, he'd still given Annette the gift of visiting his story whenever she wanted.

The trouble was, despite Patrick's speech at Lucas' retirement party, Annette had once again immersed herself in memories.

"Mrs. Slocum," Fiona asked her while watching the facts of Lucas' history replay itself for the seventh time "as unpleasant as Mr. Richardson's retirement may feel to you, don't you think it would be more prudent to spend time with the language books?"

Annette had already spent time studying the language books she'd brought back with her from *The Muse's Corner*. To deter the depression caused by Lucas' departure, Annette had practiced rigorous speech exercises. By now she had mastered Latin and Greek; brushed up on her Spanish; could speak French fluently, as well as Chinese, Japanese, Tagalog, Arabic, and Italian; and was currently trying to maneuver her fingers in sign language. Unfortunately, her focus on languages didn't destroy the depression; it was always there, lurking in the recesses of her mind, waiting for the right moment to pour even more salt onto a festering wound.

"I know it certainly doesn't help matters to have an empty office reminding you of your loss." Fiona told Annette. "Management has simply been waiting for the right individual to come along," Fiona patiently explained, grasping the back of Annette's swivel chair and pulling the muse in the yellow dress out of Lucas Richardson's colored peg and into the office. "You've sequestered yourself, Mrs. Slocum, and it's necessary to branch out."

Branch out? Annette had to laugh at the irony of Fiona's comment. The three hundred and thirty-five white envelopes and various colored pegs since Lucas' retirement had sent Annette to places that utilized her newfound knowledge in the various languages. As a result, Annette had seen more of the entire world than most had ever seen in their lifetimes.

"Say something, Mrs. Slocum."

But Annette didn't feel like saying anything. There were still many pegs to go and the space between each inspiration was excruciating. She missed Lucas with the same intensity that she missed her deceased father. She longed for her best friend the same way that she had longed for library books after Lyle had left for work. "In a few moments, Mr. Richardson's

163

replacement will be arriving in the waiting room. I'd like it if you were there beside me." Annette scoffed. "Perhaps if you shook hands with the new muse, you'd see that retirement is a process. Retirements have happened at least eighty times before, with other generations, and will continue…"

Annette zoned out Fiona now.

When she wasn't working on various languages, inspiring strangers in foreign countries, or trying to dodge Harriet in the hallway while in search of Nathaniel J. Cauliflower's mozzarella bow-tie pasta spotted with Gruyère cheese in the conference room, she would sit and stare at the life of Lucas Richardson and remember him with tenderness. Both Lucas' green peg and Adam's trench-coat were her escape; they were her way of dealing with things. What was wrong with that, Annette wanted to know? It was as if no one mourned Lucas' departure. It was as if she was the only one who cared where he went after passing through the waiting room door.

Not even Fiona's current encouragement could pry her from the swivel chair. Nor Harriet's protests about turning pegs. The brilliant compositions of Paganini, whoever he was, occasionally agitated her. Violin strings were plucked maniacally above the ceiling, rather angrily it seemed, as if the fiddler was giving the instrument a series of shiners. Annette had hoped that a colored peg would send her to a library with a computer where she would sit and research Paganini on search engines but, alas, she was only sent to random places such as to Alcatraz, Stonehenge, even to the Great Pyramids at Giza, which held little knowledge of the violinist.

"Oh for Management's sake, sit there, Mrs. Slocum, and wallow in a private pity party." Fiona exited Annette's office now, calling over her shoulder. "Someday you'll understand it's all a process! If you don't move yourself from your misery, Management will find a way to get the gears set back into motion!"

A helpful tool to dislodge her unhappiness was a certain blue colored peg. Adam the Bookseller's extensive knowledge of rare facts and his ruggedly bookish appearance often caused Annette to turn his peg clockwise. She'd promised Lucas, before he had retired, that she would find a replacement friend.

Figuring that Harriet certainly wasn't material to fit that role, Annette believed Adam seemed the perfect candidate. Every time she managed by *The Muse's Corner*, Annette made sure to run her fingers along as many books as possible in hopes of collecting as many literary trophies from the bookseller's kingdom as possible.

"Paganini, eh?" Adam consulted the various CDs in his collection on her next visit. His fingers played an imaginary piano in mid-air as he scanned the various titles. His one bedroom, one bathroom flat was modest, yet it suited him perfectly. He was a man with bookshelves stuffed with various volumes of history and stacks of CDs consisting of various composers from around the world: all of which were encapsulated in the museum of his living room.

The first time Annette had seen his apartment was right after Lucas' retirement party; Adam had made her dinner. They had continued the discussion about her love of literature, Adam had told her about his love for history and how they had both always adored picking up library books, sniffing the pages, and flipping the paper to intensify the smell. They had not discussed who she was or how she had come to exist in his world. Annette carried with her certain anonymity, which she preferred. Now here she was again sitting on the couch down deep into the cushions.

"I know I have him in my collection somewhere," said Adam, finding the CD at last. The speakers fastened to the ceiling in the living room erupted seconds later with the familiar sound of bow across string.

"Niccolò Paganini." He handed her the case that housed the CD. On the cover was a well-painted interpretation of his likeness. "One of the world's greatest violinists: said to have sold his soul to the devil."

"Sounds about right by the looks of him," Annette commented. The picture was of a tall individual, rather skinny, with gaunt features, wild hair, sunken cheeks and thin, elongated fingers that, in mid-performance, looked as if they were charming the strings of a violin the way a snake-charmer tamed serpents. "Sold his soul to the devil, you say?"

"Born and raised in Italy where he mastered not only the violin but also the mandolin at a very young age. Under the tutelage of various teachers, he surpassed them all. A real prodigy that one - they don't make geniuses like they used to."

"Fascinating," Annette said, hoping that Adam had the key to making the music in the muse offices stop.

"Still, Paganini wanted to be the best violinist in the world. He would practice the instrument obsessively for hours each day."

"What made him one of the world's greatest violinists?"

"Ah." Adam replaced the current CD with another. "Paganini's talents were bizarre."

"Bizarre?"

"Extremely."

"How so?"

"Paganini and the violin: an infamous pair. Instead of sliding a bow across the strings, he would *bounce* it across. He'd even mistune the violin to avoid switching hand positions frequently. That itself was irregular. Paganini would often employ a pizzicato technique where he would also *pluck*," Adam pantomimed playing a violin, giving her an example, "the strings, staccato-like. He had long thin fingers, you see, which enabled him to play the violin like no one had ever played it before."

"Because he sold his soul to the devil?"

"Well, that's the romantic explanation. But there was a rumor that he had a disease which enabled extreme flexibility in his joints. Ever heard of Ehlers Danlos or Marfan Syndrome?" Annette shook her head. "At any rate, riches and fame didn't really suit him all that well. He was a lush. Had problems with gambling. And one night . . ." Adam sat on the arm rest next to Annette as if sharing a dark secret, "some say a mysterious woman took him in."

"A mysterious woman?"

"An unexplained lady of title in Tuscany. For three years he disappeared from the public eye; and, in those three years, he took up the guitar . . . and supposedly sold his soul to the devil. He emerged with great techniques that literally changed the way that humanity saw the capabilities of a violin."

"A mysterious woman in Tuscany?"

"Rumors and speculations. Everyone has a story."

"Everyone has a story," Annette repeated him. Adam's interest in the history lesson was shifted to the way her eyes glazed over.

"Why the interest in the violinist, anyway?"

How could Annette tell him *why* she was so interested in the music of Niccolò Paganini without telling him that she was currently a muse? The more she kept from him about her previous life, the more she stayed quiet about being dead and inspiring the world one colored peg at a time, the more the budding relationship would remain far less complicated. How would he react if she told him about the accident in front of the library? That she was, in fact, dead? Her previous client and Lucas' public speaker, Patrick, had reacted well . . . but she cared more for Adam. She didn't want to risk losing him and feeling even more alone.

"There you go again: lost in thought."

"Seems to happen a lot, I'm afraid." She stood from the couch cushions, brushed the wrinkles from her yellow dress, and thanked Adam for his hospitality. "I have to go."

"Always running away." Adam gave a sly smile. "One of these days, Annette, you'll feel comfortable enough to stick around."

"I'm needed at the office." Annette said.

Adam shook his head, releasing a half grin. "Of course. You know where to find me."

Annette opened the front door of his apartment and fled for the breezeway. As fate would have it, another apartment door opened five doors down. Out stepped a well-dressed man in his mid-thirties wearing a black suit and tie. She had seen this individual before in the restaurant during hers and Adam's first official date. Annette nodded as she passed by him and the stranger nodded back. As she turned the corner, Annette looked back to find that the man was still watching her. Crow's feet were beginning to form beside his eyes and his hair had turned to gray. He had a fair hint of familiarity which, to Annette, was never a good sign.

How unusual, she thought to herself as she disappeared from his line of sight.

Once she was alone, Annette returned to the office where she heard the familiar instructional video from the conference room: an omen that stated Lucas' replacement had finally arrived.

"Well, there you have it," Fiona's voice said from the conference room as the video ended. The lights in the room coming up. "Shall we check out your new office, Mr. Hollinsworth?" Mr. Hollinsworth – Annette was once again overwhelmed with sadness. "The office is a green one, Mr. Hollinsworth. The light bulbs used in the ceiling help reduce and conserve energy. Even the envelopes that Management sends us are biodegradable, though Mr. Cauliflower prefers we simply recycle them. It was his idea to modernize - an 'earth-friendly operation' he called it."

Seconds later, Fiona found the replacement's office which used to be Lucas'.

"There is one thing the instructional video didn't show. Most envelopes are white, but occasionally one will arrive in your post box that's violet. Violet stands for 'very important.' No one is too great or too small, it's true, but the violet ones are the toughest of cases. They are the ones that will literally push you to your limits and beyond. If you see one of them, open it immediately, take time to assess the situation, and execute. If you fail, consequences could be disastrous."

Annette listened through the following silence, barely detecting the sound of a thumb teasing open the lip of an envelope: the replacement's first inspiration. As Lucas' former office folded and unfolded, Annette poked her head into Mr. Hollinsworth's workplace.

While she had been away visiting Adam, the drab walls had been replaced by a lawn of fresh grass that glistened with dew. On this lawn was an oak tree with a tire swing fastened to its strongest branch. There was also a porch that had been newly painted white with dark green shutters. A porch swing, two rocking chairs and a hand-woven hammock were present on the deck: each as inviting as the other. Mr. Hollinsworth's desk, water-cooler and Lite-Brite were also on the porch, overlooking the morning. An aria was carried in the manufactured morning breeze. Birds chirped from the nearby trees in these eternal moments before sunrise.

Though the transformation was beautiful, Annette couldn't help but to pout. She didn't want this interior. She wanted Lucas' balcony with his starlit sky. She wanted to see Lucas' Lite-Brite. Not Mr. Hollinsworth's productivity. It wasn't the same . . . nor would it ever be again.

Annette sauntered to Fiona's office. She had been told that Fiona usually took on the responsibility of emptying offices after retirements. Annette wondered if Fiona had a hidden vault to store the last remaining scraps of Lucas' belongings. As she approached Fiona's office, however, she was caught off-guard by Harriet who was at that moment leaving. There were no vaults nor were there any remaining treasures. All evidence that Lucas had been an occupant of the department had been eradicated. Annette was all the more displeased to find another envelope in her post box yet she still took it with waning mild enthusiasm. Inside was a green-colored peg.

After a sip of water, Annette was deposited into a bar. The time period was definitely not present day and the city, she deduced, was somewhere in Venice, Italy, as she could see gondolas bearing their passengers through the windows.

A tall and gangly man with long, unkempt hair sat on a stool with a violin propped against his legs. This man was so skinny it seemed as if there were hardly any muscles between his skin and bones. Behind his eyes, Annette could only detect pure darkness.

"Niccolò, go home," the bartender said in Italian, attempting to take the glass from the drunkard who, in turn, was not about to give in so easily. "Niccolò, enough."

"*Not* enough!" Niccolò moved from the bar in protest but, as his feet gave out from underneath him, it was clearly evident that he, indeed, had consumed one drink too many. Mortified that the grim truth could not be concealed, the musician ripped the violin out from under the bar and attempted a departure. Niccolò stumbled past the bar stools and, on his exit, someone gleefully announced in Italian, "Ladies and

Gentlemen, the Great Paganini!" An uproar of laughter followed.

Annette's heart-strings pulled her out the door to see Niccolò Paganini collapse in the street. "What Would Fiona Do" had become Annette's mantra in that moment; Fiona would have probably set beside Niccolò and taken his arm to aid in him getting back to his feet, as any great encourager would do. However, when Annette tried to do this, Paganini was far less receptive than she first imagined. "Leave me be!" he cried in Italian. His stale and alcoholic breath assaulted her senses. His face grew ashen as he turned away from her curious and concerned gaze.

*

When her oldest brother Franklin had his first child (a beautiful baby girl) Annette didn't lovingly take the baby into her arms; instead, she sat there staring at it as if the baby were about to explode. There was drool, and Annette hated drool. The fact that the baby's poo smelled as putrid as a rotting pound of road kill meant that Annette had absolutely no desire to be anywhere near it.

"Nonsense, Annette." Franklin plopped the baby in Annette's arms despite her aversion. "It's not going to kill you to be a part of this family." It was picturesque to everyone but Annette. A conversation about when Annette and Lyle were going to have children soon followed. All the while Annette clutched the squirming baby rather uncomfortably.

"How many children will you and Lyle be having?" her mother asked, as the baby exposed Annette's left breast by stretching the fabric of her shirt.

"Five." Lyle spoke with such confidence about his decision that Annette was barely sure she heard it right - they hadn't yet discussed it. "Two girls, three boys."

"Well, five children..." The number not only surprised her mother but Annette as well. "That'll be a lot of hard work."

"Oh, I'm sure Annette can handle it. I know *I* can." Annette sat there as her future was dictated. She wanted to speak up and say, "Oh sure, I can handle it, Lyle, for about ten

170

minutes until I can find a frying pan big enough to knock myself unconscious." But frankly, Annette was too stunned to say anything so Lyle kept on trying to convince himself (and Annette's mother) that five was the right number. "I mean look at Annette. With her motherly instinct?" The baby then regurgitated its breakfast on Annette's shoulder; that was the moment that Annette stopped listening.

*

Sure, her heart-strings were tugged upon seeing Niccolò Paganini for the first time but, as the inspirations never really came with a step-by-step instruction manual, Annette wondered how she was going to spark a man's endorphins when Paganini, she deduced, saw two of her. Annette did manage to pull him from the street with his arm wrapped around her shoulders; the wafting odor of his armpits forced Annette's nostrils to shrivel in disgust.

She at least had him on his feet and now she planned on inspiring him. For once, the situation seemed promising: only there was no warning that the pop-up book was about to refold. Instead, the thunderclap signaled an abrupt and unexpected end to Annette's inspiration as she, and the inspiree, were thrust back into her office.

"Um . . ." was all Annette could say. What exactly would Fiona do *now* if the inspiree was accidentally brought back? There wasn't any problem with bringing Patrick to the offices but, as Harriet had mentioned before, Management only allowed visitors for the retirement parties. But now . . . *now* Annette had committed a cardinal sin. A strong feeling that she'd caused damage to the universe prompted all sorts of malevolent anxieties.

What she needed was Lucas; however, the mere thought of her friend brought about another wave of depression. At that split second, with the body of Niccolò Paganini draped over her shoulder, all seemed hopeless. Lucas wouldn't have judged Annette and, being a Seventh Generation muse, he would've known what to do. Now there was no one she could call on for help. So she decided to throw off the depression and deal with it herself.

The plan was simple: turn the peg and send him back to his own time.

By squeezing the green-colored peg and rotating it clockwise, Annette expected the office to unfold back to Italy. Unfortunately time wouldn't budge no matter how many turns she gave the green-colored peg. Undoubtedly she had caused harm to the "space-time continuum." The situation had become even more complicated. How was she supposed to take him home if the colored peg wouldn't allow it?

Annette decided that, until she figured it out, she would stuff Niccolò Paganini somewhere in her own personal library, as she had little strength to hold him up for much longer. As she searched for the perfect hiding place, Annette's eyes finally settled on the cabinet on the second floor. She tilted her head quizzically to the side.

The cabinet with the ten digit combination lock had been opened. Though she knew it wasn't the time to entertain her curiosity, Annette couldn't help but to wonder what was inside. Certain that she didn't have the strength to drag Paganini up the stairs to the second floor, Annette decided on another force of action. Paganini, unfortunately, was not too keen on any idea Annette was haphazardly formulating as she tucked him under her desk and went to investigate the cabinet.

"Stay put," she told Paganini in his native tongue. "I'll be back in a second."

She would take a quick peek and then return to Paganini. Or at least that was the plan. As she was climbing the stairs she heard the words: "Hello, Dear."

Her head shot up, suddenly worried that she'd been spotted with the body of her inebriated client. She was even more confused when she saw the face.

"*Patrick?*"

"Quite a shock to me too."

"You're Lucas' replacement?"

"In the flesh, Dear." Patrick shrugged his shoulders. "Apparently Management liked my speech so much they waited until I passed away . . . They made me 'one of the elite.'" He stood taking stock of her personal sunlit library. "Actually, it's remarkable how all the years I lived leading up to this point feel like a dream." The desk thumped as Niccolò Paganini's head bumped the underside while Paganini attempted to stand. "Desks don't normally do that here, do they?" Patrick's question was soon answered as Annette, abandoning the stairs and cabinet, showed him the drunken Paganini. "Oh dear. Is that...?"

"That," Annette said nervously, "is Niccolò Paganini."

"Paganini?"

"A violinist." She nervously bit the cuticle of her right thumb.

"Dear, Niccolò Paganini wasn't . . . isn't . . . simply a violinist. He did . . . *does* . . . extraordinary things with a violin, or any stringed instrument, for that matter."

"Yeah, well." Annette was all too familiar with Paganini's music, as it constantly haunted the walls of her personal library and department. "Now he's underneath my desk and I need him *not* to be. I need your help."

"My help?"

"I'd ask Lucas . . ."

". . . but he's retired," Patrick finished for her.

Annette nodded. "And considering that you're the only other man that I've kept conversation with about this place . . . and considering I can't move him very far on my own . . ."

"Oh Dear," Patrick looked under the desk once more. "Only one envelope in and already my employment has become problematic."

"We need to take him back to his own time."

"First and foremost, I think he needs a trash can or, perhaps, a toilet."

It was an experience Annette would never forget as she and Patrick hoisted Niccolò Paganini off the floor and dragged him to the bathroom across the hall. They placed his head over the toilet. Seconds later something akin to what Paganini had previously eaten for dinner resurfaced.

As Annette had never been one for poo or vomit, she ran from the bathroom and shook out her disgust in the hallway. She suddenly realized she'd abandoned Patrick. "Oh . . . Patrick?"

Patrick was still behind the closed door as Paganini continued to vomit rather noisily.

"It's fine, Dear. Remember that I've had several grandchildren."

"Well, I *haven't* had several grandchildren! Lyle had every intention of having me birth five children, but it's something we never got around to!"

"I'm used to this kind of thing, Dear. Just wait outside." Annette couldn't dispute Patrick's orders so she paced back and forth in front of the bathroom door biting on a cuticle.

"Annette, staff meeting." Harriet's approach caused Annette's skin to crawl. Annette stood horrified. "Did you hear me?"

"Staff meeting," Annette nodded, once again nibbling the cuticle. Harriet's presence unnerved her. "Conference room, right?"

"What's the matter with you?"

"Me?"

"You look as if you've brought an inspiration job back to the offices or something."

"But I *didn't*," Annette corrected. "Because that would be bad wouldn't it? A worst-case scenario? Like the way some people consider being attacked by rabid wolves or a zombie infestation a worst case scenario?"

"Annette," Harriet's eyes narrowed the way they always did, "what have you done?"

"Nothing," Annette let out a forced laugh. "Nothing at all."

"Where's Patrick?"

"Patrick?"

"Lucas' replacement. Have you seen him?"

"Oh he's in the bathroom." Annette felt like kicking herself for giving away his position. Her face flushed as Harriet rapped a knuckle on the door. "He's uh . . . not feeling very well. First inspiration jitters and all that."

"Patrick?" Harriet spoke to the wood of the bathroom door. "Staff meeting."

"I'll be right there, Dear," Patrick called from inside.

"Now." Harriet turned to Annette. "*Both* of you, in the conference room."

As Harriet continued down the hallway spitting the words "staff meeting" into the doorless offices like pellets firing from a BB gun, Patrick stuck his head out of the bathroom. "What shall we do, Dear? Leave him here?"

"Leave him *here*?" Annette was suddenly flustered, whispering to her accomplice. "We can't leave him here."

"Then where?"

"I'd say we get him back to my desk, rotate his green-colored peg, and send him back to his own time, but . . ."

"But what?"

"It's not letting me send him back, for some reason."

"Then we'll leave him here and go to the staff meeting like nothing has happened." To that, Annette began to protest. "What other choice have we, Dear? Tell Fiona, perhaps?"

"No!" Annette seethed. "I'm already on the outs with Fiona. This is the sort of thing that would bring the wrath of Management down on me. No, we won't tell Fiona anything. We can figure this out."

"Mrs. Slocum." Fiona appeared from the conference room door. The other muses had already congregated in the conference room, save for Annette and Patrick.

"Be right there, Fiona," Annette shouted over her shoulder, knowing full well there was no other choice that could be made about the matter. Back to Patrick she whispered, "Leave him in the bathroom. We'll have to get him later," taking a serious bite to her pride.

"Mrs. Slocum, is there a situation that needs to be addressed?" Fiona started for the bathroom door but Annette was quicker. She grabbed Patrick and yanked him out into the hallway. She closed the door. The mess that was Paganini was "swept under a rug" to be worked out later.

"Nope, no situation. There's no situation. Is there Patrick?"

"No situation whatsoever."

"Then stop avoiding the inevitable." Fiona ushered the two muses down the hallway and into the conference room which no longer had the rectangular table, nine identical swivel chairs, and mural. Instead, the room had been elongated into a ballroom with trays of hors d'oeuvres and wine. A fine silk banner arced downward from the ceiling. "Friendship Day" was the message written with artistic care on the fabric. From a gramophone, the jazz composition "In the Mood" warmed the atmosphere.

"This isn't a typical staff meeting, as you can plainly see, Muses." Fiona explained. "As Management is always changing the way they do things and this celebration will become a regular occurrence after each retirement. It's a chance for the working muses to blend with one another and get to know what makes them each operate. A way for some of you," Fiona turned her eyes to Annette "to branch out. So what I want each of you to do is to find someone you've never before conversed with and spark a conversation."

While the other muses began searching for a new friend, Annette gripped Patrick's hand a little too tight for his taste. "Oh Management, I've stepped into Hell."

"Come on, Dear, it can't be that bad."

Fiona appeared behind Annette, cupping her fingers around her shoulders. "Mingle."

"But I-" but Fiona squeezed her fingers, pushing Annette into the crowd.

"*Mingle*, Mrs. Slocum."

Moments later a freshly hired Ninth Generation muse, Mr. Goodwin, said "Well, I've always wanted to be the world's greatest chess player." He went on and on about checkered boards and the various moves of the pieces. He certainly had great strategies for beating his opponents but all had been unrealized before his death. "Sort of a dream, I suppose, for who really makes a living pushing queens and rooks around, unless you're Bobby Fischer . . ."

Annette wasn't listening. She was too busy keeping tabs on all the muses to assure that no one escaped to the hallway.

"Some people fall into habits," Mrs. Donnelly of the Ninth Generation was saying while Annette nibbled a piece of cheese and pretended to take note. Mrs. Donnelly talked more than Lucas had. "They wake up at the same time every day, have the same old thing for breakfast, go to work, and do the same old thing for days on end. My favorite way to inspire is to create a bit of chaos if you will. Extract them from auto-pilot, stir the pot, and get them into a fresh routine. Though some don't like change it's the only way to survive . . . that's the way my life was before I was inspired. Like this one violet envelope I had; you wouldn't believe the trouble a client gave me! Out of three thousand people, she was lucky I even found them at all. I was an archivist when I was alive, you see. Working with restoration of aged documents. But I suppose that's what Management does to us all. They give us this opportunity to become more than we originally thought we were . . ." On and on Mrs. Donnelly went, until Annette politely excused herself to converse with another muse.

"I was the architect for the Titanic," said Mr. Andrews moments later, taking a third, and then a fourth, sip of wine to ease his troubles.

"Mrs. Slocum," Fiona encouraged, stepping into the conversation between Annette and Mr. Andrews. "Mr. Richardson had expressed specific interest about pairing you and Harriet. Now, I think, is the perfect time to get better acquainted."

"Acquainted?" It then dawned on Annette: this occasion was all Fiona's idea not Management's. Perhaps it was some kind of punishment to force the two women into awkward conversation. "So Harriet . . ."

"So Annette . . ."

"Enjoying Friendship Day?"

"'Enjoy' isn't exactly how I'd put it."

"Yeah," Annette gave a forced smile. "Me too." Harriet took a sip of her wine, while Annette nibbled on a piece of cheese. Annette then asked: "So did you find anything interesting?"

"Sorry?" Harriet was taken aback.

"In Fiona's office."

"Meaning?"

"All of his personal belongings have been taken by Fiona. I naturally assumed you'd gotten the first and best dibs before I did: his guitar, the moleskin journal."

"I don't believe you, Annette." Harriet shook her head incredulously and took another sip of wine. "That's the pot calling the kettle black. Lucas gave you his colored peg and you've been coveting it . . ."

"I haven't been coveting." Now Annette was suddenly on the defense.

"The least you could do is leave a little for the rest of us." That was the end of the conversation between Annette and Harriet as Harriet then spotted another muse with whom to converse.

"So tell me, Fiona, you're a First Generation muse, you must have stories." Patrick was comfortable keeping conversation with strangers, unlike Annette, who was then trying desperately to eavesdrop.

"There are so many. Where should one begin?"

"What about Nathaniel J. Cauliflower? How did the two of you meet?"

This was obviously not the greatest question to ask Fiona as she looked rather uncomfortable. Her eyes shifted to Annette and back. "If you'll excuse me, Patrick, I need to go powder my nose." Annette's eyes widened. Her accomplice was equally horrified as Fiona turned for the bathroom at the end of the hall.

Annette raced after her employer with her heart pumping profound palpitations in her chest. *"What was going to happen now,"* Annette wondered to herself.

Unfortunately, the ghostly violin music that had graced their offices so many times prior once again paid a visit. Much to Annette's dismay, the music in the ceiling then inspired Niccolò Paganini who had been half-unconscious in the bathroom. In a strange duet, the ghostly violin and Paganini's violin were one in the same; they overlapped in various techniques of plucking the strings with fingers and bouncing the bow. It was a startling composition to say the least as both instruments were plucked and teased maniacally and screeching a devilish duet. Fiona opened the bathroom door to find Niccolò Paganini sitting on the bathroom floor with the violin positioned under his vomit-coated chin, the bow flying a little too fast, as if a mischievous sprite was playing.

"Oh no . . ." Annette's whisper was barely detected over the music.

"Care to explain, Mrs. Slocum?"

The gravity of the situation, butterfly wings and earthquakes, were now weighing on Annette's shoulders. She had tried turning over new leaves and what-not, learning new languages, and attempting to sway memories. Now it seemed that she had inadvertently ruined everything.

*

"Well, worse things have happened, Mrs. Slocum." Fiona was surprisingly calm about the entire situation. "But taking Mr. Paganini back to his own time is more difficult than one might realize. Unfortunately, Management plots when a person comes and goes. That's why we pick the public speaker - then the time and date for the individual is calculated. Outside of those timelines, irregular departures upset the very fabric of space-time itself. Fortunately, there's nothing here that can't be fixed. Management has decided to keep him here until they sort everything. So, as I like to say, it will all be ironed out."

"Yeah . . ." Annette thought aloud.

"Don't be ashamed. This has happened to one other muse before you."

"Has it?"

"One muse accidentally brought back Amelia Earhart. We're not perfect, Mrs. Slocum. Muses make mistakes, as normal people do, but do we dwell on those mistakes? No we don't. We *learn* from them." Fiona then turned to leave.

Annette stopped her. "Who was it? The muse who brought Amelia Earhart to the office?"

"Harriet." Fiona smiled and crossed to the doorway of Annette's office. Stopping in mid-step, her employer turned and reached into her jacket pocket. "And another thing, Mrs. Slocum. When a muse retires, the Lite-Brite pegs fall into a pile which I personally scoop up and place in a manila envelope to be sent directly to Management. Along with the pegs, it's the responsibility of Head Muse to dispose of any personal belongings. Mr. Cauliflower keeps these items stored safely in his office of Seven Obsessions." Fiona handed Annette Lucas' moleskin journal. "I took the liberty of making sure this stayed behind." It felt odd having the scribed thoughts of Lucas in her hand now as if he was speaking through the ink, through time itself, reassuringly. "Keeping his past belongings will not bring him back, Mrs. Slocum. No matter how much we want them to. Retirement is a process, nothing more. We must move on."

"But even you have to agree that having the objects makes Lucas' departure a little more bearable." Annette told Fiona.

"Be that as it may," Fiona consoled "eventually you must leave the objects and live your own life with the same passion that Mr. Richardson had led his."

Annette stood in Harriet's doorway several minutes later watching as her enemy returned from yet another inspiration job.

"I owe you an apology." She handed the moleskin journal to Harriet whose features softened slightly as she took it. Still hesitant to have a conversation with anyone other than Fiona, Lucas, and Patrick, Annette turned and fled to the hallway. Turning Lucas' colored peg within the face of the Lite-Brite, Annette couldn't help but wonder just what sort of influence he had had on Harriet. Why had he been so determined to have them become friends after he left? What was Harriet's story? Annette decided to find out the answers to all these questions, and more, thus deciding to forgo the need of Lucas' world. Grazing a fingertip across Lucas' plastic peg, she placed it in her desk drawer.

She then remembered the oak cabinet.

Annette hurriedly made her way to the second floor and bent down to the now opened drawer. She looked at the word that had allowed access and she shook her head in disbelief. Inside, Annette found two preserved mason jars and a wooden box that had been sealed with an ornate golden lock that required a key. Also on the box was an insignia of a dandelion. Annette lifted one of the mason jars to find that it held twenty-one dead dandelions. In the second jar, which had been sealed air tight, Annette found a roll of perfectly preserved parchment. She dared not expose the parchment to the elements of her office for fear of it falling to pieces. She wondered what it had written on it. She then recalled that Mrs. Donnelly had been an archivist before becoming a muse. Perhaps Annette would ask her to take a look at it. Annette also couldn't help but to wonder what was inside the locked box with the dandelion insignia. Who had placed those three containers in there . . . and where had they kept the key?

CHAPTER 16: WHAT BECAME OF THE GREEN-COLORED PEG AND PURLIONED VIOLIN

Another transformation took place as Niccolò Paganini was nestled safely in what he thought was Tuscany which, in actuality, was the conference room made up as a replica. Brilliant blue skies and fields of green surrounded the violinist: colors so vivid as if painted by a great brush recently dipped in acrylics. The stone foundation of the villa in which he stayed was bathed in sunlight. Stones reflected the magnificent yellow star. As Paganini slept in a shaded corner, with the violin cradled in his arms, Annette stood in the conference room doorway and wondered, because of the music, what had become of Jonathan.

The colored pegs, when turned to the right, were far more interactive. With Adam, Annette was able to enjoy time co-existing with him instead of watching a slideshow. With Patrick she was able to find solace from Harriet's horrible attitude and her own memories of Jonas Rothchild. There were sunrises, bookshelves, and alliances when the pegs were turned clockwise. For Jonathan, whose peg Annette turned moments later, she remained still and listened to the strings of his instrument.

Though the notes were precarious at best Jonathan strummed them anyway reconstructing his self-assurance. With each passing day, of which there were many, the notes soft-shoed around him like childhood friends greeting him in his darkest hours. Four years passed within the blink of an eye and the sound of his violin accompanied the movement forward through time. In those four years Jonathan and the violin became one, as if the bow anticipated his intentions and the strings sang the exact notes that the violin player heard in his head.

A cobble-stoned river-walk was where Jonathan and his violin eventually found residence. It was the kind of river-walk where congregations of teenagers would stroll from store to store while slaying time, a place for young lovers to discover their likes and dislikes of one another's personal choice in ice-cream flavors. It was a modest pier with various food establishments and the occasional music, clothing, or toy retail. There were fountains that whipped wanton water into the air: water that was reflected by the sunlight or moonlight depending on when you happened by.

There was only one tunnel on this river-walk and the burrow was part of an overhang for the only hotel in the vicinity. It allowed Jonathan's violin to truly express itself and, because of that, the violin case that sat at his feet always caught currency. Just as the other passersby did, Annette stood before him irresistibly enthralled with his compositions.

No one knew him like Annette knew him: the way the music first tortured him at the kitchen table, the arrival of his father's beat-up trumpet, the afternoon before the library in the Cadillac, and the days he languished in the prison cell. But one didn't need a direct narration filled with pompous prose; one only had to listen to the violin. Each time the bow glided along the strings it reflected the fragments of his life. Each note that was ignited from the strings was as sharp as blinding rays of the sun or as soft as moonlight. Some were happy and some were downright depressing but, overall, behind the music was something that only Jonathan could play on that particular instrument: that was hope.

As the Great Niccolò Paganini manipulated the strings, Jonathan had designed his own method to domesticate the stringed device. His music inspired a hope that reassured Annette, the strolling pedestrians, and even Jonathan himself that, someday, his music would bring him back to his family; that somehow his music would inspire another or, even perhaps, that today was only the beginning of other untold adventures.

When Jonathan withdrew the bow from the strings, there was applause and he bowed. As coins and crinkled dollar bills were tossed inside the felt case, he thanked his patrons and continued playing. It was unfortunate that Annette didn't have any change to spare. She stood there, nevertheless, watching Jonathan play well into the night.

The crowd dispersed sometime about midnight. Eventually it was just him and Annette. Jonathan looked at her and silently decided that the night called for an encore. His eyes seemed to speak to Annette in saying, "This composition, right now, is for you." Jonathan didn't pluck the strings like Paganini but the sound was indeed all his own. The music pulled thoughts from her of watermelon-logged library books, raindrops on the day she received her graduation gift, and the wedding waltz on her special day. Other memories escaped from her head with the fluidity of Lyle's shirts rippling in an afternoon wind, of the crispness of pages turned in library books, and of the cherry blossoms turning into butterflies. Annette could feel a warm tear tracing the outline of her cheek and, as it did, Jonathan made sure to include its equivalent in the new song. When he finished, they stood in silence as his music echoed off the walls.

"It's you," Jonathan said.

"Yes, I'm afraid I didn't have much to say that night in the hotel room." They stood in silence now. It was a quiet that prompted Jonathan to store his violin safely inside its case and clasp it shut. Annette asked: "How are you?"

"You changed everything."

"Something happened, in the offices. I'm afraid that the music haunted you because of what I did." Jonathan stood with the handle of the violin case grasped by callused fingers. "I was worried that the music would have a negative effect."

"Had its moments," Jonathan confessed, "but overall I suspect so does everything else. When I heard the music there was something to it: something that pulled and spoke only to me."

"I know . . ." And Annette truly did but said nothing more of what she had witnessed when his peg was turned counter-clockwise.

"Coffee?"

"Oh . . ." Annette shook her head. "I couldn't possibly."

Apparently some pegs had time restrictions and some didn't: Adam's and Patrick's, no, but apparently Annette wasn't meant to spend much time with Jonathan outside of a few minutes per visit. As time roared, she saw him again a few years later. He was bussing and waiting tables. With the tips he made from the tunnel and those he earned being a waiter, he was able to afford a decent apartment and stay ahead of the rent and bills. Slowly but surely Annette watched as, over consecutive visits into his future, Jonathan rebuilt his life.

"At least I have the violin now," he told Annette, as he walked home from the restaurant one evening. Although he was in his mid-forties, Jonathan was still an attractive man, a real charmer. "I remember dreaming these horrible nightmares. The music ripped me from those dreams. And then there you were. Who was the other woman with you? I think she was there in the bar with me that day when I had . . ."

"She was." Annette sighed, deciding to change the subject. "So what're you planning to do now?"

"Well, I suppose get my wife and kids back. Elaine said she loved me once. Maybe she'll love me again. There's a patron who's thinking of setting up a benefit concert and wanted me to be the main attraction." It was at this time Annette realized she was having a decent conversation with the man who had killed her. "I hope you don't mind walking. Ever since the afternoon of the accident, I've realized I'm much happier and safer on foot. The apartment isn't that far."

The walk didn't bother her at all. It was similar to the one she would frequently take to and from the public library so she felt right at home trekking on foot through the night. Stars twinkled above them: not as spectacular as those at the retirement party but still heavenly all the same. There was really nothing to say, regardless of whether Annette had grown more social in the past hundred colored pegs.

"Know what I thought when I first saw you in my hotel room?"

"That there couldn't possibly be two women standing at the foot of your bed?" Annette said, kicking an acorn from her path.

"Well, that too." He brought a key-ring from his pocket as they approached his apartment building. "I remember how relieved I felt. I mean, I must've gone through that accident a million times in my head. I'd pictured your face and the way your body laid there." Jonathan climbed the iron stairs to a second floor loft which, even in the night, had an exquisite view of the river.

Jonathan stopped, turned to Annette and looked her in the eyes. "When I saw you, standing in my hotel room, I thought 'My God, there she is. I have a chance to apologize.' But I couldn't say anything. I was too stunned, seeing you after all that time completely intact. Then you disappeared into thin air." Jonathan fit the key into the lock and his shoulders sagged. "I'm sorry I killed you, Annette."

"Jonathan, there's no need." Now that Annette thought about it, it really didn't bother her at all. "To be perfectly honest, I'm not sorry that you did. I was stuck, immobilized in a dead-end marriage and, when you killed me, you opened me up the way I opened the windows when Lyle left for work at the used car lot. Of course, it's complicated. On one hand I'm grateful but on the other hand . . . life would've been much simpler for you. The violin was *right there* in your front seat."

"Ah, but perhaps it wasn't the time. The violin meant more when it arrived in the hotel room than on that particular afternoon." He opened his front door, switching on several lights. The violin case had its own leather recliner where it sat for the rest of their conversation. "Lyle . . ." Jonathan shook his head, starting a pot of coffee in the kitchen. Annette wasn't sure what Jonathan meant by saying her husband's name and shaking his head so she continued walking with him. "I'm telling you, Annette. If you'd been around for your own funeral . . ."

"I've been to enough funerals for a lifetime," Annette confessed. A memory flooded over her as swift as an owl snatching a mouse.

*

When Annette's father died, her mother spiraled faster and deeper into a depression. There were no amount of antidepressants or empty journal pages that could coax her from it and, to literally keep her alive, Lyle suggested over Thanksgiving dinner taking her to a mental institution.

"Mom's not crazy, Lyle." Franklin was the first to speak up. "She's depressed."

"I'm surprised you've even allowed steak knives at the dinner table," Lyle tossed up his hands. "That's all I'm saying." Even though Annette's mother was sitting at the end of the table, she was nowhere near the conversation. The glazed look in her eyes (that Annette had later inherited) gave it away. "But I would seriously consider getting rid of everything that she could use to potentially end her life."

"You know what I think, Lyle?" Michael spoke up at last, his eyes squinting in anger as he stabbed the turkey. "Since we're all voicing our opinions here, except for Annette because, let's face it, she doesn't say anything . . ." Annette looked up from her mashed potatoes defensively. Lyle's grip on his wife's hand tightened in preparation for man-to-man combat. "And I think I speak for all of us. You may have married Annette but no one really considers you family. Whenever we have you over, I say to myself, 'Maybe this time Lyle will've changed and Annette will've started speaking' or, better yet, 'maybe Lyle won't even come.' But the only time we ever see Annette is whenever you're around so we put up with you. Not anymore."

It was Lyle's turn to speak but only because he wasn't willing to let another second go by in which he would've been insulted. "I didn't cause your father's heart attack. So stop treating me as if I did."

"Oh?" Franklin threw down the fork and turned his full attention to Lyle and his handle-bar moustache. "He wouldn't have had the heart attack if you hadn't married Annette."

"He walked Annette down the aisle."

"Reluctantly," piped Michael.

"Reluctantly?" Lyle's face lit up with indignation. It was his turn to throw down his fork. "I'll have you know that heart attacks aren't caused by marrying a daughter off to a new and used car salesman; they're brought on by poor diet and clogged arteries. So I can't, under any circumstances, see how his heart attack was my fault. And as for Annette, if she's so unhappy in the marriage, she would say something." Lyle turned to Annette and all the focus was brought onto her. "Well?"

Annette nearly choked on her stuffing.

"Come on, Annette, for once, *say* something," Franklin coaxed. "Tell Lyle how you really feel. Dad would've wanted you to." But as Annette had never been one to have a family of eyes aimed in her direction, especially when Lyle was so close to her, Annette said nothing and, instead, took a sip of her water followed by a bite of casserole.

"Well, I think Annette has spoken her piece." Lyle said, obviously satisfied.

"Annette *hasn't* spoken her piece, Lyle. She didn't speak. Annette . . ." Out of reflex, Annette looked up at Franklin when she had been addressed. "Annette, say something. Your family needs you to back us up here."

"I think we've had enough. If we aren't welcome then we certainly aren't going to stay for dessert." Lyle stood and, because Annette was his faithful housewife, she stood too. Lyle then crossed to the kitchen and snatched up the pumpkin pie he'd purchased at the store. Annette's older brothers followed them to the front door where Lyle ripped his and her coats from the wire hangers in the closet.

"Annette, are you seriously leaving?" asked Franklin. Annette looked at both Lyle and her brothers. If Lyle hadn't ushered her out the front door, she would've stayed . . . she would have . . .

The next time Annette saw her family was at her mother's funeral. After Thanksgiving dinner, while Franklin and Michael were washing dishes, Annette's mother utilized a steak knife as Lyle predicted.

Now here they all were again: one big "happy" family. No one said a word to anyone else. Well most said nothing. Annette's niece was bouncing in her mother's arms mumbling incoherently with bubbles of drool on her lips. It was the last time that Annette would ever see her brothers. After the ceremony, they figured that if Annette was too whipped to speak her mind, that maybe she truly deserved to be with Lyle.

*

"Wow, when you check out you really check out." Jonathan handed her a mug of coffee. "I've been waving my hand in front of your face for at least a minute."

When she came to, time nearly knocked the wind out of her lungs as it rushed forward once again. Eventually time focused on another moment in Jonathan's future.

"You came." Jonathan sat in the dressing room chair with the violin the way he sat on the bar stool next to Fiona eleven years ago. Annette thought he looked dashing in the tuxedo he wore. His hair was combed and his face clean-shaven. "They've come several times telling me the show's about to begin but I have told them I was waiting for someone. Told them I couldn't go on stage without my muse."

"Jonathan, I'm flattered." Annette truly was.

He took her hand and led her to the stage. "Somewhere out there are my ex-wife, my children, and my ex-wife's new husband. I sent them tickets."

"If they *aren't* out there, you're still going to play beautifully," Annette encouraged. Jonathan wasn't so sure. Annette simply shrugged her shoulders. "You've come this far. Why not let yourself shine?"

Indeed, Jonathan did play beautifully. He had started off as a child struggling with mathematics and had evolved with Annette's help into the next Great Paganini. Every audience member in the house thoroughly enjoyed his personal compositions and sat enthralled as Jonathan regaled them with the same haunting music that had started it all. Annette, standing backstage out of support, was grateful that the green peg did not send her away prematurely.

After the performance, Jonathan and Annette went out to meet the conversing crowd in the lobby. There was sparkling wine which Annette declined, asking for water instead, finger food which Annette nibbled on, and eager audience members who truly admired the work they had heard and with whom Annette timidly associated. The only thing missing from this celebration was the family that Jonathan had sent tickets.

"They're not here," Annette sighed, munching dejectedly on a bit of broccoli drenched in ranch dressing.

"No they're not." His eyes fell, and his hands trembled.

"I'm sorry, Jonathan," Annette expressed, as reassuringly as possible. But she was soon interrupted by a woman in a sparkling ball gown and curly brown hair.

"Jonathan. I wanted to say that . . . well . . . I'm in awe of what you can do with a violin."

"I've seen you on the river-walk . . ." Jonathan's face grew flushed.

"Every night."

"Oh, well, thank you . . ." He coached her for her name, nervously switching the bow from his right to left hand for a more decent handshake. "Lila?"

"Mary Anne," Mary Anne winked at Jonathan's attempt to guess the name of a woman he had never met before but had only seen. Annette rolled her eyes which was only visible to Mary Anne who asked, "Is this your wife?"

"No. She's my . . ." Annette didn't expect Jonathan to call her his muse to someone else and therefore she was not disappointed when he hadn't. "My friend. Just a friend. Annette, this is Lila."

"Mary Anne," Mary Anne corrected with a smile, blushing.

"Mary Anne, of course." It was obvious how flustered her arrival had made the great violinist.

"Pleasure." Annette faked a smile and extended a hand.

"Would you . . . coffee, Mary Anne?"

"Jonathan worked pretty fast," Annette thought to herself but said nothing. She felt that time was beginning to press the fast-forward button again so Annette excused herself to disappear through the crowd in search of more broccoli.

Thirty years roared in front of Annette now and, in these years, she could tell that the relationship between Jonathan and Mary Anne developed into a healthy marriage. They had three children who each grew up playing the instruments that they wanted to play and, later, were getting married themselves. As time finally began to slow its progression Annette's breath was taken away. Everyone that played a role in Jonathan's life had aged so much that, by the time his life had slowed to a normal speed, she didn't recognize anyone - not even her client.

Jonathan was old with white hair. Arthritis ripped through his fingers, as he once again pressed his violin bow to the strings. He didn't play very long before he gave up and sat the violin in its rocking chair next to him. When he spotted Annette, the wrinkles that scarred his once beautifully young face stretched in a smile.

"Muse."

"Jonathan." Annette sat on the arm of his recliner. She was reminded of when Peter Pan visited the aged Wendy in the Darling nursery. Annette wanted to cry but Jonathan's smile kept her from doing so.

"Look at you, Jonathan. You've . . . grown up."

"I've lived . . . a spectacular life, Muse." Jonathan's words were strained yet he spoke them anyway. "Because of you."

"Jonathan . . ."

"I haven't heard the music since that night in the hotel room but somehow I always equated it with you and all that you do. Because of you, Muse, I played. And even though it didn't quite turn out how I wanted it to . . ."

"Everything was eventually ironed out."

"Yes . . . it still . . . turned out beautifully . . . like notes beautifully arranged on staves. I'm going to die soon, Muse," Jonathan told Annette and, despite her protest, he went on. "But I wanted you to know something. I want to do for you what you've done for me. Lyle . . ."

Annette didn't care about Lyle anymore. In fact, she hated him. She truly hoped that Lyle would never re-enter her life for a second act. Most likely he was still shoveling those damn eggs and completely oblivious to the fact that she was even dead. Lyle probably still read the paper at the kitchen table, assuming that Annette was still behind the printed words nibbling on her own bit of granola and drinking water from the faucet. Annette didn't want to have anything to do with Lyle. Especially now. "Muse . . . are you listening?"

"Jonathan," Annette tried her best to smile and touched his wrinkled hand. "Whatever you have to say about Lyle I don't want to know."

"But you *must* know."

191

"All I want to know is: are you happy?"

"Oh, Muse . . ." Jonathan's eyes began to tear. "I've *lived* and, thankfully, many of those years have been with Mary Anne. Did you know she went to Juilliard before we met? She plays so beautifully. So beautifully . . . but even if it wasn't for Mary Anne, even if there were difficult times . . . I *lived* . . ."

Paganini's haunting music returned to Jonathan's life at this moment. Both he and Annette listened as it played as it had so many years before. A roll of thunder somewhere in the distance told Annette that Jonathan's story was coming to an end.

"The music has finally returned," Jonathan cheered as he took his violin in hand. Annette watched the duet with reverence and was surprised when Mary Anne entered the room as well. She, like Jonathan, had aged considerably. It was clear from the confused expression that she heard not only Jonathan's music but Paganini's as well. She and Annette caught eyes with one another during the duet. Even though, to Annette, everything about this moment seemed normal, to Mary Anne it was like a scene from *The Outer Limits*. As the duet came to a conclusion and Paganini's music receded, Jonathan closed his eyes and smiled.

"My only regret, Muse, is that I never got around to meeting the violinist who sent me the music. Do you think, the next time you happen by, you might bring him with you?"

"I don't know if that's possible," Annette told him, for honestly she wasn't sure if it was. She wasn't quite sure why Adam's and Patrick's lives hadn't flashed this quickly. Perhaps the pegs showed time differently for the various clients. Annette hoped Adam wouldn't have aged to the verge of death by the time she would see him again. She could actually picture having five children with him: (with Lyle, absolutely not, but Adam . . .) Annette could picture being married and growing old with him.

As the thunderclap roared, Annette was once again deposited into her swivel chair. The Great Niccolò Paganini's violin played in the conference room, echoed by the music coming from the ceiling. "But I can sure try, to bring Paganini to you," Annette whispered, hoping Jonathan could hear her. "I can sure try . . ."

Jonathan's green-colored peg fused happily with the grid, ever-glowing in the face of her Lite-Brite. Somewhere in the world Jonathan was living all the moments in between that Annette had missed. Jonathan was *living*.

CHAPTER 17: A SEEMINGLY INNOCENT ARTIFACT

"It's at least two hundred years old," said Mrs. Donnelly of the Ninth Generation. She and Annette were standing in an office that had been made up, on Mrs. Donnelly's arrival, into a document preservation lab. Mrs. Donnelly was dressed in a tuxedo shirt opened at the collar. Over the shirt was a tan dinner jacket. Her blonde hair was haphazardly fastened with pins. She was in her mid-thirties and had a genuine goodhearted nature that put everyone around her at ease. With sterilized gloves and equipment, Mrs. Donnelly held up the parchment that Annette had discovered in one of the two jars from the oak cabinet. "What we're looking at, Ms. Annette, is a ledger."

"A ledger?" Annette leaned in to get a better look.

"Or it's at least a single page torn out from a much larger ledger. But it's unlike any ledger I've seen before. I've seen many slave registers in my days as an archivist but this one isn't a slave ledger. Nor is it a ledger to document accounts payable to a corporation. Not even by a long shot." Mrs. Donnelly examined the document even more closely now. "*This* ledger gives names, ages, and dates, yes, but it also gives cost of admittance."

"Cost of admittance?" Annette studied the document even more intrigued. "Admittance for what?"

"The page doesn't say what for. What surprises me isn't what it's *for*, instead *how much* an individual paid for the service." Mrs. Donnelly pointed to the column of costs. "Each message was worth the same flat fee of three dandelions."

"Dandelions?"

"Furthermore, there's one name that seems to reoccur," Mrs. Donnelly observed. "Recognize anyone on this ledger?"

Annette read each name to herself until her eyes finally fell onto a name she recognized: Nathaniel J. Cauliflower. She wasn't all that surprised. After all, the ten-lettered combination on the oak cabinet that had housed this artifact had his first and last name as possible solutions. What took Annette's breath away was the amount of times that Cauliflower's name was listed.

"Nathaniel J. Cauliflower, age 23, 1807, three dandelions," Annette read aloud as her fingers trailed down the single page. "Nathaniel J. Cauliflower, age 18, 1921, three dandelions. Age 37, 1945, three dandelions. Three dandelions, three dandelions, three dandelions." Annette shook her head. "The ages don't match up. How can someone be twenty-three in 1807 and then eighteen years old in 1921?"

"Perhaps he's pulling a 'Benjamin Button,'" Mrs. Donnelly offered.

Annette shook her head and said: "Because he aged twenty-four years between 1921 and 1945 when he paid another three dandelions. And then he goes backwards in age and forward again." The seventh life of Nathaniel J. Cauliflower had been scratched through by two distinct lines making the information regarding the year, age and cost illegible.

"Maybe," Mrs. Donnelly interjected "we're looking at reincarnation. Maybe what we are looking at, Ms. Annette, is the recycling of a soul and in each life he encountered . . . whomever he encountered."

"If that's the case," Annette took Mrs. Donnelly's comment and ran with it "then Nathaniel J. Cauliflower has lived seven lives. And in each life he paid . . ." she suddenly was lost in thought. Annette picked up the second jar she had found. Inside Annette could see twenty-one dead dandelions. She whispered in disbelief "It's possible. I don't know *how* but it's possible."

Annette's eyes caught sight of another name at the bottom of the page as Mrs. Donnelly was tucking the page back into its glass container.

"Wait," Annette told Mrs. Donnelly.

"Certainly."

The ledger was brought back into the light. Annette's spirits quickly sank. The man that had been listed below Nathaniel J. Cauliflower's seventh visit had been a name Annette recognized. She read aloud to herself: "Thomas Rothchild. 1959, three dandelions."

Annette had a sickening feeling that the Thomas Rothchild that had been mentioned on the page had been a relative of her adversary, Jonas. Annette couldn't help but to wonder if perhaps the man that had been listed was Jonas' father. She had only seen Jonas' father once, long ago, in the new and used car lot when she had first met Lyle.

"I need to think," said Annette. "Excuse me."

Mrs. Donnelly tucked the parchment back into the jar and screwed the lid tight. Without saying another word, Mrs. Donnelly respectfully handed Annette the jar and returned to another document. Annette stopped at Mrs. Donnelly's doorway and said "Thank you for taking the time."

As Mrs. Donnelly nodded in appreciation, Annette's eyes fell upon the new artifact that was about to be examined: the letter that had been written in French that Fiona had shown her many colored pegs ago. Annette almost wanted to hover over Mrs. Donnelly's shoulder to uncover the mysteries of the Head Muse. But there were already too many closets with skeletons that had been opened for one day. As she made her way back to her office and set the mysterious treasures on the edge of her desk, Annette's most notorious skeleton shook its rotten, yellowed bones like demented wind-chimes caught in a hurricane.

*

There were days in her marriage to Lyle that Annette forced herself to commune with the world around her while protected by a rickety shopping cart in the nearest grocery store. With her champagne-colored Beetle nestled at the far end of the parking lot, Annette took her list and silently gathered what she needed as if stocking for Armageddon. Annette would pick three cartons of eggs, checking each egg-shell inside for flaws, the way a geologist inspects diamonds. Milk, of course, was next, and she would buy two gallons. Annette would also purchase refrigerated slabs of bacon, pancake mix, cantaloupe, granola bars, and fixings for the various meals that were typically eaten in the Slocum household.

In the same fashion as she adored sifting through various library books, in life Annette had a private passion for the coffee section. Though she never truly enjoyed the taste, she could have spent hours standing before the various coffee beans, absorbing the various scents. As she had done with the pages of library books, Annette lifted the bags of coffee beans up to her nose and sniffed, imagining the aroma brewing in the coffee pot while she crisped Lyle's bacon. The spice racks were also something that made her nostrils flare with elation. Annette didn't care if one was a far less pungent odor than the one before. She loved them all and stocked up on them whenever she could. The laundry detergents were her guilty pleasure: the sterile scent of soap was enough to keep her near the shelves for at least half an hour.

With her shopping cart filled with amenities, Annette prepared her envelope of coupons. How horrible then that, on a particularly nice afternoon, as Annette wheeled her cart up to the automated check-out counter, she discovered Jonas watching her from afar. Annette tried not to make eye contact. Especially as she scanned the toilet paper and tampons.

As she scanned the cantaloupe and shoved it deep in a plastic sack, Annette was mortified to find that the circular fruit had other plans. It somehow rolled out of the bag and across the tile where she found Jonas' foot stopped its escape. Out of the corner of her eye, Jonas bent down and picked it up as effortlessly as if it were nothing more than a soccer ball. He then nonchalantly walked up to her with it between the palms of his hands.

"Dropped something, Annette." He offered her the cantaloupe but it reminded her of the watermelon slice under the tree. Annette dared not take it. Jonas accepted defeat and opened the plastic bag from which it had bounced, only to notice the box of tampons that Annette had hoped would remain invisible.

Jonas uncomfortably stuffed the cantaloupe inside the bag. Annette stood perfectly still. "Saw the announcement in the paper about your wedding. Congratulations."

Annette mumbled something beneath her breath that could've been interpreted as a thank you.

"The other announcement, too. About your dad. I'm . . . uh . . . I'm sorry." She started scanning the last of her items, hoping that Jonas would catch the hint for him to ditch the scene. Unfortunately, Jonas lingered instead helping to bag the last of her groceries. "Need any help carrying these out?"

Annette shook her head, swiping her husband's debit card with one hand while attempting to shelve each bag in its place in the shopping cart with the other.

"If you ever need someone to . . ." Jonas laughed, bringing a hand up to rub his eyes. "How foolish of me." Annette took a moment now, waiting for Jonas to finish his original thought. Certainly he wasn't about to extend a shoulder for her to cry on. They stood awkwardly in the grocery store until Annette broke the pause and wheeled her cart back out into the sunlight. "Nice talking to you!" Jonas' words were cut short by the sliding doors which closed with finality behind her.

*

Annette had told Mrs. Donnelly she needed to think but the department had a way of causing thoughts to become downright crippling. Instead of staying in the offices to recollect, Annette felt proper consolation in the arms of her bookseller. And that was where she promptly found herself. While Adam lay on his back staring up at a mid-afternoon sky, clouds drifted. Annette lay in the crook of his arm. Her eyes fluttered open after a short doze.

"Sleep well?" Adam asked, a thumb gently stroking her elbow.

"How long was I asleep?"

"Not long." Adam turned his eyes back to the clouds drifting above. "You were mumbling in your sleep. Something about a library donned in a tuxedo and how Lyle probably wouldn't even notice as you left with a suitcase."

198

"Funny thing, dreams." Annette brushed away the subconscious conversation she had with herself as nothing of trivial importance. Inside she was unsettled that her subconscious had said too much.

"You were also mumbling something about a cantaloupe and a jar of twenty-one dandelions."

Annette blushed, turning her attention to the sky as well, hoping to divert the conversation. They were on the rooftop of *The Muse's Corner* which allowed a spectacular view of not only the sky but of the city as well. She couldn't remember the last time she'd tried to equate the cloud shapes with animals and, considering that the *new* Annette had decided to make new memories to substitute for the old ones, she made up new names as well.

"Decilpherogus."

"Ah, see, it was on the tip of my tongue, Annette. But you're too quick for me." Annette was thrilled that Adam was invested in the game. She was even more so when he pointed out another animal. "Fart-lunger."

"Picklagorgenhip."

"Yiggleumpro."

"Borselfinmeierfarfergaloogen."

"No kidding? I thought those were extinct. Very good eye." And so they lay there for the longest time, simply enjoying the afternoon. "Annette?" Adam asked finally.

"Adam . . ."

"Shouldn't you be going?"

"I'll stay for a minute longer."

"Not that I mind," Adam grinned, "but why the sudden change of heart?"

"Let's just say I watched a life flash before my eyes before I came back here."

"A life." Adam nodded then, teasing a strand of her hair. "Yours?"

"No, someone else's."

"Whose?"

"Jonathan, the green-colored peg with the violin." The moment Annette uttered the words she sat up, the blood rushing to her head.

199

"Green-colored peg?"

"I have to go." She should have known it would slip eventually. She thought to herself, *"you relax in the arms of the bookseller and then you say things you shouldn't."* The solace of her lover's arms had been compromised and she hated that. Annette wasn't sure where this rush of emotion was coming from. It was as if all the emotions that she had kept secure, like the dandelions and 200 year old parchment, had suddenly been exposed.

"Wait a minute," Adam scrambled to keep her on the blanket but to no avail. "Annette!"

"I have to go. Management only knows how long I've been away from the office."

"At least half an hour, maybe more."

"Half an hour, maybe *more?*" *"Harriet's going to kill me,"* she festered within, her face red as the stripes on an American flag.

"Annette."

"And Harriet's probably standing in my office doorway, right now, *wondering* where I am." Annette shook wrinkles from her yellow dress. Behind her, in the sky, a dark storm cloud crept closer overhead. "Then I'll never hear the end of it." Here she was, making herself look like an idiot, but she was too consumed with worry to stop.

"Annette, look." Adam propped himself up with his left arm. "We were having a perfectly nice afternoon, right?"

"Perfectly nice," Annette nodded. She looked in his eyes and felt momentarily centered.

"So why don't you forget the office, lay back down and enjoy the rest of it?"

"Because that's not part of my job, Adam," Annette tried to explain. "None of this is part of my job. I'm supposed to be in the office awaiting envelopes that have colored pegs so that I can . . ."

"Can what?"

But apparently in trying to explain, she had explained too much. "Gah!" Annette was flustered once again. "I can't keep anything a secret from you, can I? I just look at you and the words just come *flying* out as if I've lost all sense."

200

"Is that such a bad thing?" Adam's hand reached up to touch hers now. Once his skin touched hers, Annette closed her eyes, allowing him to make contact. He tugged her down to the blanket now, her rigid body soon growing limp. "Now, lie back down. If you're worried about saying something you shouldn't, don't talk."

"Don't talk?"

"Sometimes it's okay not to say anything . . ."

"What kind of woman would I be if I didn't talk?" Annette thought to herself. *"Not talking to anyone was what had caused this mess to begin with."* The sunlight that warmed them was soon covered by the storm cloud. A cool breeze teased a strand of Annette's limp hair from behind her ear to her left cheek.

"Vergilniffers," Adam sighed, his warm fingers coaxing the strand of hair to behind her ear. "They always spoil the fun."

"Yeah . . ."

"Well, right on time; it's been a minute."

"Has it?" Annette sighed.

"Disappear like you always do."

Annette frowned, stood from the blanket and exited through a stairwell door out of Adam's sight. She'd tried so hard to keep her comings and goings a secret from him. For how could she possibly explain her disappearances without giving anything away?

Once again Annette was deposited into her office where the swivel chair, inbox, and water-cooler were cold to the touch. There were also thirteen white envelopes waiting in her post box. Unfortunately also waiting for her, with the air of presidency and sitting in the swivel chair on the opposite side of the desk, was Harriet.

"Annette, Annette, Annette." Harriet eyes squinted, fingers locked like an overturned book below her chin. "Thirteen now."

It had become a regular habit between the two women: Annette would turn a peg and Harriet would be waiting for her. Annette had about had it with Little Miss Priss but said nothing as she organized the pile of envelopes. If she had had a coconut cream pie, Annette would have thrown it into the snot's face.

The possibility of whipped cream choking her adversary's nostrils was enticing. Instead, Annette quietly and embarrassingly went to work with Harriet watching. Harriet folded her arms and narrowed her eyes even more.

Annette traveled to Ireland, Spain, Bogota, Tokyo, Milwaukee, sand dunes in the Nevada desert, and Chicago. She even managed to inspire great figures like William Shakespeare, Charles Dickens and Harry Houdini. Alas, however far of a distance Annette traveled or whatever time period in which she found herself, there was no escaping Harriet who was always there to greet her when she returned. Annette was glad she had recently had lunch with Adam before naming cloud formations. Otherwise she would have had very little energy.

Thirteen inspiration jobs later, Annette sank into her seat content to know that all her tasks were efficiently completed. That is, until another envelope was delivered into her post box. Nathaniel J. Cauliflower was elusive as ever in his role of postman. Annette dared not groan in petulant exhaustion as both she and Harriet stared at the envelope. Harriet's eyes watched Annette like a hawk and Annette turned her eyes back to Harriet. For a moment the two of them sat staring maliciously eye-to-eye with a wave of silence passing between them.

"Alright, Harriet, what do you want from me?"

"I beg your pardon?" Harriet's eyes opened wide as if this question was the greatest insult in her entire employment.

"How many inspiration jobs do *you* have at a time? Twenty? Thirty? A hundred and fifty-seven?"

"At least I don't *neglect* my envelopes."

Annette had felt childish emotionally exploding in front of Adam but found it easy to release her feelings in front of Harriet who, in Annette's mind, deserved the full force. With that, Annette let Harriet have it.

"Certainly not you, oh Miss *Perfect*. You who never do anything wrong! I'll bet you execute them with perfect timing and agility. I'll bet your Lite-Brite board is just *full* of them. And you, oh Miss *Wise One*, would never bring a client back to the offices by accident. Oh wait! Aren't we forgetting your little mishap with Amelia Earhart? Or allow Jonas to drench the pages of a library book with watermelon juice, *or* marry the wrong man when you're obviously in love with another!" Annette, realizing that two of the three things she mentioned had nothing to do with management envelopes, began to blush. As if all the pent-up frustrations had finally found an outlet, Annette tried desperately to stuff all of her emotions back from whence they came. "Now if you please, if you're so hell-bent on keeping up with the Joneses, why not sit in your *own* swivel chair, in your own drab little office, and leave me alone?"

Her father had once told her to talk like a main character; to fight with words rather than barbaric fists. Though she had finally stood up to an enemy the right way, there were no trumpet fanfares or processions, no confetti falling to the ground and no balloons descending from the ceiling.

Harriet, obviously affected by Annette's emotional outburst, turned and stormed out of Annette's office in her own fury. Annette stood up from her swivel chair and crossed behind her desk, picked up the envelope, and gave the water cooler an extra punt. She heard a click from her post box again. She was not surprised to see that it was blue.

Mrs. Slocum,
Step into my office for a moment.
Sincerely,
Fiona

"Oh, Harriet the princess has gone to complain," Annette thought to herself. As if matters couldn't get any worse, Annette simmered even more when she saw Paganini headed back to the conference room from the restroom. He had in his hands another artifact that Annette had been familiar with: Lucas' guitar. Fiona sat behind her desk as Annette lurked in the doorway. Her employer's pearl earrings sparkled in the lights of the art gallery office.

"Mrs. Slocum. Please, have a seat."

"Rather stand."

"Sit down, Mrs. Slocum."

"I'd rather stand." Annette spoke through gritted teeth.

"For Management's sake," Fiona's lips pursed. "If I wanted teeth to grit at me I would have hired a half-starved Doberman to reside in your office. I won't ask a third time."

Annette slumped into a spare swivel chair.

"Explain."

"You gave Lucas' guitar to Niccolò Paganini?"

"I thought we'd closed the conversation about Lucas' belongings," Fiona said very matter-of-factly. "It wasn't getting any use when Mr. Richardson was here; it's getting use now that he's retired."

"It wasn't yours to give!" Annette's exclamation was completed by the sound of Paganini's mitts strumming Lucas' guitar in the conference room.

Fiona told Annette: "Detox, Mrs. Slocum, is no easy task, but it seems that his newfound likeness to the guitar makes it easier."

"Uh huh . . ."

"Think of it this way, Mrs. Slocum: Mr. Richardson would've wanted Paganini to have it. He would've wanted it to go to someone who would enjoy playing it as much as he had." Annette rolled her eyes. Fiona intentionally ignored the behavior of the muse in front of her. "Speaking of Mr. Richardson. Before retiring, he mentioned that you and Harriet might hit it off as friends."

"Me and Harriet."

"You and Harriet."

"As friends." Fiona nodded. Annette tossed her hands up. "Boy, that's rich. Great conversation at the Friendship Day, by the way."

"I know that the two of you did not have the greatest start. But I must ask you give her another chance. The two of you are more alike than you might realize."

"Fine," Annette surrendered. "But she has to make more of an effort as well."

"She knows this," Fiona told Annette. "The sooner the two of you make amends, the quieter things will be in this office. When two muses are at odds with one another it risks the efficiency of the department. That will not do. I also believe it will be best for your own well beings."

204

Annette nodded as if she had been paying attention but Annette's mind had wandered back to how she had left things with Adam.

"You seem to have a lot on your mind, Mrs. Slocum. I wonder if there is an even deeper dilemma from which your worries are stemming?"

"You wouldn't understand," Annette told her.

Fiona then turned her eyes from Annette to the young man that had been framed in the many portraits along her white museum walls. "I think you'll find that I understand more than you realize." Fiona stood gracefully from her swivel chair and stepped closer to the nearest portrait. "His name was Alexander Thibodaux and we had once been in love. I was no ordinary woman when I had been alive, Mrs. Slocum. There are those who had seen me do things, strange things and, due to that, it was Alexander's father who had accused me of being a witch. On the day that I died, his father forced my beloved Alexander to light the fire. Even on those last moments, when all around me had been flickering flames, I could tell that Alexander was suffering as much as I was. Snow fell on Alexander's cheeks as I departed the world. And then I found myself waking up here, in this office, where I was given a cream-colored pants suit by Management." Fiona went on. "And after three thousand colored pegs, I was given a single yellow peg that took me back to him. I rotated it so many times until at last his life came to an end. Eventually I couldn't rotate it any further and eventually I had to let him go. So I sealed up his yellow-colored peg in an envelope and gave it to Mr. Cauliflower for safe-keeping." Fiona then fell into silence.

"I'm not used to feeling so strongly about things," Annette confessed. "I haven't felt this much emotion since . . . I don't think I've ever felt this much emotion! Everyone else here seems so even-keeled. Why can't I feel that way like I used to? What's wrong with me?"

"Nothing is wrong with you, Mrs. Slocum. You care very deeply about those around you: be they clients or fellow muses." Fiona then turned away from Alexander's portrait. She once again regained her Head Muse composure. "You have to find a way to channel that passion into positive construction instead of burning bridges with blowtorches."

After considering Fiona's words, Annette said "I feel like I'm a trapeze artist without a safety net, Fiona."

"I know," Fiona couldn't help but to smile warmly. "Isn't it wonderful?"

*

On September 11th, 2001 Annette was sitting in a plastic chair affixed to the wall of the car wash waiting room watching the champagne-colored Beetle pass through one large window after another. She could've flipped through the uninteresting selection of greeting cards or spied the less appealing hood ornaments or bottled car scents, but instead her attention was fixated on the wax sealant being applied to the hood of her car.

A ray of early morning sunlight erupted from the docking doors as Jonas brushed through. "Well, we meet again," said Jonas, who took a seat in the chair to the right of Annette and watched as the tail of her car passed through the far left window and the hood of his appearing at the far right. "I uh . . . read in the paper about your mom's death."

Annette sniffed.

"Sorry to hear about that. Not a very good year for you, is it?" He cracked his knuckles and shifted the position of his tennis shoes, but Annette didn't feel like speaking. Instead she kept her eyes on Jonas' sedan as it had passed through another window behind the rear bumper of her own. Although it was originally rusted, Jonas had restored his vehicle. Annette was impressed by his handiwork but said nothing. They sat in awkward silence for the entire process: she with her hands resting on the lap of her plain housedress and he anxiously shifting one of his tennis shoes on top of the other and back again.

"Still giving me the silent treatment?" Jonas said as he shook his head. He would've gone on badgering her but the waiting room was suddenly ablaze with commotion as the car-wash technicians turned up the volume sitting on the small television on the counter. Annette and Jonas stood with the attendants as they huddled around the television screen to find that the World Trade Center had been struck by a plane followed by a second attack. For once, Jonas was silent in Annette's presence.

*

"Why are all the details so convoluted," Annette thought to herself while reaching out then retracting her hand from Adam's peg. She reached out again and recoiled. Adam's peg called to her the way books did in the library. She wondered what harm it would do to see him for one more minute. Would she apologize for being flustered earlier? Would they get into another argument? Would he even talk to her? Would Harriet be waiting for her? Perhaps if she lingered in the shadows, gathering the unique idiosyncrasies of his behavior, Annette would possibly gain a better understanding of the bookseller.

Annette eventually bit her lip and grazed the peg clock-wise. It thrust her back into Adam's apartment. It was almost too perfectly timed: the way the knobs were turned in the bathroom as if Adam had been waiting for her to arrive to take a shower. As water gushed through a faucet behind a closed bathroom door, Annette seized the moment to further inspect the habits of her bookseller.

There were photos in the apartment: many of them caged behind glass, some on the fireplace mantle, others sat atop the bookshelves that held his history books, some on side tables, while others hung on the walls. They were photos of family in which Adam was, Annette assumed, probably wielding the camera. Fourth of July picnics, birthday parties and school photos were documented. Though she didn't know their exact names, Annette deduced that her bookseller had three sisters. Then there was his mother Gwendolyn, a father, and an abnormally large extended family.

In his kitchen, Annette found a well-stocked refrigerator. On the countertops were several cookbooks that looked as if they'd been rifled through many times before. Annette flipped through one in particular that she pulled from his collection. Gwendolyn Mansfield had compiled a grand anthology of her personal recipes on neatly handwritten with pages protected by plastic pockets. He was a guy who loved his mother, that was for sure, but there was nothing wrong with that. Annette figured it added even greater charm to his disposition.

All was quiet in the bathroom now save for a few splashes in the tub. Apparently Adam was also the kind of man who preferred baths instead of showers. Trying desperately not to imagine how handsome his naked body would look in the bathtub, Annette turned her attention to another area of his apartment.

On his bedside table Annette found a small collection of journals, which she cautiously picked up and inspected his handwriting. Annette sniffed the pages. The smell of ballpoint was faint but recognizable along with a hint of musk. Unaware of how long she stood taking in the smell of his journals, Annette was startled by the sound of Adam standing up from the water. Side-stepping around the bed to place the journals back into position, Annette fled back to the living room, stubbing her toe on the coffee table. She let out a yelp of pain along the way.

"Anyone there?" Adam called. Annette slinked further into the apartment's shadows as he appeared. His toned hairy chest glistened with bathwater. A dark green towel was wrapped around his waist accenting the muscles in his abdomen. "Annette . . . is that you?"

The telephone rang somewhere in the kitchen and continued to ring as Adam was on the hunt for Annette. She dared not say anything for fear of an argument about her intrusion or, worse yet, more disapproving words about her fleeing the cloudy afternoon. Adam was inches away from her hiding spot behind his curtain as the answering machine clicked on.

"Adam, Mom calling. Wanted to make sure you're still on for this weekend. The whole family's getting together at the house at three." Adam stretched out his hand hoping that, by reaching into the shadows, his fingers would touch the hem of her yellow dress. "Have you talked to Annette? We'd like to have her over; she's all you talk about." Retracing his footsteps, he then retreated into the kitchen and pulled the phone from the cradle.

Annette's heel, which had touched carpet seconds ago, found a well-mowed lawn of grass. Turning, she found that time had fast-forwarded and there, in the backyard of Adam's parents' house, was a Fourth of July picnic. Blistering sunlight caused her to shield her eyes as she ducked beneath the shade of a Bradford pear tree.

"Because she's a private woman, Mom." Adam was dressed in a polo shirt and jeans. He had a spatula in one hand prodding a hamburger on the grill.

"Well, any woman who's important to my son is important to this family. I don't care how private she is," Gwendolyn told Adam as she cooked the hot dogs. "Dad and I want to see you settle down."

"Right now I'm just trying to get her to stay."

"Spoken as if she were a dog."

"Annette's not a dog, Mom. She's . . . perfect." He stacked several hot dogs and hamburgers on a plate. "A little insecure, secretive, modest... and she certainly knows how to disappear. Quite literally. But still perfect. I can tell that she's stressed. I want to help her be more relaxed. I want her to trust me with whatever secret she has." Closing the lid of the grill, Adam turned to the rest of the yard and held the plate aloft. "Soup's on, family!"

From behind the Bradford pear tree, Annette once again spied the Well-Dressed Man in a Black Suit and Tie watching her from the road. He raised a hand and waved and Annette, out of reflex, waved back. *"Who was this chap,"* Annette wondered to herself as an open-faced hamburger on a Styrofoam plate appeared from around the bark of the tree.

"Fancy meeting you here," Adam told her. "One of these days you'll explain everything to me: the way you appear and disappear from my life. You're not an illusionist, are you?"

"Illusionist?" Annette was instantly at ease upon seeing him look at her.

"It would be okay if you were, you know. I happen to like magic tricks. Want to see one?" Annette gave a half smile as Adam swung around the tree breaking the line of sight between her and the strange man. Adam extracted two unlit sparklers from behind his back making a bigger production out of it than it was. "When the sun sets, what say you and I light them together?"

"Adam . . ."

"Hamburgers, hotdogs, chips, an afternoon of family fun, and then sparklers."

"I don't have time for sparklers."

"Don't have time for sparklers?" Adam's brow furrowed playfully. "It's the Fourth of July. Everyone must make time for sparklers."

"Everyone but me," Annette replied, trying to free herself from his close proximity.

"And for my next trick, ladies and gentlemen, I'm going to make Annette here disappear." Adam called after her as she darted from behind the tree. ". . . Again."

Annette spun defensively.

"Unless the audience wishes that I perform an even greater feat and make you stay . . ." Behind him, Annette could see his entire family where all had grown silent to watch the next act. She turned her attention back to the road where the stranger had since abandoned then turned back to Adam.

"Stay, you say?"

Adam nodded and Annette finally gave in, allowing herself to spend an afternoon with the Mansfield family. Though the wind was warm and the sun unrelenting, the upside was that the chips were crisp, the hamburgers juicy, and the sprinkler jets beside the house were on and gently misting. Casserole dishes weighted down the plastic checkered tablecloth, napkins with images of American flags occasionally fluttered to the manicured lawn and bees buzzed industriously. Plugged into an outside outlet a CD player proudly produced the processions of John Phillip Sousa. There was also a bubble machine to add an even greater gaiety to the occasion. Considering that she was still uncomfortable conversing within a large crowd, especially family members of the man she'd been seeing, Annette stayed quiet and listened.

The Mansfield clan were all Cancers; though initially shy themselves, they found it easier to escape the confines of their "shells" when around one another. The Mansfield Cancers were simply laid back, as if the world outside of Adam's mother's backyard didn't exist. They acted as if they weren't even celebrating the Fourth of July at all. That this kind of gala was just a private Mansfield ritual, nothing more. For a moment, Annette found herself forgetting about the chaos of the department and thinking not of Lite-Brite boards, colored pegs, and water coolers. Instead, Annette thought of Adam's hand near hers while they held their respective sparklers as the sun ducked below the horizon. As the twin wicks erupted in orange and white sparks, Adam smiled. His fuzzy cheeks were accented by the light.

"There truly are sparks between us, Annette. You can't deny that."

When the sun finally set, the Mansfield family lounged in lawn chairs on the rooftop of *The Muse's Corner*. Adam and Annette snuggled on a blanket watching the show.

"The stadium sets them off," Adam told her "but I've always preferred to watch them from up here. Much more . . ."

". . . much more quiet." Annette's words overlapped his but the conversation fell short as they watched the rest of the fireworks in silence. Adam's hand grazed Annette's. Annette allowed herself to feel it. She then carefully took his hand in hers and held it there for the rest of the evening. Red, orange, purple, green, blue, yellow, and white with pink fluttering sparks; the fireworks reminded her of a giant Lite-Brite board. The sight reminded her of the time. As the sky once again fell dark, with clouds of smoke lingering before the stars, Annette sat up as she'd done at the end of her previous visit.

"Running away again, are we?" Adam inquired playfully.

"Only for a little while." Waving goodbye to his family, Annette took several steps to the stairwell as if time were about to refold there. Adam stayed alongside with her their hands clasped together. And it was then that Annette finally said, "I'm sorry."

"You were here all day today, Annette. You've made me very happy."

"Time to say goodnight, then."

"Goodnight, then," said Adam, leaning in to kiss her.

"Goodnight." Annette wanted to kiss him and feel his prickly facial hair against her smooth skin but something held her back causing her face to move slightly to dodge the bullet. Adam took a few steps back now to allow the illusionist ample room to disappear which she took by stepping further onto the stairs vanishing through the darkness. She had been an emotional mess but Adam still wanted her. Annette took comfort in knowing that, even on bad days, she was still thought after with caring and loving thoughts.

It wasn't to the Lite-Brite board and musing office that she was sent. Instead, Annette found herself standing in the breezeway of Adam's apartment complex. It was the same July evening as Annette could still detect a hint of sulfur lingering about the clouds. Standing in the shadows with her was the Well Dressed Man in the Black Suit and Tie.

"Annette Slocum?" His voice was as mysterious as a whisper. It was elusive as the purring of a great panther.

"Do I know you?" Annette asked him.

"There's no easy way to explain this, I'm afraid," he replied.

"Oh?" Annette raised an eyebrow.

The stranger pulled out a newspaper clipping from his jacket pocket unfolding it with his coarse fingers. Holding it up to a key-ring flashlight, Annette recognized it as an obituary . . . *her* obituary.

For a split second, it felt as if a firework had exploded within her heart. She cautiously inquired: "Why are you showing this to me?"

"According to this obituary, Annette, you've been dead for three years."

"I think you have me mistaken for someone else . . ."

"Uncanny resemblance. I thought that too, at first. But the more I followed you, the more I stared at your face, that hair, that yellow dress . . . I knew it had to be you. *How*, I'm not quite certain but, the point is, this seemingly innocent artifact can cause quite a stir if handed to the wrong individual," he threatened, menacingly.

"What do you want from me?"

212

"For you to return back to where you came from, Annette. Or I'll be showing this to your bookseller."

"Who are you?" As he smiled, pocketing the obituary, Annette knew exactly who he was. Although it had been a little under ten years since they'd seen one another last, the darkness in his eyes, the sharp curve of his cheeks, even the smirk on his lips was unmistakable. "Jonas . . . ?"

Time wasn't about to allow him to answer. The breezeway folded and unfolded back to the offices. Jonas was no longer a series of wretched recollections. He had been there watching her every move around the bookseller since the first time she set foot in *The Muse's Corner.* Annette then realized how dangerous the situation had become with Adam.

Things didn't bode well for Annette. If Fiona's relationship with Alexander Thibodaux had caused the Head Muse so much grief, and if Nathaniel J. Cauliflower's relationship with Evangeline had brought about so much destruction due to a misplaced letter, Annette wondered how much damage would be inflicted on her if she turned Adam's peg one time too many. Certainly it didn't help matters in knowing that Jonas lived only five doors down from her bookseller. It wasn't stress that fed upon her emotions now. It was pure terror.

213

CHAPTER 18: FUNNEL CAKES AND OTHER HESITATIONS

Annette paced back and forth before her desk in her private office library, nervously biting on a cuticle. Certainly Jonas Rothchild was not aging well. He was beaten-down by stress but still the same man who had tortured her relentlessly when she was alive. It didn't come as much of a surprise that he would somehow, once again, bulldoze through her life. But things were slightly different than they had been before. She could've bowed-out gracefully and sworn to herself that, due to Jonas' attempts to devastate what was shared between the muse and the bookseller, she'd never turn the blue-colored peg again.

As Annette thought about it, she created a slight tread in the floor beneath her feet and wondered if perhaps a relationship with Adam the bookseller was worth the trouble. With the jury still out, a staff meeting was promptly called to order. To which all nine muses efficiently and begrudgingly congregated inside the larger office at the end of the hall. Management had reconstructed the conference room into a giant stage with acoustics for Niccolò Paganini to fine-tune his techniques while plucking happily on the strings of Lucas' guitar.

Nine swivel chairs were set into a circle around center stage, all facing inward, as if the muses were attending a support group gathering. The violinist Paganini strummed a few of the strings as Fiona stood regally from her swivel chair.

"Friendship Day was a success and for that both Management and I are appreciative. As you are all well aware, Niccolò Paganini is still with us, pending a date on which Management can send him back to his own time. To those of you who have made him feel welcome, thank you. To those of you who haven't, please do so." Fiona circled the outer area of the swivel chairs now with hands behind her back.

"I, Mr. Cauliflower, and Management wish to thank you for becoming more aware of your inspirations and setting aside your memories. Unfortunately, there's a *new* matter of importance that I feel we must discuss and that's 'peg-rotations'." Fiona stopped behind Annette, casting her eyes toward the muses.

Annette's face suddenly grew pale.

"Now, I'll be the first to confess, Muses, that *I* have turned a few pegs in my day. There's nothing more enticing than seeing the product of our handiwork. However, the reason we're *able* to turn the pegs isn't a reason we *should*. Turning the colored pegs is the responsibility of Mr. Cauliflower. Your job, Muses, is to simply inspire the person and move on to the next. Management has sent me a letter . . ." Fiona once again reached into her cream-colored pocket, revealing a blue envelope, which she carried while continuing to circle the swivel chairs. "Expressly forbidding any and all future peg-rotations forthwith. For some of you," Fiona turned her eyes to Annette's, but did not address her personally, "rotating the pegs has caused a lapse in inspirations. And that will not do.

"As far as the peg-rotations are concerned, Management has decided to keep a close watch on it. If anyone rotates a peg forward and/or backward after this point in time, Management will alert me and I'll be alerting you." Fiona took a breath now, pocketing the letter into the folds of her cream-colored pants suit jacket pocket. "I've personally spoken to Management about this particular issue and they've allowed each muse seven more rotations before receiving reprimands. In those seven rotations, finish whatever activities you have set into motion. Or there will be consequences."

"Consequences?" All eyes were once again back on Annette.

"Something to add, Mrs. Slocum?"

"What's going to happen if we turn the pegs again after the seven grace periods? What's the consequence?"

"A violet envelope," Fiona said rather plainly. The rest of the muses (including Annette) felt more than mildly uncomfortable. "For *each* peg you turn. I'm serious. Peg rotations is strictly forbidden from here on out. Make those last seven rotations count and focus on the jobs at hand."

The staff meeting was dismissed but Annette stayed in the swivel chair. When all but she and Fiona had cleared the conference room, Annette finally asked what had been buzzing about her head. "Why are you doing this, Fiona?"

"Management thought it necessary."

"Necessary."

"That's right, Mrs. Slocum."

"You're the one who's been trying to pull me and Adam together and now you're going to give up? Seven more peg rotations, Fiona."

"More than adequate."

"Seven, and then I'll never see him again."

"Never see him again?" Fiona looked concerned. "Who said anything about never seeing him again? All I said was 'a violet envelope for each rotation of a peg'."

"What are you saying?"

"That eventually you're going to have to make a choice, Mrs. Slocum. A relationship with Adam Mansfield during an employment of never-ending violet envelopes . . ." Fiona then shrugged her shoulders. ". . . Or not?"

*

For her first of seven peg-rotations, Annette figured that she'd put to bed the story of Doris the waitress. Perhaps if there was a happy ending with Doris there would be one for her and Adam despite Jonas' interference. Thus, she rotated the white colored peg with red polka-dots clockwise to find hundreds of funnel cakes sitting atop Doris' kitchen counter, dining room, and coffee table.

"Funnel cakes?" Annette asked aloud.

"Yes, funnel cakes." Sitting next to the oven in an apron, Doris stood; her hair all askew, thick black glasses on the bridge of her nose. When Doris saw Annette she nearly leapt over the

216

table. "My God! It's you! I mean . . . it's you! My own personal Jiminy Cricket! Only bigger."

The last time Annette had seen Doris, a series of unrequited Valentine's Days and failed relationships had raced by with a fateful encounter involving a dropped donut. The last time that *Doris* had actually seen Annette had been in the backseat of Doris' car at the funeral attended by the Man with the Eggs. And, from the looks of things, Doris had been busy. "Can I get you anything? Water? Funnel cake?"

"Water's fine." Annette figured she could skip the funnel cake as funnel cakes had never really been Annette's thing but Doris wouldn't have it. She sat her muse down on a stool and piled at least three funnel cakes into a makeshift mound of powdered sugar and crisp-fried batter. Annette couldn't help but wonder how many inspirations she would rip through on the high that such a frail delicacy would employ but said nothing.

"I did what you told me, Jiminy Cricket," Doris went on, "I figured that life was too short to sit around and watch him. So I thought long and hard about how I could show my secret affection."

"Did you think about writing him a letter?" Annette asked as she pushed the funnel cakes several centimeters away.

"Yes but, frankly, why would I write him a letter when I've never known exactly what I wanted to say?" Doris, thinking Annette's pile of funnel cakes wasn't big enough, piled. two more pushing them back to her muse.

"Flowers?"

"Flowers wither and die."

"So do funnel cakes," Annette sighed. As Doris flew through the kitchen with such excitement, Annette wondered how many funnel cakes the waitress herself had eaten before the muse returned for the second half of the story. "So you've made the Man with the Eggs funnel cakes."

"Yes, yes I have. When I was a little girl my parents would take me to various festivals and, no matter how heart-broken I was, I'd find joy in a funnel cake. So, what better way to pass it on to the man who visited the diner?" Somehow the peg didn't show this tidbit of Doris' life but Annette went with it anyway.

217

"And he's eaten them?"

"Not exactly." Annette wasn't quite sure she understood the point of the funnel cakes. Doris picked up on her confusion. "Well, they sit there on his front porch."

"And disintegrate." Annette failed to see the logic. "Why on his front porch? Why not hand them to him at the diner?"

"Because after the funeral he stopped coming in."

"But his porch . . ."

"Yes. If he decided to go out on his porch one day, he'd find a funnel cake."

"Decided to go out on his porch . . ." Annette stewed in confusion. "How would he even know they were there? Did you ring the doorbell?"

Doris stood defeated now and the same unhappiness that Annette first spied in the diner returned once again. In a fit of fury Doris threw all the funnel cakes, including the ones stacked on the plate before Annette, into a trashcan. Then came the tears. Annette had never been one for poo, or vomit, but she was definitely the woman to supply a shoulder to catch tears.

"Aww . . . Doris, come on. You need a game plan."

Doris continued to sob into the frills of her apron. "I've always been too afraid to ring the doorbell. Because what if he actually came *out*? What would I *say*? What would I *do*? What would I . . . ? I've had horrible luck in relationships."

"Well, let's find out what he'd say!"

"What?" Doris was in shock now as Annette pulled her to her feet, spying the trashcan.

"Obviously those are defective, but I have a feeling that the next one'll be the winner."

The two women prepared a fresh bowl of batter and discussed what they were going to do with the funnel cake once it was powdered and ready. They even took turns playing the various roles of the situation. Annette even had Doris laughing when she took on a manly voice for the character of the man.

"'Oh, a funnel cake,'" her voice was as deep as it would go. "'Come on in and let's get it on at the kitchen table'."

"Oh Jiminy Cricket, how horrible!" Doris squealed, trying to hide a smile. In a few short minutes, Annette had transformed into a social (and downright humorous) friend.

"No! No, wait!" Annette grabbed a towel from one of the drawers, rolled it up and stuffed it between her legs. Now the man from the diner was considerably well endowed. "Okay, start again." Doris pretended to ring the doorbell and Annette, playing the ever-so-hung Man with the Eggs, answered. "'Well, hello there, pretty little thing. Got any extra powdered sugar we can *sprinkle* about?'" Both women erupted in laughter but, when the oven bell dinged, they fell silent.

"It's done." Doris said in horror. Like two surgeons standing over a body with their various tools, Annette dramatically called for the powdered sugar then called for the car keys.

Doris' Honda Civic didn't protest as much as the Beetle Annette had driven to the library on the day that she had died. As they drove through town, both women sat in silent anticipation for the main event. Doris, more filled with dread, navigated while Annette drove the rundown vehicle. When they pulled up to the driveway, Annette's foot caught the brake. The tumbleweed-type bush by the mailbox at the end of the road was all too familiar. Not very long ago, Annette had stood at this driveway fetching the mail in her house-slippers. And, while she had fetched the mail, she had noticed Fiona in her cream-colored pants suit for the first time waving like a passenger on a great ocean-liner.

The Man with the Eggs was not the man with the eggs; he was the very same man she had longed for ten years to escape.

"Are you sure we have the right address?" Annette asked Doris. Her heart was thudding wildly in her chest. Doris verified that this was, indeed, the address of the man from the diner because after the funeral she had followed him home. Annette tried to remember the first time she had stepped into the diner. At first glance, she hadn't recognized anyone, yet there was the sliver of familiarity about the lonely man sitting in the booth. His head, if she remembered correctly, was bald. But the handlebar moustache that had literally made him Lyle had been missing. Therefore, Annette had mistaken him for another random person. How could she not have seen this before? Was he truly that different? Another colored peg had even taken her into the man's house! Their house! It wasn't a house that had a similar floor plan; it was the exact same abode that she'd spent cleaning after he had left for work!

"Had Management truly pulled the wool over my eyes that much," Annette wondered. *"I hadn't even recognized the details?"*

Annette was absolutely furious. Here she was meant to inspire Doris to put her heart and funnel cake on Lyle's doorstep when all Annette wanted to do now was turn the car around. That's exactly what she did. Annette, without a single word, put the Honda Civic into reverse and headed back down the street from which they had just come.

"Where are we going? I thought you said we were going to drop off the funnel cake." But Annette wasn't listening. She was too busy nursing her fury. Annette wasn't quite sure why she was enraged. Maybe it was because Lyle was mourning his loss, as if he actually *noticed* she was gone after years of pretending she wasn't there. Maybe it was because Management obviously thought it was some kind of demented joke to send a peg to her own husband's life (ex-husband's, actually, now that she reminded herself that she was dead). Or maybe it was the sheer fact that Doris had once again found herself a man who wouldn't treat her right and would, once again, wallow in her own loneliness.

"Jiminy Cricket, slow down!" But Annette had absolutely no intention of slowing down. What would it matter now if Annette ran into a tree? *She* certainly wouldn't die but Doris would. And, in Annette's mind, that was a far more hopeful future than the one she would ever have with Lyle. "I think that was a patrol car you passed."

Indeed, it was a patrol car. Within seconds it was racing after them with its lights flashing and its siren set to a banshee-like scream. All Annette wanted to do was get to the library and hide in the thousands of books; a library that was only a five-minute ride away. So she pressed on the gas.

"Are you crazy?" Doris protested the increase in speed. The funnel cake flew from her lap and showered her front with white powder. Perhaps Annette *was* crazy as things were certainly falling apart in all directions.

Annette then decelerated. If Doris was going to die it certainly wasn't going to be today. If Management felt it necessary to put Doris into a situation where she would suffer then Annette had to trust that it would progress positively. Things had worked out with Jonathan so perhaps there was hope. With the car pulled to the side of the road, and the window rolled down, the officer peered in wearing sunglasses. The brown aviator lenses hid his eyes from view. "License and registration," he said casually.

Thankfully, time did its fast forward thing taking Annette from the scene and leaving the front seat of Doris' car unoccupied. Moments later, Doris sat at the end of Lyle's driveway with the messed-up funnel cake in hand. The engine of the Honda Civic purred happily.

As before, Annette sat in the front passenger seat of Doris' car in silence.

"He was too stunned to write a ticket. It's not every day a person disappears like that... as if they never existed. He waved it off as a warning and stumbled off as if he'd seen a ghost." Doris had tears in her eyes. All hope was lost to her at this point. Without Annette's encouragement, how the hell was she going to ring Lyle's doorbell and give the funnel cake to him?

"I'm sorry," whispered Annette. "It's just . . . do you really want to get mixed up with a guy like that?" Her eyes were glistening with tears as she remembered all that she wanted to forget. "What if he's not the Prince Charming you think he is?"

"Well, what does it matter now that the funnel cake's ruined?" Doris' doubt had once again deflated her.

"Let's make another, then," Annette told her. And so they did. Later that afternoon the wind had picked up considerably and the car was in front of Lyle's driveway. Annette and Doris walked up to the front porch with the new funnel cake in hand; this was the same front porch that Annette had spent so many mornings going up and down to retrieve the morning paper and the afternoon mail. "You can do this, Doris," she encouraged.

"I can do this, Jiminy Cricket." Doris told herself as she stood like a waitress balancing a plate of appetizers. She pushed the doorbell but there was no response. "Okay, let's go."

"Try again."

"Come on, Jiminy Cricket . . ."

"Try again." Doris pushed the doorbell but it pained her to stay and wait. "Would you feel more comfortable if we left it on the porch?"

"Yes," Doris confessed. With the funnel cake left on the porch, Annette gave the doorbell one more ring (for good measure) and they ran like children back to the car where they peered over the hood in hopes that Lyle would come out to play.

However, it wasn't Lyle who came out to play. It was Annette's former self who answered the door. Annette finally remembered the extent of the experience with the Man with the Eggs: how she had stood in the living room unable to speak or make objects move, eventually opening the door herself where she had found the mysterious funnel cake. Annette wondered what she had done with the funnel cake once she had closed the door. Had she put it down or had she taken it with her? Did it fall to the foyer floor? Is that what happened?

"Who was that?" Doris wanted to know, as soon as the front door was closed again.

"It was me . . ."

"You?"

"It's sort of a long story."

"What were you doing inside of his house?"

"A colored peg took me there."

"A colored peg?" Doris was exasperated.

"Sort of like space-time continuums in *Back to the Future* . . . trying to explain it can be a little tedious."

"Well?"

"Well, what?"

"Did you give it to him or not?"

"I can't remember, Doris!" Annette was all of a sudden on the defense. "When the inspiration job is done, there isn't a voice that says 'set the funnel cake on the kitchen counter, the pop-up book is about to refold'."

It looked as if Doris was about to hyperventilate.

"Listen, Doris, I've got to get back to the office. Make him another funnel cake and *this* time stay by the door when he answers." Annette didn't want Lyle to have a happy ending but that certainly didn't mean Lyle didn't deserve one.

"Jiminy Cricket!"

"Stay by the door, all right? Promise me."

"Fine. I promise." By the time Doris looked back from the car to see if Annette was following her down the driveway, Annette had disappeared back into the offices.

*

She spotted Patrick in his office moments later with his head between his knees. Annette wondered what sort of malady had occurred. Clutched in his fist was a piece of paper which he used to fan himself. It was violet paper . . . an opened violet envelope. Apparently he'd recently returned from its perils. "Patrick?"

"Annette . . . Dear . . ."

"What's happened?"

"Did you know these things fall even if you don't rotate the pegs?" The water cooler in his office gurgled as Annette filled a cup of water handing it to him. "It was awful, Dear, awful. I'm only five pegs in and didn't quite expect for one to arrive so soon. But it arrived in my post box nonetheless. Such a beautiful color for those ignorant of its trials…"

"Where did it send you?"

"To a museum."

"That's okay," Annette patted his back. "Museums are a naturally quiet place."

"On field trip day."

"Oh . . ." *"What kind of sick game was Management playing at?"* Annette thought to herself as she refilled Patrick's cup of water.

"There were hundreds of children. About twenty to thirty groups with tour guides."

"Didn't your heart-strings tug?"

"Not at first. No one ever truly prepares you for the violet envelope. So on your first you begin to panic. Your

223

breathing becomes shallow, your vision narrows, and it feels like the walls are going to cave in on you. It certainly doesn't help having a distant thunderclap warning you of an impending expiration."

"What did you do, Patrick?"

"Stood still, Dear. Figured that Management had placed me in that specific spot for a reason. Considering the museum had three floors, I wasn't about to go exploring. Because they didn't give a name or a picture or age, I couldn't figure out if it was a child, parent, teacher, tour guide or the guy that mops the tile and places the wet signs to warn of the potential hazard. The thunder roared but, of course, I was the only one that heard it. It shook the walls and, with its vibrations, rotated the statues on their pedestals. If I didn't do anything and fast, the pop-up book was going to fold and unfold back into my office without the slightest bit of difference in evolution."

"And?" Annette, being the ever-so-imaginative person she was, could picture the chaos in her mind. She wondered what she would do if she were in that position, regardless of how much she didn't want to be in it.

"And then, before the building refolded, I spotted him. He was five years old and standing right in front of me - right in front of me, Annette! This entire time I'd been looking up, or searching the surrounding walls and banisters, not even aware that he was at my feet.

"'Are you lost?' I asked him. The little boy nodded his head. 'Let's see if we can find your mother' I said, and together we walked through the lobby. Each step I took was precarious as the floor itself was starting to give way. The boy felt nothing. And as I brought him to a painting, I felt a tug. So we stopped and stared up at it. It was something modern, definitely a work of art that I have never seen in my lifetime, but it was enough to catch the boy's attention. I have a feeling, Annette, that by taking his hand and going in search of his mother that an inspiration took place. This was my final thought as the pop-up book folded and unfolded."

"But you're winded," Annette didn't understand how taking a boy's hand would lead to the head between the knees and a violet envelope fanning the sweaty face.

"If violet envelope inspirations aren't bad enough, imagine how amplified the pop-up book is when it's over a thousand people instead of one. When the white envelopes fold, it's like a page turning in a novel. But when the violet envelope folds, it's something akin to an avalanche."

"An avalanche?"

"Whatever you do, Dear," Patrick took another sip of water, "avoid doing anything that might prompt an unexpected violet envelope."

Patrick's words held little aid in her recent encounter with Jonas, for how could she possibly make an informed decision about Adam with him blackmailing her with the obituary? To see past the murkiness, Annette knew her next step in her employment: to rid herself of the seemingly innocent artifact. She figured that if there had been hope for Doris, perhaps there was hope for Annette. Rescuing the obituary was a fool's errand, she knew. But she at least had to try.

CHAPTER 19: HARRIET'S STORY, OR A CHOICE OF CRUNCHY VERSUS SMOOTH

"As much as I hate to admit it," Annette told Harriet. A desk, inbox and Lite-Brite was between them. "We're much more alike than we'd probably prefer." Harriet said nothing, her eyes squinting, fingers propped against her lips. "I need help with a certain project and I don't feel comfortable confiding in Patrick."

"A certain project."

"You're an Eighth Generation muse, so you've suffered through plenty of envelopes." To which Harriet nodded. "Have you ever encountered a locksmith? Or perhaps a thief?"

"A locksmith or thief?"

"Who may or may not have given you some clue as to how to get inside a locked apartment door?" Annette blushed at the absurdity of her question but held tight to her guns anyway. "There's a man out there, living five doors down from Adam, who has something I need."

"Something you need." Harriet's face suddenly lit up with revelation. "Your obituary."

"How'd you guess?"

"I'm not too keen on the idea of thievery or sending you out on yet another peg-rotation." Harriet tossed up her hands. "Can't help you. I'm sorry. Find someone else."

"What do you have against peg-rotations?"

"Rotating pegs isn't our place. It's reserved for Nathaniel J. Cauliflower and Nathaniel J. Cauliflower alone."

"Did you give Lucas this much grief about them?" Mentioning Lucas' name struck a chord with Harriet, whose eyes squinted even more. "Yet he rotated them anyway, didn't he?"

"When a colored peg is rotated, Annette, a window in time is opened and I would hate to see a muse get stranded somewhere."

"Happened before, has it?"

"Yes, and I'm sure it will happen again. Rotating pegs is all fun for you and Lucas, but it's business, Annette. A serious business. And yes, I asked him not to rotate the pegs, but he turned them anyway. You're as stubborn as he was."

"We have a common ally." Annette decided to change tactics. "You're the only one I can count on." Harriet shook her head so Annette decided to switch tactics again. "Okay. Fine. Be safe inside this office experience nothing that might further your evolution." Annette stood up from the swivel chair but was stopped as Harriet spoke accepting Annette's bluff.

"I have encountered a thief." Harriet pursed her lips and repositioned the inbox on her desk a centimeter clockwise so it was flush with the edge of the desk. "I'm not the tyrant you make me out to be, you know." Harriet's words still dripped with disdain but underneath was something different. Something hidden. Harriet took a moment to consider her next words. "But I suppose people are the way they are because certain events have caused them to be . . ."

"Certain events?"

"If you and I are truly going to pair up and rescue your obituary, you need to understand where I come from." Annette nodded, though she was unsure how the next conversation would direct itself. "Lucas was there for me during a very dark time, you see. I'd like to show you."

From her unfolding fingers, Harriet produced a purple-colored peg and placed it on the desk. Annette recalled the color from Lucas' personal instruction booklet. The purple peg stemmed back to Melpomene, the Muse of Tragedy. Annette took it into her fingers, holding it up to the energy-efficient light bulbs. As Annette had six turnings left, she decided to sacrifice one for a good cause, turning to the doorway of Harriet's office only to find that Harriet wasn't following.

"Did you want me to rotate it alone?"

"I've already lived through it," Harriet frowned. "If you're still interested in having help afterward, you know where to find me."

With six turns left to administer before the great consequence, Annette sat in her own swivel chair and stared at the purple-colored peg pinched between her fingertips. Niccolò Paganini's violin screeched in the auditorium and the water-cooler gurgled a few bubbles in accompaniment.

Lucas, though retired, left imprints wherever he went. Whether notes in a moleskin journal or the facts of his existence before and after his inspiration, Lucas had taken extra steps to insure Annette's survival. Harriet had been nothing but a beast, that was for sure, but if Lucas had felt a perfectly good reason to form something between her and Fiona's assistant, then it was good enough reason for Annette.

With a sip of water, she reluctantly inserted Harriet's peg into one of the few remaining spots in her Lite-Brite board and waited for the show to begin. Harriet's peg bellowed like a ravenous lion around Annette and finally paused to an empty classroom where Harriet, nine years old, sat looking up at a chalkboard in thought. She returned to reading the book in front of her. A calendar on the wall read 1973. Several dates were marked off in anticipation of the upcoming holidays.

Outside the window it was a gray mid-afternoon. Snow drifted in abnormally large flakes. Sounds of snowball fights and crunching footsteps were audible outside the glass window, but nine-year-old Harriet didn't take any part in it. The image forth a recollection of Charles Dickens' *A Christmas Carol*, as young Harriet sat in the solitary company of the schoolbook. That is until fate, quite forcefully, intervened: a boy, no bigger than Harriet, with flushed cheeks, a stocking cap with a fluffy green yarn-ball on top, bulky mittens, and a fleece scarf around his neck entered the classroom with his snow-caked boots clumping heavily on the tiled floor.

"Harriet?" said the boy.

"I'm reading, Harold, go away."

"Harriet, would you like for me to walk you home? We don't have to talk or nothin.' Heck, you can read while we walk. I just want to walk you home."

"Harold, I wouldn't walk home with you if you were the last boy in the world."

Harriet then proceeded to walk herself home alone, wrapped in a large navy pea-coat, thick boots and suede gloves, with her nose pressed in the pages of the book. Time raced forward to the middle of the afternoon for the next fifteen years. A total of four thousand and fifteen times, the ever-growing Harold asked the ever-growing Harriet if he could walk her home. Each time Harriet always hurried home alone, eyes glued to the printed words before her. That is, until one afternoon when Harriet was sixteen years old and she had had enough.

"All right, Harold, yes, you can walk me home." And so, with book in hand, with red-bud trees, dog-wood trees, and forsythia bushes in full bloom around her, Harriet read the pages that were opened to the sunlight while Harold finally walked Harriet home.

"Boy, I sure am glad you finally agreed to let me walk you . . ." Harold said in earnest but Harriet was too busy reading a book to even notice the features of the now-handsome young man who was walking beside her. "Harold, you're blocking the sunlight."

Home for Harriet was a storey house with a white picket fence and well-scythed lawn. A beautiful house, save for the red pick-up truck in the driveway which, as they approached, caused Harriet to close the book and tuck the literature away in her backpack. The red pick-up truck obviously meant something bad to Harriet, but Harold was too much of a gentleman to ask why.

Prom night was next and far more entertaining. Here Harriet was wrapped in a baby blue dress as a man, who wasn't Harold, attached a corsage on her wrist. Annette was reminded of her own high school prom when her mother and father had chaperoned. The high school version of Annette had stood as a wallflower by the punch bowl, nibbling on dinner mints and salty cashews. But now, Annette told herself, was not the time for such memories.

Teenage Harriet danced with her date and, after countless hours that whizzed by in seconds, they ended up in the front seat of his car overlooking a lake. It was a typical variation on the ever-popular Lover's Lane, where poplars were painted perfectly in moonlight and fireflies flitted in a desperate attempt to mimic the stars.

Harriet's date was trying to get "fresh" and she certainly wasn't going to have it. What started as a playful tickle progressed into an argument about how she "wasn't ready," which ended up with Harriet's date driving off leaving her by the side of the moon-lit lake.

Sitting there staring at her silvery reflection in the surface of the water, Harriet sighed and turned her face up to the moon. There were tears on teenage Harriet's cheeks and, somehow, secretly and selfishly vindictive, Annette was glad to see them. *"If life came with a soundtrack,"* Annette once again thought to herself, *"the scenic background would have to be overlapped by a sad lament of a cello driven by a dramatic swell of a full orchestra."*

From the night's shadows emerged a fully grown Harold who, Annette thought, cleaned up rather nicely in a tuxedo. His bow tie dangled loose from his neck and the top two buttons of his shirt were undone revealing a slight hint of a wife-beater. Harold stood about two yards down the shore of the lake staring at his own reflection. After several minutes he seized a perfectly round stone and skipped it across the surface.

"Harold?" Harriet addressed him after the skipping rock jostled her from her reflection.

"Oh, hello, Harriet. Did you have a nice evening?"

"No, actually. It was horrible."

"Oh, I'm sorry to hear." There were no cars in the area which prompted the next question. "Harriet, where's Gil?"

"He left me here." Harriet continued to stare out over the water at the moonlight that lay on the water like melted Swiss cheese on a frying pan.

"Can I walk you home?" Harold asked. In response she looked up, hesitantly extended a hand, and together they walked down the road.

"Why do you want to walk me home, Harold?" Harriet inquired as he wrapped his tuxedo jacket around her shoulders to keep her warm.

"Because I like spending time with you."

"But you don't know me."

"I'd like to think I know you plenty."

"But you *don't*, Harold." Harriet looked down at her feet and kicked an acorn with her shoe. "There's a history about my family I've never told anyone."

"Well, if you feel uncomfortable telling me, that's fine." Harold, once again being the gentleman, didn't press the subject; he concluded it with "As long as you let me walk you home once in a while, I'll be a lucky man."

Shared silence transpired for the rest of the walk back to her front porch. Teenage Harriet was obviously uncomfortable spying the red pick-up truck in the driveway, but Harold said nothing. Once at her front door, Harold said goodnight and, because he was a well-raised man, didn't beg for a goodnight kiss. He simply smiled his "Harold grin" and tipped an imaginary hat.

"Sleep well, Harriet."

"Sleep well, Harold." Then, suddenly realizing she still had his jacket, Harriet stopped him after descending her front porch. "Harold, wait. Your jacket." Shoulder pads, buttons and pockets in the tuxedo jacket stood between them.

"Goodnight, Harriet."

"Goodnight . . . Harold."

An uncomfortable "friendship" between Harriet and Harold now raced before Annette's eyes. In the years that followed, they both shared an unspoken love for one another. But the friendship suffered when one or the other decided to branch out to other people. Time stopped several years later with Harriet staring at herself in an oval mirror. Her hands glided along the satin of a wedding dress. There were bridesmaids there in their own slightly more hideous dresses fitting the veil's net. "Beautiful," said one.

"Isn't it, though?" came Harriet's reply. "Do you think James will like it?"

"What happened to Harold?" Annette wondered and, as if the peg could detect the question, the walls dematerialized showing the back of the hall from which Harriet planned to proceed.

Harold stood fixing her veil when Harriet asked "How do I look?"

"Exquisite." Harriet smiled, her face slightly obstructed behind the veil. She processed down the aisle with Harold on her arm.

"Harriet should have married Harold," Annette thought to herself and was distraught to discover that Harriet's husband to be was a man named James Flournoy. Opening doors, eating delicious meals served in bed, laughing and tickling fits filled her world then. However, as all honeymoon periods eventually do, the situation turned sour. James began to change; he became physically abusive several years into the marriage. Whether it was the stress of his job or the fact that James wasn't ready to have children, whether his aggression was genetic, his abuse grew worse as the days went on.

"I've become my mother," Harriet said brokenly to her reflection in the bathroom cabinet mirror every morning when James would go off to work.

As much as Annette feared to watch it, Harriet was abused quite frequently, bruising not only the skin, but the soul. After ten painful years, it was another man whom she met at the grocery store who guided her to safety. Annette nearly gasped as Lucas appeared out of nowhere in Harriet's past while trying to decide on the kind of peanut butter he desired.

"Excuse me . . ." Lucas said to the past version of Harriet. Annette reached out to touch her friend's face but realized all attempts to touch his cheek were pointless. "If you were peanut butter, would you be chunky or smooth?" The past Harriet said nothing. She simply stared at Lucas as if he had seven eyes. The first question didn't elicit a response, so he asked another. "Peter Pan or generic then? I would *hate* to get myself into a sticky situation by picking the wrong peanut butter, 'cause once you pick the wrong one, it doesn't really work with the *jam* you thought you'd try it with. Then the whole sandwich is ruined, you know?"

The past Harriet simply stood and stared at the peanut butter. It took a few seconds for Lucas' question to take effect but soon Harriet's pupils lit up.

"Smooth."

"Smooth it is. Now, Peter Pan or generic?"

"Peter Pan."

"Good choice. Peter Pan *flies*, you know? Gotta love a man who flies. I've always had this dream where I'm standing on a great cliff then I *kick* myself into the air and soar with eagles . . . anyway." As Lucas went on with his wild tangent, Annette watched in remembrance. Oh, how she missed his conversations! He had warned her over their first meal that he was a talker, and Annette recollected even that exchange fondly.

"It's interesting that whenever *Peter Pan's* acted on stage it's always by a woman," continued Lucas. "So, in actuality, it's the *woman* who flies." Even though the past Harriet couldn't detect it, Annette felt the slight roll of thunder as Lucas winked and said, "Anyway, I've got to go. Good luck with the smooth Peter Pan." And then he exited into another aisle.

Before Annette had any time to process what any of this meant to the past Harriet, time once again jetted forward. Once again, James had given a shiner to Harriet. His wife ripped through the closet and the exposed hangers swished on the pole on which they dangled. "Don't you get it, James? You're the *crunchy* and what I need is *smooth!*"

"Don't you put those dresses in that suitcase, Harriet! If you know what's good for you!"

"I do know what's good for me, James, and what I need is *not* in this house! Or in this marriage! It's not with you!" This new found wave of confidence was bewildering to the former version of Harriet but, as the pile of dresses accumulated in the suitcase on the bed, she felt compelled to continue. James took the suitcase and threw it against the wall. Its contents scattered along the floor. Harriet then debated if it was even worth it to retrieve them. "That's fine. I didn't need them anyway."

Harriet went to the bathroom where she rummaged through the medicine cabinet for her toothbrush and face cream. James slammed the medicine cabinet shut with his hand. "You aren't leaving this house, Harriet."

"I certainly am, James." Harriet promptly surrendered her toothbrush and face cream to the tyrant and headed for the stairs. James wouldn't hear of it and instead grabbed Harriet by the shoulders shaking her several times. When that didn't work, he slapped her so hard that she toppled down the stairs to the first level of the house.

For a moment, James and Annette thought past Harriet was dead. But James was soon disappointed as she straightened, stood and stared back up the stairs to her husband. "Harriet?" said James, who started down the stairs after her.

Annette had to race down the stairs behind James to see what happened next. The past Harriet soared through the living room where a low flame was flickering in the fireplace, then to the foyer where she almost unhinged the front door with super-human strength. A strong evening wind almost touched her cheek but James was indomitable on seeing that she didn't leave. Thus he grabbed her by the hair. Husband and wife went back inside the living room. Even though Annette tried to keep James from attacking Harriet, she still went straight through with the consistency of the dead. Fancy that this was the one peg in which the post-inspiration *wasn't* interactive. The toughest lesson Annette learned then was that some things needed to happen, no matter how terrible.

Now the past version of Harriet grabbed a fire-poker and, finally with the upper hand, took it down hard on James. Blow after blow, it become eventually evident that James wasn't getting up.

"I . . . need . . . smooth . . . James!" Each word was accented by her blows with the fire poker as she gave back James all the pain she'd received from him. Finally, the past Harriet stood in silence with the fire crackling close by. Triumphantly, she then climbed the stairs and gathered her dresses, toothbrush, and facial cream in peace.

As the night roared on and abnormally large snowflakes began to drift down, the sick feeling in Annette's stomach subsided. Past Harriet traipsed through the snow and found herself on Harold's doorstep. When he appeared at the door, she didn't fall into his arms. She simply asked "If you were peanut butter, would you be crunchy or smooth?"

"Smooth." The answer was apparently what Harriet needed to hear.

Throughout the night, the guest bed in the house was occupied and, by the morning, the guest bed was still taken. All through the afternoon, through the evening, and the next morning, as the snow continued to fall, Harold wanted to go in and check on Harriet. As he was still been the perfect gentleman, he didn't feel it right to disturb her. It was as if Annette could see two sides of the story co-existing together. In the guest bedroom, past Harriet was sleeping. And in the hallway just outside Harold waited by the door for the moment she would part from the sheets.

"Wake up, Harriet." Annette whispered but it seemed that her words were a waste of breath. In Harriet's case, it seemed there were no more breaths to be had. The pop-up book that was Harriet's life hesitated; time stood still as Harriet's body grew limp. It was obviously the last moment of Harriet's life but, as Annette hadn't been thrust back into Harriet's office, there was obviously more to come.

The bedroom and hallway were replaced by the waiting room, the water cooler, the two doors, nine chairs and the stealthy second-hand gliding on the single clock's face. When the door opened to reveal Fiona in her cream-colored pants suit, Annette was absolutely captivated.

"Mrs. Flournoy?"

"Harriet," the past Harriet looked up. "Just Harriet."

"All right, Harriet. Would you follow me, please?" One instructional video later, and one lecture on violet envelopes, Harriet was given an office, a Lite-Brite board, and an empty inbox.

"I don't get it," Annette said. "How does the peg still consider our deaths part of our lives?"

As Harriet's story ended and Annette was once again deposited in her office and swivel chair, all was quiet and still. The events of Harriet's life were changing Annette's entire perspective. Annette found Harriet in her own swivel chair. Harriet's eyes were glued to the hallway where she could see the edge of the post box by her office door. There were only ninety-two pegs left in Harriet's employment and the grid was beginning to fill up rather quickly with various colors leaving only three and a half rows left to fill.

"How did you . . ." Annette stepped into the doorless office. "What I mean to say is . . . why didn't you wake up?"

"A torn aorta." Harriet turned her eyes to the desk's surface. "Happened in the fall down the stairs. Humans are monstrous," Harriet told Annette. "It's safe here."

"But they can also be filled with hope and capable of wonderful things," Annette replied. "A good friend with a violin taught me that."

Harriet looked away from the ceiling now, turning to Annette.

"Perhaps the field trip will be good for you." Annette said.

Harriet scoffed.

"Trust me, Harriet. If at any time you don't feel up to it, you have my permission to return back here where it's safe."

"Fine, Annette. Let's rescue the obituary." Harriet stood from her swivel chair, tucking the chair underneath her desk and circling around to the door. There was a height difference between the two and Annette marveled at how a woman taller than she was more frightened of the world outside these walls. "Fiona was right about you, Annette. You certainly have changed since you first arrived."

"Life can't all be smooth, Harriet." Annette guided her out into the hallway. "It's suffering the crunchy moments that truly makes us who we are."

236

CHAPTER 20: IN THE HALL OF THE METEOROLOGIST KING

As Annette watched Adam Mansfield sleep, she longed to lift his arm and curl under it to feel the heat of his body against hers. The moonlight shining through his open bedroom window painted the muscles of his cheeks, neck, and forearms perfectly. The sight was so inviting and so tempting. It was one of those perfectly warm summer evenings with a slight breeze. A birthday card, signed by his mother Gwendolyn, was on his bedside table with a note inside that read "to savor the memories of you and Annette." There was an empty picture frame beside the birthday card which she could only deduce was the actual gift: a silver frame that might one day hold a picture of the woman who had died three years before.

But Annette had other plans that pulled her from its appeal. The plan was simple. Steal the obituary. It seemed the only logical solution really, for how could she possibly make a well-thought-out decision with Jonas Rothchild's blackmail? There were two alternatives. One, she could steal the obituary from Jonas three years earlier – but, then again, her death was more fresh back then and he could easily steal another. The second was to steal the obituary from the current time, three years later, when it would be far more of a challenge for Jonas to find another copy. So the plan was set into motion. Annette and Harriet would turn Adam's peg clockwise, jimmy Jonas' lock while he slept, steal the obituary, and end Annette's suffering.

Putting the plan into action, however, caused the knot in Annette's stomach to tighten even more. Watching Adam sleep was a subtle reminder as to her reward, so she quietly slipped out of the bedroom, abandoning the bookseller and the empty silver frame, passing through the history book collection that was his living room, carefully tiptoeing so as not to stir him. Harriet stood up from the couch in the living room. How frail she looked in the moonlight like an ice sculpture slowly melting. The door-chain was latched in place. Cautiously scraping the tiny brass ball against the track, Annette unhinged it and let it dangle in a pendulum fashion.

When she tried the door it was stuck. So she tried pulling harder, until it gave a sound akin to fat buttocks suctioning off of a plastic beach chair. Trying to make as little sound as possible it seemed that Annette caused far more noise than anticipated. She could hear Adam stirring in the bedroom and knew that if he caught her all hopes would be lost. Annette, followed by Harriet, snuck out of the open door and into the breezeway. Stars in the night sky shone shyly from between the passing clouds and a light sprinkling of dew glistened on the tree leaves and grass below.

They crept along the breezeway with the stealth of lions on the hunt for a lone zebra. Recognizing the fifth apartment door down as Jonas' Annette stood aside and allowed Harriet to put her knowledge to good use. Harriet's hair was always up in a bun but tonight a single tendril hung down to her back as she removed one of the hairpins. She fit it into the lock.

There was a click from both the dead bolt and the regular keyhole below and, as the door slid open a crack, both women peered in to find pitch darkness. Harriet used the hairpin as tweezers and carefully managed to unhinge the chain that kept the door from opening further. For the most part it was quiet inside. No lights on at all. But there was a sound of a deep snore bellowing from the bedroom. Slipping into the shadows of Jonas' apartment, Annette turned to find Harriet standing motionless in the breezeway.

"Coming in or staying out?"

"Staying out," Harriet nodded. "Yes, I think that's the best thing." Harriet's perfect demeanor was slightly unraveled by the loose tendril of hair. Annette waved, closed the front door behind her, and began the hunt for the obituary.

Moonlight aided in her search as she first inspected the living room and kitchen saving the bedroom for last. Jonas' apartment layout was identical to that of Adam's but the two men had entirely different tastes in décor. Jonas' living room had a large screen television, a digital cable box, and a single VCR. Stacked within an entertainment system was a hefty collection of movies and television series. One single video tape poked out of the VCR. Labeled with a date three years prior, Annette pushed it into the machine. Half out of curiosity, Annette switched on the television immediately lowering the volume to mute.

Although she couldn't readily hear the words, Annette watched his marriage to a woman she'd never before seen. The man on the video was certainly not the man blackmailing her with the obituary. What had transpired in his life to alter his demeanor so dramatically? Jonas continued to snore in the bedroom so, in the greater glow of the television screen, Annette decided to continue snooping for the obituary.

Jonas apparently ate only microwave dinners and didn't even have the decency to recycle the cardboard boxes in which his meals were contained. Oversized pizza boxes, crunched up grease-spotted fast food sacks, Styrofoam cups, and dented soda cans filled his small living room beside the recliner. How he managed not to have clogged arteries and still managed a decent shape Annette only wondered. Jonas was a man who read newspapers and the crisp documents were stacked haphazardly all over on the kitchen table. Like Adam, Jonas was a historian of sorts, who focused on history more closely related to him. Flipping through various newspapers, Annette was happy to find that none of them were dated anywhere near her death but, instead, were far more recent. On the dining room table, she dug even deeper into Jonas' life as she spied pay stubs. It was in this moment she discovered his occupation: a meteorologist. Annette then found divorce papers and letters regarding custody hearings. Turning her eyes to the video on the television screen, all the pieces were starting to glue together.

In all the excitement of rifling through the papers, Annette failed to realize how quiet the bedroom had become. Jonas had stood up from the edge of his bed causing the springs to squeak slightly. He crossed into the narrow hallway between the bedroom and the bathroom. Annette caught sight of his ghostly figure. She felt the hair on her forearms begin to rise. Jonas, though slightly ruffled and obviously naked, was still too half-asleep to see her. The light of the television did, however, catch his attention.

Annette stood perfectly still next to the television, knowing full-well that if she darted, Jonas would catch her. Thankfully, just the right amount of shadow was keeping her hidden from his half-glazed eyes. Trying not to stare at his naked physique, Annette felt a wave of disgust. She had never found him even the least bit attractive, and now, with adulthood tacked on to his physical features, she was even less enthralled by his attributes.

Wondering what his television was doing on, Jonas approached it. His eyes focused on the screen and the muted words. Annette hoped he wouldn't look an inch or two to the left or else she would be spotted. Jonas reached for the television remote and switched it off plunging the living room back into darkness. With Jonas wandering to the bathroom and switching on the exhaust fan, Annette didn't want to think about what he was about to do and, once again, found herself facing two alternatives. One, she could abandon the mission and resign herself to the fact that her enemy had won or two: search his room for the obituary while he did his business. Reluctantly deciding on the latter, Annette tiptoed to the bedroom while Jonas picked up a newspaper from the bathroom counter. She could hear the heavy stream of his urine which was a perfect sign as to his movements while she stealthily searched his nightstand.

There, in the moonlight, she found her old repaired library books: Tolkein's *The Hobbit*, Stoker's *Dracula*, and Hugo's *Les Miserables*. She even found his copy of *The Picture of Dorian Gray* by Oscar Wilde. She picked it up and flipped through its pristine white pages. After ten years it still looked brand new . . . but now was not the time for memories.

From inside the bottom cover, the tattered obituary that caused all her worries fluttered to the floor. She placed *Dorian Gray* onto the nightstand and reached for the make-shift

240

bookmark. Annette took it in her fingers and held the announcement up to the moonlight. It seemed it had been forever since she had been hit by Jonathan's Cadillac in front of the library yet here was the obituary, much like the copy of *Dorian Gray*, which was perfectly preserved for sinister purposes.

As the toilet flushed in the bathroom and Jonas crossed the space between the bathroom and bedroom, Annette spun. There wasn't anywhere for her to hide. If she didn't find a spot in the next few seconds all attempts to steal the obituary would be futile.

The bedroom door quietly slid open as he entered. Without any other option, Annette slid under his bed into the tight space between the floor and his mattress. The weight of the mattress pressed down upon her now as he climbed into bed and there they coexisted for several uncomfortable minutes: the meteorologist and the muse. Suffocating, yet clutching the obituary, Annette once again longed for a deep breath. Feeling pin-pricks in her fingertips and pressure on her lungs, Annette wondered if perhaps it was possible for her to die a second time. Was she truly immortal as a muse? Was she a ghost or simply given another shot at life with the same body she'd had for the previous thirty years? All these questions and more filtered through Annette's brain as she began to lose consciousness, the last bit of air escaping from her nostrils. The last memory of Jonas came to Annette like a swarm of fire-ants climbing about a giant mound of dirt.

*

Three years into her marriage with Lyle, Annette had already fallen into a healthy pattern of waking up at five fifteen, showering with soap and shampoo with a twinge of peppermint, retrieving the morning paper in her housedress and slippers from the tumbleweed-type bush that haunted the mailbox, preparing Lyle's bacon and cantaloupe, and pouring the coffee. Although she had received a copy of *Les Miserables* as a belated wedding present from the stranger who performed miracles on dismantled library books, Annette still had not yet discovered the identity of the individual who had repaired it.

One spring morning, birds were chirping somewhere in the distance and both white and yellow dandelions were sprouting from the front lawn among the clovers and grass. Ants already began their marches through the terrain and a bumblebee was hovering menacingly over a potted plant on the kitchen windowsill. Annette was sitting at the kitchen table taking a bite of her granola and drinking tap water as Lyle was devouring a slice of cantaloupe. His handlebar moustache was wet with its juice. It was the first day that she began to notice that Lyle didn't seem to respect the meal offered to him and it was the first moment that she realized he probably wouldn't offer groans of satisfaction for any meals that followed. Life had become stale and eventless. She had fallen into a monotony that wouldn't be broken until seven years later, when Jonathan's blue Cadillac would change everything.

As usual, Lyle was wearing his lucky tie and dress shirt, ironed dress pants, and leather shoes. He kissed his wife on her cheek and opened the front door to greet the morning.

"Is Annette in?" Another man's voice came as quite a shock to Annette since on the previous mornings the front of the house was usually quiet. Annette stood up from the kitchen table and peered through the curtains of the kitchen window to find Jonas standing in her front lawn with a book in his hand.

"Who's wanting to know?" asked Lyle, standing between Jonas and the front door of the house.

"Jonas . . . just Jonas. Annette and I went to school together, years ago."

"And?"

"And I recently read an interesting book and thought she might like to read it."

Lyle considered taking the book from Jonas but, instead, his handlebar moustache fell framing a frown as a revelation crossed his features.

"If I could just see her for a second..."

"You were the one on that rainy day with quite a few nasty words, in my car lot. You're Thomas Rothchild's son."

242

"Yes, sir." Jonas suddenly looked as if he was embarrassed by his actions. "Consider the book a peace offering. When you see her next, will you tell her . . . tell her I was wrong about burning *Les Miserables*." Jonas held out the book between them. Eventually Lyle took it. Jonas looked as if he was about to turn, climb back into the used car, and leave them forever, but his eyes caught sight of Annette in the kitchen window. "Annette? Is that you?"

Annette closed the open kitchen window and shut the curtains, but it did little to shield her from the following conversation.

"No, no sir. My wife isn't interested in talking to you."

"But if she'd only give me one minute to explain-"

"You've brought your book . . ."

"Annette!" Jonas' voice was raised above Lyle's. "Haven't you ever wondered who stitched up those library books?"

"That's enough, Mr. Rothchild . . ." But Lyle's words couldn't deter Jonas.

"*The Hobbit, Dracula, Les Miserables* . . . for the longest time I couldn't place it - until I saw him, Annette!" Jonas' face was slightly distorted by the closed fabric of the kitchen window curtain yet it was unmistakable. "This book, right here in my hand, Annette, was shoved through a paper shredder, a single page at a time, and now here it is, completely intact!"

"Kindly step away from the porch." Lyle tried his best to keep Jonas from Annette, who then opened the curtain to see the state of the book. Indeed it looked as if it had been stitched together in the same way as all the others.

"Miraculous to say the least wouldn't you say?" Flipping through the paper, he fanned the pages like cards in a rolodex. The three of them stood in their respective places, two men on the lawn and Annette in the kitchen, all eyes affixed to the wonder of the rescued book. "So I tried it again. But this time I didn't use the paper shredder. I flung it into wet cement where it was buried . . . buried! And still, he was able to stitch it back together as if nothing had happened to it at all. Grease stains, spilt wine, shears, a lawn mower, the sharp tips of sewing needles . . . whatever I did to the pages, the book was . . . over a certain amount of time and with meticulous care . . . fixed."

Annette then cracked open the kitchen window which allowed fresh air to circulate. Jonas approached the kitchen window with the book holding it up to her as if it were a rose and he a prince attempting a rescue. Lyle remained on the lawn watching Jonas and his wife survey the book yet he said nothing.

"Come with me, Annette," Jonas told her. "Together we'll ask him how he does it." Annette and Lyle met eyes at this point, her lips tightening pensively. "What's wrong?" Jonas looked to Lyle, then back to Annette. "Don't tell me you're gonna stay in this house . . . and . . . when you can go out and find out the answers!"

"That's exactly what she's doing," Lyle finally piped up, taking the repaired book and shoving it into his enemy's shoulder, pushing Jonas back to the road. "From the first moment I met you, I've known what kind of influence you've had on Annette. From now on, I'd appreciate it if you'd let her be happy."

"Happy?" Jonas had scoffed as Lyle opened the front door of Jonas' car. "Annette's never been happy. Annette, come with me, I'll protect you; and keep you safe!"

"Enough," interrupted Lyle. "Now, in the car if you will please." It was more of an order than a request. Lyle shoved Jonas into the car seat. Defeated, Jonas disappeared from Annette's life as his car rolled down the street and out of sight beyond a patch of trees. Lyle turned back to Annette who still stood in the kitchen window. He smiled and Annette smiled slightly in return. Jonas had been vanquished . . . that was, until ten years later.

*

Now here Annette was, crushed beneath Jonas' mattress and feeling the last bit of air leave her lungs. She tightly gripped the obituary determined between her fingers. Thankfully, when Jonas climbed up from the bed, he released the grip on Annette's figure. She took in a deep, yet precarious intake of breath. As he shuffled his way into the kitchen, Annette herself shuffled out from under the confined space realigning the symmetry of her body. She was trapped inside his bedroom now with the obituary in hand; although she'd planned the beginning of the rescue mission, ending it was quite another matter entirely.

How could she get the obituary out of the apartment with Jonas in close proximity to the front door? That was Annette's main concern as she peered out of the bedroom door to the living room where a rectangle of light from an open refrigerator humbly glowed. Thirty-three year old Jonas' naked form was illuminated as he stood with a glass of milk holding the book that so many years ago he'd tried to offer to her. Deep in the night when he couldn't sleep, Jonas had apparently flipped through the pages of *Dorian Gray* in an attempt to better understand how it had been reconstructed so often.

Jonas held the answer as to who had repaired her library books and the mere possibility of uncovering the mystery was too thrilling. But if she announced herself, chances were she would forfeit the entire operation. If she was meant to know who had stitched her book together, she'd find out another day.

There was a look that suddenly appeared in Jonas' eyes for now he was completely awake and understanding the current situation. In a sleepy daze, he'd simply switched off the television, but how was it initially turned on? Her heart was racing as he examined the television, then the front door, where he carefully fit the chain back onto the track. Then he sniffed the air. Annette couldn't hide in the remaining shadows fast enough as Jonas rushed into the bedroom only to find the muse attempting to shred the screen of the bedroom window in hopes of escape.

"What the hell are you doing here?" he asked her. But Annette was silent. Her heart was thudding in her chest as Jonas' eyes locked on to the obituary. "I should've known you'd attempt to steal the evidence. Now let's not do anything stupid Annette. Hand it over."

Annette dodged around the mattress at this point, shoving her full weight into Jonas' naked body. As he'd just recently stirred, Jonas wasn't at the top of his game, sending his shoulder blade into the corner of his dresser while Annette raced out the door to the living room. She didn't care how much noise it made to attempt to remove the chain lock on the door but, in all her nervousness, her fingers fumbled several times. Jonas, now wearing a pair of boxer shorts and wife beater, snatched her left wrist which held the obituary. In a battle for possession, the muse and meteorologist spun from the living room to the kitchen to the living room again, sending his empty pizza boxes, daily newspapers, and video recordings of his weather reports into a maelstrom.

"Give me the damn obituary, Annette!" Jonas bellowed but Annette held firmly onto the newspaper article. On top of the raucousness in the apartment, Harriet was beating on the other side of the door, twisting the door handle. "Why can't you," Jonas held Annette several inches into the air against the kitchen cabinets, the muscles in his forearms stretching. Several pots and pans clattered to the floor. "Just . . . stay . . . away?" His face was red and his nostrils were flared. Snatching the obituary from her fingers, he dropped Annette to the floor. He towered over her now. The shadows on his skin took awkward shapes by the overturned lamps in his living room. "This is mine! Do you hear me, Annette?"

In the craziness, Harriet had once again managed to unlock Jonas' door and this time swung it open striking the meteorologist from behind. Taking one of the pots, Harriet wielded it. Before Jonas could stop the attack, the muse knocked him unconscious. Annette watched as Harriet extracted the obituary from Jonas' motionless fingers and grasped Annette's hand. She yanked Annette to her feet and pulled her along behind her toward the breezeway. Their footsteps, which had been so quiet moments before, now thudded on the cement. Out under the stars, moon, and dew-dappled foliage Annette and Harriet found sanctuary in Adam's living room, closing and latching the door behind them. Annette slumped by the front door reading the obituary and studying her rather unflattering picture. Harriet sat beside her even more ruffled than before.

"Everything okay?" Adam appeared in the living room now offering the muses a hand up from the floor. With a sly smile, he beckoned Annette the muse into his arms where he held her and felt the rhythm of her anxious heartbeat. "Nice to see you too, Annette." How she held on to him, so tightly, knowing that Jonas couldn't possibly explain how she'd been dead without proof . . . proof that she had in her hand. Proof that Adam then discovered. "What's this? A love letter?"

"Adam . . ." Adam teased the obituary from her fingers, switching on the living room light. The sly smile on his lips faltered as his eyes scanned the message. "I can explain, I can..." But his living room folded and unfolded revealing the office and water cooler that so often greeted her.

Annette collapsed into the swivel chair tasting blood on her lower lip. Upon further inspection she found she had a paper cut from the disturbed newspapers in Jonas' living room. Though her body truly had been smeared across the pavement before the library, and though for a brief moment she held the obituary that proved it, the muse in the yellow dress discovered then that she was still as easily bruised. Harriet was sitting in an opposite swivel chair.

Annette didn't know which was worse: fifty-seven white envelopes in her post box or the fact that Adam had found the stolen obituary. Either way, she did what any good muse would do. She began opening each envelope with the cut on her lip becoming more pronounced as she set out to inspire others despite her own woes.

CHAPTER 21: REMAINING ROTATIONS

Following the rescue attempt, Annette and Harriet managed their friendship well despite their differences. While Annette concocted a list of her last remaining rotations, Harriet attempted to avoid comments about the envelopes in the post box Annette neglected for more than thirty seconds. While Harriet ordered the meteor shower for Mr. Andrew's retirement party, Annette tried her best to stay out of trouble. They reminisced about Lucas over the water cooler in the hallway and sat and listened respectfully to the concerts that Niccolò Paganini put on in the conference room while he strummed the strings of Lucas' guitar. But whenever they set out to inspire their respective clients they did so alone.

Annette made sure to redeem herself with the other muses, first apologizing for her one "bad day" and then attempting to forge new friendships. She found that she actually enjoyed being around Mrs. Donnelly and her outgoing nature. Annette made sure to bring Mrs. Donnelly various dishes that Nathaniel J. Cauliflower had delivered; she did this in the same fashion that Lucas had done with Annette in the very beginning. Annette did her best to make Patrick feel more at home than before by sitting and talking with him on his personal front porch office. And finally, once Annette stopped fighting her feelings about Paganini wielding Lucas' guitar she discovered that she rather enjoyed listening to him play.

Between her last few remaining rotations, Annette inspired ninety-two individuals and took extra care in delivering the best customer service possible. She took extra heed not to involve herself in any more stories aside from those she had been already invested in which pained her on several accounts. Knowing the details of a person's life before and after an inspiration had complicated things, yes, but the temptation had been sometimes too great to ignore.

With her list of remaining rotations prepared, Annette intentionally repositioned the respective colored pegs further and further down the grid for easier access. Annette planned to deliver Niccolò Paganini to Jonathan before returning the violinist back to his own time which probably would've required two turns all together. Because Paganini had not yet been given a time to depart, Annette skipped that turn on her list and moved on to the next.

There were two alternatives for her next departure and neither of them sounded appealing: the first was to rotate Lyle's colored peg clockwise and get him to answer the door when Doris rang the bell and the second was to face Adam and his reaction to the obituary eventually having to tell him goodbye. She figured that it was probably the best for both of them. Chances are, now that Adam knew she was dead, he wouldn't want to be with her. Picking the lesser of two evils, Annette found Lyle's colored peg and rotated it, sacrificing one of her last turns for not only Doris but her former husband as well.

Annette still wasn't convinced that Lyle would be the best match for Doris the way he guzzled his coffee and masticated his eggs without reaction. Doris the waitress had waited a long time with sorrow. She deserved better, much better than Lyle Slocum. It wasn't up to Annette to question what Management had set into motion, nor was the situation really for Annette to manipulate after the initial inspiration, now that she thought about it. She did it regardless.

*

It was raining when Annette returned once again to the Man with the Eggs. How she wished that he had simply been the Man with the Eggs instead of Lyle but Management (whether she liked it or not) played unfairly. When she first arrived to the house she noticed that she was still invisible. No amount of waving her hands in front of Lyle's face would have pried him from his misery. Annette puzzled over how ghosts do it, wondering if she could coerce a penny to scoot up a doorway. Annette even tried whispering a subtle encouragement in Lyle's ear. There was nothing she could do. Lyle kept watching *Wheel of Fortune* with the same blank stare across his eyes.

Annette breathed deep deciding to switch tactics.

"Management?" For the first time, she felt she had enough confidence to address her employer personally. The rain fell heavier now with a slight hint of fluttering envelopes breaking forth from the water droplets. "Management, you've gotta give me some help here. I know that you don't encourage rotating the colored pegs, but please . . ."

It was then that Annette suddenly felt more in the space than ever before. She actually felt the carpet beneath her feet, smelled the mildew on unwashed dish-rags, and even heard the rain drops outside more succinctly. Management had answered her prayer by performing a nonconventional miracle. Lyle, sans the handlebar moustache and comb over, was still sitting in his recliner staring into the shadows when Annette stepped into the muted rainy afternoon light. He jumped as her hand touched his shoulder from behind.

"Annette?"

"Yes, Lyle, it's me."

"Are you really here?"

"Yes Lyle, I'm here." The house, now that she gave it a closer look, was exactly as she had remembered it, only with many more dirty dishes and much more wrinkled laundry strewn about. "Lyle, haven't you hired a maid?" Figuring that this was her last moment with Lyle, and also considering that at any moment now Doris would be ringing the doorbell with yet another funnel cake, she flew open the doors and windows, despite the rain, and gutted the house of its stench.

Lyle was in awe as Annette piled dishes and carried them to the sink where they came crashing down like clashing cymbals.

"Annette, you look good. Radiant, actually. Considering you've been dead for a few weeks." Radiant wasn't quite the word she'd use but she took the compliment regardless. In a mirror she spotted the yellow dress she'd worn since visiting

250

Patrick's before Lucas' retirement party. She had to admit that the transformation from the housedress did suit her quite well. But now was not the time for such thoughts as she stuffed trash into black bags and recyclables into the blue.

"Thank you. I wish I could say the same for you. You've fallen into depression, Lyle, and that can't happen."

"Annette." Lyle held open a trash bag as Annette scooped crumbs from the kitchen counter into the palm of her hand dumping them into the receptacle. "Can we talk?"

"Oh," Annette couldn't help but laugh. "Now you want to talk. After ten years of marriage, shoveling your damn eggs and reading the paper, and ignoring me day-in-and day-out! Now that I'm dead, you want to talk!"

"Yes." He followed behind her now with several coffee mugs. He grasped the handles with shaking hands.

"Fine, Lyle. Talk. What is it that you have to say?" The dishes, covered by water and soap, were not visible under the bubbles.

"I . . . wasn't a very good husband," he confessed.

Annette overfed the washing machine with shirts and turned the dial. She really didn't want to hear what her husband had to say. She was determined to accomplish only one thing: to get him and Doris together according to Management's designs.

"No, you weren't a good husband," she agreed, rushing then to the bedroom where she removed the bed sheets and replaced them with new ones. Though they were the words she had longed to hear for ten years in their marriage, they were meaningless now. "I wasn't a very good wife, either, I suppose," she admitted.

"No, Annette. You were a great wife. Waking up every morning at five fifteen, cooking breakfast, doing the housework. But I gave up on you." With these words, Annette ceased all motion. There was a roll of thunder that shook the house at that moment. Without his handlebar moustache, Lyle looked like a completely different person. Yet his voice was the same. "I've been going over it again and again wondering what I should've said or done to eventually get you to open up to me, but after a while I sort of gave up. I shouldn't have given the guy at the emergency room my business card. I should've let you stay with

251

your family at Thanksgiving. I should never have mentioned the butter knife. Annette." When he grazed her face with the side of his hand, Annette closed her eyes and allowed herself to feel it. "Had I known it was going to be your last morning . . . before I kissed your cheek and left for work, I would have called in sick. I would have tried so hard to get you to talk to me."

Annette shrugged and said "It doesn't matter now."

"Imagine how hard it was when I found out that one of my own used cars hit you."

"I met him, you know." Annette finally came back to her senses and brushed his hand away. "Jonathan was . . . *is* actually a decent guy. Yes, he made a few mistakes. But he learned from them. He grew. I saw my own corpse, too, at the mortuary. There's nothing quite like looking at yourself once you've died." Was it what Annette said or the whirring of the washing machine that once again lulled Lyle into a silence? She wasn't sure. Had he even changed? Or would he stare at her speechless until she eventually left for the office? Annette figured she'd said enough to spark a dialogue so she continued to clean in silence.

"Annette, would you like some breakfast?" Even though she had despised him for the way their marriage had failed, Lyle still managed to catch her by surprise. Annette straightened the house room by room; changed all the burnt out light bulbs; straightened the hanging pictures; scrubbed the commode; fluffed the pillows on the couch; and stacked the newspapers. Lyle cooked breakfast in the few pots and pans that weren't speckled with crusty leftovers or soaking in the sink.

When Lyle asked why she was doing all of these things to their house, Annette responded "You have company coming over soon."

"Company?"

"Yes, company." But Annette, spotting a *Playboy* magazine by the nightstand, suddenly wasn't all that interested in telling him anything more.

After a while, Lyle emerged from the kitchen with two plates of vigorously scrambled eggs, five crisp strips of bacon, and a stack of waffles coated with thick syrup. The only thing missing was a small bowl of fresh cantaloupe and the coffee (probably because Lyle hadn't stopped at the grocery store in the past weeks since Annette had died). Husband and wife sat at the table and endured one another's company as she regaled him with stories of her journeys since her body had been hit by Jonathan's used car in front of the library.

Lyle listened, shocked, and tried his best not to seem freaked out as she told him of her death and the adventures that followed. She told Lyle about Jonathan's desire for the violin and his disappointment when he received his father's old trumpet instead. Annette told him about Lucas; Harriet, her foe turned friend; Patrick, the man with the sunrises, and Fiona with the cream-colored pants suit. Lyle was especially intrigued about the retirement parties and the special visit from Saturn and cherry blossoms. As Annette told him her stories, she barely even believed herself that she was the main character in all of them. How miraculous it all was with hindsight. Finally, she told him about Adam and how she had fallen in love with him and about the obituary three years in the future with thirty year old Jonas' blackmail.

"This Adam sounds like a great guy for you, Annette," Lyle confessed, carefully biting a bit of egg from the fork. "On the other hand that Rothchild kid has been trouble since the very beginning."

"Adam found the obituary, though." Annette's shoulders sank. "Management only knows what he'll think now . . ."

"He'll think what I'm thinking now," Lyle told her "that you are a beautiful, radiant woman. Even after all you've been through Annette, how can you not see how incredible you really are?"

When breakfast was over, Annette switched the laundry and set the washed dishes back into the cabinets. As she did these next tasks, she told him of all the influential people she had inspired including those from around the world. She told stories of Paganini's music in the conference room and of helping to discover the key to unlock Emily Dickinson's poetry. Annette continued telling him of her adventures well into the afternoon and early into the evening. The rain clouds began to part revealing a sunset that bathed the inside walls of the living room.

"So you see," Annette told her husband as they both watched his shirts ripple in the breezy sunset, "answering the doorbell is top priority."

"But I've never been a fan of funnel cakes."

"It doesn't matter, Lyle. Eat the funnel cakes; don't eat the funnel cakes. The point is it's time to get over my death and move on."

"I have to tell you, Annette . . ." Lyle turned sullen once again. "It took you leaving to realize just how much I needed you. At your funeral I actually begged you to come back so that we could talk about Tolstoy's *War and Peace* and John Steinbeck's *Grapes of Wrath*, and for a chance to change history, to keep you safe instead of visiting the library on that day."

"But there's really no way to change history, Lyle. Management orders events for a reason. You must understand that."

"I swore I'd change if you only came back for one more day."

"You can still change, Lyle. You can live your life. You can be happy again."

"But you're dead, Annette. I can't live my life without you."

"No, but you can live your life with Doris."

"Doris?"

"All you have to do is answer the door when she rings and take her to dinner. Try a new restaurant; someplace you've both never been. Explore as much as possible. Time to let go of all the memories and propel yourself forward."

"I'm too old to propel forward, Annette."

"You know something I've learned, Lyle? No one is ever too old to be inspired. No one is too great or too small. I took a risk by coming to see you today and, so help me, you're going to follow through. Stop wallowing! The envelopes Management and Nathaniel J. Cauliflower send have great plans for you." As fate would have it, from inside the house Annette could detect the faint chime of the doorbell. Lyle could too. "It's a new opportunity, Lyle. Take it."

Lyle frowned, turned, and started for the front door, turning back one last time to see once more his former wife, whose yellow dress shone in the sunlight.

"Annette?"

"Yes, Lyle?"

"Do you think things would have been different if we were like this in our marriage?"

"What does it matter now, Lyle?" Annette shrugged, feeling a bit like Fiona when Annette asked about her own inspiration before the first envelope arrived in her post box. "Circumstances have changed. Go."

"Adam would be a fool to cast you aside. I know I certainly was for doing so."

As time raced forward, Annette found herself watching from the tumbleweed-type bush at the mailbox as Doris stood ringing the doorbell one last time. Annette wondered if Lyle was ever going to answer that damned door but it pleased her to know that he eventually did.

Lyle looked smaller, insignificant from a distance; so did the funnel cake that Doris offered. Annette couldn't hear what Doris was saying but she could tell that things were going to turn out just fine.

Time raced forward and Annette watched the couple as several uncomfortable dates roared by. They ate at new places that were far from the beaten path, they shared movie popcorn and they played miniature golf. Soon their dates became even more spontaneous and unpredictable. Each outing was an escapade for them both. As time progressed, Lyle fell in love with Doris and Doris fell in love with Lyle. Annette made sure that Lyle treated her sufficiently even after they married and had a baby girl. She was named after the muse who had changed everything.

*

Mr. Andrews' retirement party was equipped with all the fine fixings that had come before. Cherry blossoms turned to butterflies when the wind scattered them. The great body of water was also present. Under the surface, one could make out

255

the sea creatures varying in size from minnows to whales. The nine original muses danced in the field that was once Fiona's office as Patrick paced nervously, awaiting the time the public speaker would need to be retrieved. In the daylight hours, Mr. Andrews inspected an exact replica of the Titanic making audible notes to Management about all that needed repair. Yes, the deck of the ship looked too cluttered but there were plenty of lifeboats in case of emergency along with many other details that Annette would never be able to remember.

"I just spent time fixing my ship and finally making it perfect only to learn a lesson." Mr. Andrews said as Annette followed him around, "Once you die, you begin to wonder how you could have changed things: done things differently or said something differently. The truth of the matter is, what's done is done."

"What's done is done . . ." recited Annette. And she truly believed it.

The banisters were polished, the deck was scrubbed, china plates were sparkling with sunlight, engines had fired and eighteen muses watched as the giant ship embarked on its great journey towards the horizon. Standing on the terrace, overlooking the sea, Mr. Andrews said to no one in particular, "*Now* she is a perfect ship . . . and I can finally let that obsession go."

A compilation of all of his inspirations played in the conference room while the band that had played in the last few moments of the great ship's sinking accompanied in song. Paganini stood with them strumming a melody on Lucas' guitar that wove in and out of the musicians' masterpieces. Saturn passed the horizon now along with Harriet's meteor shower and Jupiter's stormy sphere.

"It truly was a retirement party to remember," Annette thought to herself. She wasn't in much of a mood to listen to the public speaker so she stood on the terrace and watched the stars chase one another across the heavens. It was at these moments, in the quiet of the retirement parties, that Annette missed Lucas. Remembering him with his friend Gabriel, feeling Adam's trench coat around her shoulders . . . the first moment she and the bookseller had kissed. Sometimes it was hard for her to

forget the memories, no matter how hard she tried. *"But what's done is done,"* she thought to herself. Harriet joined her on the balcony now and both women stared up into the brilliant universe.

Mr. Andrews blew out his candle on the cake and, waving goodbye to his comrades, passed through the blinding white light beyond the waiting room door. All was slowly beginning to return to normal, it seemed, as Annette then took her seat in her swivel chair and stared at the now stocked bookshelves of her personal library office. She waited patiently for the time Paganini would be sent back. She was putting off her final goodbye to the bookseller. It wasn't worth the violet envelopes to keep visiting him if he decided not to be with her anymore. Now that he had seen the obituary, Annette made up her mind that the next turn would be her last.

Violet envelopes horrified her. The idea of thousands of people surrounding the one she was meant to inspire, the avalanche of the inspirations that followed, made her skin crawl. Avoiding violet envelopes altogether seemed the only logical method of prevention. There were only sixty-eight colored pegs to go before her own retirement and she hoped that all of her envelopes would be white.

Friendship Day went by while *In the Mood* played. Afterward, Niccolò Paganini gave a final performance to the muses tucking the violin under his chin and applying the bow to the G string. The performance was stirring, as Annette knew it would be. But like the events in her employment it hadn't lasted long. Fiona stood in Annette's office moments later with the muse and the violinist, and handed Annette a cup of water from the cooler. Annette turned a green-colored peg, hoping that Fiona wouldn't know the difference.

The great violinist Paganini and Annette found themselves in the living room of Jonathan. But they had come too late. The room was cold, dark, and empty like a tomb. Most of Jonathan's belonging's had been cleared away save for the violin Annette had procured for him during her very first inspiration. She carefully took hold of the violin. She could hear a wake from the next room. It saddened her to know she had waited too long to come back. She could've taken Lucas' guitar back to the office, to hold on to it, but Annette knew she didn't need it anymore. Nor did Niccolò Paganini. Time roared forward to the graveyard where they found Jonathan's grave. Annette had Paganini ceremoniously set the guitar down, propped against the engraved limestone, allowing herself to give up the last shard of Lucas Richardson.

Annette still held the violin and bow from her first inspiration. As she stroked the strings of the purloined violin she recalled having handed it to Jonathan in the hotel room, having heard him playing it night after night, and having understood how much hope a single instrument had given him. Time then rewound back to the aforementioned initial inspiration in 1987, where time promptly stood still once more. Annette then slid the instrument and bow into the violinist's fingers. It was as if it hadn't even been stolen.

Paganini was taken back to his own time, three years into his own future, after presumably being "taken in by a lady of title in Tuscany," after which he stunned the world with his newfound techniques on violin and guitar. When Annette returned to her office she found that Jonathan's peg was still glowing as if he were still alive.

"Because, Annette," Harriet told her when the question arose, "what the peg shows us is several *minutes* in a single lifetime. There are so many others that he's still experiencing. There are countless single moments to profit from in a single lifetime."

*

Returning to her bookseller was the hardest thing that Annette felt she had to do. Still, Annette once again found herself standing in the apartment firmly clutching his trench coat. She intended to hand it to him and say goodbye but the bookseller had other plans. He wrapped a blindfold around her head. "Can you see anything?" Adam asked in her ear.

"No."

"Good." He led her out the front door and down a flight of steps. He told her to stand still while he opened a car door and clicked her seatbelt into place. The drive to wherever they were going was completely pitch-black to Annette and it lasted years. "Jonas came to me the same night that you brought the obituary. He told me everything. And I must say, I was stunned."

"I want to let you know," Annette interrupted. "I'm not an average woman one might meet in a supermarket or a car wash."

"No, you certainly aren't."

"If I told you what I was . . ."

"Yes?" he interrupted.

"Would you still love me?" she asked.

"Love you?" Realizing she'd said the word love Annette blushed horribly. Annette tried lifting the blindfold but Adam was in control and kept it that way. Therefore, the blindfold remained and he did not answer her question – verbally, that is. His hand suddenly resting on hers came as quite a surprise but Annette held it anyway soon finding pavement below her feet. With the blindfold still shielding her eyes in the suspense-filled silence he rotated her. He removed the fabric.

Annette was brought to tears when he removed the blindfold: Not because she was unhappy - no, it was quite the opposite. Her hands cupped around her mouth as she gasped. Her legs felt all wobbly. Fellow passersby wondered as to the purpose of the unusual spectacle.

"Do you think they're having a sale?" one customer asked her husband.

"What do you think it means, Patricia?" asked another. But Annette knew what it meant and that was all that mattered.

"Annette," Adam whispered into her ear as her eyes studied every square inch of the largest tuxedo bow tie she had ever seen draped around *The Muse's Corner*. It was breath-taking and wonderful as she had first imagined it would be, with the bow right above the front door. "Of course I would still love you and there's nothing that you could say or do to have me think otherwise . . . stay."

*

259

For a brief moment it seemed that everything in Annette's employment had been "ironed out," as Fiona mentioned it would. But there were still sixty-eight envelopes left to go. While Annette finally succumbed to staying with Adam, Fiona stood in the door frame of Annette's office, arms folded, with Harriet beside her. Nathaniel J. Cauliflower stood at Annette's post box siphoning violet envelope after violet envelope into the slit.

"This isn't punishment, is it, Fiona?" Harriet asked with her eyes focused on the last few violet envelopes that were delivered.

"No." Fiona shook her head. "Not punishment at all. Mrs. Slocum has utilized her last seven rotations perfectly."

"Then why so many?"

"Only Management knows, Harriet."

"How many violet envelopes does a muse get in a typical employment?"

"Nine at the most, unless you're Head Muse."

"And in all your Generations how many have you worked?"

"Thousands, but this many violet envelopes for one particular muse at one time is highly unusual."

"But all sixty-eight and in *her* post box?" Harriet shook her head. "What does it mean?"

"I'm sure Mr. Cauliflower knows what he's doing," Fiona turned to Nathaniel J. Cauliflower now. "Don't you Mr. Cauliflower?"

Nathaniel J. Cauliflower shook his head in disbelief, looking serious. "I hope she's ready." His eyes landed on the two jars and wooden box with the dandelion insignia that Annette had carelessly left on display next to her Lite-Brite board. With a touch of fury, he shoved the sixty-eighth violet envelope into Annette's post box. He frowned, approaching the two jars and wooden box. Evident unpleasant memories passed before his eyes.

"She found them in the oak cabinet on the second floor not too long ago," Harriet told him.

"How did the cabinet get there?" he wanted to know.

"It just appeared. Or so she said." Harriet then took a step forward. "I can put them away."

"No," was his curt response. "She took them out. She can put them back." He then exited the department leaving the two jars and locked box right where he had found them.

Harriet stood alone in the doorway now. "Wherever you are, Annette . . ." Harriet whispered to the colored pegs in the grid of Annette's Lite-Brite board, "hurry."

CHAPTER 22: AFTER THE NIGHT

Annette's eyes fluttered open at five fifteen, just as they had when she was married to Lyle. The sheets which encapsulated her bare skin were cold and soft. Adam's body was warm against hers and the slight intake of breath from his nostrils were barely audible as he slept. The morning was quiet with a chirping bird somewhere in the neighboring apartment complex. A car engine tiptoed down the pavement of the road along with a subtle morning breeze tickling someone's wind chimes. She was content in Adam's arms recalling the various details of the night before.

"You smell nice," Adam had told her, kissing the side of her neck while they made love the previous night. "What is that? Fresh-cut cucumbers?"

"Shampoo from the musing department."

"Ah . . ."

Annette then took in his scent, holding him closer. "What do I smell like?"

"Ink print on paper..." Her response had not been particularly romantic, unlike Adam's, but it was a memory that she relished now as she watched the morning sun peek over the horizon.

Life was peaceful here; it was hushed, with no threat of Lite-Brite pegs and violet envelopes. As if finally waking from a dream, Annette realized the dour truth and wondered how long had she been away from the office. How many envelopes were waiting in her post box? Both of these questions and more caused her to suddenly sit up clutching the covers. The bookseller stirred.

"What's wrong?" What was wrong, Annette thought, was that in that split second she had remembered her obligation and had made her decision. Though it was hers alone to make Annette didn't particularly enjoy what she was going to have to do but knew it had to be done.

"Everything . . ." Annette's heart sank as her fingers clutched the yellow dress that was crumpled at the foot of his bed. "I came here to tell you goodbye."

"Goodbye?" Obviously Adam hadn't completely regained consciousness, shaking himself from sleep.

"When I came to you yesterday, I was going to stay for only a minute to bring you back the trench coat and then return to the office. Unfortunately, I stayed much longer than I'd planned. I wish I could stay but I have a responsibility to the rest of the world, Adam, to inspire."

"Why it took you so long to tell me this, I'll never know." He climbed out of bed, kissing the back of her neck as she fit the yellow fabric over her figure. "My own private muse."

"The world is a large place, Adam, and considering that time is circular for the department, the world is even bigger than one might imagine." Annette shuffled into the bathroom where she found his brush and combed her hair as if piecing together a lamp that had been broken in two. "That and I've tried really hard to be a good muse for Fiona. I've told you before of the violet envelopes, I'm sure."

"You have."

"If I were to continue to visit you, Management had threatened those violet envelopes. I can't take that kind of warning lightly."

Adam's naked reflection in the bathroom mirror was tempting but Annette wouldn't have it. Abruptly, she turned away from their reflections.

"What are you saying, Annette? That you're choosing the musing office over our relationship? Why can't you have both?" Annette said nothing, setting the hairbrush back on the counter top. "You'd choose to avoid having to deal with violet envelopes than be with me?"

"There are many other factors involved, Adam."

"No," Adam frowned, surrendering to her decision. "I understand. I'm one out of many *clients* that need your expertise."

"You're much more than a client, Adam."

"Don't patronize me, Annette. I've fallen in love with you. The fact that I'm still sticking around you after you've been dead for three years says a lot." Annette turned to face Adam now. "Running from me isn't the answer anymore, Annette. If you truly wanted to be in this relationship, you'd find a way to get over your fears of the violet envelopes, or any other fears that are keeping you from happiness."

"That's asking a lot."

"Is it?"

"Have you ever been on a violet envelope?" Annette asked defensively.

"Have *you*?" Adam's words, like the sound of his voice, stung as if dipped in poison. Finally, Annette was silent. Her eyes cast down to the floor. "I'm done fighting for us . . . 'cause what's the point if you really don't want to be here?" How she wanted to hold him and abandon the musing office. She wanted to live a conventional life and tell him that she would do anything for him. She would have done this and faced any violet envelope Management sent her way if she believed she could. But Annette instead said nothing.

"Go, Annette. I only hope the white envelopes waiting in your post box are worth it."

Regrettably for Annette, the sixty-eight envelopes that waited in her post box were all violet. As her office folded and unfolded, once again depositing her into the swivel chair, she felt utterly alone. With trembling fingers, a beating heart and an anxious stomach, Annette hesitantly dove into the violet envelopes. As each seal was broken she felt a piece of her heart ripped right along with it.

Just as she'd feared, the violet envelopes were truly outlandish. In the first ten violet envelopes alone, Management had sent her on a wild chase for the inspiree in several dreadful situations. She first was sent to a DMV on a rainy Tuesday morning and everyone there, from the old people waiting to get their licenses renewed to the clerks themselves, were miserably unhappy. She was sent to a Civil War battlefield in Virginia to inspire a Union soldier who faced a gun aimed by his own rebel brother serving in the Confederacy, though thankfully Annette was there to redirect the bullet. She was sent to Japan to divine the identity of her inspiree during the wake of a tsunami and to New Orleans, where the recent devastation of Hurricane Katrina was truly mind-boggling as Annette herself attempted to aid in the relief. She was sent to witness the great speech of Martin Luther King Jr., in which he claimed, "I have a dream," and Annette inspired only one in a crowd of thousands. She was delivered to the set of *Wheel of Fortune* where she was invisible but could at least whisper letters into a contestant's ear to help solve one of the puzzles so that the contestant was able to win a trip to Hawaii. When she was sent to a bustling farmer's market, Annette spotted her inspiree just beyond a fresh batch of ripe red tomatoes. At the Kentucky Derby she inspired a horse to win the race rather than its jockey. Rowing her own punt in Oxford, England, Annette attempted to inspire a young man three boats downstream. The worst inspiration job was to a midnight book release of J.K. Rowling's seventh Harry Potter installment; an event that caused her anti-social behavior to quiver; however, like a good muse, Annette pressed on.

What followed was more of the same and more daunting. Annette attempted to inspire a tightrope walker a hundred feet in altitude as she desperately avoided looking down at the audience below. She went to teach patience to an intolerant individual during five o'clock traffic and attempted to inspire someone as she held the suction tube under a dental patient's tongue while half the patient's face had been numb during a root canal. Swarms of bees buzzed happily around the nervous Annette as she inspired a beekeeper. As she forged ahead to inspire a scuba diver inspecting the Coral Reef her house dress was drenched and her lungs ached. She was sent to a Jewish concentration camp to instill hope. Later she floated above the ground in a hot air balloon and clutched the basket as she held back a wave of nausea. She was sent to a roller coaster where she had been fastened in but felt it difficult to express any kind of encouragement as the ride jostled and groaned. She was sent to *Riverdance* where she was barely able to distinguish the tap dancers against the roar of thunder that signaled the end of the inspiration. She immediately went to a contemporary church service where she experienced the approach of a splitting migraine during the rise in volume of synthesized sacred music.

There were tribal drums in Africa and squealing bats in underground caves. There were cockpits in airplanes along with the rickety elevator of the Saint Louis arch. There were ancient ruins of time-eroded castles paired with grand cathedrals where the voices of castrati kissed decorated buttresses. Annette stood in oil rigs confined to the middle of oceans, museums of forgotten treasures, bars during happy hour, concerts of Amadeus Mozart, and other well-known composers. Annette even inspired a participant for American Idol.

The violet envelopes spared no expense in exhausting the muse assigned to them.

If the violet envelopes weren't bad enough, in between was the avalanche that Patrick had mentioned. It was as if she were a plastic ball in a bingo hall being turned over and over in the machine. Sometimes Annette even felt off balance as if trying to country-line dance on a moving carousel while at other times the final moments of thunder were so loud they deafened her. Annette felt that she'd truly lost her mind for everywhere she turned there was chaos.

There was also something increasingly peculiar about the inspiration jobs. She wasn't quite sure if the envelopes were getting progressively harder to open or if it was just her imagination. In the past, the flaps usually only needed a gentle nudge with her index finger. But now it seemed that nothing less than her fingernail acting as a make-shift letter opener was enough. In addition, as she inspired it seemed that the time allotted for the jobs was creeping shorter by a few seconds during each job until by the time the thunder roared on the sixty-fifth one, she was barely even sure she had inspired the right person.

Her assumption that perhaps the window of time for each inspiration was closing faster by the second was soon realized as she lifted the last three violet envelopes that rested on the bottom of her post box. She prepped her fingernail but it wouldn't puncture the paper. Her heartbeat raced even faster at the horrifying prospect that perhaps she might not be able to open it. Could it be that this particular window was going to cause her the greatest grief of all? The threat of butterfly wings and earthquakes weighed upon her now.

It *had* to be a violet envelope that wouldn't open, didn't it? That was the thought which raced through Annette's mind as she ripped open the drawers of the bathroom cabinets in search of something sharp. A nail-file, fingernail clippers, nose hair trimmer, shoe-horn, anything . . . but she came up empty-handed. Annette raced to the conference room where, on several occasions, there had been forks, knives, and other utensils that could aid her in the quest to extract the colored peg. However, Nathaniel J. Cauliflower had taken the liberty to prepare a candy shop with chocolate truffles and other such sweets that could cause a diabetic to drop dead. There were no utensils to be found.

"Something wrong, Mrs. Slocum?" Annette heard Fiona ask from her office.

"No, nothing's wrong." She snapped at Fiona. Annette went back into her office and tossed the violet envelopes on the desk. "All right, you. Give me some kind of sign. How the heck do I get you open?" The violet envelopes did nothing to help but simply sat on her desk as all violet envelopes are prone to do. The water cooler gurgled encouragement then. "Water..." Annette's eyes flashed with realization.

She ripped a cup from the water cooler in her office. The water cooler gurgled happily, as if thinking it was some kind of game. Annette filled the Styrofoam cup with liquid. Like a scientist measuring units in graduated cylinders, Annette held the violet envelope at eye level and tipped the cup. Annette watched happily as the violet envelope drowned in the water, its hue darkening slightly as it had when Lucas' tear pelted his own.

Annette seized the violet envelope and hoped that the paper would rip. But it didn't. The violet envelope remained completely intact. Annette tried using her teeth but still the paper wouldn't budge.

Harriet sat in her swivel chair moments later with Annette across from her. On the desk were the three unopened violet envelopes.

"And you say you've tried water?"

"And trying to rip it with my teeth and hoping it would rip in half with the weight of my desk."

"A nail file?"Annette nodded her head. "Fingernail clippers," she nodded her head again. "Nose hair trimmer?"

"It's like the bathroom knows, you know?" Annette sat forward in her swivel chair, eyes squinted and forehead furrowed. "And Nathaniel J. Cauliflower had to try his hand in candy-making today . . ."

"Then there's only one thing left to do." Harriet stood from the swivel chair. Annette followed with the three violet envelopes clutched in her fingers. As the two muses stood in the doorway of Fiona's office, Annette swallowed her pride.

"Mrs. Slocum." Fiona stood up from her swivel chair and crossed around the side of the desk with a smile. "I'm glad we ran into one another. Management and I were talking about your predicament."

"You were?"

"Seems that the two of us have a very important situation that needs addressing," Annette turned to Harriet, who ducked back out into the hallway and left the Muse and Head Muse to discuss the matter privately. Annette held the three violet envelopes out to Fiona. "When it comes this close, we can't afford to waste another minute. Am I right?"

"I suppose not."

"I've been in the Head Muse position for centuries. Management sends me cases that are far tougher than any violet envelope a regular muse could encounter. With each case, over the span of time, I've been fortunate enough to execute each inspiration with the utmost care." Annette nodded, hoping Fiona would cut her monologue short. "Great masterpieces of literature, art, and music have been cultivated from my efforts. Lovers have united; vast measures in history have unfolded; the very core of inspiration itself blossoming as Management

268

needed it to. Along with inspiring those cases, I order all the miracles for retirement parties. When I'm not invested in inspiring those outside of these walls, I'd like to say I run a fairly well-oiled operation. But this . . . truly takes the cake."

"It was a mistake to be gone from the offices so long," Annette flushed. "I'm sorry. But surely there's something you can do."

"I'm afraid, Mrs. Slocum, I can't." Annette stared at its purple exterior dejectedly. Fiona led Annette into the conference room where they once again sat as they had on the first day. Fiona then removed the remote control from her jacket pocket and the mural disappeared behind the movie screen. Annette hoped that perhaps Fiona would show her a video on how to rip open a stubborn envelope. What followed, unfortunately, was something that Annette had already seen.

"'*Musing and You*' brought to you by . . . Management. Narrated by Nathaniel J. Cauliflower."

"Fiona, what does the instructional video have to do with my situation?" Fiona hushed Annette so Annette pursed her lips and sat watching the video.

"Since the beginning of time, muses have been inspiring the world around them . . ." The instructional video continued but Annette eventually stopped listening. Things had changed considerably since the two of them had sat here last. Annette wasn't watching the video. She was watching the light from the screen before them dance on Fiona's cheeks. ". . . Which means that if you are watching this training video, you are now one of the elite. You, dear muse, are a Ninth Generation muse. Now we know what a muse is, so let's talk about what a muse does and, more specifically, how they do it." The longer they sat here watching this poorly drawn animation again, the shorter the amount of time would be allowed Annette to complete the inspirations, even if they could release the colored pegs. As Nathaniel J. Cauliflower continued his spiel about the Lite-Brite board, dread poured through Annette heavier and thicker. "There are several things to think about before venturing forth, dear muse . . ."

"Pay close attention, Mrs. Slocum." Fiona's words overlapped Nathaniel J. Cauliflower's voice. "We're coming up to the most important information of it all."

". . . Therefore, don't be surprised if you're inspiring a person suffering from vertigo to bungee jump with his friends one moment and, then, inspiring the painting of the Sistine Chapel the next." Annette wasn't quite sure how that bit of information was supposed to be helpful. "Third and most importantly, do not, under any circumstances," now Fiona was talking along with the narrator emphasizing the words. "Leave an envelope unattended. The window of time, or the page of the person's pop-up book, is only open for a limited interval and can only be opened by you." Fiona lifted the remote control and skimmed back a few seconds. ". . . Window of time, or the page of the person's pop-up book, is only open for a limited interval and can only be opened by you."

"I get the point," Annette seethed but Fiona considered it necessary to repeat it yet again driving the point home. "I said I get the point, Fiona."

When the instructional video ended, the screen disappeared and the lights in the room came up to a full brightness.

"So . . ." Fiona prompted Annette. "What have we learned from this situation, Mrs. Slocum?"

"That after a while," Annette fumed "an unattended envelope can't be opened."

"No," Fiona corrected. "That's not the lesson."

"That an unattended envelope can't be opened, that's it."

"It means, Mrs. Slocum, you need to try a little harder because only you can open them." From the hallway, Harriet brought in a rolled-up leather tool pouch. She set it on the conference room table and unwound the suede straps that bound it. The three muses peered down at seven tools resting underneath leather straps. "Now, what say *you* get these violet envelopes open?"

The first tool, which Annette figured would do the most damage, was a well-sharpened machete. Annette had to use both hands to wield it. The last knife that she'd used was the paring knife used to slice Lyle's cantaloupe, so she had to get used to swinging the machete around several times the way a child does a stick to a piñata. However, when the blade collided with the paper, a crease was all that developed. The three violet envelopes remained intact.

The second tool was a pair of polished broad scissors and when Annette plied them the violet envelope broke the scissors in two.

"Durable little suckers, aren't they?" Annette said of the violet envelopes to Fiona, who sat in a swivel chair enjoying one of Nathaniel J. Cauliflower's chocolate raspberry truffles.

The third object was a hole-punch. The metal surface reflected the light of the conference room. Annette prayed that when the hole-punch clasped the envelope, a hole would appear. She squeezed. Annette continued to squeeze harder. After a few dismal seconds, she tried another corner, then another, even using the desk as leverage for the hole-punch's handle. But no amount of pressure applied to the handle could break the paper. Annette sighed disappointedly and figured the fourth tool might do wonders.

The fourth tool was a colored peg which, after a sip of water from the water cooler, brought Annette to a laundry room with a potentially useful tool: an iron which steamed when plugged into the wall. It seemed promising but the envelopes were only mildly cooked and the colored pegs were still trapped within.

Annette removed another blue-colored peg, from the strap and considered that it might send her somewhere or, more specifically, to someone who could help. She pocketed the violet envelope, took a drink from the water cooler, and plugged the blue-colored peg in to the conference room's Lite-Brite board. Transported to a vacant study, Annette discovered a paper shredder with its cord plugged into an outlet. When she switched on the piece of machinery, its gears made an awful grinding sound. She slipped one of the violet envelopes through the shredder, pleased to hear the crunching of paper; however, inside the bin, Annette was disappointed to find that the violet envelope had only severely dented and the paper still remained as durable as concrete.

271

A red-colored peg, the sixth tool, sent Annette to a stormy afternoon in a giant field. Looking rather ominous and twisting in rage on the horizon was an F5 tornado. Annette had been caught in a few storms during her life, but she had never stood before an actual funnel cloud. Still, it was the sixth out of seven objects in the tool pouch, and solutions were limited. Swallowing her fear as the swirling column ripped through the field, Annette held the violet envelopes up and allowed the wind to rip her off the ground. Annette didn't fear death, especially since she'd been dead for awhile now, so she decided that she might as well enjoy being in the heart of a tornado while it lasted. The pressure reminded her of being trapped beneath Jonas' mattress as she had attempted the rescue of the obituary.

As half of a house raced by, Annette seriously hoped that the wind was strong enough to pull the paper of the violet envelopes apart. When the tornado quit its rampage and ascended into the sky, all that it had been carrying suddenly fell to the ground. Annette was also thrown to the earth where she groaned unhappily. She caught sight of the violet envelopes. They fluttered about around her as undamaged as they had been before she had come to the field.

Deposited back in the swivel chair with the impenetrable envelopes, Annette unearthed the seventh and final tool: a lighter. As the tiny flame licked the paper, she pleaded with the violet envelope before her. "Please . . . I beg of you . . . not when I'm so close to retiring. They're just paper, for Management's sake!"

As she held the flame under the violet envelope, she knew she'd never see Adam again, that all was truly lost despite her best efforts. A life without Adam was far worse than any violet envelope that wouldn't open. A life unlived, shackled by anxieties of the unknown, was a far greater punishment than Management could have conceived. She had lost everything save for the little pieces of stubborn violet paper that were resolute on remaining whole. If only there were some way to go back, she told herself, she would instill all her well-earned knowledge in her previous self and change the course of events. Annette wondered if things would have turned out differently.

Much to Annette's surprise the three violet envelopes finally turned to ashes and revealed three colored pegs: one blue, one purple and one cream-colored with red polka-dots. Now that she thought about it, Annette pondered which was worse: the violet envelope not opening or the fact that she now had the colored pegs and would actually have to face the inspiration jobs represented by them.

CHAPTER 23: HE WHO REPAIRS LIBRARY BOOKS

A pungent odor of stone and earth hung in the darkness. Various glass jars secured with metal lids rested on dusty wooden shelves. She could feel as cobwebs clung to her sweat-covered cheeks and knew that thin threads of silk held tightly to her hair like a hairnet. The soles of her feet shuffled loose piles of dirt and eroded stone and her eyes took in very little. For a moment, Annette wondered if perhaps Management, as consequence, had buried her in a tomb of some sort, in the manner that Egyptians had been buried with their personal treasures. As she felt around ahead of her with the palms of her hands, she gathered even more of the geography of her location and finally deduced that the first of three violet envelopes had delivered her to an underground root-cellar. The only question was why?

Isolated, Annette feared the very worst: that perhaps the time of inspiration had come and gone. Her client may have eventually skipped the scene without her intercession. As her eyes adjusted, she could detect a fraction of sunlight skipping down a flight of cement stairs like a silver coil rapidly tumbling down toward her. With a new path laid out, Annette took timid steps upward and bent awkwardly so as not to scrape her scalp on the low stone ceiling above. At last finding the exit, she touched the wooden doorway. Its surface was as cold as ice but the sunlight peeking through a knot-hole was warm and reminded her of sparklers at the Mansfield's Fourth of July celebration.

Unfortunately for the Ninth Generation muse, the door was latched on the opposite side. The plot of her adventure was kept in forced hiatus and the world around her was beginning to rumble now: a declaration of the limited remaining minutes. Annette wondered if perhaps she'd really messed up this time. Would the universe end right here at this very moment? Would the stars collide and the astral rotation of planets in the Solar System redirect?

From beyond the door came the sound of shoes urgently crunching grass. Annette stepped away from the doorway and hobbled down the cement stairs as a hand took to an outside latch releasing the barrier which kept the door from opening.

The mysterious second party clicked a chain at the top of the stairs and suddenly the stone cellar was pleasantly lit by a yellow artificial light. A breeze of fresh air flushed through the root-cellar heightening the surrounding smells to an even greater level. As a figure descended the stairs, Annette stood on the floor of the root cellar taking in even more discoveries. The glass jars contained olives, green beans, corn, tomatoes and other vegetables that had been stored throughout various seasons. A small wooden table and a single chair were stationed nearby as a make-shift workshop.

The boy who descended the stairs was no more than eight years old. His pupils were magnified nearly three times their normal size by coke-bottle lenses which were as hideous as those of Doris the waitress. They were fitted into large black frames. His hair was neatly combed to one side with a clearly defined part, his pressed shirt was white cotton, and his pants were khaki. Due to his poor eyesight, the boy didn't notice Annette at first although she was clearly visible in the room. Setting a mass of torn pages onto the surface of the small table, he pushed the glasses up over the bridge of his nose, then brushed his hands clean of sweat and dust. His fingers gently stroked the paper as if it were made of cat fur.

Annette recognized the book immediately: it was the very same library book Jonas had tossed into the street so many years ago. The boy, suddenly detecting a hint of yellow in his peripheral vision, looked up from the book, examining the small space before him.

"Who's there?" asked the boy, cleaving to the dismembered novel for its own safety. Annette's mouth suddenly went dry, her lips remained immobile. The answer to the question that had puzzled her for years was finally revealed. "Look, whoever you are, you're trespassing on private property."

"How do you do it?" Annette finally asked, squatting down to his eye level.

"Do what?"

"Repair the books."

"Oh, that . . ." said the boy, his eyes now turning back to the pages, shrugging his shoulders. "I dunno. Just sort of happens, I guess." A rumble of thunder emanated from the walls now, louder than before: an approach of a storm on the timeline's horizon.

"What sort of tools do you use?" Looking around the room, there were certainly very few instruments that could aid in him repairing a library book.

"Tools?"

"You . . . don't use tools?" The little boy shook his head. "Then how does it happen? How do you take a library book that looks like this . . . and turn it into something else?" Once again, the little boy shrugged his shoulders in a movement accentuated by another roll of thunder. "Look, there isn't much time, so I need to make this quick." Annette bit her lip but said what was on her mind anyway. "Management sent me here to inspire you."

"Inspire me?" Obviously, the boy was confused. "Management?"

"If I inspire you, will you show me how you do it?"

"I don't know if I can. It's only happened once before."

"Once before?" The boy nodded his head. "How? What happened?"

"Well, there I was…"

"Yes?"

"Setting a small sailboat out to sea in the pond by our house," the little boy continued stroking the pages of Young Annette's copy of Tolkein's *The Hobbit*. The boy went on to explain that a ways down the current he had found a single

276

leather-bound book from an encyclopedia, which had already been damaged by the water. The ink on its pages had already turned blotchy. Even the pages themselves had the weight of water-logged rags. Where it had come from, the boy wasn't sure but, as he had sat there watching the small sailboat drift along the water's surface, he had flipped through the pages of the volume. Suddenly the boy fell quiet.

"What happened then?" Annette asked.

"And that's when they arrived."

"Who?"

"The Sisters."

"Come again?"

"They had this tent, you see. And it floated on the water as if it was on its own little island. But it wasn't on any island. The tent sat atop the surface of the water. And there was this sign that said 'Admittance, three dandelions.'"

Annette's face suddenly went pale.

"And there was a small patch of dandelions on the water's edge where I was standing. I swear they weren't there before. It was as if the dandelions just appeared."

"And what did 'the Sisters' do for you? What did you pay them for?"

"They told me I had the ability to repair things, especially things like the book I had found in the water. And I was instructed to bring it home and repair it. So I did. I brought it back here," the boy said with a sigh, "set it down on the table and stroked the pages of it. Like trying to bring back to life a dead frog."

"A dead frog." Annette repeated, trying to understand.

"And that's when it happened," the boy said.

"What happened?"

"My fingers, they began working all by themselves, it seems, like they had the Devil in them." Annette turned her eyes to the boy's hands which looked perfectly normal to her but the reassurance could barely hold at bay the chills that washed over her. "They worked for hours, piecing it all back together . . . until finally, there it was."

"There it was?"

277

The boy then knelt to the floor where, from underneath the shelf with the jars of vegetables, an object wrapped in cloth emerged. He held the wrapped object up to Annette who then touched the fabric with her fingers. The single leather-bound volume from the backyard pond was meticulously stitched together, as all of her other library books had been. The letters "Sl-Sm" were scrawled neatly on the cover and spine, labeled by a calligraphy pen. Though she was almost certain she'd never seen the volume before, there was still a haunting familiarity. The weight felt as if it had been lifted by her hands before. It was remarkable to her how real yet distant this object was to her. Like a memory she'd forgotten. A memory that, no matter how hard she tried to remember, would never resurface.

She thought about perhaps opening the book but decided against it. The roll of thunder only gave so much time and now was not the time to read. Covering it up with the fabric she handed it back to the boy who stashed it back underneath the shelves.

"I've tried several times. I've brought back several damaged books, but it's like the first time never happened. Trying to repair a book that's that bad off is impossible." The boy slumped in the chair now, dejectedly. "When I saw Jonas toss the girl's book into the street, and saw her face as it was ripped apart, I thought I'd at least try. So when the girl left the library book in her room during dinner, I opened her bedroom window and brought it back here."

"So here it is."

"Yes Ma'am . . ." The thunder that only Annette could hear was growing louder. The stones beneath her feet and around her began to shake violently. Even the sunlight seemed to jostle. "It's impossible, isn't it?" asked the boy, his eyes looking straight into Annette's.

"Some people would like to think so, yes." Annette then smiled. "But some would say that time travel is impossible, too, and they're wrong, aren't they? I've seen time travel. I've seen the books you'd repaired in my past. This library book, Tolkein's *The Hobbit*, was mine. You did it . . . honestly. It was miraculous, truly miraculous. And maybe I was meant to come here to inspire you and to encourage you to believe that even

278

things that may seem impossible can happen." Her time with him was beginning to end and Annette knew that she wasn't going to be given the opportunity to see the boy's fingers as they repaired the pages.

"Do you really think so?" asked the boy. Annette nodded. "I'm Nathaniel, by the way. Nathaniel J. ..." He raised a hand to hers but as she reached and before he could say his last name, the root cellar folded and delivered the now-bewildered muse back into her swivel chair.

"Nathaniel J?" Annette looked up from her desk to see the office chef then pass by her door on his way to the conference room in his usual white pressed shirt, khaki pants and suspenders. He had a bald head and glasses. He was carrying various food trays hoisting them high overhead. She heard the clinking of silverware – silverware would have been useful moments ago!

She found the answer to a question that had been lingering within her for years while also introducing several others. She thought about introducing herself properly and asking Nathaniel J. Cauliflower if he could show her how he had repaired the library books. Considering that there were two more treacherous tasks ahead of her, Annette decided against it. *"Another time,"* Annette thought to herself. *"Another time."*

CHAPTER 24: THE UNFORGETTABLE TEMPEST

The thunder greeted Annette immediately as the next-to-last of the sixty-eight colored pegs deposited the Ninth Generation muse into a storm. Unable to differentiate between Management's warning thunder and the storm's rumbling in the sky, Annette realized she was standing at Adam Mansfield's and Jonas Rothchild's apartment complex parking lot. It was one of those spring afternoons where blue horizons were crowded over by menacing sea-green storm clouds like great gods caught in war over conquered territories. If Adam were here, Annette thought he would call these clouds Virgil-niffers or perhaps something else. She wasn't sure.

The threat of the storm was on a determined path, although the storm had not yet reached the parking lot where she stood. The temperature was warm but an arctic zephyr combed through the trees like a mother eager to untangle her child's hair with a brush. Clouds stretched into the heavens as grand thunderheads signaled the vast gale. A bolt of lightning erupted in the sky spreading electric tendrils in an upward arc. Another flash followed striking the ground somewhere far away. Annette stared up at the storm in wonder. The fabric of her yellow dress swished this way and that in the draft. Strands of her hair brushed to and fro about her face. This was a perfectly magnificent storm, Annette thought to herself, absolutely brilliant: that is, until she caught sight of her inspiree standing to her left.

Jonas stood watching the storm as well, dressed in his usual black suit and matching tie. His charcoal gray dress shirt was clearly visible beneath the unbuttoned jacket. If she'd never met him before, Annette would have pegged him as a decently handsome thirty-five year old. But she knew better. This was the same persecutor who had caused her grief for years and he would always be a villain to her. Her heart-strings were tugged, disappointedly so, for who would want to inspire someone like him?

Catching sight of her wind-whipped yellow dress, Jonas found Annette. His lips stretched into a deep grimace. "You couldn't stay away, could you? Always have to come back like a stray in need of leftovers!"

"Aren't you supposed to be playing weatherman?"

"Not my shift," Jonas turned his eyes to the sky. "Good thing, too. Looks like it's gonna be a busy one. And the term is *meteorologist*, Annette," he spat. The two stood in the parking lot, separated by a little over a hundred feet. They made little advancement toward one another. She could see that his dress shirt underneath was stained red with blood. He asked her: "Why did you come back?"

"I had to," Annette replied. She kept her eyes fixed on Jonas and worried about any sudden movements on his part. "You know you've been a real jerk, Jonas," she said, antagonizing him deliberately.

"Have I?" Jonas smiled. "That's your interpretation."

"Interpretation?"

"My motives have always been in your best interest," he said. "Even now, you still can't see it." The storm inched closer. The noise was more menacing and the lightning was hungry. "When I first saw you sitting under the tree with that stupid book in your hands, I knew there was something off about you. You were part of the world but not part of it. You were wasting your life and gliding along without splashing any proverbial puddles. That's not the way to live life, Annette."

"No, it's not."

"No one gets anywhere staying comfortably locked inside their own private worlds. No one *evolves* by playing it safe."

Annette crossed her arms, defiantly.

"Ever feel, Annette, that there are certain things in life that you can't change? No matter how much you want to

281

manipulate the state of affairs, some things are just out of your control?" A flash of lightning allowed Jonas a dramatic moment before continuing. "Before I found you under that apple tree, that's all life was to me. Everything was outside of my command but then there you were. Saving Annette Slocum became my personal project."

"Oh, what a saint," Annette snapped uncharacteristically but fully indulging in sarcasm.

"Unfortunately, over the years, things changed. Growing up does that to you, I guess. The world really isn't a place you'd want to live. It changes you but not in a positive way. Gets under your skin, into your blood, like thick tar."

"So you think you're a martyr?" was Annette's caustic reply.

"Where *are* you now, anyway?" Jonas asked.

"Employee for the Uninspired, for Management." Jonas nodded when he heard this, although he didn't completely understand what she meant. "They sent me here, to inspire *you*." Annette chuckled at the irony.

"Inspire *me*."

"That's right."

"You're a muse." Jonas laughed at the idea. "*You*: a muse! Why?"

"Management sends me to different people to further the evolution of civilization," Annette said with confidence.

"Interesting occupation, if I do say so, especially for you," he remarked, laughing. Jonas turned his attention back to the storm and, for several seconds, several rain drops began to fall.

"I've always had your best interests at heart," Jonas sighed as several more raindrops fell from above. "Working as a muse, you probably think the world is one big happy place where everyone gets a chance to be who they really want to be." Annette shook her head. "The world's not glossed over that easily, Annette. The world is full of war, destruction, assassinations, terrorism, heart-break, hunger, divorce, *murder...*" He took several steps closer to her. Raindrops began to fall hard on their skin and lightning flashed above them. Suddenly, a flash struck a nearby tree. "I was wrong, Annette. I

282

wanted you to see the world a long time ago when we were both naïve and impressionable. When we finally got out in it, though, and you had died in the car accident in front of the library, I was happy for you."

"Happy for me?"

"You managed to escape before history began to change. No one will ever forget where they were when President John F. Kennedy was assassinated, the day the Challenger exploded, or when the Towers were attacked on 9-11. There are other events that seemed to have completely missed you. And when I saw you again, Lazarus from the dead and with your precious bookseller . . . I wanted to protect you from this already rotting existence."

"You are the one who blackmailed me with the obituary."

"I was trying to keep you safe from a world that had become so jaded, disfigured, and infested. I felt responsible for fixing you, Annette. I still do." Jonas was centimeters away from the muse. The two of them were standing in the rain with thunder roaring above. The lightning brightened the sky and was reflected in the puddles at their feet. "So you see, Annette, everything that I've done, even with the obituary, has always been in your best interest . . ."

It was no longer safe standing in the rain as the lightning grew ever more threatening.

"Everything you put me through, when I was dead and alive, was for my best interest?" Annette shouted to him. "You've no idea what Management has given me. They didn't take me out of the world: they immersed me in it! And because of that, I can see how beautiful it is. Even in the darkest moments, there's still hope."

"Do you ever question what Management does?" he asked her without taking her previous remark into consideration.

She shrugged in reply, exasperated by the conversation, as a crack of thunder erupted from the sky. The ground now began to vibrate beneath her and the panorama of the parking lot began to fragment. Time, for the muse, was running out. "When the colored pegs are rotated, it doesn't show every single moment of a person's life," she explained. "It only shows the pivotal moments. All the hours in between sort of whiz by."

"How do you mean?" he asked.

"Individuals spend too much time worrying over things - the meaningless moments when life doesn't seem to progress forward and the days where nothing seems to happen. But things are happening all of the time. Life may seem to move slower some days but life still moves."

"So why are the moments even there? If the colored pegs, when rotated, push those moments to the sidelines, why are they even there?"

"Because," Annette said with authority, "that's part of the journey. We need those meaningless moments to take us to the ones that truly change us. I wish you could see what I've seen. I wish you could understand."

The world was flickering wildly and Jonas grabbed her arm.

"If the office where you work is so perfect, you're going to take me with you," he shouted.

"Let go of me, Jonas!"

But Jonas wasn't about to let go. The muse and meteorologist stood locked together in a tussle, as lightning struck weathervanes atop the apartment complex. She spied Adam running toward them with his feet splashing in the rain. With her morbid imagination, Annette imagined her bookseller getting struck by lightning, and that wouldn't do; however, Adam didn't care what the weather was doing as long as Jonas took his hand off Annette's arm.

"Rothchild, let go of my muse!" cried the bookseller. Jonas sneered.

"You're going to take me, Annette. I'm so *sick* of this world and the people in it. I'm going to find out why the world is the way it is!" Annette tried to pry herself from Jonas' grip but he held strong. "And to maybe *fix* it, if I can."

"Management has my best interests at heart, Jonas: *Not yours*." Annette wrenched her arm from his just as the bookseller punched the meteorologist. The two were battling one another on the ground: tossing a few kicks and throwing a few punches. Annette stood above them screaming for the two

284

men to stop but the storm and the inspiration were coming closer to their ends and roared even louder. She jumped into the fray and then pried Adam from the rain-soaked ground. "Let Jonas go, Adam. Let him go." Together they soon distanced themselves far enough from Jonas' broken nose and blood-spattered cheeks. And thankfully so.

"Take me with you!" Jonas screamed to Annette then craned his neck to the heavens. "Do you hear me up there? I need to know!"

In a split second, as the bookseller held his muse in the dry breezeway, far enough away from the meteorologist and his bellowing, a bolt of lightning ripped from the storm clouds and struck Jonas. A brilliant white light filled Annette's sight and a sound the same as thunder, if not greater, struck her ears. The hair on her head and arms stood on end and her heart nearly skipped a beat. But the end result was final. Jonas' body laid on the ground, his black suit licked with flames, his skin burnt, and his form motionless. She was too stunned to say anything and too exhausted to revive him even if she had been willing.

As the backdrop began to shift maniacally around her and the ground began to break apart, Annette remained close to her bookseller and whispered, "I should have stayed. And I'm sorry." Adam led her back to the apartment with their hands locked together. Soon she broke free of his grasp and the inspiration. Annette grieved as she beheld what could only be construed as the severing of their bond and the end of the final chapter of their affair.

CHAPTER 25: A PIVOTAL WEDDING RECEPTION

Annette stood in the bathroom with the hair dryer poised over the yellow dress but her skin was flickering in and out like a television picture during a thunderstorm. She'd never been this disoriented. As the seconds crawled by, she felt as if she were losing control of her memories, of her mind, and even of her soul. The fingers that held the hair dryer were solid one moment, transparent the next, then solid again. Annette wondered if it was due to the close proximity of the lightning storm in the previous inspiration or if it could be caused by something worse.

This would be her last adventure. Her clothing was now dry and she found herself at a wedding reception where not one, but two families, each with their own impressive lineage, were celebrating a union. Live music emanated from a piano where a trained accompanist played an unrecognizable melody. A catering staff milled about the room with wine for the adults, punch for the children, and finger foods. Annette grabbed a quiche from a plate. Immediately there was a roll of thunder.

Hundreds of family members of all ages, ranging from those running around in a game of hide-and-seek to the feeble and wheel-chair bound matriarchs, could be her inspiree and were more than intimidating to Annette as she heard the foreboding boom of thunder. Her eyes scanned the room. She wasn't sure how much time she had so she surveyed speedily and hoped that her heart-strings would tug her in the right direction.

Was it the great-great-grandmother who, from the looks of things, thought that the day was all about her as she tried to get anyone's attention? Perhaps the inspiree was a member of the wait staff who stole a sip of wine from a glass when he thought no one was looking. Then again, it could've been the best man as he scooped peanuts into his hand from the buffet table.

There were so many individuals to choose from - too many in fact - and the sickening feeling returned to the pit of Annette's stomach. Much to her dismay, the tugging of heart-strings never occurred. She had no inclination as to where she should proceed and simply stood on the dance floor in her yellow dress looking foolish . . . until she spied the bride and groom who, with a single knife attempted to cut a piece of their wedding cake. Beyond the icing on both of their faces, Annette knew who they were and the prospect of it nearly took her breath away.

Annette watched her mother and father along with the rest of the family.

Her parents, before having three children and living as examples for them in the years to come, were young and in love. They were the happiest she'd ever seen them. Annette wondered if this was her parents' Heaven. Had Management placed them in a time capsule where one of their happiest moments was relived after their deaths?

If she hadn't spent the last some-odd years inspiring people, if she had stumbled on to this scene with ignorance, Annette could have believed it. How she wanted to believe it! However, as she had spent a good while with the pegs from sixty-seven violet envelopes, Annette had a strong feeling that this was going to be a happy experience for everyone but her. A great roll of thunder shook the wine glasses and caused a few cake crumbs to dance happily about the reception table. As time was running out, Annette began to feel another sensation swell deep within her.

As her presence in the moment flickered, all the memories that she'd collected over the years and through past inspirations were finally starting to fall down and separate, like potted flowers on a shelf disturbed by a roll of an earthquake, which really didn't help her current situation at all. She hadn't existed at this point in history and, therefore, had no memories of it, but there was one specific memory she was trying to find. The only problem with going on a cave spelunking adventure through the cavern of her old memories was that the rocky innards of her mind began to break apart with erosion. Annette took a mental scythe whacking at the jungle of the Mansfield experience and Doris' funnel cakes, through a lifetime of Jonathan's desire to play the violin, through to her death, then to the marriage with Lyle. Alas, as she sifted through the memories, she was quickly forgetting them . . . as if they hadn't even happened at all.

A roar of thunder then began to shake the dance floor. As time passed farther and farther from her, Annette then realized that if she didn't do anything now that perhaps she may not even exist in the timeline. What was she sent to her parents' wedding to do? Why was she even sent there? Then she began to wonder about her own identity. It was as if she was experiencing a serious case of Dementia. All these questions and more exasperated and confused her as she plummeted deeper and deeper into madness.

At last, thankfully, Annette found the day she had been hunting for in her memories: her father's toast to the new Mr. and Mrs. Lyle Slocum. The guests had hoisted their glasses high at the end, but how would this memory help her? Something about "if it hadn't been for . . ." whatever "it" was led to Annette growing up like . . . Another roll of thunder ripped Annette from her memories. It was a sign that soon, and very soon, the wedding party would disappear. That meant that even though Annette didn't have to endure this torture much longer, there would be still enough time left to send her over the edge.

Annette wondered, as the speeches were given, what sort of consequences would arise if she failed. Would she be erased from history? Would the story end in Deus ex machina, rescuing her from peril? She wasn't quite sure how it was supposed to go down but she had a good idea that if the inspiration job thrust her back into the swivel chair now, it would mean that Annette and all the great work she'd done would never have happened. If she couldn't have married Lyle or died in the middle of the street, which meant that she wouldn't have been hired as a muse. Which meant that every single person she had inspired wouldn't have taken her advice. The consequence was no end to the problems for everyone she had inspired in the some-odd years she had been a muse. Her life, though now spiraling southward, had purpose. Despite all of its pitfalls and disappointments, all of its sadness and perplexities, life finally meant something in the end . . . not only for her, but for those around her.

Thunder signaled the swift approach to the end. As it did, Annette suddenly knew what had to be done. Even though the rumbling rolled more frequently and with far greater vigor than before she wasn't behind in her time. In fact, she was exactly where and when she needed to be. Annette no longer fretted about the disappearance of her soul or the other consequences that would follow. Trusting that Management would eventually straighten things out, Annette switched the frown to a smile and asked her father to dance.

"Would you mind?"

"Not at all," said her father who was considerably younger than she'd ever seen him. But the soul that Annette admired was the same. "Whose side of the family are you on?"

"Both the bride and the groom's side," Annette smiled as they waltzed to the sound of the piano.

"I suppose that is the case," her father smiled, "as we are now a family."

"A family . . ." As they danced, Annette was able to have a last moment with her father in replacement of the one that had been taken from her so abruptly on her honeymoon. Conversation was mainly one-sided as Annette entertained him in many of the life lessons she had learned along her journey: the words of encouragement given to her by a loving father, reassurance by her employer Fiona, and finite details of life given by Lucas Richardson before his retirement. As they glided along the dance floor, the piano music was lost momentarily in the maniacal thunder.

The ground beneath Annette was beginning to give way now causing her steps to become disjointed and her words studded with insecurity. The more she talked about what she had learned, the faster the faces and lives she'd previously encountered were beginning to reform. History was beginning to right itself, thankfully, but there was still more to be said. Alas, there were other women who wanted her father's attention and she couldn't hold on forever.

"One more thing . . . if you ever have a daughter," she told her father, pressing him closer, her lip on his ear, "if she's really quiet and seems detached . . . know that everything you say to her will change her entire world. And though she'll never truly say it . . . she'll love you forever." There were tears in her eyes and even her throat began to swell up. It was time to let her father go and to say goodbye.

"Are you alright?" He could see that tears were beginning to form in Annette's eyes.

"Promise me," Annette found it harder to breathe as the precious inspiration was nearing its end and the very life that had been given to her was finally slipping away. "Promise me that, even if she marries a new and used car salesman, a man that you won't think is right for her . . . that you'll support her. And when you think you've lost her forever . . ." Oh, how Annette wanted to preserve his face and to be with him without time constraints, ". . . you won't. She'll come back . . ."

The final thunder clap separated Annette from her father as she was once again deposited into her swivel chair. She no longer flickered in and out of time. She was completely solid yet still felt a void deep within. Oh, how wicked were the ways of time, Annette thought to herself, as she wept uncontrollably into the hem of her yellow dress. The clients of the violet envelopes were inspired and her employment had finished. So the Ninth Generation muse curled up beneath her desk where it was cool, calm and peaceful, where she closed her eyes and slept.

*

There came a subtle knock at Adam Mansfield's apartment door. Thinking it was Annette, the bookseller tore himself from the couch where he'd immersed himself in a book of Greek mythology and slid the chain. Only it wasn't Annette in the doorway. Instead, Fiona stood wearing her cream-colored pants suit with matching heels. Her hair was radiant and air authoritative yet warm.

"Mr. Mansfield."

"Yes?"

"I believe you know of my employee, Mrs. Slocum." Adam's eyes widened, looking beyond Fiona's shoulder. "I'm afraid she isn't here. Nor will she be with us much longer. May I come in for a moment?" The bookseller led Fiona into the apartment closing the door against the storm that still raged in the sky above. "I'm Fiona, from Management, Mr. Mansfield. Have you heard of me?" Adam nodded and Fiona continued. "We have thousands of candidates to be public speakers for Mrs. Slocum's retirement. Patrick is our newest muse and he hasn't found the right speaker. So he came to me and asked if I would do it."

"Kudos." Adam's voice was sour as he sat in the shadows. "I'm sure you know she chose your office over our relationship, right?"

"Yes, I'm aware."

"Then why are *you* standing in *my* living room?"

"I've tried to put you two together for years, Mr. Mansfield. On the afternoon of the plane ride to Las Vegas, where you first met her, I played the role of gate announcer and kept the door open long enough for you to catch the flight. You may not remember me, Mr. Mansfield, but I've played *many* roles, put on many disguises, applied various faces to ensure the two of you meet. And so I'm here to try, one last time, to bring the two of you together again."

Adam looked on in disbelief.

Fiona nodded. "I've been there, and so has Management, every step of the way." She offered an arm to escort the bookseller. "Will you please be our public speaker, Mr. Mansfield?

CHAPTER 26: A RETIREMENT PARTY FOR A NINTH GENERATION MUSE

"Annette?" The voice called to her gently and a warm hand tugged on her left shoulder which prompted Annette's dream to dissolve. In her fantasy, Annette was laying in a field, looking up at the clouds with Adam Mansfield. *"Perfection,"* she remembered thinking until there came another great tug on her shoulder. "Annette, wake up."

Annette awoke at five-fifteen and again found herself in Adam's bed. The hint of wind chimes jingled somewhere beyond the open bedroom window and songbirds chirped. All was serene and unruffled. Annette thought the pillows smelled of her bookseller: even the sheets had the distinct aroma of paper as she lay with her eyes closed and curled deeply into the covers.

"No, Annette," protested the voice beyond the bed sheets. Hands then began to part the covers. "You don't want to miss your retirement party, do you?" Annette opened her eyes suddenly in recognition. She tossed the covers to find Lucas sitting on the bed in his usual argyle sweater, tight jeans, and sandals. "Looks like you've come out of everything relatively unscathed," he observed matter-of-factly.

Annette squealed with delight, cleaving on to her best friend. She said nothing, just felt his heartbeat thudding gently in his chest. Lucas had returned, as she had hoped he would. Annette didn't even care how long he stayed as long as he was here for the moment.

"From the looks of things, you've been busy, you know?" he continued.

"I've had sixty-eight violet envelopes!" Annette told him with her voice muffled in the proximity of the hug. "Not to mention all the others in between. I have so much to tell you."

"Later. For now you've got to prepare for your retirement party. Fiona took the liberty of picking out another dress." In Adam's apartment Annette ambled into the shower and silently lathered herself in soap bubbles and generic shampoo that gave off a fresh hint of peppermint. Meanwhile, Lucas stood by the bathroom door and listened to Annette tell her stories of Jonathan and the violin, about inspiring Lyle and Doris and about the last encounter with Jonas and how he was struck by lightning. "Boy, I retire and miss all the excitement, you know?"

Minutes later, she abandoned the towel for the yellow-sequined evening gown and white opera gloves that had been dangling from a brass hanger on the back of the bathroom door. Beneath the gown, Annette found the black hoodie that had once been kept in the department bathroom. As always, Annette looked radiant in yellow and, as the morning sun peeked through Adam's apartment windows, she put even the sunrise to shame. She realized that Adam's apartment wasn't exactly how it was in real life: some of it was his while other rooms extended into the house where she had spent ten years in an eventless marriage.

"It's like walking through a dream," she told Lucas, surveying the land. "It's all here and stitched together."

"And it's only the beginning."

Standing in front of the stove in a perfect replica of the house she'd lived in during her married years, Annette smiled as she noticed the cooked breakfast Nathaniel J. Cauliflower had laid out before she had awakened. As it had been on every morning, the meal consisted of two vigorously scrambled eggs, five crisp strips of bacon, a stack of waffles coated in thick syrup, a small bowl of sliced cantaloupe, and a cup of coffee for each person which, by her count, consisted of a party of five.

"Morning, Annette." A male's lips kissed her cheek and brushed against her skin with stubble. It was undeniably surreal to see her father, her mother, and two brothers suddenly appear from the sidelines like actors playing their roles in a production.

Annette's family sat together at the table and Lucas served up the breakfast. When the plates arrived at the table, Franklin, Michael, and her parents all waited in anticipation. "I hear that Nathaniel J. Cauliflower is a great cook," said her father. Annette nodded carefully, not truly accepting the reality.

Management had constructed her family so perfectly that, during breakfast, it seemed like nothing had changed before Lyle had entered the picture. Annette knew something had changed however. Annette was far more talkative and the animosity between her and her brothers had been erased. Life was as it should have been: a decent happy ending to a tumultuous employment. As breakfast ended Annette was reluctant to see her family go but Lucas reassured her there was much more to see . . . much more, indeed.

The soothing sound of rippling fabric drew her to the back yard. Lyle's shirts were hanging to dry in the morning sunlight and Annette allowed herself to be enchanted by the sound. Cherry blossoms kissed Annette's cheek then. Beyond the fabric she could see fields of pink-spotted trees that swayed in the morning breeze. So far, the retirement party was exactly what she wanted it to be and as it had started for all the others.

"Are you pleased, Mrs. Slocum?" asked Fiona who stood with Annette in the back yard now. Her cream-colored pants suit was replaced by a blue that mimicked the sky just as Annette preferred.

"It's perfect."

"You've been so busy that we've barely had enough time to assess your desires. If there's anything missing, please let me know."

"Actually, now that you mention it," Annette whispered into Fiona's ear a specific request.

"Management will provide it."

"Thank you, Fiona."

In the hallway, Annette found that the retirement party had continued extending the space to several fiction aisles of the library where all her adventures had begun. The library donned in a spectacular bow-tie and cufflinks as she'd imagined. Her champagne-colored VW Beetle was parked on the terrace and beautifully restored. Annette even spied the spice and coffee racks from the grocery store and she and Lucas found themselves uncapping and savoring the various aromas.

In the green field that was once Fiona's office, a small family band was setting up for a concert. While his children and wife sat preparing their own instruments, a thirty year old Jonathan took to his own violin and began the composition. Niccolò Paganini joined in, enriching the music. Jonathan didn't need a tunnel before the front doors of a hotel to cause his music to sound great as Management had adjusted the acoustics in the field appropriately. While the nine modern-day muses, the original muses, and Lucas stood on the lawn, the various instruments evoked a different feeling in each guest.

The notes started off quietly and built to a regal climax which Annette equated with the happenings of her own life. The intensity would rise, then fall, then increase again. To Annette it reminded her of the emotions she encountered during her employment. As she listened, Annette studied her other muses. The music captured the essence of a collection of reverence, requited joy and hope which surrounded the field. When the original music came to a dramatic conclusion, the three suns rose to their highest points in the sky. Temporarily blinded by afternoon light, Jonathan's family dissolved as if they were made of the consistency of vapor.

With too much food to fit in the conference room, various tables of shapes and sizes that Annette had seen in her various inspirations appeared in the field. All of the delicacies that Nathaniel J. Cauliflower had provided in the time of her employment reappeared on the mismatched tables and chairs, which were linked together and reminded Annette of the tea party scene in *Alice in Wonderland.* Included in the delightful banquet were the meals that she had longed to taste during the inspiration jobs: like Jonathan's mother's meatloaf and the bran muffins and donuts at the diner, or during her lifetime, like the Thanksgiving dinner that she never got a chance to thoroughly enjoy because of the argument over her mother's mental state. There were even meals that had been eaten by the fictional characters from the library books she had so often read. The muses enjoyed the bountiful feast with voracious appetites. Paganini's music even narrated part of the event with the bow

295

on string actively imitating the buzz of bumblebees picking pollen from petals and the sound of chirping birds.

Present also were fragments of the entire world such as the great columns at Alexandria, the lost island of Atlantis, the Pyramids at Giza, Big Ben, and the bustling streets of Tokyo, all mapped out like storefront windows which she and her friends frolicked through and re-discovered.

The greatest surprise was a display of all the library books that were repaired in the history of Annette's life. She expected to find Nathaniel J. Cauliflower standing by the table. Instead the booth remained empty.

"Is he here?" she asked Fiona.

"He wanted to be, but something came up."

"Oh." Annette was obviously disappointed but tried her best not to dwell on it. "Tell me something, Fiona. How is it that Nathaniel J. Cauliflower rescued my library books as a young boy but exists here in the office as a thirty-something year-old man?"

"My dear Mrs. Slocum, you must remember that time is circular."

Annette still wasn't satisfied with her employer's answer but nodded anyway. If their paths eventually crossed again, Annette made a mental note to ask him personally.

"Mr. Cauliflower did want me to tell you congratulations and that you've been a great asset to our cause." Annette, once again, nodded to Fiona's words. Just then she spotted Adam watching from under a Bradford pear tree similar to the one in his parents' back yard. Although they knew a relationship was impossible they held each other and named the clouds. They marveled at Saturn's rings appearing and becoming more defined in the afternoon's horizon.

"You've touched so many lives, Annette," Adam told her, placing her hands in his. "Especially mine. Before you came along, I was sheltered. I only knew history from books but you've helped put it all together and opened my eyes." The Mansfield Fourth of July was next on the agenda filled with sparklers, fireworks and the smell of sulfur lingering in the sky.

The retirement party roared on and Saturn was once again outdone in beauty by Fiona's meteor shower accompanied by a spectacular aurora. Eventually the spectacle would end. She would have to say goodbye to everyone and move on regardless of whether she wanted to or not. So Annette reserved her sadness and uncertainty of the future. For now Adam had his arms around her and it would have to be enough.

As Harriet stood on the veranda watching the meteor shower, a single tendril of her hair loosened and flapped in the breeze. She was surprised to feel a hand touching her on the small of her back. She turned to find Harold who was dazed by the dream he thought he was having.

"Harriet?"

"Harold?"

Harriet's and Annette's eyes met for a moment from afar. Harriet gave a small smile and mouthed the words "Thank you" to her new friend. Annette blushed and mouthed the words "You're welcome." Annette was happy that Management could work her one request in so quickly. Annette had then thought of another request. Though she wasn't quite sure how to put in an inquiry, she simply closed her eyes and imagined it happening. And thus her thought came into fruition.

Fiona, who had been standing on the veranda overlooking the party she had planned, was suddenly joined by Alexander Thibodaux. Fiona, whose demeanor had always been controlled, was suddenly awash with tears of joy. Fiona turned to thank Annette but Annette had already turned and walked with Adam through the other spectacles.

Annette spotted Doris and Lyle who had made a quick appearance (hand-in-hand and happily married, with a baby girl in their arms) to congratulate her on her achievements. Annette lifted the baby and held her triumphantly to the meteor shower cooing in the toddler's ear. She no longer feared poo or vomit; instead she took in the clean scent of the child's skin and the bright blue eyes that reflected the stars above. Yes, it was the perfect retirement party.

"Annette?" It was Patrick who pulled the couple's attention from the meteor shower. "It's about time for the speech."

As the crowd gathered in their seats in the conference room, Annette and Adam held hands. The podium did not remain empty for much longer as Fiona reviewed her notes. Her new baby blue colored pants suit looked even more radiant as the stage lights illuminated the material.

"Welcome, friends and employees, to Mrs. Slocum's retirement party. As most of you know, when it comes time to picking a public speaker, Management provides a rather inclusive list. Mr. Hollinsworth is our newest muse which meant that he had the responsibility of picking our public speaker. Out of all of the colored pegs, Mr. Hollinsworth didn't find one that would be significant enough for Mrs. Slocum's party. So he came to me and asked if I would do the honors." She looked out into the audience where Adam sat with Annette. "In my place, I asked Mr. Mansfield if he would like to be the public speaker but he humbly declined . . . so, on such short notice . . ."

Fiona consulted several index cards.

"To fully comprehend the events of the day Annette Slocum died, one would have to examine how she lived the first thirty years that preceded it. Annette Slocum lived most of her life in solitude but, after her death, she soon discovered that the world needed her much more than she had realized. Very plain-looking Annette did not stand out in a crowd and, more often than not, blended into the wallpaper or couch cushions at parties. After her death, we forced her to interact and she blossomed. She's realized that she had been meant for much greater things than cooking Lyle's eggs or washing the stains from the crotch of his underwear. She knows that she was destined for a life outside of the pages of the books that she so desperately relied upon for escape. Her actions were meant to be seen, learned from, and examined."

But Fiona's speech was suddenly interrupted with a simple word.

"Wait." And that word came from Annette. The spotlight turned from Fiona to the guest of honor. Annette shared a look with Adam before she approached the stage. As Annette stood behind the podium, Fiona offered her the floor. Annette smiled politely to her employer and mouthed the words "Thank you" to Fiona. She then addressed the audience without aid.

"Hello. My name is Annette Slocum. I suppose you're wondering why I interrupted Fiona's great speech. And . . . I guess . . . it didn't feel right to sit there quietly without sharing what I'd learned myself. That's something the old Annette would do." Annette turned her eyes to Fiona who, in turn, never looked prouder. Annette went on. "What makes a hard-working muse? Is it a Lite-Brite board with colored pegs? Is it white and violet envelopes? Is it an office with a water cooler? Certainly these objects help but let's not forget the true purpose of a muse. One only needs to take an active interest in the world and evoke the spirit that exists within each of us. So often we become slaves to time, dwelling in pitfalls of monotony or fretting over the small things that, in the greater picture, mean very little. Living in auto-pilot or within the nature in which our worlds become fraught with mundane details is the weakness of all.

"Why does Management do the things they do? We are bound for great things. To create masterpieces in every aspect. To influence not only ourselves but others. To encourage, to reassure and to give hope. It's all about a leap of faith. Management does not expect us to be miserable continually; instead, Management desires for us to learn, to grow, and to experience new things; to evolve, to utilize our full capacities, and to change the world.

"That is the true rhapsody of a muse and of the individuals who inhabit the universe. And I hope that, as you each go your separate ways, you'll remember that you have the ability to affect the world around you. We are all connected. All living things in this world need support. No one is too great or too small to inspire. You can, and will, inspire anyone."

Applause was followed by a standing ovation. Fiona stepped towards Annette and offered one last revelation. "Mrs. Slocum, you once asked if I'd suffered through any violet envelopes. I answered yes, thousands to be exact. One of those was yours. My how you've grown, Mrs. Slocum. You've faced your memories and overcome mounting obstacles. You've helped others in additional peg turns when it wasn't required. With impressive dexterity you were able to work through sixty-eight violet envelopes. I couldn't be more proud."

Moments later, Adam stood in the conference room staring up at the mural of nine beautiful muses dancing with laurel leaves around their heads. Down the hallway, at the waiting room door, Annette found the cake. It was not just any cake: it the very same wedding cake from her marriage reception with Lyle which signaled the end of the retirement party. A single candle served instead of a miniature husband and wife topper.

Annette knew that her wish was going to determine her eternity. As the meteor shower disappeared on the horizon and Saturn's rings smiled down upon her, Annette said "Lucas blew out his candle at the end of his retirement, I remember," to Fiona.

"Before the retirement party, I like to sit down with the muse and lay out several options. Most only have two but in your case there are three. Considering we haven't had much time before this moment, would you like to hear them now?"

A collection of her peers were standing in the hallway. Patrick's wrinkles were accented by the light of the candle and Lucas' eyes reflected the flame. But now it was just her and Fiona: two women whispering privately.

"The first, ascending to Management, or to Heaven as you call it. It's different for everyone, really and, in your case, Heaven would be a quiet library filled with books in all the languages of the universe. When you ascend, there'll be no need for the language books to decipher linguistics as the knowledge will accumulate within your mind through osmosis. The shelves are stocked with books that you've only dreamed, books that have been around for centuries, books that have been lost or forgotten in pillages and fires, and books that have yet to be written. You'll have no one there to bother you. It will be you and the pages: no complicated love affairs, no school bullies, nor worries of time, no violet envelopes or other commitments, only pure bliss."

Annette closed her eyes and tried to envision the library that Fiona described. The aroma of ink on paper stirred something within her. And the quiet . . . no more pegs, no more having to be social. Life could return to normal.

"There are comfortable chairs there as well so you'll feel as if you've slipped into a cloud of feathers. You could even have Lyle's shirts there rippling in the wind. You'd like that, wouldn't you?"

"It sounds wonderful . . ." Annette sighed happily.

"The second," Annette opened her eyes. The image of the universal library faded away. "Is to go back and live on Earth again."

"With Adam?" Annette was suddenly alert.

"No, Annette. Once you do this, you will not remember being here. All knowledge that you've gained will be swept clean. You'll start a brand new slate. You'll have no previous knowledge as to the perils or triumphs that have already occurred. Between the two of us, no matter where you go, you'll lose Mr. Mansfield. So please don't let your relationship with him affect your decision."

"But you brought us together . . ."

"Retiring is a whole new venture all together, Mrs. Slocum."

"Management won't send me back as something like a rock or a candy-bar wrapper will they?"

"No, Mrs. Slocum. You'll be human." Annette nodded her head. So far, the first sounded the most promising. "And third, you can stay here and take my position as Head Muse. You'll oversee the new employees, control the instructional video, monitor peg rotations, plan retirement parties for the exiting muse, including Saturn's rings and the Edge of Creation if you so wish and you'll speak directly with Management. You'll mentor the other muses. If you stay here, life will be too busy to keep a relationship with Mr. Mansfield."

"What of Harriet?"

"Harriet will also have this option."

"And those are the three choices?"

"Yes, Mrs. Slocum. Those are the three choices. The library in Heaven, reincarnation, or become Head Muse." Annette watched the flickering flame on the wedding cake for a moment considering her three options.

"Either way I lose him," she whispered. Fiona nodded. "Then I've made my decision."

Annette took in a deep breath snuffing out the candle. A bright light exuded from beyond the waiting room door causing the hallway to shift playfully as if the walls were the inside of a kaleidoscope. Adam's attention was then pulled from the mural

301

and his eyes turned to the end of the hallway where Annette reached for the door handle of the waiting room. Annette quickly felt as light as the morning breeze that ruffled Lyle's shirts on the backyard clothes line.

"Know that once you walk through the other door in the waiting room, Mrs. Slocum, there's no turning back. You won't remember anything."

"I know, Fiona." Annette started for the door then turned back to her employer. "Though I wasn't too keen on being a muse at first . . . becoming one has been the best thing that has ever happened to me. Thank you."

"You are most welcome, Mrs. Slocum." Fiona's pearl earrings were ablaze and, to Annette, resembled miniature spinning galaxies.

Annette turned to Harriet who seemed about on the verge of tears on seeing Annette go. "Remember, Harriet. Crunchy isn't always a bad thing."

"It's those crunchy moments that truly help make us who we are," Harriet recited the adage that Annette had once told her. They embraced like two old friends. This connection pleased Lucas to no end.

Annette then turned to Patrick. "Here's to sunrises."

"To sunrises," Patrick told Annette as he embraced her.

Annette gave Mrs. Donnelly a hug and thanked her for her help in uncovering the mysteries of the two hundred year old parchment and for their brief friendship.

Finally, Annette turned to Lucas.

"At first I didn't understand how you could've been so calm when you retired, Lucas. But I understand it now. Like you once said to me… 'it's time.'"

"I love you, Annette Slocum. Wherever you go, I'll always be with you."

"And I'll always be with you," Annette told her best friend, touching his cheek with affection. As Annette opened the waiting room door, Adam yelled out her name. His feet clumped heavily on the floor below. The blinding light swirled.

Annette remembered waking up from her death and finding herself in this waiting room staring up at the stealthy hand on the wall clock. She remembered hating the water cooler and seething over the fact that Fiona had destroyed the familiar rhythm to which she was accustomed. Passing back through the waiting room, she was a completely different person . . . or perhaps she was even more of a person than she had been before.

"Annette, wait!" Adam cried but Annette was already going into the light. Annette wasn't so certain about anything now. What was certain was that Annette now delighted in the unknown rather than fearing it. Several steps more into the light, Annette disappeared from the waiting room completely. "Annette!" screamed the bookseller.

"Mr. Mansfield," Fiona was telling him, "I brought you here under false pretenses. Not to be the public speaker but to make a choice . . ." Her eyes were then cast to the door through which Annette had exited. "If you wake up in your apartment, you'll always remember her no matter where Management sends her. She won't remember you. So why not forget together? Would you like to go where she's going? Management always finds a way to iron things out, you see." Adam considered her words then raced after Annette disappearing into the great swirling light at the end of the waiting room.

Fiona turned back to the muses in the office as the illusions were already fading. She then entered Annette's office. She fit the two mason jars and the wooden locked box inside the oak cabinet on the second floor of the library shutting the drawer and securing it with the combination. She then returned to Annette's desk where she emptied the Lite-Brite board. As she did this, the office that had been Annette's began to slowly dematerialize back into a space with four drab walls.

Before exiting, Fiona took one last look at the office and, brushing away a single tear, said a prayer for her retiring muse and her bookseller. Thus, Annette Slocum's employment had come to an end.

303

CHAPTER 27: REQUIEM REVISITED

It was Christmas Eve and the snow had begun to fall at a rapid rate. It coated the trees, it blanketed the sidewalks, it stacked above mailboxes and vehicles on the side of the road. The carolers trudged through, determined to sing their hymns and spread their joy of the season from one house to another. They were bundled in mismatched stocking caps and scarves bound tightly in trench-coats, pea-coats and other outerwear that made them look far plumper than they originally were. Their cheeks and noses were red and, as they sang, they could see their breath. But that didn't stop them from journeying on.

Annette Redmond stood amidst her fellow carolers wishing she'd brought a better pair of boots. The snow that she'd kicked up had gotten into her boots and had become sludge. But not even that could deter her from enjoying herself. *"It was just part of the season,"* she told herself. She had two pair of wool socks on anyway.

Annette was in her mid-thirties with striking red hair that glowed almost orange whenever there was sunlight. She had green eyes that twinkled almost as bright as the colored lights on the houses that night. Freckles dotted the cheeks of her slim face. She always smiled, despite the commonplace woes of life. She managed to keep a sense of optimism and tried her best to instill that in the many friends with whom she associated herself.

As they approached the next house, Annette felt something. She wasn't sure what. Was it the name "Slocum" on the mailbox? Was it the tumbleweed type bush beside the mailbox that had struck a tiny chord within her? Or was it the front porch of the house? As Annette stood with her carolers, she couldn't help but to study the multicolored lights that had been fastened to the porch and roof. They reminded her of a toy she had once played with as a little girl . . . a Hasbro Lite-Brite board in which she had pieced together many multicolored masterpieces. No other house had sparked this memory from within. Why was this house any different, Annette wanted to know?

A man in his late forties with a handlebar moustache stood with a woman who wore thick black-rimmed glasses. In between them was a five year old girl who looked equally overjoyed to be visited by the singers.

It pleased Annette to see that this family looked content. It gave her a sense of peace, though she wasn't quite sure why. As she stood there singing the ballad of Good King Wenceslas, Annette's mind was suddenly elsewhere. It was as if she was recalling a dream that she had once had, many years ago, but the images were indistinct.

"Merry Christmas," Lyle Slocum said to the carolers as they then dispersed.

Soon the only caroler that was left standing on the porch was Annette. She looked at his face with a hint of recognition. There was something about the mother as well and the little girl. Annette had seen them somewhere before she was sure of it.

"Merry Christmas," Annette said awkwardly. Shaking off these thoughts like brushing away snow, she left the porch and joined the carolers, but not before turning around a final time. The husband lovingly guided his wife and child indoors where it was warm. No doubt to prepare for the arrival of Santa.

They passed by the cemetery not too long after. She would have kept going if it hadn't been for the two figures she had seen walking through the plot. The carolers went on but Annette lingered. There was a woman in a baby-blue pants suit and a bald man in a white shirt, pressed khaki pants and suspenders. Neither one of them wore anything over themselves to keep warm which Annette thought was irregular. They didn't even seem to mind the cold which Annette thought was even odder.

As the caroler's version of Carol of the Bells drifted farther and farther away, Annette tip-toed through the snow to investigate further.

"I grow so tired, Nathaniel," said the Woman in the Baby-Blue Pants Suit.

"I know you do, Fiona," said the Man in the Suspenders.

"Why is it so difficult?" Fiona inquired. "You would think that after almost ninety retirement parties, I would learn to not take their departures so personally. I remind myself it's all a process, I put on a brave face, but . . ."

"I know, Fiona," the man named Nathaniel said comfortingly.

At last, the man and the woman found a specific grave and stood there for a moment out of respect. "Out of all the muses, I miss her the most." To which, Nathaniel said nothing. But Annette Redmond could see, even in the pale light, that he had missed "her" as well. "Do you think Mrs. Slocum's happy, wherever Management sent her?" Fiona asked.

"I'm sure she's right where she needs to be."

Fiona continued to look at the gravestone. Nathaniel's eyes turned up to find Annette standing several graves away. Not knowing quite why, Annette raised her hand and waved. The man named Nathaniel waved back. Nathaniel then brought his attention back to Fiona and guided his friend away from the grave. It was almost as if they had both disappeared into the snow, stepping out of the world, out of time.

As Annette walked home, she heard the bells chime in the tower of the Methodist church. Christmas had finally come. All was quiet, all was calm. Eventually she passed by the library where she had vaguely recalled the afternoon of the accident with the woman named Annette Slocum and the Cadillac. It had been many years ago but Annette remembered looking down on the woman and watching the life leave her eyes. Tonight it was just another street covered with snow.

It was then that she caught sight of the only other individual outside that late. Underneath the glow of a solitary street light, he stood carving an ornate statue of a woman out of ice. The statue's hair had been topped with chiseled glittering glacial laurel leaves. The toga, which was as slick and as

306

translucent as the rest of her icy figure, seemed to ruffle in the midnight wind. With each delicate blow of the chisel, the man's work became all the more prominent. As she stood there watching him work, the man looked up and greeted her with a nod.

"Merry Christmas," said Annette.

"Merry Christmas," he told her. He was in his mid-thirties as well with a lean figure despite his trench coat. He had a full head of hair and a bushy beard. For a split second, Annette thought she recognized him from somewhere but, the longer she stood there, she realized that it was impossible. She'd never seen this man before in her life. The man studied Annette with a look in his eyes that told her that he was thinking the same thing.

"Does she have a name?" Annette asked.

"I call her Polyhymnia," the man replied. "She was the original Greek muse of sacred music."

As Annette nodded her eyes caught sight of a tiny object resting at the foot of the great statue. She leaned down to pick it up with her gloved fingers. Annette held in her hand a single orange Lite-Brite peg which she curiously turned this way and that. Meanwhile the artist opened his tool box and offered Annette a second chisel. "Care to join me?"

And not knowing quite why, Annette said "Yes, I would love to."

"I'm Adam, by the way," he said as he fit the chisel into her hand.

"Annette," she told him. "Pleased to meet you." And so, on that cold winter's night, Annette's and Adam's work had begun.

CHAPTER 28: TWENTY-TWO ENVELOPES LATER

"There are several things to think about before venturing forth, dear muse: the first is the water cooler. Water is a conduit, a necessity for traveling from place to place. Drinking the water lubricates the transition of traveling through these passages. Without it, the journey would be excruciating. Second," the narrator marshaled "time for the muse is circular, which means that you can travel both forwards and backwards through time. Remember that past, present and future exist both harmoniously and simultaneously. Therefore, don't be surprised if you're inspiring a person suffering from vertigo to bungee jump with his friends one moment and, then, inspiring the painting of the Sistine Chapel the next.

"Third and most importantly, do not, under any circumstances, leave an envelope unattended. The window of time, or the page of the person's pop-up book, is only open for a limited interval and can only be opened by you . . ."

The instructional video went on the fritz again as it had done moments before repeating the words "Can only be opened by you" seven more times.

"How about now?" Fiona's voice was muffled as the top half of her torso was engulfed by a hole in the conference room ceiling tiles.

Harriet frowned. "Still doing it." Fiona grunted displeasure, continuing to fiddle with the wiring. "Perhaps we should ask Nathaniel to fix it, Fiona. He's truly a wonder with these kinds of things."

"We don't need to call Mr. Cauliflower for everything that goes wrong in this office, Harriet. All it needs is a little more encouragement."

"It's a piece of machinery," Harriet sighed quite audibly. "And doesn't *need* encouragement."

"How about now?"

Harriet turned her attention to the instructional video again only to find that the picture and audio were once again not on the same wave-length. "Now it's in French, Fiona!"

"What about now?"

Harriet shook her head. "Tagalog now."

"And . . . now?"

"Now it's playing it in Japanese and upside-down." Harriet tossed up her hands. "This is impossible!"

". . . Butterfly wings and earthquakes," continued the instructional video this time in English and playing in the right direction. "So finish a job and move on to the next. You now play a vital part in humanity, dear muse. No one you inspire is too great or too small. No task is ever out of your control. You, by yourself, hold the reigns to inspiration. You can, and will, inspire anyone."

"We're good to go!" Harriet called up to the Head Muse, who seconds later descended the ladder. Fiona's baby blue-colored heels matched her baby blue-colored pants suit; the baby blue jacket which matched the ensemble was draped across the back of a spare swivel chair. Fiona wore a cream-colored camisole allowing the fabric to trace the curve of her breasts. Though her head had recently hovered in the catacombs and air-ducts of the ceiling, Fiona's hair still waved radiantly. While the Head Muse closed up the metal ladder, Harriet was reminded of the WWII campaign posters with the woman bulking up a bicep with the words "You Can Do It!" but said nothing.

"Now what were you saying about the instructional video not needing a bit of encouragement?" The more words Fiona spoke, Harriet could detect a subtle British accent.

"The energy efficient light bulbs, the instructional video, the water coolers, you treat them as if they're just as important as our clients."

"Ah, but they *are* just as important as our clients."

309

"But they don't have skin, brains, a beating heart, souls..." as Harriet went on, Fiona carried the ladder out of the conference room and down the hallway past the other nine doorless offices, Harriet in toe. "They don't have a projected purpose Fiona but you're acting as if they did."

"Just like one of our clients, Harriet," Fiona told her assistant, opening the door to the waiting room where she instead found a utility closet, into which she stuffed the ladder. "If one little cog is missing, broken or obsolete, then circumstances would change. Management has things just the way they like it are for a reason, from a client that we inspire down to the energy efficient light bulbs in the hallway. Everything that we encounter deserves recognition."

"I'm not trying to be difficult, Fiona."

"Not being difficult at all, Harriet." The two women turned back to the conference room.

"Only one more peg to go before I retire and, if I'm going to take over your position, I need to know these things."

"When I started as a First Generation muse, Harriet, and was employed as Head Muse after the initial employment, do you think anyone passed down a guide book? Sure there was the demonstration about the Lite-Brite board but I personally formulated my own procedures as the need surfaced."

"Management must have taught you *something*, Fiona."

"There are many things that Management taught me, Harriet . . ." the muse in the baby blue-colored pants suit frowned, "and many things I wish they had but didn't. Alas, like the lives our clients, we are only given just enough to continue on our own path. It's up to us, as it is for them, to figure out our own answers." The two women passed by the office that used to be Annette Slocum's. Both women paused in commemoration. It was no longer a personal library with sunlit stained-glass windows and polished wood floors. The office had been transformed into a hall of nine thunderstorms. The wood on the floors, banisters and columns of this office had been stained black. Beyond the archways were nine distinctly different thunderstorms forever caught in the moments before their approach.

"Do you miss her?" Harriet asked.

310

Knowing who Harriet was slyly alluding to, Fiona still played coy. "Who?"

The two muses stepped away from the office door as it folded and unfolded depositing Annette Slocum's replacement back into the Hall of Thunderstorms. Continuing down the hallway to the conference room, Harriet wasn't about to let the conversation go.

"You know who."

"Retirement is a process, Harriet."

"Yeah, but you don't miss her even a little bit?"

"One shouldn't become emotionally attached to one's employees."

"Where do you think she is now?"

"Exactly where she needs to be."

"With Adam Mansfield?"

"What does it matter, Harriet?" The two women found themselves back in the conference room seated at a rectangular table with nine chairs and a mural of nine naked muses with laurel leaves between them on the wall. "Mrs. Slocum has moved on to bigger and brighter things so why not celebrate that she was ever here, has achieved her goal, and has moved on? Why mourn?"

"Ever since she left and *he's* arrived, it's difficult not to."

"Your reservations about the new muse stem from the fact that he isn't Mrs. Slocum."

"No, my reservations about him stem from the fact that he's a creep."

"He is not a creep, Harriet." But even Fiona's words could not mask her insecurities behind the statement.

What made him a "creep" in Harriet's eyes was not his musing techniques or the way he would slurp the water from the water cooler. It was not the way he would eat the delicacies Nathaniel J. Cauliflower would supply in the conference room. What concerned Harriet the most was the way he would look up from his desk if anyone passed by his door with his cold eyes boring holes into one's skin. The women in the office often wore extra layers of clothing and the men hurried past his door to and from the restroom. The overall demeanor of the new hire was negative and not even Fiona could refute this fact.

The new muse stepped into the doorframe. He wore a black suit, gray shirt, and licorice-colored tie. Though he was only in his mid-thirties, the stress and worry on his face caused him to look well beyond his years. He had a head full of grey hair and crows-feet in his skin spread out from his pupils. He watched them intently with a glacial stare.

"Mr. Rothchild, is there anything I can help you with?" Fiona suddenly realized that her baby blue jacket was still draped across the back of the swivel chair; an article of clothing that she now wrapped around her shoulders to preserve her compromised modesty fitting her arms into the sleeves.

"Hello Fiona . . ." said Jonas, then turning his eyes to Harriet, he acknowledged her presence. "Harriet."

"Jonas." Harriet uncomfortably positioned the fabric of her own cardigan, covering herself more.

"My first violet envelope," Jonas smiled as Fiona finished buttoning her jacket. "Came away from it still intact."

"Wonderful, Mr. Rothchild," but the moments preceding Fiona's words were not so wonderful. They stood in prickly silence, the three of them. Mr. Rothchild's stare was deadening. "Well, good to know that you're first violet envelope went well."

"Oh, I wouldn't say it went well, Fiona."

"No?"

"Perhaps it would be better to say that nothing happened at all." These words caused Fiona's head to lean to the left quizzically. "There I was, standing in my violet envelope inspiration, when it suddenly occurred to me just how much I shouldn't be inspiring the client at all."

"Mr. Rothchild, when we're given envelopes, we don't neglect our clients."

"Ah yes, I'm afraid I've sinned."

"Well, there's no harm done. Hand over the violet envelope; we will get everything squared away with Mr. Cauliflower."

"Yes, I suppose that would fix it all, wouldn't it?" Jonas' face grew grimmer, if it were even possible. "Unfortunately, I cannot hand it over to you."

"I'm not sure I follow," Fiona's demeanor did not falter. If anything, it was enhanced.

"I'm taking the violet envelope with me."

"Taking it . . . ?"

"With me. My exit is a bit dramatic but there's just no other way. After twenty-two envelopes, I've heard and seen enough. The operation that you run here is worse than I ever anticipated. A world of disease, pestilence, plagues, starvation, rot, disappointments, war, famine, terrorist attacks – man is a beast, and a ravenous one at that. And this grand evolution of the species that you so often promote is nothing more than a hoax."

"What are you saying, Mr. Rothchild?"

"For years before my death I had prayed to Management for answers. Why does Management put us through turmoil? We are all Job from the Bible and the world is getting worse by the minute! Now I know it's all because of Management! Because presumably *they* know what's best!" He craned his lips to the ceiling where the sound of fluttering envelopes whispered in protest.

"Mr. Rothchild, I want you to take a breath and think about what you're doing."

"I *have* taken a breath, Fiona, and because of Management's world, I had the wind knocked out of me." His bitter eyes were even more frozen as he ran his fingers along the door to the waiting room as if stroking the spine of a great leather novel. "How it taunts me, Fiona, this door. How is it that only Nathaniel J. Cauliflower enters and exits from this door on a normal basis while the rest of us are trapped in here like rats? Even the walls of Babel had to eventually crumble..."

Fiona then stepped forward: "Mr. Rothchild, please hand over the colored peg and violet envelope." From inside his black jacket pocket, he produced the violet envelope, as if actually considering surrender. From inside the envelope a small blue peg toppled into the palm of his hand. Jonas licked his lips, hungry for destruction. "There are moments that we all go through, Mr. Rothchild, where we question the motivations of Management. All will be forgiven."

"No," Jonas pocketed the blue peg and the violet envelope.

"There's no reason to be ornery, Mr. Rothchild."

"No," Jonas smiled like a petulant pyromaniac poised with a metaphorical match.

The other muses had congregated in the hallway to watch the great show, fueling his confidence. The time had come for Jonas to make his great escape.

"What's gotten in to you, Mr. Rothchild?" Fiona wanted to know.

"What's gotten in to me?" Jonas turned to the Head Muse. "The world, Fiona. Everything about it sickens me, and knowing that Annette Slocum is out there somewhere unprotected . . . I'll no longer placate Management and all the manipulation as if I were a marionette with strings." He reached for the doorknob, which turned, but the door seemed stuck. *"Every . . . little . . . moment,"* his words punctuated by his attempts to open it. *"Will need . . . to be . . . rectified!"*

Finally the door was swung open. A blinding white light erupted from the waiting room which accented the Great Discourager's wrinkles. His gray hair caused him to look all the more malicious. Fiona raced toward him but the glacial stare in his eyes caused her to stop.

"How do you know what's on the other side, Mr. Rothchild? What makes you so confident?" Fiona wanted to know.

When Jonas turned back to them, Fiona could see that Jonas had something around his neck – an old key with a dandelion insignia dangling from a necklace. "The Dandelion Sisters have shown me everything, Fiona. There is so much work to be done. Or undone, rather."

He turned to the light now, carrying the violet envelope within his jacket pocket.

"Mr. Rothchild, I beg of you . . . at least tell us a time period of where it sent you? A name! Anything!" None of which he supplied. Instead, after one final kiss into the hallway's air, Jonas stepped through the hallway door. Kicking the waiting

314

room chairs aside, his silhouette was erased like an ink-stain in bleach. Upon his exit, the energy efficient light bulbs in the office flickered out, the Lite-Brite boards lost their illumination. The hands in the typical wall clock of the waiting room wall ceased its rotations. As the light at the end of the waiting room tapered out, the other eight muses stood in shock. All was quiet and still.

"The key that was around his neck," Harriet asked Fiona. "Wasn't that hanging in Nathaniel's office not too long ago?"

"I'm afraid so."

"Then what was Jonas doing wearing it around his neck?"

Fiona then crossed into the Hall of Thunderstorms to find the old oak cabinet that was half hidden in shadow in the far corner. The frames of the muses had been turned picture side down. The drawer with the ten-lettered combination had been opened. The mason jars had been unsealed. The twenty-one dead dandelions had scattered in the pre-storm breezes of the office. The box that had once been sealed had been opened. Fiona looked inside to find the contents were still there: a bound volume labeled *The Lives and Times of Nathaniel J. Cauliflower*. No doubt Mr. Rothchild had thumbed through it. She had no doubt that its information played a role in his defiance.

And then the colored pegs, without the envelopes to encase them, descended. Not just one or two, not the thousands Fiona had encountered in all her generations or the sixty-eight Annette Slocum encountered in hers. No, the numbers were far greater; hundreds at first, then thousands, then billions. They fell from each office ceiling like shards of multi-colored hail. Desks were dented and water coolers were overturned by great force. One after the other, the inboxes overflowed, the post boxes were knocked off kilter, yet the colored pegs kept falling. The floor was littered with them and, in the flood of colored plastic, the eight scrambling muses found themselves wading through the multi-colored madness in order to take proper shelter from the onslaught.

"That's not possible . . ." Fiona whispered as the ceiling then fell quiet. There were piles of them, swamps covering the

315

office and hallway floors. "Not possible . . ." but it was. And the nightmare had only begun. It wasn't the last of the colored pegs that were to descend. From the ceiling came a sound that warned of more on their way, like a string of devastating tropical storms headed straight for a solitary island surrounded by tempestuous waters.

"Well . . . I suppose it's going to take a lot more than encouragement and a ladder to fix *this* mess," Harriet said to her employer as the last of the light escaped the office plunging them deeper into the disaster.

ACKNOWLEDGEMENTS

There are many people who have helped make the story of Annette Slocum possible. First off, I would like to thank Lewis O. Powell IV who was there in Annette's first days and for JD Nichols who was there to support her through the last. I also want to thank my mother, Deborah Jacobs, her wife, Anne Marie Bills, my sister, Amanda Stone, my father, Delton Jacobs, my step-mother, Janie Jacobs, and the rest of my family who have always been there to support, inspire and encourage in any and all creative endeavors.

A huge amount of gratitude to Carisa Schuster, Beth Holt and Julia Chappelle-Thomas for taking a chance on Annette and helping to edit out all the tangles. Thank you to Don and Angela Ovens, Samantha Lee Wallace, Susan Summers, Susan Baker, Chris Hays, Leslie and Mark Stock, DeeDee Folkerts, Erin Kolks, Meg Phillips, Bev Pfeffer, Robin Morrison, Martha Bollinger, Angela Mason and Earl Coleman who always seem to be there, with unbridled positivity, when I need them the most. Thank you to the teachers that inspired me to write and appreciate music: Mrs. Thrasher, Mrs. Sisson, Nick Norwood, Sally Hook and Dixie Holton. Thank you also to the members of the writer's group circle: Geoff Blackwell, Erika Woehlk and Aaron Young. My love and appreciation goes out to the managers and crews at both the Barnes and Nobles in Columbus, Georgia and also Columbia, Missouri. Thank you to all of my friends and comrades, both onstage and off, involved with Columbia Entertainment Company. Thank you to all of the friends, family, other random individuals, and coffee houses with outlet plugs in both Columbia, Missouri and Columbus, Georgia who have helped to make this book a success.

A personal thanks goes to the random stranger who played the violin to his friends outside of my apartment that long ago night. Thank you to Hasbro for inventing the Lite-Brite along with all the colored pegs that go along with it. Thank you to Mother Nature for all of the inspiring thunderstorms that came my way. Thank you to Corgi who was always there, peering over the couch cushions, while I wrote Annette well into the night. Finally, in closing, an unconventional "thank you" to those who have passed on: Lisbeth Yasuda, Renee Kite, David Kent Toalson and Miss Norene Wood - a woman who was, and always will be, the greatest muse who ever lived.

About the Author

When David is not writing, he enjoys ghost hunting and can often be found acting and entertaining audiences on the community stage. He also loves to draw and paint, finding comfort in anything creative.

David lives in Columbia, Missouri.

Contact the Author

https://www.facebook.com/DavidPJacobsAuthor/

Twitter:
@DPJMuseAuthor

www.davidpjacobs.com